"*The Julian Secret* is thought provoking and Loomis lets his readers form their own conclusions. This is a lively and stimulating thriller you do not want to put down. The surprise ending is great—a light moment from the serious questions on life. Dan Brown's fans will find *The Julian Secret* a delight."

—I Love A Mystery

THE PEGASUS SECRET

"[*The Pegasus Secret* has] more intrigue and suspense than *The Da Vinci Code!*"

—Robert J. Randisi, Bestselling Author
of *Cold Blooded*

"The international setting and fast-paced action grip . . . [Readers] looking to repeat *The Da Vinci Code* experience will be satisfied."

—*Publishers Weekly*

HANGING BY A THREAD

Lang clung to the rope, an umbilical cord that held him above a drop of thousands of feet. The swing ended abruptly as his momentum slammed him into a protruding stone, perhaps the top of another gun port. The impact knocked the breath out of his lungs and blurred his vision with colorful spots that spun in front of his eyes. Gasping to refill his lungs, he felt his grip on the line slip before his concentration could return.

He drifted back and forth in space. His shoulder muscles were in rebellion, sending pain radiating from neck to wrist. Hands beginning to spasm from the physical tension, he forced one after the other to inch his way up the remaining few feet of rope toward the gun.

He was almost there when he felt an almost imperceptible slack in the line. The swinging motion had somehow loosened the knot in the rope. It was coming loose.

If it did, the next stop would be nearly a half mile below . . .

GREGG LOOMIS

The Bonaparte Secret

Dorchester
Publishing

To Frank Loomis.
We choose our friends, God our families.
Frank was the best of both.

DORCHESTER PUBLISHING

May 2011

Published by

Dorchester Publishing Co., Inc.
200 Madison Avenue
New York, NY 10016

ISBN 13: 978-1-4285-1112-5
E-ISBN: 978-1-4285-0964-1

The "DP" logo is the property of Dorchester Publishing Co., Inc.

Printed in the United States of America.

Visit us online at www.dorchesterpub.com.

The Bonaparte
Secret

PROLOGUE

Syria, near Damascus
October, 322 BC

All one hundred or so inhabitants of the small oasis gathered to watch a sight never before seen and unlikely to be seen again: sixty-four mules pulled what Diodorus, a Sicilian Greek historian of the first century, would subsequently describe as an Ionic tomb made entirely of gold, twenty feet long and fourteen wide. Inside, the king's mummified body, preserved in honey, rested in a golden sarcophagus. The weight of the hearse had required specially designed wheels and suspension. Even so, six miles a day was the greatest speed it could attain.

The honor guard of one hundred Macedonian cavalry made no secret of the fact that the king was being taken home to Macedonia. He had died the year before in Babylon. The sheer size of his empire, stretching from Greece to India, had required over twelve months to divide among his generals before they could turn to the disposition of their former ruler's remains. Chief among them, Perdiccas, had decreed the body was to be entombed next to the king's father, Philip. The order was not entirely popular, for Macedonian tradition held the first duty of the new king was to bury his predecessor, but the king's only son was a half-wit and Perdiccas was an ambitious man.

But no more so than Ptolemy, known as Soter, the savior, because he had been chief among the king's generals who had saved Egypt from the tyrannical rule of the Persians.

Ptolemy had his eyes on Egypt, now part of the empire. More importantly, he had his army of several thousand blocking the funeral cortege's path northwest to Macedonia.

The villagers watched in eager anticipation of bloody entertainment as Sertice, commander of the honor guard, wheeled his horse to climb the slight rise where a single figure sat on horseback in front of a line of a dozen or so war elephants. Behind them, men armed with spears had already formed phalanxes, the Greek battle formation of close ranks and files.

Reaching the crest, Sertice removed his helmet so the other man might more clearly see his face.

He dismounted and knelt before the other's horse. "Sir, you do me honor to join my small force in escorting the king home."

A smile creased the weathered face of the man on horseback. Despite Sertice's flowery words, he knew the cavalry commander was fully aware of what was happening.

"Honor is due you, Sertice. But I come to join you not in taking the king back to Macedonia but to Egypt as he wished."

"But my orders . . ."

"Your orders are countermanded. Do not force me to slay my fellow comrades in arms."

It didn't take Sertice more than a second to make up his mind. A little over a year ago he would not have given the superior strength of an adversary a second thought. Had not the king's thirty thousand Macedonians routed ten times as many Persians? Had the king not consistently defeated armies far larger than his own? But the king was dead, there was no clear chain of command and it had been over ten years since he had seen his wife back in Macedonia, ten years of forced marches, combat and privation until the army had finally mutinied, refusing to go farther than the Hindu Kush. They all wanted to go home. What purpose would be served by losing a hundred brave men now?

He stood, head bowed. "My life will be forfeit when Perdiccas hears of this."

Ptolemy barked a harsh laugh. "Then come with me to Egypt. It is a rich country and I have need of men like you." He noted the man's hesitation. "Have no fear for your family. I will send swift riders to bring them from Macedonia to Egypt."

With no small disappointment there would be no fight, the villagers watched the two groups merge, shift the marching route from northwest to southwest and slowly disappear over the ridge.

From the diary of Louis Etienne Saint Denis, secretary to Napoleon Bonaparte, commanding general, Army of the Nile; edited and translated to the English by Henri D'Tasse of the University of Paris

Alexandria
19:01, August 23, 1799[1]

We left at night so the troops would not be disheartened. Fortune had frowned upon us. After Nelson the Englishman destroyed our fleet at Aboukir Bay[2] a year ago, he sailed away to Sicily, leaving Captain Sidney Smith in command of the British fleet. If anything, Smith was worse

---

1 The French Revolution worshipped "logic" over religion. Consequently, the Gregorian calendar was scrapped and the Jacobin system adopted. The year was proclaimed to begin on September 22, with twelve months of thirty days each. Leap year included a five- or six-day holiday. Even the names of the months were changed to words more "natural," such as Vendémiaire, or "vintage," for late September–October, followed by the words for mist, frost, snow, rain, wind, seed, blossom, meadow, harvest, heat and fruits. Napoleon abandoned the system in year XII, 1804. In this translation I have used the actual dates rather than the Jacobin.

2 The battle, August 1, 1798, was close enough to Alexandria that the explosion of the French gunship *L'Orient* lit up the night sky of the city.

than Nelson. He defeated us at Acre and challenged the general to a duel, a madman.

Control of the sea by the enemy has stalled our campaign here, so there is little choice but to leave General Kleber to make terms with the English and the Turks who joined them. The revolution at home is in chaos and the commanding presence of the general is needed there.[3]

With us in the longboat that ferried us out to the ship in which we will make our voyage are only a few savants[4] and confidants. Three more such craft follow as a nautical baggage train. One of these the general himself loaded with only his manservant to help. In addition to a number of small antiquities, there is a parcel wrapped in sheep's skin. From its size, I would have supposed it to be a small statue of one of the pharaohs of whom the general has become quite fond. But such an object would be carved in stone and far too heavy to be carried under the general's arm.

I asked the general what such a parcel might contain but he was understandably in no mood for trivial matters and turned my query aside with the rudest of grunts. Then, his mood swinging as abruptly as the wind, he unbuttoned his uniform tunic to show me a small gold cross he wore about his neck. Knowing his attitude toward the Church, I was obviously surprised.[5]

---

3 Whether Napoleon was needed or not was made moot by his coup d'état on November 9. In 1804 he crowned himself emperor.

4 Not only did Napoleon take an army and navy to Egypt. He included 160 "savants," scholars in fields as diverse as botany, languages and art. One of them was the father of Ferdinand de Lesseps, the builder of the Suez Canal. Another preserved the Rosetta Stone for the future translation by Champollion, a feat that unlocked the secret of hieroglyphics. The studies of the savants were published in the monumental, multivolume Description de l'Égypte in 1809. The ancient glories of Egypt were generally unknown in Europe before then. Each volume caused a sensation.

5 The French Revolution not only overthrew the monarchy but the powers of the Catholic Church, whom the revolutionaries viewed as much an oppressor of the people as the king and nobility. The official policy of the French government even today is regarded by many as anticlerical.

"It was given me by my mother on the occasion of my first communion," the general said, another surprise, since he rarely spoke of his humble beginnings on the island of Corsica.

"The people," I noted, "might adversely view such an adornment."

By the flickering light of the boat's sole torch, I saw him smile. "Such is the reason I wear it under rather than outside of my tunic. It is dear to me, not as a object of religion, but as a reminder of my origins. On Corsica I was also given life and with that life I was also given a fierce love for my ill-starred homeland."[6]

He held the cross up for a moment to catch the shifting light of the torch before returning it inside his tunic. "It is but an ordinary object but one I shall always treasure greatly, along with a few others from the past. I wore it that day when, as a mere general, my epaulets still new, I defended the Convention."[7]

It was a rare moment when the general actually spoke tenderly about his life before some star of destiny called him to lead his nation's army and one I would have enjoyed, had we been attacking rather than fleeing the British.

---

6 Despite such language, Napoleon did little to further the cause of Corsican independence. The island is still French today.

7 A royalist uprising in Paris almost disrupted the National Convention. Napoleon, who had recently been promoted to general but was out of favor, was the closest officer available. He dispersed the royalists with what he would later describe as "a whiff of grapeshot," killing about a hundred of them. Most scholars attribute his rapid rise to this incident.

CHAPTER ONE

Chin Diem, undersecretary for foreign relations of the People's Republic of China, admired the view. Spread out below the mansion's picture window was the city, its lights cradled below the mountain like a handful of jewels. Fortunately, far below. Far enough that the stench of open sewers, uncollected garbage and burning charcoal that had assaulted his nose upon his arrival could not reach him. Neither could the flies and mosquitoes that seemed the country's most populous fauna. Up here the residences were multimillion-dollar mansions on multiacre lots. Their owners shopped regularly in Paris or Milan. The residents of Pétionville owned over 90 percent of what little wealth Haiti possessed. And that had come largely from offshore, untraceable investments originally funded mostly from foreign aid, money that had seen the beginnings of schools, the foundations of hospitals, projects never finished as funding trickled into well-connected pockets.

There was no din of hucksters up here, selling everything from carved figures with grotesquely enlarged penises to fly-ridden food to black market–discounted gourdes, the national currency, which proclaimed itself to equal twenty-five cents American but was actually without value outside the country.

The night and distance also blotted out the movement. Port-au-Prince was a city in constant action. No Haitian, from naked children to shirtless men to skirt-wearing women, young or old, was ever still. Not unless they were squatting beside the ubiquitous charcoal fires on which they prepared every meal on the filthy, noisy streets in front of rickety shacks or apartments.

Or, perhaps, were dead.

But Chin Diem had not come to this diminutive country for socioeconomic observations. His government jet had intentionally arrived after dark, when the prying eyes of what few foreign news correspondents remained in this poverty-ridden corner of the Caribbean would be unable to see who was disembarking. A Mercedes with darkly tinted windows had met him on the tarmac and he had been whisked here rather than to the alabaster capitol building in downtown Port-au-Prince. Had anyone been curious enough to check the aircraft's number against flight plans, a process made ridiculously easy by the Internet, they would have ascertained the aircraft, registered to a Swiss company, had departed Geneva, its previous stop.

Nothing more.

Secrecy was imperative if his visit to this humid, stinking place was to be successful. Secrecy and a great deal of diplomacy, for he was dealing with a madman, a leader of a country, every bit as volatile, egotistic and unpredictable as that lunatic China could barely control in North Korea. Fortunately, though, Tashmal duPaar, another in the dreary and endless procession of Haiti's "presidents for life," lacked power outside his tropical domain. He had but a small army and no nuclear weapons. In short, he lacked what Diem was prepared to provide.

It was not particularly remarkable that duPaar had managed to seize power from the duly elected president. He had been the senior officer of the country's military. As such, he simply marched a dozen men armed with outdated but deadly U.S. Army–surplus rifles into the capitol building and dismissed the president, his cabinet and the sitting parliament.

It had been an all-too-familiar move in Haiti and one of which the rest of the world, particularly America, had grown weary. Demands that the United Nations peacekeeping force withdraw were complied with in an eager expeditiousness that bespoke the futility with which the international community viewed the country. A condemning resolution ricocheted around the halls of the UN, the world's most useless debating society. The former Haitian ambassador to the United States, along with his UN counterpart, had sought sanctuary rather than return home, and the matter had died a short and unproductive death. Countries that exported little other than their own citizens tended to attract little attention. As for the people of Haiti, they were far more concerned about the next meal than the next politician to occupy this sumptuous home above Port-au-Prince.

Diem's thoughts scattered as an Uzi-carrying bodyguard entered the room, followed by a small black man in a uniform literally sagging with the weight of medals—duPaar.

Diem turned from the window and bowed deeply. "Mr. President."

The president for life acknowledged him with a wave of the hand before sliding behind a mammoth, gilt-edged Boulle partners desk that made him look even smaller. "Good evening, Mr. Secretary."

Since duPaar spoke no Chinese and the Chinese diplomat certainly knew no Creole, the blend of mangled French and West African dialects that is the language of Haiti, the men would converse in English.

Diem nodded toward the armed guard. "My understanding was that this meeting would include only us."

DuPaar shrugged. "My enemies will do anything to get at me, even a suicidal attempt. The man is deaf. He will hear nothing to repeat."

Chin Diem refrained from pointing out that even his casual appraisal of the presidential palace on arrival had revealed security befitting the leader of a country under siege.

Nothing less than an armored or airborne division could penetrate the walls, gun emplacements and security cameras he had seen. He assumed there was a lot he had not seen, too. Instead, he indicated a French wing chair, one of a pair upholstered in blue silk that was showing both stains and its age. He raised an eyebrow in a question.

"Yes, yes, of course. Please sit."

Chin did so, reaching into a pocket inside his black silk suit.

Instantly, he was looking down the muzzle of the guard's Uzi. Gingerly, he removed his hand, holding a pack of American Marlboros. "May I?"

In reply, duPaar opened a desk drawer and produced an ashtray with the words *Fontainebleau Hotel Miami Beach* on two sides. He smiled slyly as he slid it across the desk's inlay top. "As you can see, I, like you, have traveled widely."

Once again, Diem said nothing as he busied himself with lighting a cigarette.

Then, nodding to a painting behind duPaar's head, he asked, "That is a Bazile, is it not?"

For the first time the president for life smiled, showing teeth the color of old ivory. "You know Bazile?"

"I know of several of your country's painters. Bazile reveals himself by his use of several shades of green, more green than all other colors combined."

DuPaar produced a cigar from somewhere, bit off the end and spit out the tip. He spoke between puffs as he applied a wooden match. "The green mirrors the lushness of the country."

Not if the pictures of Port-au-Prince's neighboring countryside Chin had seen were accurate. The surrounding mountains were eroded dirt, the trees having been long ago stripped away to make charcoal. "I see."

DuPaar leaned back in his chair, his feet on the desk. Chin noticed his short legs barely reached. "Well? You did not come this distance to speak of artists."

Chin's inhale nearly turned into a choke on the smoke of

his cigarette. Most diplomatic conversations started with a compliment to the host or his country, meandered through the participants' families and their comparative health, took a leisurely stroll along a simple outline of the problem to be addressed, all before the business at hand was even mentioned.

DuPaar's feet hit the floor as he snapped forward. "I am a busy man, Mr. Secretary. Please come to the point."

Chin Diem could not remember being addressed in such a manner, but he swallowed his indignation. His mission was to come away with what he wanted, not put this penny-ante tyrant in his place.

"My country has long wished to expand its business interests to this hemisphere. We would like to begin in Haiti . . ."

DuPaar was leaning forward, feet firmly planted on the floor, his hands clasped on the desktop. He spoke around the cigar clamped between his teeth. "You have already begun. The company that operates the Panama Canal is owned by your government. Specifically, your army."

The man might be crazy but he was no fool.

"True," Chin conceded, "but the Canal Zone is quite small. Our international competitors, the Russians, for example, already are forming alliances with Venezuela, Nicaragua, even preparing to return to Cuba."

"Countries where the United States is disliked by those in power. Chavez in Venezuela, for instance, would do business with the devil to stick his thumb in the Americans' eyes."

Chin shifted in his chair. "My country is more interested in economic expansion than sticking fingers in eyes. I am authorized to propose opening manufacturing plants in your country."

"Manufacturing what?"

"Clothes, textiles, light manufacturing to begin with."

He definitely had duPaar's attention. "And then?"

"And then we will see."

DuPaar made a steeple of his fingers and rested his chin on it. "And what would I get?"

"Get?" Chin pretended to be puzzled, knowing full well what the president for life meant. "You would have employment for a number of your people, money they lack today."

DuPaar made a guttural sound, a sound of dismissal. "Do not play me for an idiot, Mr. Secretary. You know precisely what I mean."

Chin took the opportunity to stub out his cigarette. "Well, for starters, as our American friends would say, I would anticipate five or six thousand Chinese soldiers would be stationed here to protect my country's investment, prevent any further, er, abrupt changes in government."

DuPaar shook his head. "The Americans would never allow Chinese soldiers on their doorstep."

Chin smiled. "The Monroe Doctrine, the policy that the United States would tolerate no country out of this hemisphere to meddle in the affairs of a country in the Western Hemisphere, died in 1962 when Kennedy agreed not to invade Cuba again if the Russians would remove their missiles from the island. Their present president believes talk, not action, is the solution to all problems. In the end, the Americans will do nothing."

DuPaar's eyes narrowed. "These troops, who would command them?"

Now came the time for the vagueness that characterizes the accomplished diplomat.

"They would, of course, serve under their own officers. But who commands the officers . . ." He trolled the idea implicit in the unfinished sentence like a baited hook.

DuPaar leaned back in his chair again, puffed out his chest. "You will not be surprised to know I am well versed in military command. Not only did I serve as my country's highest-ranking officer, I have read all the military works, the campaigns of Alexander, Caesar, Napoleon, Frederick the Great, Stonewall Jackson, Rommel, Patton . . ." DuPaar inhaled deeply. "There are those who say I am the embodiment of those men. I believe I am their souls reincarnated in one body."

Either the president for life had been smoking something other than his cigar or he was farther down the road to insanity than Chin had been informed. But then, mental problems had historically been an issue here. François "Papa Doc" Duvalier had believed the dogs and cats in the streets informed on his enemies, and acted accordingly. Crazy or not, if this fool thought the People's Republic of China was going to trust him to command Chinese troops . . . Well, he was thinking just what Diem had been instructed to make him think. By the time he found out to the contrary, China would have a foothold within a few hundred miles of the American coast, a base from which its aircraft and navy could reach any place in the Caribbean, a sea that the Americans regarded as their own lake.

"Such a command would restore the glory of my country," duPaar continued, "reminiscent of Toussaint L'Ouverture . . ."

"The former slave who defeated Napoleon's brother-in-law and chased the French out of Haiti forever." Along with a hefty helping hand from yellow fever, to which the indigenous population had some degree of immunity.

DuPaar smiled again. "You are acquainted with my country's history. You see the similarity between me and the great Toussaint."

More like his successor, Henri Christophe, tyrant and self-crowned emperor who ruled as Henri I. Believing he was too great a man to die a normal death, he shot himself with a silver bullet rather than be torn apart by a mob. It was he who started the practice that would ultimately make Haiti the poorest country in the Western Hemisphere: subdividing already-small parcels of arable land to distribute to his supporters. The predictable result was that few Haitians owned more than tiny plots, hardly enough to feed their families. He also bestowed empty titles, among which were the Duke of Marmalade and the Viscount of Beer.

But Diem said, "My superiors are aware of the parallel."

Both men were silent for a moment, duPaar basking in imagined glory before he spoke. "I will agree to your proposal, but I need a sign of your country's good faith first."

Diem had been prepared for this. His government had authorized a bribe of up to ten million dollars to be paid into the president for life's Swiss bank account. "And that would be?"

"I will need you to retrieve a very special object for me, one that will symbolize my might and grandeur, something that will proclaim my status to the world."

Diem swallowed hard. He dared not think what this madman had in his twisted mind. The Holy Grail?

DuPaar was staring at him. "Did you know Haiti and the Dominican Republic were the same country in colonial days? It was known as Saint-Dominigue. It is my ambition to reunite us."

The sudden change of subject caught the Chinese diplomat off guard. It took him a second to realize the tourist and agricultural industries of Haiti's neighbor were worth billions of dollars, a good part of it from investors in the United States. If anything could provoke the American president into military action, this would be it.

"You have reason to believe the Dominicans wish such a reunion?"

DuPaar snorted. "When they see Haiti's might, when they see the great symbol of military prowess you are going to bring me, they will have no choice."

Military prowess. Diem relaxed a little. That would seem to exclude the Holy Grail. "What is this object you desire?"

DuPaar told him.

Shock stripped away the diplomat's facade of calm. "But no one knows where such a thing is to be found. Or even if it still exists!"

DuPaar stood, took two steps toward the door through which he had entered and stopped. "When you have it, come back and we will discuss the terms under which you may build your factories and where you may construct such military facilities as you desire."

He left the room without another word. The guard gave Diem a blank stare and followed. The Chinese diplomat sat for a full minute, sorting through the most unusual negotiations in which he had ever participated before getting up and heading for the waiting Mercedes.

Venice
18:20, February, the present year

Lang Reilly was not fond of Venice. The city was like a movie star long past her prime. Faded stucco peeled from stone walls like a woman unable to replace her makeup. The *acqua alta*, high water from the Adriatic, relentlessly flooded most of the city in its persistent effort to reclaim what had been taken from the sea.

It was a city of tourists, twenty-one million in 2007, as opposed to only sixty thousand residents remaining of the one hundred twenty thousand of twenty years ago. Many of the historic palazzos were now hotels, an increase in visitor accommodations of 600 percent in the last ten years. Claustrophobic byways, more alleys than streets, were far too tight for conventional vehicular traffic even if the city allowed it. They were so narrow they remained in shadow even during the day, perfect places for muggers or worse. Indeed, the city boasted a Street of the Assassins, reflecting a cottage industry of the city's past. Many of the street signs, where there were any, were in the Venetian dialect, rendering a map useless. The numerous canals caused perpetual dampness and musty smells, adding to the reasons he and Gurt had chosen a hotel on the powdery sands of the Lido, a strip of beach-

front a five-minute boat ride across the lagoon that it separated from the Gulf of Venice.

The hotel's boat, resembling a perfectly restored Chris-
Craft from the 1950s, complete with teak decking, wallowed
in its own wake as the driver reversed, then cut the twin
engines a few feet from what would have been steps up to
the Molo San Marco had they not been under water. As it
was, the craft's passengers had to balance their way on a
makeshift gangplank.

From dockside, Lang could see the winter rain was adding
to the flooding of the Piazza San Marco, already several
inches under water from the seasonal high tides. A clumsily
raised platform, specially erected for Carnevale to host mu-
sicians, acrobats and other entertainers, was draped with a
sagging banner proclaiming Coca-Cola the *"cocktail ufficiale
di Carnevale."* The banner across the Campanile also demonstrated commercialism was a prime theme of the festivi-
ties by advertising a popular Scotch whiskey. A network of
raised boards gave access to the glass shops and restaurants
lining the square. The emptiness of the tables and chairs
outside the latter added a deserted moroseness where laughter and music belonged.

The somberness seemed to have spread even to the
square's famous pigeons, whom tourists delighted in feeding.
Instead of gathering around and on anyone crossing the
square, their mournful cooing from under the eaves of buildings only added to the gloomy scene.

The weather had done little to dampen the early-evening
enthusiasm of the revelers of Venice's famous twelve-day
Carnevale, however. Elaborate costumes were everywhere,
most rented with deposits in excess of ten thousand euro in
case of a drunken dip in a canal or other disaster. Partygoers
flocked through and across the square. All seemed oblivious
to the drizzle that, under the streetlights, wrapped the city
in a glowing gauze of moisture. The impression was of an
anthill just kicked over, its inhabitants scurrying in all

directions to balls where the admission price could exceed eight hundred euro. Lang wondered if the celebrants were aware that the hook-nosed masks so popular here mimicked the masks worn centuries ago by those charged with burying those dead of the plague.

"You do not seem happy." Gurt, in the costume of a seventeenth-century lady, was walking beside him as they dodged a puddle and turned right.

They were following what resembled a fretwork of loggias and arcades below a pink Veronese marble building of vaguely Gothic style.

"I'm smiling aren't I?"

"Your smile is painted on your face along with the red rubber nose."

"The clown outfit was your idea."

Before the conversation could continue, they arrived at the back of a line of elegantly costumed men and women closely huddled under an awning, which ended at a pair of massive wooden doors, the Porta della Carta, the original main entrance to the Palazzo Ducale, the Doge's Palace.

"You did remember the tickets?" Gurt asked.

Lang fumbled in a pocket of his piebald outfit. "If the rain hasn't melted them."

"I would hate to have come this distance and not get in."

"For what the foundation contributes to Save Venice every year, we could buy the place."

Only a slight exaggeration. The international charity, Save Venice, Inc., contributed millions each year to preserve and protect the city and its art and architectural treasures from being reclaimed by the Adriatic. The Italian government had spent even more on plans for a tidal gate, which had become a political football that no one thought would ever see more than lip service, inflated contracts and political patronage. In return for its efforts, the charity was permitted to hold an annual masquerade ball in the Sala del Maggior Consiglio, the huge third-floor council room from which the independent city-state had managed an empire that embraced northeastern Italy, the Ionian Islands and a good part of the Adriatic's east coast.

Although not a fan of Venice, Lang realized its historical value. As CEO of the Janet and Jeff Holt Foundation, he honored his sister's memory with generosity to her favorite city. She and her adopted son, Lang's best ten-year-old pal, had died several years ago in a fire caused by one of the world's wealthiest and least known organizations. It was Lang's threat of exposure that had forced the very same group to fund the foundation that bore his sister's name.

He frowned, wishing it were Janet, rather than he, who had been coerced into standing in the cold dampness, waiting to arrive at a ball he didn't really want to attend. The fact he had only himself to blame did little to improve his mood. Like an idiot, he had mentioned the invitation to Gurt, who had made it quite clear she was going with or without him.

Inside, a canopy protected partygoers as they crossed a small piazza and climbed the Giants' Staircase, carved from marble in the fifteenth century and crowned with statues of Mars and Neptune, symbolic of the city's power on land and sea. At the top, an usher clad in seventeenth-century knee britches, complete with shoes with shiny silver buckles, directed them toward the sound of music. To Lang, it sounded like a replay of, perhaps, "String of Pearls" or "Pennsylvania 6 5000." It was certain the band was unaccustomed to the swing music of the thirties and forties.

Gurt took his arm. "It is Glenn Miller, no?"

"About the right band for this group," Lang muttered, an allusion to the fact the foundation's membership was largely elderly. Young people had better things to spend money on.

"You grousing again, Reilly?"

Lang turned to see a white-haired, elfin man attired in hip-high leather boots, balloon sleeves and a cap with a feather. A sword hung at his side. Gorin, Gowen, something like that. The man spoke with the genteel twang of the American Northeast. He came from a family of such wealth that no one was quite sure where it all had come from to begin with. He had dabbled in politics, actually getting appointed to some cabinet post Lang had forgotten along with whoever had appointed him. Lang had served on the board of several charitable organizations with him.

What the hell is his name?

More interesting was the woman whose hand he held. She was young enough to be, but certainly was not, the man's granddaughter. Lang suspected the diamond necklace draped across inviting décolletage was not costume jewelry, either.

Gowen/Gorin turned to Gurt and actually gave a bow. "Since this lout isn't going to do it, let me introduce myself. I am Andrew Gower." He indicated his companion. "And this lovely lady is Angelia Sprayberry. You must be the current Mrs. Lang Reilly."

Gurt rolled eyes at Lang before returning the bow with a curtsy. "Gurt Fuchs, the *last* Mrs. Lang Reilly. It does me glad to meet you."

Gower gave her a knowing look. "The modern woman: keeps her own persona as well as her name. Good for you." He turned back to Lang. "Don't you find it exciting to be in the very city where Marco Polo began his extraordinary journey?"

Lang glanced out the window, noting the drizzle had turned to full-fledged rain. "I can understand why he left."

Unfazed, Gower continued. "And in the very building where the great lover Casanova was imprisoned?"

"Lucky him; he escaped."

Gower had to reach up to give Lang's back a pat as he brayed a laugh. "Always the comedian! Now where are you two staying? Angelia and I are at the Gritti Palace on the Grand Canal."

"We're at the Motel Six on the beach."

A flicker of a smile came and went, a man unsure whether or not he was the butt of the joke. He forced a chuckle, dropping Angelia's hand long enough to rub his own hands together. Lang remembered he did that a lot, one hand rubbing the other as though washing them.

"Well, perhaps we can do lunch at Harry's."

Harry's American Bar, located nearby, past the southwestern corner of the Piazza San Marco. The owners were named Giuseppe or Antonio or anything but Harry, the only Americans to be seen there being those willing to pay an exorbitant price for a very good lunch of typical Venetian fare. And the place was a restaurant, not a bar, though it boasted two elegant wooden bars behind which were possibly the only bartenders in Italy who knew that a proper martini contained more gin than vermouth. Make that *dry* vermouth.

"C'mon, Drew. I want to dance," Angelia whined.

Gower smiled apologetically, showing teeth several generations younger than Lang guessed he was. "Duty calls." He took a step toward the music and stopped. "By the way, you know Metaccelli died?"

The longtime Venetian contact for Save Venice, Inc.

"So I heard."

"It's not well-known, but he was very friendly with the current pope. Old pals."

Reilly waited expectantly. When nothing further was forthcoming, he asked, "And?"

"The patriarch of Venice will say a requiem mass for his friend in Saint Mark's tomorrow."

"The church invited us specifically," Angelia chimed in. "And Drew isn't even a Catholic."

"During Carnevale?"

Gower shrugged. "Metacelli loved Carnevale. Besides, it's the one time of year when many of his friends from Save Venice can attend, since they're here anyway."

"Drew . . ." Angelia's lips, Botox pouty, were frowning.

Gurt was still holding Lang's arm. She tugged him to-ward the music. "Let us go while they are still playing some-thing we can dance to, before they start that . . . What is it, hip-hop?"

Lang seriously doubted the band was going to play any-thing to this audience that Sinatra hadn't sung, but it was a good excuse to terminate the conversation. "See you later!"

After three hours, even Gurt's enthusiasm had waned. She let herself be led to the eastern edge of the room, where a number of white tablecloths floated like ships adrift on the dark wood of the floor. On the nearby wall, Tintoretto's huge *Paradise* depicted a congregation of saints.

She fanned herself with her hand. "It is hot!"

Lang ran a hand across his forehead, surprised when it came away dry instead of wet with sweat. "Let's take a walk outside."

She looked apprehensively at those still dancing.

"Don't worry," Lang assured her. "We can come back."

She picked up her purse, a bag the size of a small suitcase, slung it over her shoulder by its strap and followed him from the room.

Outside, the rain had stopped and a chilly breeze flitted from building to building. Careful not to step off the planks that served as the only dry paths across the Piazza San Marco, they turned right to walk north, stopping in front of a basilica bathed in light.

Its multiple domes and arches were far more Byzantine than Gothic. Not surprising, since Venice had always looked east to Constantinople rather than west to Rome for its alli-ances, customs and, in some respects, religion. The cardinal of Venice, for example, was referred to as the patriarch, a title usually reserved for the Eastern, or Orthodox, church.

"Look." Gurt pointed.

At first, Lang thought she was calling his attention to the mosaic over the door. "It shows Saint Mark's body being smuggled out of Alexandria, past Muslim guards. Two Venetians hid the relic under slices of pork."

Gurt shook her head. "No, the door. It stands open."

Lang had thought it was merely shadows playing tricks, but closer inspection showed the door was cracked open.

"Had no idea they left the place open at night," Lang said. "Let's take a look."

The inside was lit by low-wattage bulbs. Even so, it was obvious that the ceiling and walls were covered in gold mosaics, more like the churches Lang had seen in Istanbul than those in Europe.

He was about to comment when he heard a low whine.

"What . . . ?" Gurt whispered.

"Maybe they're getting ready for the requiem mass tomorrow," Lang suggested softly.

"With an electric drill?"

It was only then Lang recognized what he was hearing. He and Gurt instinctively moved closer to the wall, where the shadows were deepest. Moving from column to gilded column, they made their way toward the altar, which sat in the center of a dim spotlight, its two hundred fifty golden panels shining in spite of the low light.

At first mere shadows, forms moved back and forth under the alabaster altar canopy like ghosts. As Gurt and Lang got closer, the shapes took on distinct human shape. Both peered around a column.

"Why are they drilling?" Gurt asked just loudly enough to hear over the whine.

Lang shook his head, having no idea. "I don't know, but the fact they they're working at this hour tells me it's probably not kosher."

"And that they are not Italians."

"And maybe we're intruding on something we weren't intended to see. Let's go."

Lang was walking backward, keeping an eye on what was

going on as he moved toward the exit while feeling his way. Gurt was a few feet closer to the altar.

With the next step, something hard and cold was pressing against the back of his head, something very much like the muzzle of a gun. Freezing, he slowly raised his arms.

He almost stumbled as he was roughly shoved forward. By the time he regained his balance, he was pushed again. Whoever was behind him wanted him to head toward where the drilling was going on.

Years of Agency training kicked in. When you have no choice, cooperate, don't give someone an excuse to kill you. But keep your eyes and mind open. Use whatever assets you have.

Like Gurt.

Instead of going directly to the source of the noise, Lang moved cautiously along the row of columns that had guided him before being taken prisoner. Even in the dim light, anyone could see his hands raised in surrender.

Including Gurt.

He was hoping that the dusky twilight, the deep shadows, had prevented his captor from seeing her, leaving her free to go for help once they passed the spot where he had last seen her.

It had never occurred to him he might need a weapon at Carnevale. He had left the Browning HP 9 mm in his bedside table back in Atlanta. Damn! How dumb could he get? Arriving by the foundation's Gulfstream, neither he nor Gurt were subject to security screening. Either or both could have brought the firearms he wished they had. On the other hand, had the Browning been in the small of his back, he could well have gotten himself killed trying for it. But Gurt . . .

His stream of self-condemnation ended with the sound of a very solid thump, an expulsion of breath and the sound of metal hitting the marble floor. The gun was no longer against the back of Lang's skull.

Spinning, he caught sight of a man trying to regain his balance as he took a second blow from Gurt's handbag, swung on its strap like the weapon it had become. Now Gurt was between Lang and the light. He could only see her silhouette as she moved forward on her victim.

The man yelled something in a language Lang didn't understand, but he heard Gurt clearly say, "The gun, get his gun. He dropped it."

There was a grunt as Gurt's adversary apparently launched a counterattack.

Had it been any other woman, or most men, Lang would have felt compelled to protect her. Instead, it was her opponent who was going to need protection, he guessed. At the top of her martial-arts class of women in the Agency, she had insisted on practicing with the men. The only problem was finding competition after breaking one man's arm and the ribs of another.

Lang contented himself with a hands-and-knees search of the area as he heard flesh meet flesh and a very masculine yelp of pain. He found what he was looking for and came to his feet just in time to see the man make a slicing motion toward Gurt's throat with the heel of his open right hand.

It was his final mistake. Ducking under the blow that would have seriously damaged if not crushed her larynx, she grabbed the hand, snatching downward, diverting the force of the blow and sending her assailant headfirst into a nearby pillar with a clearly audible crunch of bone versus stone. He slumped to the floor with a fluid motion that almost denied his status as a vertebrate. He didn't move.

Lang slid back the slide on the automatic, checking with a finger to make sure there was a bullet in the chamber. "Hope you didn't have anything breakable in your pocketbook."

Gurt was peering into the gloom in the general direction from which the noise of the drill had ceased. "I should have thought of that."

With the hand not holding the gun, Lang took Gurt's. "I'd be surprised if someone didn't hear that guy yell. Let's get out of here before—"

A shot split the quiet, filling the basilica with sharp echoes. Marble chips from a pillar stung Lang's face. Both he and Gurt dropped to the floor, where they merged with the inky darkness.

"You see where that came from?" Lang whispered

"No."

Lang took a second to think. On the floor, he and Gurt could remain hidden in a darkness as deep as Jonah must have experienced. They could move on their bellies commando-style but to get out of the church they would have to navigate a puddle of light just where narthex met nave. He had little doubt whoever had been drilling would come looking for the man lying beside the column and then for whoever had left him there. There was equal certainty that that person would also be armed.

"Give me your purse," he whispered.

"Now is not the time to be checking for damage."

He told her what he wanted.

"On the count: one, two, three . . ."

He was never quite sure what object she had removed from her purse and looped overhand in the general direction of the altar. Whatever it was, it smashed against something with a gratifying clatter.

The response was a second shot, a noise that again sent sound caroming from wall to wall. But there was also a muzzle flash, a pinprick of light in the gloom.

Lang was on his knees before the echoes stopped. He fired three quick rounds at the place he had marked as the source of the shot and violently rolled to his left. The reply was a scream and more shots that filled the air with malignantly humming fragments of stone. Lang noted there were at least two shooters.

"They'll spread out and try and find us," he said. "I'll give you cover. Run for it."

"And you?"

"I'll think of something. Right now, you best get moving or our son will be an orphan."

She needed no further incentive.

Lang spread three rapid shots toward the same spot where he had fired previously. Before the second, Gurt was up and dashing for the exit. She drew two shots which, as far as Lang could tell, damaged only the church's interior.

Moving quickly before his opponents could fire at the source of his volley, Lang was at the edge of the lighted place at the entrance. He heard a footstep behind him and to his right, another from his left. However many of them there were, he could not be sure, but the fact they had distributed their forces was bad news. It meant they were probably professionals, not some random thieves using the distraction of Carnevale to loot the church.

Professional or not, Lang was going to draw fire the instant he crossed that lighted spot. Either that or stay here, hoping Gurt could bring help before they found him.

Then the lights went on.

Not brilliant illumination, but bright enough in contrast to the murk in which he had been. It was also enough to momentarily blind him.

Instantly, he understood.

That was the purpose! Gurt had somehow found a light switch and blinded whoever had been shooting at them.

He leaped across the space between himself and the narthex like a running back stretching into the end zone.

The impact with the floor knocked the breath from his lungs as two bullets ricocheted from the place he had been a split second before.

Gurt tugged him to his knees. "Hurry! They may be right behind us!"

He didn't need the encouragement. Staggering to his feet, he stumbled the few feet to the door out onto the lighted piazza, just behind Gurt. Once outside, they both flattened themselves against the basilica's facade rather than present a target to whoever might choose to fire from the church's door.

After two or three minutes, Lang asked. "Guess our friends aren't willing to step out into the light. Want to go back to the dance?"

Gurt pointed. "You will go nowhere with that in your hand."

Lang had forgotten he still held the gun. He looked at it for the first time he could actually see. "Tokarev TT30. First time I've seen one of those in a long time."

Gurt snorted. "Seven-point-six-two millimeter with an eight-round box clip. Based on the Colt .45. Used to be the standard Russian sidearm."

Agency training included a working knowledge of small arms—recognizing them and using them.

"Underpowered piece of crap, if memory serves. But reliable in the worst of conditions." Lang was examining the weapon more closely. "But this one isn't Russian."

He held it up for her inspection.

She pushed it down out of sight. "If someone sees you waving a pistol, the police will not care whether it is Russian or not."

Lang took a brief glance around the square, confirming its only occupants were a group of very drunk couples staggering at the far end of the Procuratie Nuove toward the long-closed Museo Correr, too far away for them to notice what he might have in his hand.

"Not only not Russian, it's Chinese. I can see the characters on the barrel."

"During the Cold War, the Chinese manufactured a number of Russian small arms for their own army, the AK-47 for example."

Lang held the weapon flat against his leg, invisible to any passerby. "But why would anybody use a gun that dated? I mean . . ."

"You wish to go back inside and inquire?"

"Not that curious."

She took his hand. "I have had excitement sufficient for the evening." She looked at him under half-lidded eyes, an expression he found sexy if not provocative. "Come, let us take the boat back to our hotel and I will provide even more."

"That's an offer I can't refuse." His hand went to his face. "My nose!"

Gurt looked at him inquisitively. "Your nose? It does not seem to be hurt."

Lang's eyes were searching the paving around him. "My clown's nose. It must have come loose when I hit the floor." He touched his bare head. "And my clown's hat, too."

She gave him a tug toward the canal and, hopefully, the old Chris-Craft. "You have been clown enough for tonight. Drop the gun into the canal before you have to explain it to the police."

Calle Fiubera 32, Venice
The next morning

Lang looked down the short, narrow street to the point it ended in a *corte*, or courtyard, in which a small limestone church, San Zulian, perched like a Baroque wedding cake on a platter. It was one of the few in the San Marco district Gurt had not dragged him into to see paintings and sculpture by Bellini, Giorgione, Tintoretto and a dozen or so more names he could remember no better than he could pronounce them. He offered up a brief prayer of thanksgiving as Gurt entered the shop paying no particular attention to the church.

Inside, the place had the same sweet, musty smell he re-called from two days ago, when he and Gurt arrived to be fitted for the costumes she had reserved by e-mail months before. Somehow using electronics to visit an event that had its roots in the Shrove Tuesday celebration of the republic's 1162 victory over the patriarch of Aquileia seemed anachro-nistic. The older Lang got, the more that word came up.

The shopkeeper, himself in Carnevale costume, exam-ined the set of hangers Gurt handed him, his eyes going to a ragged tear in the bodice of the copy of the seventeenth-century costume. He tsk-tsked when he noted Lang's hat was missing. The nose Lang had had to purchase, it being not reusable "for sanitary reasons," the first time he recalled ever hearing that phrase used in connection with anything Venetian.

Reluctantly, Lang agreed to the deduction of a hundred and fifty euros from his deposit.

"Rip-off!" Lang growled as they left. "The damn hat couldn't have cost more than fifteen, twenty bucks and it will take less than that to sew up the tear in your costume."

The store's door had hardly closed behind them when the merchant began punching numbers into his cell phone as he read them from a slip of paper. "The clown costume you wanted to rent?" he asked in English. "It has been returned. Yes, just this moment . . ."

As Gurt and Lang crossed the Piazza San Marco, she said, "We do not have to meet the plane until this afternoon. We have time to terminate."

As a native of Germany, Gurt's grasp of the American idiom was less than perfect.

Lang groaned inwardly at the prospect of another church. He had viewed all of the martyred saints, ascending virgins and bleeding crucifixions he wanted.

"Time to kill."

"How would you 'kill' time? It does not live."

"We haven't ridden the vaporetto . . . water bus," Lang

said, hoping to foreclose additional exposure to religious art by changing the subject. "It's a great way to see the city."

"Why not a gondola?"

Lang remembered the last time he had been in one of the romantic if expensive boats. He had been here with Dawn, his first wife. He had met her while still employed with the Agency, one of the few careers open to a liberal-arts graduate. He had anticipated all the excitement of a James Bond film. As is often the case, experience did not meet expectations. It wasn't even close. Instead of the Operations Division, he had been assigned to Intelligence, where his duties consisted not of slinking about the capitals of Eastern Europe and seducing the beautiful female agents of the opposition but of reading newspapers and monitoring TV broadcasts from behind the Iron Curtain from a dingy suite of offices across the street from the Frankfurt rail station. There he had met Gurt and had had a brief affair that terminated when she was transferred to another station.

Then he had met Dawn and married her. With the collapse of the Soviet Empire, it became clear that opportunities and advancement inside the Agency would be limited. Lang resigned and went to law school while Dawn worked. After his practice of defending white-collar criminals began to flourish, he had taken his wife to Italy as a very small reward for her labors.

She had fallen in love with Venice. Where Lang saw fetid, malodorous canals, she saw romantic waterways. When Lang pointed out that the persistently higher tides had encrusted the lower parts of most buildings with a salty layer of slime, she regarded it as a sign of antiquity. She even endured, if not enjoyed, the endless hawking of the glass merchants in their efforts to persuade tourists to take a "free" trip to their factories on the island of Murano, a place from which no one returned—not until purchasing at least one set of the artfully colored Venetian glass.

Lang supposed the set of six pale blue martini stem glasses

had perished along with his other possessions when his condominium had been blown up in an attempt to kill him at the beginning of what he thought of as the Coptic Affair.

Within months of their return home, Dawn had received a death sentence from her doctor. For months Lang had sat at her bedside, making plans for a return to Italy they both knew would never happen. Years after her death, he encountered Gurt again while tracking down the deadly Pegasus organization. A stop-and-go relationship became permanent with the unintended birth of their son, Manfred.

"Lang?"

Gurt's tone made him realize he had tuned out the present.

"You do not wish a gondola ride?"

Lang nodded toward the basilica's doors, where a small crowd had gathered. "What's going on now?"

He changed his direction, giving Gurt little choice but to follow. She caught up with him as he spotted Gower and the heavily endowed Angelia.

Lang now could see uniformed police coming and going from the church.

"Isn't it exciting?" Angelia cooed. "They say the priest found blood on one of the interior columns when he opened the church for early mass. Like somebody had been injured."

"Injured?" Lang tried to seem curious. "Do they know who?"

"I don't think so. He wasn't hurt too badly to get away. The police think he might have been involved in a theft."

"Oh? Of what?"

Gower interjected, "I understand some holy relic was taken from under the altar."

That answered the question of the need to be drilling late in the night. "Saint Mark's bones? They're under the altar." Lang was perplexed. "Who would want Saint Mark's bones?"

"Saint who?" Angelia asked.

*   *   *

At the same time, back at the costume-rental store, things were not going so well for Pietro, the proprietor, despite the windfall of being able to pocket part of the American's deposit.

When the man, clearly Asian, had walked in, the owner assumed he had another customer for the clown suit and another sale of the bright red rubber ball of a nose that went with it. Instead, the man had asked to see the American's credit-card receipt, an unusual request, to say the least. When met with a polite denial, the man, the customer, had grabbed Pietro by the neck of his costume, twisting it into a choke hold.

It didn't take the Pietro long to realize the prior customer's privacy or identity or whatever the Asian wanted wasn't worth his life. Besides, the customer's name wouldn't be on the receipt, and all but the last four digits of the card appeared as Xs. What harm could be done with that? A great deal less than Pietro faced if he didn't give this madman what he wanted.

At the Piazza San Marco, the crowd was beginning to disperse when it became obvious that there was nothing more to be seen. Gurt and Lang said their good-byes to Gower and his lady friend.

Lang glanced at his watch, noting they still had several hours before the foundation's Gulfstream would arrive at Marco Polo International Airport to pick them up for the trip home.

"Now what?"

"The boat from the hotel . . . Why do we not ask the driver to take us on a tour of the canals?"

Lang looked around at the gaudy displays of the square's shops. "First, I need to get Manfred something. I promised him a souvenir."

Gurt shook her head, smiling. "You have already gotten him a puppet, a model of a gondolier and a nice leather jacket he will outgrow before spring. Do you believe another toy will diminish your guilt at leaving him at home?"

She had hit the mark and Lang knew it. He had resigned himself to being childless until, like a miracle, Gurt re-entered his life with a son he had not known existed.

"He's your son, too," Lang observed defensively.

"If you continue to smother him in gifts, he will be my spoiled son."

It was an argument without end or rancor. Gurt certainly loved their son but she was a no-nonsense martinet. Like so many men who had a child comparatively late in life, Lang tended to give in to his son's whims, to tolerate behavior Gurt discouraged.

Realizing the futility of the debate, Lang changed the subject. "You said something about a ride in the hotel's boat?"

The boat driver had made this suggestion when they first arrived. The price was well below that of a gondola and the trip far more inclusive. It had seemed a good idea at the time. Within minutes, Gurt had used her cell phone to call the hotel, and the small craft was on its way. From the tour, they would return to the hotel on the Lido, collect their bags and be ferried to the airport.

Lang stood at the Molo San Marco, his back to the canal as he took in a last view of the Doge's Palace and the facade of the basilica. A man loitering a few feet away between two columns drew his attention. Tall, definitely Asian. Lang had seen him . . . where?

He nudged Gurt. "Without being obvious, take a look at the guy in the tan windbreaker over there by the columns. I've seen him somewhere before."

Gurt was more interested in a wedding party disembarking from a *motoscafo*, a smaller, sleeker and faster version of the water bus, no doubt headed for a service at the basilica. "He is perhaps Japanese. There are Japanese tourists everywhere."

"Can't be. He doesn't have a camera."

Gurt gave him another glance. The object of their attention was suddenly interested in something that required him to turn his face away. "He was shopping the windows near the place we returned our costumes."

Now Lang remembered. He had noted at the time the single, tall man with Asian features. Most Asians in Europe either were low-level employees, kitchen helpers and the like, students or tourists. The man was too old to be a student and not with a tour group, to which the Japanese clung like life preservers. If he had a job in someone's kitchen, why was he standing around here when the lunch trade would be in full swing shortly? Stereotypes existed because they were correct more often than not. And this particular stereotype was an aberration from the norm like a junk car parked in a ritzy neighborhood or a street beggar with an expensive wristwatch.

For the moment, Lang forgot him as the sleek little wooden speedboat from the hotel nudged its way between gondolas and other craft.

Helping Gurt and Lang aboard, the driver began, "I understand you want a canal tour, yes?"

They did.

"We start here, the Rio del Palazzo, the Canal of the Palace, which, as you can see, runs along the back, or eastern side, of the Doge's Palace. We take this canal, join some of the smaller ones and we come out on the Grand Canal to come back here."

Gurt's elbow gave Lang a sharp nudge as she whispered, "Don't look so bored! You might learn something on this tour of the canals of Venice."

The man spoke excellent English as he continued, pointing to an enclosed bridge. "This is the Bridge of Sighs. It connected the Doge's Palace, which was where criminal court was held, with the prison. The bridge takes its name from the sighs of prisoners as they were led to trial. Now, if you look to your left . . ."

Lang was more concerned about the motorboat that had entered the canal behind them, a fiberglass Italian-made Riva. The craft's slow speed matched their own, bow level rather than raised as would be the case on open water. He could see two men on board, but the distance was too great to make out facial features.

What made him think he knew what one of them looked like?

The hotel's boat turned left onto a canal not fifteen feet wide. Even at their slow speed, a sluggish wake washed over steps to doors less than a foot above the water. The houses themselves formed the banks of the canal. The height of the reddish ochre buildings, three to four stories, provided perpetual twilight. What Lang noticed most, though, was that this hundred-, hundred-and-a-half-yard stretch of canal was empty of any other craft.

As though his mind had been read, the roar of throttles pushed forward echoed from plaster facades more used to the songs of boatmen and the oohs and aahs of tourists.

Lang and Gurt's guide turned to look over his shoulder. "He crazy! Not allowed to make wake here!"

Its bow pointed well above the water now, the Riva was closing the distance between them quickly.

"Never mind the wake," Lang shouted. "Get us the hell out of here!"

"But signor . . ."

Lang didn't have time for a debate. Shoving the astonished boatman aside, he leaned over the control panel and slammed both throttles forward as far as they would go. It was as if the small craft had been shoved by a giant hand. The Cris-Craft look-alike stood on its stern like a rearing horse as twin props dug into the water. A quick look behind him showed Gurt clutching the starboard gunwale for all she was worth. More gratifying, the rate at which the following craft was gaining was diminishing rapidly.

The man from the hotel wasn't going to give up so easily.

He was trying to wrestle the wheel from Lang when a staccato burst of gunfire reverberated against the surrounding buildings, and splinters of what had been the boat's control panel whined past Lang's face.

Terrified, the guide let go of the wheel, off balance just long enough for Lang to hit his legs with a jerk of the hip that sent him flying into the canal. Lang had a split-second view of a mouth open in a terrified scream he could not hear above the motors' roar before the man hit the water.

Another fusillade of automatic-weapon fire stitched across the boat's stern. Up ahead was a right-angle turn into another canal, one even more narrow. Lang took it at full speed, the boat heeled over so steeply that the left gunwale seemed to scrape the water's surface.

Squarely in front was a gondola, black, curved bow and stern and taking up the middle of the waterway.

Gurt saw it, too, and squeezed her eyes shut, yelling, "Look out!"

Lang cut savagely to the right, missing the gondola by inches, though it did the gondolier little good. Standing on a raised platform at the stern of the flat-bottomed craft designed for shallow and placid waters, holding onto nothing but a single long oar, the wake of the speeding craft that all but swamped it rolled it with a violence that sent him into the canal also.

Dividing his time between looking ahead for more canal traffic and keeping track of the pursuing craft, Lang saw it also dodge the gondola, this time sending both of its passengers, a white-haired man and woman, splashing into the water.

So much for their romantic tour of Venice by gondola.

He sniffed the air. There was something besides that odor of a salt swamp Venice carried like a lady's favorite perfume. He looked around for an answer. A thin white trail of smoke was streaming from the craft's exhaust. A look at the ruins of the instrument panel told him why: there was next to no oil pressure in the starboard engine. A bullet must have severed an oil line or the crank case or pump, or any number of vital parts of an internal-combustion engine. Worse, highly flammable fuel could be leaking into the engine compartment beneath his feet, waiting for the right temperature to set it off. His options were to shut the motor down or keep pressing it to the firewall until heat and friction froze it.

Not much of a choice.

"We're going to have to end this pretty quick!" he yelled at Gurt.

"Is OK with me," she hollered back. "The quicker the happier."

Lang was not sure where he was but he guessed the Grand Canal that swept through the city like an reversed S was somewhere off to his left. To seek the crowded waterway and, perhaps, the police was tempting but unrealistic. There was too much traffic, and the consequences of hitting another craft would be just as deadly as the gunfire from behind.

He was going to have to think of something else.

And fast.

Before the engine quit.

Torcello
The same time

Wan Ng had chosen this small island northeast of Venice for a number of reasons. It, not Venice, had been the leading city of the lagoon for hundreds of years. It boasted the magnificent seventh- and eighth-century Romanesque cathedral of Santa Maria dell'Assunta and had been a thriving port and commercial center. Then its canals had silted up, sending commerce to Venice. Malaria had claimed a good number of those who remained.

Few tourists took the trouble to ride the vaporetto to the stop at the other end of one of the few remaining canals from the basilica. In fact, in this, the days of Carnevale, visitors were more likely to stay in Venice itself anyway. The innkeeper of the small hotel in sight of the cathedral's tower was as willing to accept the explanation that the four Chinese men were from a university here to study the twelfth- and thirteenth-century mosaics as he was to accept advance payment in full.

Ng couldn't have cared less about mosaics, the cathedral or, for that matter, Venice itself. He had a job to do. He had no idea why it had been necessary to steal a box sealed under the altar of San Marco, but that is exactly what he and his men had done. Had it not been for the untimely intervention of the man in the clown costume and the woman, the theft might well have gone undetected. Now, short a man, he had been ordered to take care of both of the intruders in spite of the serious doubts he had expressed to his superiors that there had been sufficient light for the clown and his female companion to recognize any faces, let alone be aware that the thieves were Chinese. That had been the reason that the body of his former comrade had been removed from the basilica where his neck had been broken and unceremoniously dumped in a canal after making sure he had no identifying evidence on him. By the time the police got around to comparing his face to any surveillance-camera pictures that might have been taken when he presented his false American passport entering the country, Ng and the others would be long gone.

Ng was used to carrying out orders he did not understand, and these would allow him to avenge the loss of the man the woman had killed so easily. He thought about that for a moment. The woman was obviously an expert in martial arts—kung fu, judo, jujitsu, the lot. The dead man had been trained in them as all Ng's men had, but the woman was simply faster and better. What kind of female was that?

At least he was now forewarned that the woman, if not the man also, could be dangerous.

He only hoped his remaining two men succeeded in the task of eliminating the couple before it was necessary to use the information he was seeking on the laptop in front of him. Hacking into the credit-card company's files had been surprisingly easy. It was a wonder the identity theft of which Americans constantly complained was not even more widely spread than it was. Once into the database, it was simply a matter of viewing all charges made that morning in Venice, Italy, at a specific costume shop during the time it took the Americans to return the clown outfit and the woman's costume.

He stopped scrolling and smiled. There was only one. Here it was now: the card belonged to Langford Reilly. Accommodatingly, the list also provided an address in Atlanta, Georgia, USA.

If his men did not succeed in taking care of the pair today, Ng could look forward to a trip to the States, something he enjoyed. He had learned English, a requirement of his service, and had had ample opportunity to polish it at China's American Academy. The institution was a requisite for his service and turned out fluent, American-idiom-speaking graduates conversant in rap music, sports teams and other singularly American institutions. He had been told he had the accent of the American Midwest.

He almost looked forward for a chance to use it again.

Venice

Reluctantly, Lang flicked his eyes at the oil-pressure gauge. It was almost at the bottom of the dial. He didn't have a lot of time before the right engine went belly-up. He was slowly losing ground. The craft were about equally powered, but he was zigzagging erratically to throw off the aim of his adversaries, while they had the luxury of a straight path.

The small speedboat careened around the corner of another intersecting canal. This time the side of the craft scraped a set of steps with a protesting crunch of wood against stone. Without reducing speed, Lang continued the turn, completing a 180-degree sweep and almost swamping the ship. He had no sooner straightened out before his pursuers rounded the turn. He passed them before they could react.

The windshield shattered as bullets whined evilly past his head. Reflexively, he ducked, losing sight of where the boat was headed. Within the split second before he could see again, a four-story palazzo loomed above him. He just had time to spin the wheel, but it was close enough for him to see the expressions of faces pressed against a window.

A lot of people had to be looking out onto the canal, attracted by the sound of gunfire. One or more of them had called the cops, he guessed from the sound of sirens. By the time the police found the right place in this watery spider-web of canals, they would be too late.

The starboard engine gave a cough and went silent.

Lang yelled directions at Gurt and she dove overboard. Turning the boat around again, he aimed it at the spot he guessed the Riva craft would be seconds later. Then Lang took a dive himself, beginning to swim as fast as he could the second he was in the water. His head came above the greasy green surface just in time to see the Riva veer wildly to avoid the boat Lang had just vacated. They missed the speedboat by inches, started to regain control and smashed head-on into the steps of one of the residences.

Lang ducked back underwater when he saw the collision was inevitable. Even so, the resulting explosion was clearly audible and seemed to shake the water itself.

He resurfaced to a sea of floating debris, some of it burning. There was no sign of the two men.

Ahead of him, Gurt was dragging herself onto a set of stairs that led to an old wooden door with signs of rot at the edges. He noted her purse was slung over one arm, and as she climbed out of the water, she still had her shoes on.

The latter was hardly surprising. She had just purchased

the pair of Pradas before leaving home. Gurt was very fond of the brand.

Lang pulled himself up beside her. "And what did you learn on our tour of the canals of Venice?"

Later that evening, after Gurt had retired to the Gulf-stream's small but comfortable bedroom, Lang found himself staring at the same page of the novel at which he had been looking for several minutes. Sleep aboard an aircraft, even a luxurious private one, was next to impossible for him. Gurt and others had pointed out to him that there wasn't a lot he could do about an engine failure, fire or other disaster at thirty-five thousand feet asleep or awake, and that he had a superbly trained crew no matter whether he slept or not. It did no good. A couple of drinks and a fine wine from the galley with dinner were no help. He simply couldn't doze off. The drone of the engines should have acted as a sedative. Instead, they were a stimulant to his nervous system.

He sighed, put the book down and looked out into the Stygian darkness of a night over the ocean. There were questions bouncing around inside his head like Ping-Pong balls, questions for which he had no answers. The Chinese weapon in the church, the obviously Asian man in the square. For reasons he would not like to try and explain, he would have given odds the men in the pursuing boat had been Asian, perhaps Chinese, too. Long ago Lang had learned to reject coincidence, an explanation used by weaker minds. He was right 90 percent of the time.

The only reason he could come up with was that the afternoon's affair had to do with his and Gurt's interruption of last night's theft of Saint Mark's relics. But why? Whoever had wanted the bones had apparently succeeded in making off with them. Perhaps the thieves feared he and Gurt could recognize them, give a description to the police, even though he would have needed a cat's vision to see facial features in that darkly lit place. And if the theft plus the Asian man were connected, what would an Asian want with the remains of a Christian saint?

He smiled in spite of the questions he could not answer. The face of the elderly woman who had answered the persistent banging on her door to the canal was worth remembering. With typical Italian hospitality (or was it curiosity?), she had offered towels to the two wet, bedraggled people who had mysteriously appeared on her doorstep. Manners of another age prevented her from asking questions, and she had simply accepted that the fates had sent her two people very much in need of help, or at least admission to her home.

Or had it been the tradition of *fregatura?* There was no exact English translation for this uniquely Italian concept. *Fregatura* was an act somewhat less than entirely legal but short of egregious. It also had the hint of getting away with something, as their elderly hostess would be doing by not notifying the police that the people they were undoubtedly looking for were right here in her parlor.

Once toweled off, Gurt and Lang had declined her offer to send a servant for dry clothes, explaining their hotel was nearby and only a misstep along the canal had resulted in their falling in. The graciousness of a bygone era prevented the signora from inquiring about the explosion that had surely rattled the shelves of Venetian glass against one of the walls of her centuries-old home. Perhaps she had been too deaf to hear the wailing of the sirens from the police boats.

The concierge at their Lido hotel had given them an astonished expression as the two wet, rumpled guests, still trailing wet prints from soaked shoes, trudged through his lobby. Obviously, the hotel's boat driver had not made it back there yet.

"Signor Reilly?" he had asked.

"Your boat had engine trouble," Lang said just as the elevator doors shut. "We had to swim for it."

CHAPTER TWO

Law offices of Langford Reilly
Peachtree Center
227 Peachtree Street, Atlanta
Three days later

Lang Reilly tossed the last of the pink telephone-message slips into the trash and turned on his desktop computer. Sara had taken most of his e-mail but there was enough requiring his attention to keep him busy most of the morning: a notice of hearing on a motion to suppress evidence in the federal court here in Atlanta, a judge's questions about a pretrial order he had filed in another case, a bond hearing in the local state court. He shook his head at the last. The client, one of the inventory of pro bono clients Lang kept, couldn't afford a lawyer. He surely couldn't pay the bondsman, no matter how low the bail. A total waste of time but one of the procedures the court required.

The phone on his desk buzzed. A quick glance showed the intercom between him and the outer office was the line being used.

"Yes ma'am?"

"The Reverend Bishop Groom is here."

Sara's voice bristled with resentment, no doubt at the bishop's failure to make an appointment. A white-haired prototype of someone's grandmother, Sara had served as surrogate mother and would-be social director before Gurt's arrival. She still was secretary, accountant, office manager and a zealous guardian of his time. "Can you see him now?"

The question was for the visitor's benefit. Sara knew exactly what Lang was doing at the moment.

"Send him in."

The Reverend Bishop William Groom was, as far as Lang could tell, self-ordained. His nondenominational church in one of Atlanta's bedroom communities had grown from a few hundred members to well over six thousand, necessitating no less than four services every Sunday and several during the week, plus a televangelical ministry on Sunday nights. More significantly, donations had shown a commensurate increase. Had a number of his parishioners not become disenchanted with both a lifestyle that could only be described as opulent and a more-than-priestly interest in a number of church members' wives, he might have remained beneath the IRS's radar indefinitely.

Currently, Lang was anticipating federal indictment of the good bishop for multiple counts of tax evasion, conspiracy to evade taxes, fraud, mail fraud and a laundry list of related offenses. It would seem Lang's client had not only been dipping his pen into the company inkwell, his fingers had been in the church's purse as well.

Groom came through the door, hand extended. "Thank you so much for seeing me without an appointment."

Lang stood to shake hands. "Glad I was available." He sat behind his desk, indicating one of two leather wing chairs separated by a small French commode. "What can I do for you?"

Groom was tall, over six feet, with a shock of silver hair he constantly swept aside, a gesture Lang had noted he did with dramatic flair at crucial points of his televised sermons. Still standing, he gazed upward. "First, let us pray."

Lang always felt a little uncomfortable when his client spent a good two or three minutes invoking the Lord's favor on whatever he happened to be doing at the moment as well as seeking heavenly retribution upon those who were persecuting him. Idly, Lang wondered if a brief prayer had been said preparatory to each seduction of one of his flock. It was certain the time spent communicating with the Almighty was duly noted and added to the time spent in legal counseling to be charged against a very generous retainer.

"Amen," the bishop said, and sat down.

Lang looked across the desk expectantly.

"I've been thinking about this matter of the church vehicles. They say . . ." The man's otherwise-angelic face contorted into an expression that looked like he tasted something extremely unpleasant whenever he referred to the prosecution. "They say I misused church funds to buy vehicles. Do you know, Mr. Reilly, that the Cathedral of the Holy Savior uses its vehicles, mostly buses, to bring to God's house those who otherwise would be unable to attend services?"

Lang suppressed a sigh. He had been here before. "Does that include the Ferrari and the turbo Bentley?"

The bishop hunched his shoulders, a man deeply offended. "Someone in my position needs to display material wealth. Success is a sign of God's favor, as I constantly preach. We are in very serious trouble, this country of ours, when the Philistines can persecute the faithful because they succeed."

Another synonym for the prosecution. He was partially correct, though. The government moved with an uncharacteristically light hand when dealing with religious mountebanks, charlatans and others who saw the First Amendment as license to participate in otherwise-illegal activity. It was only when it became clear someone was using a church as a personal bank account to evade taxes, utilizing the mail to solicit funds that clearly went to private uses, or the church and its pastor became indistinguishable that criminal charges were brought.

Lang kept the observation to himself.

"And then there's the matter of the church's ownership of homes in the mountains and at the beach. Do you realize how many conferences and retreats the church elders have there every year?"

As far as Lang had been able to ascertain, there were no church elders, deacons or other persons charged with any office that related to financial decisions.

He leaned forward, his elbows on the desk. "Elders?"

"Why yes, of course. You certainly don't think one person can run an organization the size of the Cathedral of the Holy Savior, do you?"

Lang reached for a pad with one hand and took a pen from a cup filled with them. "Just who are these elders?"

"Well, there's Jamie Shaw . . ."

Lang put the pen down. "Your son-in-law."

And so far, unindicted coconspiritor.

"And Lewis Reid."

Nephew.

"And, of course, Lois."

Wife.

Lang leaned back in his chair. "The government will contend since the elders are all family members, you don't have to meet at million-dollar homes in resort areas. How many times a year do you, personally, use those facilities?"

"A man under as much pressure as I am deserves an occasional long weekend away some place." He smiled. "Besides, I've composed some of my best sermons at the beach."

"It might be a little better if the beach to which you refer wasn't at Sag Harbor in Long Island's Hamptons. That's pretty high-octane real estate. And it doesn't help that you arrive there in a private jet."

"We simply charter the airplane." Bishop Groom looked offended.

"Actually, if I recall, the church purchased a set number of hours on a Citation for the last four years."

"Tending to a flock as large as mine requires transportation."

Lang shook his head slowly. "You have members of your congregation in places other than metro Atlanta?"

"We are always looking to expand the word of the Lord." The bishop slid forward, sitting on the edge of his chair. "Mr. Reilly, you sound as though you think I'm guilty as charged. That's not the attitude I want in my defense counsel."

Lang didn't think his client was guilty; he knew it. That was not the question. The issue was whether the assistant United States attorney could convince a jury of it beyond a reasonable doubt.

Lang picked up the pen and walked it between his fingers. "Bishop, you didn't hire me for my opinions, nor did you retain me to prove you innocent. Only not guilty. There's a huge difference."

The bishop thought this over for a moment. "Any chance of a deal?"

Lang shrugged. "There's always a 'deal.' Whether you find it acceptable or not is the question. So far you haven't authorized me to ask. Shall I?"

Groom gave this some thought also. "I'll pray over it and let you know." He stood, extending a hand. "I find things come easier to me if I take them to the Lord."

"Let's hope this is no exception," Lang said dryly.

Lang stood at the door between the outer office and the building's hallway and bank of elevators, watching his client's departure.

"I hope you checked to make sure you still have your watch on your wrist," Sara snorted from her desk.

Lang closed the door. "That's no way to talk about a man who dropped a hundred big on us."

Sara swiveled in her chair to face her computer monitor. "A million dollars wouldn't make him any less of a thief, a liar and a . . ." Her expression indicated she was trying to think of an acceptable phrase to describe the man's sexual exploits. Her strong disapproval of anything not condoned by the Southern Baptist Church restricted both her world-view and vocabulary.

She settled for *adulterer*.

"He may be all that but he sure had his fun while it lasted."

Lang didn't have to look at her to see her bite back a sharp reply.

"I'm about to improve the moral quality of my companions. I'm having lunch with Father Francis."

As he shut the door to his office, he heard her mutter something like "It'll do you good!"

Forty minutes later

The Capital City Club is the last remnant of what once was the heart of Atlanta's business, financial and legal communities before flight farther north abandoned the central city streets to winos, beggars and the rare tourist unfortunate enough to lose their way between the Georgia Aquarium and the Martin Luther King Jr. Historic District. Housed in downtown's sole remaining private clubhouse, a veranda-fronted, tree-flanked, four-story anachronism, it squats between towering skyscrapers. Even though an epidemic of political correctness has made the club no longer the exclusive domain of white, Anglo-Saxon males, a near-life-size portrait of Robert E. Lee is the first thing a visitor sees upon entering the foyer.

Lang entered the dining room, glanced around and spotted Father Francis Narumba seated at a table with a view of Peachtree Street. A native of one of West Africa's less desirable countries, the priest had been educated in an American college and seminary and assigned to one of Atlanta's parishes with a rapidly growing African population. He had been Lang's sister's priest after she had inexplicably not only joined the Catholic Church but a congregation where English was a second language. Lang was not particularly religious but he and Francis had become fast friends in the years after her death.

Men in clerical collars were not uncommon guests at the downtown club, but they were more frequently seen exchanging them for golf shirts in the locker rooms of the club's two courses outside the city limits.

Francis stood, the flash of a white smile splitting his face. "How was Venice? *Incudi reddere.*"

Francis, like Lang, was a victim of a liberal-arts education. Latin had been an obvious language choice for one planning to enter the priesthood. Lang had no explanation as to why he had chosen the dead tongue. The end result was that the two friends exchanged Latin aphorisms on a regular basis.

"I have indeed returned to the anvil," Lang said, sitting and shaking out the linen napkin. "To start with, I just had a visit from the Reverend Bishop Groom. You've been reading about him in the paper?"

Francis wrinkled his nose as though it detected an open sewer. "I have indeed. The fact he has come to see you tells me he's in the trouble that he richly deserves . . . How many of his parishioners claim he seduced them?"

Lang signaled to the waitress. "If seduction were a crime, we would be building high-rise jails instead of condos. It's the fact he's using his church as a tax dodge that has the U.S. attorney's boxer shorts in a wad. *Vectigalia nervi sunt rei publicae.*"

Francis took the menu proffered by the waitress. "Cicero was right: taxes are the sinews of the state. But I could forgive chiseling on taxes."

"You're in the forgiveness business, remember?"

Francis ignored him. "It's using the church's money for vacation homes, fancy cars, that sort of thing."

"Obviously the Cathedral of the Holy Savior doesn't require a vow of poverty," Lang observed pointedly. *"Divitiae virum faciunt."*

The waitress was hovering. Both men ordered large shrimp salads.

Francis watched her retreat toward the kitchen. "Riches may make the man, but think of the good that man could do if he shared some of them with people like those guys." He nodded to the window where two shabbily dressed men were panhandling passersby.

"So they could buy a better brand of wine by the pint?"

Francis's reply was a snort. "You can be quite difficult, you know."

"Be thankful this is one of my better days. I can also be impossible."

Francis shook his head. "OK. Moving past our disagreement on social and economic issues, I repeat: how was Venice?"

"You wouldn't believe what happened."

"Try me."

Lang waited for their salads to be placed in front of them before beginning his adventures.

When he finished speaking, Francis was silent for a moment, thinking. "I read about the theft of the relics from Saint Mark's in Venice. I should have known if there was trouble within a hundred miles, you'd be involved in it somehow."

"Dessert, gentlemen? We have some freshly made peppermint ice-cream cake." The waitress was hovering again.

Lang looked up. "My spiritual advisor here will no doubt take whatever you offer. He gets only bread and water in his monastic cell."

Francis rolled his eyes. "And you?"

"As a normal human being whose natural aging process has produced a metabolism that manufactures a hundred calories for each one consumed . . ."

Francis looked up at the bewildered young woman. "He means, no thank you. As for me, yes indeed, I will have the peppermint ice-cream cake. And add a dollop of whipped cream, could you, please?"

A few minutes later, Lang watched Francis dig into a concoction that would have stilled the most demanding sweet tooth. "How is it I bust my ass working out and put on a pound if I even look at sweets and you never gain weight, yet you eat anything that isn't nailed down? Can you pray off calories?"

"'Blessed is the man that walketh not in the counsel of the ungodly, nor standeth in the way of sinners nor sitteth in the seat of the scornful.' First Psalm. For you heretics, there isn't a lot of hope."

Lang sipped a cup of coffee as Francis used the edge of his fork to scrape the last of the confection from his plate. "You can have seconds, y'know."

Francis looked up, not quite successful in hiding a smile. "I couldn't do that to you." He seemed to think a moment. "Back to that excitement in Venice. You know, there's a good chance what was taken weren't Saint Mark's bones at all."

Lang was debating if the extra caffeine in another cup of coffee would make him jumpy all afternoon. "Really? And whose bones might they be?"

Just then the waitress handed Lang the check for signature and member number. He scribbled both.

Lang gave his friend a look that said he knew his leg was being pulled. "OK, I'll bite, even if I see another of those 'who's buried in Grant's tomb' jokes. Who's buried in Saint Mark's?"

Francis lifted his arm, checking his watch. "I'd tell you but you'd want an explanation, and I have a meeting with the bishop. Gurt was kind enough to invite me for dinner Friday night. I'll explain then."

Both men got up from the table, Francis reaching to shake Lang's hand. "Thanks for the lunch. I'm a little embarrassed I can't pick up my share of the tab here."

Lang grinned. "Why? In all the time we've tossed a coin for

the check, I don't recall you ever losing. Sooner or later you will. This way, I'm spared the suspense of guessing when."

Outside, wind was chasing trash down the sidewalk between canyon walls of glass and steel. Lang had left his overcoat at the office and was glad his walk back to work would be less than a block. Everyone else on the street seemed to share his hurry to get out of the wintry blast.

He stopped long enough to wave as Francis drove out of the parking lot in the parish's aged Toyota, crossed Peachtree and disappeared down the ridge, the spine of which forms Atlanta's most famous street. Turning back toward his office, he stopped. Across the street was one pedestrian who was in no hurry. His coat collar turned up concealing most of the face, the man seemed to be staring at Lang. Perhaps suddenly realizing he had been noticed, he hurried into the revolving door of a nearby hotel.

Lang's first impulse was to follow. He took a couple of steps and stopped. Overactive imagination? Had the stranger been looking at him or simply taking in what meager sights the city had to offer? He looked around, spotting no one who showed any particular interest in him, not even a street bum. Still, ingrained paranoia wouldn't let go, a paranoia that had saved his life more than once.

Once he was back in his office, Sara was waiting for him with another stack of messages. He soon forgot the man on the street.

Beijing Olympic Tower
267 Beisihuan Zhonglu
Haidian, Beijing
The day before

Less than a week after the end of the 2008 Summer Olympics, the space occupied in the new sixteen-story building by the committee that had organized and operated the games was vacated. The colorful posters and photographs of the athletes that had festooned the walls were replaced by officially sanctioned pictures of the holy trinity of Sun Yat-sen, Mao and Chou En-lai. China's burgeoning bureaucracy, ever hungry for more room, now filled the building overlooking the Birdcage, the popular name for the unique Olympic stadium.

Not that the view from the fourth floor this afternoon was one that might adorn the cover of a magazine, thought Wan Ng. Beijing's brownish haze had reduced the landmark to a mere chimera even though it was less than a quarter of a mile distant. A combination of coal-fueled industry, vehicle emissions and lethargic natural circulation rendered Beijing's air among the most foul on earth. A system of alternating days when the massive number of government employees might drive into the city, a lottery for license plates to restrict the number of vehicles on the roads and a requirement that all autos and trucks must have an "environmentally friendly" sticker to enter past the Fifth Ring Road had done little to ameliorate the air quality. The fact a thriving black market dispensed the stickers to anyone willing to pay was only part of the problem.

Poisonous air was the least of Ng's concerns this afternoon. The tone of the call he had gotten from Undersecretary Chin Diem summoning him here had lacked the congratulations for a job well done. True, Ng had lost the men assigned to him and had made international news for the chase through the canals of Venice. But he had brought the object of the mission back with him even though its theft had caused a worldwide uproar.

So what?

The men he had left behind could hardly be identified as Chinese nationals. Even if the Italians possessed the technology to compare their features with scans of their American passports, it would be months before the authorities realized the papers were forgeries.

Still, Diem was unhappy for some reason. Not knowing that reason made Ng nervous. One thing was certain: meeting the undersecretary here rather than in Diem's sumptuous office with a view of Tiananmen Square and the Forbidden City beyond, haze permitting, meant there would be no record of either the meeting itself or the subject to be discussed, a rarity in a society where the affairs of the lowest citizen were subject to scrutiny.

Uneasily, Ng watched a procession of three Shuanghuan CEO's, midsized SUVs, pull up to the building's entrance below. Four dark-suited men got out of both the leading and trailing vehicles, scanned their surroundings and nodded to the driver of the second car. Crime in Beijing was almost as nonexistent as political dissent. The number of cars in the caravan of a high-level official was more a testimony to his importance and current standing in the governmental hierarchy than his need for security. Should a bureaucrat who had formerly rated three cars appear with a single-car escort, his status was clearly waning. Decline to a lone SUV augured an immediate and involuntary retirement from government service.

Ng could see the portly figure of Diem below as one of the men held the door open. He was carrying a thin attaché case.

Ng turned around, facing a double bank of elevators. The one on the far left whispered open and four black suits stepped out, followed by Diem.

The undersecretary glanced around, fixing an expressionless stare on Ng. "Follow me."

He led the entourage down a short corridor and opened a door at the end. Motioning his men to remain in the hallway, he ushered Ng inside.

Here the walls still bore Olympic posters. A metal desk and chair faced two uncomfortable-looking seats. The office was devoid of the normal photographs of wife and the single child allowed each family, or any other personal effects. Clearly, this office had been borrowed just for this meeting.

Ng was pondering the significance of that fact as Diem rounded the desk, sat and snapped open the attaché case. Wordlessly, he motioned Ng to be seated. Reaching into a jacket pocket, he produced a pack of American cigarettes—Marlboros—and then a gold lighter, a knockoff of a world-famous jeweler's design. He shook out a cigarette and lit it without offering his guest one, not a good sign.

His head circled in blue smoke, he removed a thin folder from the attaché case, opened it and began to read. Ng would have bet the undersecretary had the few pages memorized. It was a common tactic among the Party's elite. The theatrics enforced the fact the subordinate did not rate the time it would take for his superior to read the file in advance.

From somewhere behind the desk, Diem produced an exceptionally ugly porcelain ashtray and set his smoldering cigarette down. "How did the Americans know you were in the church?"

Ng felt his throat go dry. The implicit accusation could be career ending. In fact, if he was even suspected of revealing his mission, prison or worse was likely.

"I do not believe they did, Comrade Secretary."

The use of the honorific, though passé, showed respect.

"Explain."

"Had they known my men and I were in the church, I doubt they would have entered so obviously. They made no effort to conceal themselves."

Diem picked up the cigarette, took a puff and returned it to the ashtray. "Do you not find it coincidental that two members of American intelligence would just happen by late at night when the church would ordinarily be closed?"

"Do we know they were American intelligence?"

Diem snorted, smoke erupting from his nose. "The woman obviously had military training, did she not? And if she had the capability to not only defeat but kill one of your armed men, we must assume her companion did also."

"Comrade Secretary, my subsequent investigation of the credit-card records shows the man, Langford Reilly, is some sort of lawyer living in the southern United States."

"An intelligence operative would have such cover, would he not?"

Ng had no answer.

The undersecretary was studying the short stack of papers in front of him. "Intelligence or not, the man and woman could well have seen the faces of you and your men. They could have told the police the men robbing the church were Chinese."

"The interior of the church was too dark to see faces."

Diem was reading from the file again. "You are Yi, are you not, from a small village in Yunnan?"

Ng hoped his face didn't show what he felt. It was no surprise his background had been duly recorded. A file existed on every person born in China, one of the reasons for the bloated civil service. There would be a more detailed dossier for those considered to be in sensitive positions. His uneasiness came from the mention of the fact he was a member of one of China's fifty-five ethnic minorities, people the government viewed with xenophobic suspicion.

Ng recalled his childhood in the tiny village: the walled, plank house with a sod roof held on by stones shared with his parents, his grandparents, uncles, aunts and cousins. As well as a number of livestock far too valuable to be left out in the elements. Neither the Great Leap Forward nor any other proclaimed program of rural modernization had reached the place. The last time he had visited, there still was no electricity or running water. It had taken hard work from sunup till dark to wrest a living from the stony soil of each family's single small field allotted by the local commissar. Army life had been luxurious by comparison. He felt nostalgia for the place along with a strong desire to never have to live there again, a real possibility if he failed to follow whatever agenda the undersecretary had in mind.

Diem continued. "Major, People's Liberation Army, transferred to Special Branch, Department of International Affairs three years ago, commendation for successful completion of unspecified mission eight months ago . . ."

Again Ng kept quiet.

Diem's eyes flicked over the top of the file. "And I see you graduated from the American Academy."

"That is all correct, Comrade Secretary."

Diem nodded as though an issue had been resolved. "Yes, of course. Do you feel comfortable operating in America?"

"I have been so trained, Comrade Secretary, as you have just noted."

The secretary paused long enough to put out his cigarette with an exaggerated stabbing motion. "Good. You are to choose such men as you think best fitted and travel to the United States, where you will observe this Reilly person and the woman. If you are convinced they have no connection with an American intelligence organization, you are to so inform me." He held Ng's gaze. "You will be certain before you make such a decision."

"And if they are?"

Diem leaned across the desk. "If such is the case, we may be assured they have passed along the fact that the People's Republic may have been involved in the Venice affair and change policy accordingly."

"And if not?"

The undersecretary shrugged; it was a matter of no consequence. "Either way, what they might have seen presents a future risk. Eliminate them."

472 Lafayette Drive, Atlanta
19:42 the next evening

Lang Reilly was sprawled into his favorite chair in the house's paneled library/den, a Waterford crystal tumbler containing the remnants of a scotch and water on a leather-inlaid desk beside him. The flames danced across shelves of polished spines of leather-bound books Lang had collected and read. Works of Scott, Burns's poetry . . . All were in English, not the Danish or Swedish popular for decorative purposes sold in antique stores. From the sound system, John Denver was extolling a Rocky Mountain high. The singer, dead these many years, had been a favorite of Dawn's and a voice Lang associated with a particularly happy part of his earlier life. The music was more nostalgia than entertainment.

He was watching his six-year-old son, Manfred, seated on the muted Kerman rug in front of a fire crackling behind a brass screen. Opposite the boy, Francis sat splay legged, holding a deck of oversized cards. The priest dealt slowly, faceup, one on top of the one before. At the appearance of a jack, both attempted to be the first to slap an open palm on it as it hit the floor, thereby claiming not only the knave but the stack of cards beneath.

The disproportionate size of the piles accumulated by the competitors was attributable to Francis's reluctance to slap the jack with full force for fear of hurting Manfred, plus the fact the latter's shorter arms and unrestrained enthusiasm gave him a distinct advantage. Curled up touching Manfred, Grumps, the family's dog of undetermined age and breed, opened an eye, either the blue one or the brown one, annoyed at each shriek his young master gave as he claimed another jack.

Lang stood up, crossed the room and stood at the built-in bar. "One more scotch before dinner?"

Francis looked up, card in midair. "No thanks. I'm afraid it'll dull my competitive edge."

Lang helped himself before nodding toward the relatively small stack of cards the priest had won. "What competitive edge?"

John Denver was imploring the country roads of West Virginia to take him home.

"Abendessen!" Gurt was standing in the doorway to announce dinner. When possible, she and Lang spoke German around their son in hopes of preserving his bilingual abilities.

"Aw, Mom," Manfred protested in words and tone familiar to any American six-year-old's parents. "I was beating the socks off Uncle Fancy . . ."

Francis slowly got up. "And I expect you will after dinner, too."

Gurt shook her head at her son. "I will bet you did not whine so at coming to dinner while you were staying with Mr. and Mrs. Charles while your father and I were gone."

She referred to their next-door neighbors, who had a son slightly less than two years Manfred's junior. Even though the difference between four and six is large at their ages, the two boys had been fast friends since Lang and Gurt's participation in rescuing the younger from kidnappers the year before. The Charleses, Wynton and Paige, were more than eager to babysit as a small return for Lang and Gurt's efforts, a return both Lang and Gurt insisted was not due.

"But Mom," Manfred said innocently, "Mrs. Charles is an *awesome* cook."

Lang tousled his son's hair, speaking English for Francis's benefit. "Meaning from what I heard that you and Wynn Three had a steady diet of hot dogs, hamburgers and peanut butter."

"And the best apple pie in the world!"

Smiling, Gurt led her son to his seat in the dining room. *"Auf Wiedersehen* apple pie and peanut butter; *wie geht's* roast chicken and vegetables?"

Having outgrown his high chair, Manfred climbed up on top of two sofa cushions that got his head and shoulders above table level.

Sitting, Lang turned to Francis. "OK, padre, see if you can finish saying grace before dinner gets cold."

When Francis had completed an admirably brief blessing,

Manfred piped up. "Why does Uncle Fancy always do that, thank God for the food, when Mommy buys it at the store herself?"

Francis gave Lang an amused look. "Your son's spiritual education seems to be somewhat lacking."

Gurt and Lang exchanged glances before Lang looked back at Francis. "You said the blessing; you explain."

Francis cleared his throat. "Well, we thank God that your mother has the ability, the money, to buy . . ."

The phone rang.

Family custom decreed a ringing phone be ignored during dinner. If the call was important, there would be a message. If unimportant, why bother to answer in the first place?

This time, though, Lang wiped his mouth with a napkin and stood. "Excuse me. The federal grand jury was meeting this afternoon, and the indictment of the Reverend Bishop Groom was one of the things they were considering."

"I thought grand-jury proceedings were secret," Francis observed.

Lang was headed back to the den and the ringing phone. "They are. That's why I need to take this. My source isn't free to call at just any time."

Lang noticed it the second he put the phone to his ear, a faint hum that had not been on the line when he used the telephone earlier that evening. "Hello?"

Silence.

"Hello?"

"Mr. Dean?" a man's voice responded. "Is this David Dean?"

The humming seemed to waver like an echo with each word.

"Just a moment," Lang replied evenly.

Leaving the cordless receiver off its base, he went to the two windows closest to the street. The curtains were already pulled for the night. Reaching up behind the heavy drapes, Lang grasped a handle. He pulled, lowering a metal sheet. He repeated the process at the other window.

When he returned to the phone, the caller had gone. So had the hum.

As he returned to the table, Gurt studied his face. "Who was that, a wrong number?"

Lang shook his head. "I don't think so."

"Then, who . . . ?"

Lang's expression said he clearly didn't intend to discuss it in front of Manfred or Francis.

Thirty minutes later, the two men were back in the den. Now, with thudding guitars, the more-recently deceased baritone voice of Johnny Cash was lamenting his confinement in Folsom Prison. Francis was watching as Lang carefully decanted a bottle of twenty-five-year-old vintage Graham's port.

"What makes a certain year 'vintage'?" Francis asked.

Lang's eyes were on the remains of crumbled cork collecting in the silver port filter along with the residue, or "mud," of crushed fruit with which the distilled wine had been fortified before being stored in oak barrels. "A vintage year is when one vineyard declares it. That's why the year of this Graham's, say, might not be declared a vintage by another house, say, Sandeman's, Cockburne's or Fonseca."

"What's to stop a port manufacturer from declaring every year a vintage? I mean, the price of a vintage is double or triple that of a late-vintage ruby or other port."

Lang placed the full decanter on the bar. "Nothing except the fact that if a house puts out an inferior year's product as vintage, it won't keep its customers long." He filled a small crystal glass, holding it to the light to admire its ruby color. "You might say the free market keeps the port makers honest."

Lang handed the glass to Francis, who took a tentative sip. "As always, delicious!"

Lang poured and sampled a glass of his own. "You're right, it is good but . . ."

"But what?"

Lang looked longingly at the coffee table where a mahogany humidor sat. "It would be better with a good *cubano*."

Francis shook his head slowly as he sat on the sofa. "Don't even *think* about going back on your word."

When Manfred arrived in Atlanta, Gurt and Lang had made promises to each other concerning the child's health. Not wanting to set a bad example or subject the little boy to potentially harmful secondhand smoke, they agreed they would not smoke in front of him. That proved difficult for Gurt, leading to clandestine Marlboros smoked in the yard, the odor of which was clearly detectable upon her return inside. Lang, a lover of Cuban cigars, which he had ordered specially by an indirect route, only consumed one or two a week anyway. It had been easier for him to smoke less although more difficult to conceal, since he refused to throw away a cigar only half-smoked. The things cost nearly twenty-five bucks apiece. The ultimate resolution had been for both parents to simply quit—if there was anything simple about giving up a lifetime pleasure.

"What word was that?" Gurt had returned from her turn to bathe Manfred and put him to bed.

"Our mutual smoking ban."

She looked at her husband with mock suspicion. "A year into an agreement and you are already looking for hoop holes?" She shrugged. "It is not easy, being married to a lawyer, always the hoop holes."

"Loopholes," Lang corrected.

"Is one hole in an agreement not as good as another?"

For an answer, Lang poured a third glass of port and extended it to her. "At least we didn't give up port."

She accepted the offering with a mock curtsy. "For small favors I am thankful."

Johnny Cash bewailed being named Sue.

Francis smiled. "Always found that song amusing. What I don't understand, though, is your choice of music."

"I suppose you would prefer Gregorian chants?"

"Not necessarily. What I meant was, you obviously enjoy history." Francis pointed to the overburdened bookcases. "I see everything from Gibbon's *Decline and Fall* to Will Durant's *Story of Civilization* and Churchill's *Second World War.* I see works by Dickens, essays by Emerson and a bunch of contemporary novels."

"And?"

"I don't get it: someone as obviously well-read as you likes country music?"

Lang nodded. "Yeah, I do. At least some of it. I can understand the words and it actually has a tune I can whistle. Try whistling Beethoven."

An hour or so later, the port exhausted, Francis stood and stretched. "As always, a magnificent dinner, wonderful port and delightful company."

Lang also stood. "You are easily amused."

Francis sighed. "Not as easily as you think. It's been a long time since you broke bread at the parish house." He lowered his voice conspiratorially. "Mrs. Finnigan, my housekeeper-cook, bless her heart, is a fine woman and a good Catholic but a horrible cook. *Deorum cibus non est.* Food for the gods it ain't."

"Doesn't sound like a fair trade-off to me," Lang said, walking his friend to the front door. "Why not get someone who is a decent cook, then?"

Francis stopped, facing Lang. "She's been at Immaculate Conception longer than I have. I can't just fire her like that."

Lang reached to open the door. "Maybe you'll be canonized someday for your martyrdom in suffering heartburn as the price of Christian charity."

Francis stepped around Lang to give Gurt a hug. "In addition to being a heretic, your husband is a wiseass."

Gurt hugged him back. "Be grateful you do not have to live with him."

"I include thanks in my daily prayers."

They watched him pull the Toyota into the street. In following it with his eyes, Lang noticed a sedan parked at the curb to his left. The people who lived there had an ample yard in which to park cars, so the automobile was not a visitor's nor was it one he recognized as his neighbor's. For that matter, the humble Ford was not the type transportation preferred by the residents of affluent Ansley Park.

Its sheer ordinariness stuck out like an automotive sore thumb.

Lang took a little more time closing the door than was necessary. He thought he saw a flash of movement. Someone was in the car.

Why?

Lang thought he had a good idea.

It was then he realized he had forgotten to ask Francis about his cryptic remark at lunch the other day concerning the true occupant of Saint Mark's tomb under the altar in Venice. Oh well, he saw the priest on a regular if purely social basis. He'd get an answer the next time.

Upstairs, Lang cut off the bathroom light and was approaching the bed where Gurt was an indistinct pile of covers.

"Who was it on the phone?" she asked as he pulled back the covers to climb in.

"Someone who wanted me to think they had a wrong number."

"Why would someone want to do that?"

"There was a hum on the line."

The blankets fell away as Gurt sat up. "A parabolic listening device? That could make wireless electronics like a cordless telephone hum. Someone with the thing trained on the windows to pick up the vibrations of the glass caused by the human voice. It can also pick up both sides of a telephone conversation. They were testing it."

"That's why I pulled down our custom-made privacy shields before I got in bed."

In remodeling the old Ansley Park home, Gurt and Lang had spared no expense to retain its early twentieth-century charm while modernizing a number of features. One of these additions had been a security system that would shock their more conventional neighbors, and one many military bases might envy.

With the past they shared, neither wanted to risk a former enemy's reappearance. The house contained a complete privacy system designed to thwart the most sophisticated listening devices, in addition to a number of other surprises, such as oak bolted to two-inch case-hardened steel for doors, a central control system that could remotely seal off any part of the house and real-time surveillance cameras.

Gurt turned on the light by her side of the bed. "They called to make sure their device was operational."

"Not as good as tapping the phone but not as risky, either. And they can follow conversations anywhere within a hundred yards just by focusing the antenna."

"But why would someone want to . . . ?"

"To enjoy my brilliant wit?"

Gurt's frown showed that at the moment, she wasn't enjoying it at all. "What should we do?"

"Not much. Far as I know, there's no law against eavesdropping as long as no wiretap or trespass is involved. I'd say someone is more interested in learning about us than doing us harm."

Gurt nodded. "For now."

"For now." Lang turned to open the top drawer of the bedside table and verify his Browning HP 9 mm was where he kept it. "At some point they—whoever 'they' might be—are going to either find out whatever they want to know or give up. Then they'll either go away or move to the next step."

Gurt was crawling out from under the covers.

"Where are you going?" Lang asked.

"Downstairs to make sure all the locks are on and so are the motion and impact detectors."

"Don't forget the motion-activated cameras."

Lang knew the house was as secure as modern technology could make it. He still had a hard time getting to sleep.

From the diary of Louis Etienne Saint Denis, secretary to Major General Napoleon Bonaparte

Chateau Malmaison
September 22, 1799

The general will not see his wife. We arrived in Toulon[1] from Egypt near a week past and hastened to Paris and then to this small palace nearly in the shadow of the grandeur that was Versailles before it was sacked by the mob. It is the news received in Egypt that lent wings to our heels, the open secret of the many affairs of the general's wife, known to all but, it would seem, the general himself. Had not General Junot told him, all would be well.[2]

Now, he sulks in the upstairs of this petite palace, which he provided for Joséphine,[3] not allowing her to his bed despite the most piteous wailing and tears. The general married this woman but three years past and it has appeared to all close to him the marriage has been unsatisfactory from

---

1 Joséphine thought her husband was to arrive at Le Havre and rushed there to meet him in hopes of squelching the news of her multiple adulteries. Napoleon was in Paris before she caught up to him.

2 Junot was the only general of Napoleon's staff at this time who did not eventually achieve the rank of marshal of France. Could it be Napoleon blamed him for his wife's indiscretions, a killing of the messenger?

3 She was born Marie-Josèphe-Rose Tascher de La Pagerie. "Joséphine" was the name Napoleon gave her.

the start. The widow of an aristocrat who fell victim to the guillotine, she escaped the same fate only by the overthrow of Robespierre.[4] *She is the daughter of a plantation owner in the West Indies*[5] *impoverished by a hurricane. Older than the general by several years, she is far from beautiful but has a charm and grace that, according to gossip, have enslaved many of her lovers.*

From the beginning, she treated the general with scorn, while he adored her. Now things are upside down, she begging forgiveness while he ignores her.

I can do nothing to improve his dark state and have quit trying lest I draw his ire. Even remarking that we will not miss Egypt's searing heat brought forth nothing more than a glare. Other than meeting daily with his staff and walks in the small garden,[6] *the general keeps to himself, reading and dictating letters to me. He has become fascinated by the history of Alexander the Great. Only this morning, he commented to me that a great battle*[7] *had been fought along the Nile for possession of Alexander's body, for it had been prophesied that the nation that possessed the remains of the god-king would never be defeated.*[8] *Though he does not say, he believes himself to be a second Alexander, his conquests in Europe rather than the East.*

---

4 Robespierre was overthrown and sentenced to the guillotine himself. A much-admired orator, he was on the scaffold addressing the mob when someone shot him in the jaw. He went to his death mute. Thus ended the Terror.
5 Martinique.
6 Small by the standards of Versailles, perhaps. Even today the formal garden surrounding Malmaison is impressive.
7 In June or July of 320 BC, Perdiccas arrived on the banks of the Nile to do battle with Ptolemy to retrieve Alexander's mummified body. He was defeated by a combination of better intelligence by Ptolemy, having to cross a river with tricky currents and the voracious appetite of the Nile crocodiles, who fed on the living and dead for days afterward.
8 In spite of the mania for "logic" and "science" in postrevolutionary France, Napoleon had his personal astrologer, whom he consulted on matters both military and civil.

The only constant in the general's life is the mysterious
box he brought from Egypt. It is never out of his sight.

Law offices of Langford Reilly
The next day

Gurt was the only person who regularly called Lang on his
cell phone while he was at work and then only if she had
reason to short-circuit Sara's phone-answering duties. So
why was she doing it now?

Lang pushed back from his desk, where he had been
proofreading a motion to be filed the next day, dragged the
cell from a pocket and pressed "start."

"Yes ma'am?"

"Lang, there is someone in our house."

It took a second for her meaning to register. She wasn't
referring to Allard, the man who did twice-a-week cleaning,
and he couldn't recall anyone else who had a key. "You
mean, like a burglar? In broad daylight?"

Her voice was perfectly calm, the way it always was when
she was facing danger. "I took Manfred to kindergarten,
went to the grocery store, came home and the red light was
blinking."

Another of the home's security features was a series of
perimeter sensors that illuminated small warning lights dis-
creetly placed beside front and rear doors.

"Any sign of entry? Our locks aren't the kind that can
easily be forced."

"Whoever is inside the house had to have special equipment. The locks on both doors are intact and I can see no
broken windows. Shall I call the police?"

Response time for Atlanta's emergency services had been
the subject of TV and newspaper articles after several houses
had burned to the ground and one or two home invasions
had taken place between notifying 911 responders and arrival

of the police. Callers had an equal chance of being put on hold or having the emergency crews sent to the wrong addresses. The director of the service blamed budget cuts. Most citizens realistically blamed stupidity and the city's civil-service system, which made death almost the only cause to terminate inept employees.

"Whoever's in there isn't going anywhere and he might be armed. I take it you're not."

"I do not carry weapons to drive Manfred to kindergarten, no."

"Call 911. I'm on my way."

Less than twenty minutes later, Lang parked in front of his home. It must have been a slow day at the 911 number. Already, the driveway was filled with police cruisers, lights flashing and the street filled with curious neighbors. A van bearing the logo ATLANTA POLICE S.W.A.T. TEAM was disgorging a number of figures in paramilitary dress carrying M16 rifles, who were running toward the uniformed officers already surrounding the house. Lang climbed out of his Porsche just as a tall black man in a suit exited an unmarked but obviously official car.

"Well, Mr. Reilly! I shoulda knowed this be your house, the place where there always some kinda trouble."

Lang smiled. "Good to see you again, too, Detective Morse."

Morse shook his head as he followed Lang up the path to the front door. "Reckon I should be thankful you called us, someone in your house, instead of you bagging him yourself like usual."

Lang didn't break stride. "Be fair, Detective. The only times you've arrived after someone got hurt was when I had to defend myself."

Morse shook his head. "Still a mess. Between somebody taking a walk off your twenty-fourth-story balcony at your condo, blowing up your car, killing a professor down to Georgia Tech, you just plain trouble. Not to mention your condo exploding."

Lang spied Gurt in conversation with a man who appeared to be the leader of the SWAT Team. "At least it's never dull, Detective."

"Maybe ain't dull but sure gonna make retirement enjoyable."

Gurt recognized Morse and turned from the other man. "Ah, Detective! So glad you could come!"

"Ain't by choice, ma'am, tell you that." His eyes focused on a small blinking red light under the mailbox. "That gizmo there what tell you somebody inside? Hate to think we got all these folks and hardware out here 'cause of a false alarm," he added dubiously.

"I made sure . . . ," she began.

Reaching past her and the detective, Lang flipped open the mailbox beside the door and pushed a small button. The back of a very ordinary looking postal receptacle fell away, revealing a small TV screen. The picture was black-and-white. It showed a figure pacing up and down a room, a gun in his hand.

"Our foyer," Lang explained. "You can see there's someone there."

Morse's eyes widened. "So we seeing a burglary in real time? But why ain't he trying to get away? He gotta have heard the sirens."

"He can't. The minute he stepped into the room, activating the security system, steel screens dropped down from the ceiling, trapping him in the foyer. Same thing would have happened if he had broken in anywhere else."

Morse gave Lang the expression of a man who thinks he may be the butt of a joke. "Get outta here!"

"If you liked that, you're gonna love this."

Lang pushed another button and a panel next to the video mailbox popped open, revealing what looked like a small speaker. Those standing close by could hear the footsteps of the man inside.

"Voice activated," Lang explained as he leaned forward. "You, in the house!"

The figure on the screen froze for a second before turning around, looking for the source of the voice.

"You! You've got exactly ten seconds to drop your weapon, lie down of the floor and put your hands on your head. Now, nine seconds before we shoot in the cyanide gas."

The man seemed paralyzed.

"Seven seconds or you'll be dead in less than thirty."

That got his attention. He did as ordered.

"Now what?" Morse asked.

Lang produced a key and opened the door, standing back to let the SWAT team enter. Its leader glanced nervously at Lang.

"The gas was a bluff."

Morse watched the men enter, cuff the intruder and drag him to his feet before speaking. "Who the hell's the architect for your house, Mr. Reilly, James Bond?"

Lang chose to laugh rather than explain how many close calls he had had in the last few years. Morse was aware of a number of them.

Conversation stopped as the SWAT members dragged the invader toward the open doors of a van.

"Caught in the act—*in flagrante delicto*, as you lawyers say," the detective observed. "Even the Fulton County DA should be able to get a conviction if the sheriff can hold on to him."

He referred to the fact that the current county prosecutor's office chronically saw criminals go free for reasons of failure to timely prosecute, misplaced evidence and general incompetence. In the last year, several high-profile suspects had walked out of the county's jail by simply giving a false name to sheriff's deputies. In Atlanta, Fulton County, Georgia, the wheels of justice did not just grind slowly, they frequently ran with stripped gears.

Lang was more interested in the man being shoved into the back of the paddy wagon. "Detective, when was the last time you busted an Asian like that guy?"

Morse looked at him suspiciously. "You asking on behalf of the ACLU or somebody?"

Lang shook his head. "Not at all. Just asking because I'm curious."

The detective rubbed his chin. "Dunno. Most them Asians around here too busy working for a living to do something like break in a house. Now, out to DeKalb County, they got theyselves a problem with some Asian gangs, but here, they run their businesses an' what all." He grinned. "Don' know if you notice, but ever' year the paper runs pictures of the top graduate of ever' city high school. Most of 'em are Asian kids. Kids who finish top of their class ain't got time for gangs, crime or anything else."

The detective watched the van drive away with its prisoner. "That perp, Vietnamese or whatever, didn't do his homework before he tried to break in here. Just random luck, his bad luck he chose your place." He turned to face the house's open door, where several uniforms were watching Gurt demonstrate how the steel curtains worked. "Fact is, he'd a known who you were and the sorry-ass history of people trying to fuck with you, he would've chosen another house, that's for sure."

"I appreciate your confidence."

But Lang felt anything but confident the break-in was random.

472 Lafayette Drive, Atlanta
That evening

Lang had finished putting his freshly bathed son to bed despite the little's boy's every effort to negotiate a few more minutes. Lights out, Grumps already snoring gently on the hooked rug, Manfred now breathing deeply. Lang stood at the door, observing the scene limned by the hall light. He was perpetually both astonished at and grateful for the domestic turn his life had taken in the last two years.

After Dawn's death, Lang had reconciled himself to a life without the children he had wanted so badly. His resignation to an existence alone had deepened when his sister Janet and her adopted son had perished in a bomb blast in Paris, what, five years ago? To his mind, Gurt's unexpected reappearance with a son he didn't know he had was nothing short of miraculous.

Now, if only he could shake off the troubles that seemed to follow him like stray dogs, he could settle down to a life of pleasantly dull domesticity. His existence would be as close to perfect as he could wish.

Or as I think I might wish, he added as he flipped off the hall switch and started down the stairs. Running a charitable foundation was, at the best of times, a source of little excitement. The practice of law, even dealing with characters like the Reverend Bishop Groom, was at its most rewarding repetitive, and constant repetition soon equaled ennui and boredom. Job satisfaction among those of Lang's peers who had the keenest of minds took a definite downward turn after ten to fifteen years of doing basically the same thing over and over, whether it be in the boardroom, the closing room or the courtroom.

OK, he conceded in the ongoing self-debate, *what is it you want: a fabric of life into which is woven the occasional bright hue of action, a stew, bland other than the odd piquant morsel?* Most of his contemporaries accepted the colorless existence, the tasteless portion.

Not that he had a choice, he realized. Interrupting grave robbers in Venice, the chase through the canals, just happened. Like getting drenched by an unpredictable summer thunder shower, he and Gurt had just chanced to be there by some random process, call it luck, fate, karma or whatever. Now, for reasons he didn't understand, his home was under surveillance and had been invaded.

His guess was that the intruder had seen Gurt leave and had anticipated the house would be empty, carrying a weapon only against the possibility of her returning earlier than expected. He had little doubt the job had been thoroughly reconnoitered. But to what end? Hardly some dopehead, desperate to rip off a flat-screen TV to exchange for a few flakes of crystal meth. Even if the law did not recognize a causal relationship because of the mere proximity of events in time, common sense did. What had happened in Venice had precipitated the break-in; he was sure of it.

But why?

The doorbell chimed as he reached the bottom step. He saw Gurt squinting through the peephole before she opened the door. He was surprised to see Detective Morse cross the threshold.

The policeman nodded to Gurt. "Evening, ma'am. Sorry to bother you."

Lang grinned inwardly. As usual when the detective wasn't on duty or around the other cops, the deep Southern-black accent dropped away like a discarded garment. Lang supposed the dialect was a device to disarm suspects, to conceal a sharp mind and a quick sense of observation.

"Well, Detective," Lang said, "this is a surprise. I don't recall a visit from you that wasn't in response to some sort of mayhem."

Morse was looking around curiously. "Tell me about it! This isn't a social call, though."

"Well, you're welcomed nonetheless." Lang gestured. "Come on back into the den. Can I get you something, perhaps an adult beverage?"

"Thanks but I won't be staying that long. I've got a couple of questions, though."

Lang led him from the foyer, past dining and living rooms and into the den. "I'd be surprised if you didn't." He went to the bar and poured himself a shot of scotch. "Sure you won't join me?"

Gurt sat on the sofa and motioned the policeman into a chair across a glass coffee table. "Perhaps a Coke?"

Morse shook his head. "Mighty kind of you, but no thanks." Reaching into a pocket, he produced a small notepad. "Don't suppose either of you have ever seen the perp that was in your house?"

Both Lang and Gurt shook their heads no.

"Should we have?" Lang asked, adding ice and water to the glass.

The detective gave him a long look, the stare of someone who thinks he is perhaps not hearing the entire truth. "The question you asked me, the one about Asian criminals. Almost like you weren't surprised at being burglarized by someone other than some homey looking for something to fence in a hurry."

For not the first time, Lang realized the man's perceptiveness was usually hidden behind his speech. He said nothing as he sat on the sofa next to Gurt.

"The guy's Chinese, best we can tell. Least he seemed to understand one of our guys who speaks Mandarin, though he wouldn't respond to it. And a pro, like he's been in a police station once or twice, I'd guess, and I don't mean to contribute to the Policemen's Benevolent Association, either. No ID on him. A real hard nut. Only words he's spoken since he was busted has been to ask for a lawyer, fellow named Wan who practices in DeKalb County. Mostly defends gang members. Why do I think to you all this isn't news?"

Lang shrugged. "Detective, I can assure you, we were not expecting to be burglarized, not by a Chinese or, for that matter, a Frenchman or Sherpa."

Morse gazed around the room. "For someone got his house secure as Fort Knox, you weren't exactly expecting Girl Scouts selling cookies, either."

"Last time I looked, Detective, a man's house is his castle. He's free to use any security measure he chooses unless it's illegal like a spring gun or something else that potentially could injure emergency personnel."

Morse gave him another long look. "You're right, counselor. But you can understand why I might be curious as to the, er, rather elaborate precautions. I mean, what other house you know got steel curtains drop down from the ceiling, cameras and an intercom? And I'm far from certain the cyanide gas was just a bluff."

Lang sat back, crossing his arms. "You know I seem to draw trouble, Detective."

"Like sugar draws ants."

"Now that I have a family, it seemed only reasonable to take certain . . . precautions."

"OK, conceding that you're just a cautious man, why would some Chinese guy be interested in your house?"

Lang rattled the ice cubes in his glass and took a sip. "Until you told me the man's nationality—or should I say ethnicity—he could have been any number of people of Asian descent."

Morse stood, stuffing the notepad in a jacket pocket. "See if I got this right: you had no reason whatsoever to think you'd be burglarized, and even less by a Chinese."

Lang stood. "You got it."

The detective glanced upward, perhaps checking this room for cameras also. "These real-time TV cameras that showed the perp in your foyer. I don't suppose they make a tape, too."

Lang shook his head. "No need. The purpose is to be able to see an intruder, not produce evidence."

"You sure about that?"

"Very."

Morse's eyes narrowed. "Let me be very clear, Mr. Reilly. You hiding something pertinent to my investigation, I won't hesitate to charge you with interfering with an investigation, obstruction, spitting on the street, parking overtime or whatever."

Lang smiled disarmingly. "So you've told me."

Morse pointed an accusing finger. "Ever' time, there's something I feel you aren't telling me. This time . . ."

Lang crossed to the doorway between the hall and den, his good humor undiminished, a clear indication the conversation was at an end. "Thanks for stopping by, Detective. Anytime."

Between drawn curtains Lang and Gurt watched Morse climb into his car and depart.

"You had a reason to tell him not about Venice and to lie about the tape?" she asked as the car's taillights disappeared around a turn.

Lang let the drapes fall back into place. "What good would it have done? We can't establish the break-in was related to Venice. As for the tape, I didn't lie. The camera records on a *disk* on a twenty-four-hour cycle. If I'd told him one existed, he'd demand we hand it over. As it is, I've got a much better use for it. In fact, I'll remove it now."

"To do what?"

"See if some of our former friends can identify our visitor."

Gurt turned to go back into the den. "What do we do now? The next time may be more than a burglary."

"Perhaps. The listening device, the surveillance, even the break-in when you weren't at home, tells me someone is after information."

"But what, who?"

"That is precisely what I'm going to try to find out."

Lang went to a broom closet in the kitchen. Behind brooms, mops and a vacuum cleaner he had every intention of repairing someday was a small metal door resembling a box housing circuit breakers. Inside were a slot and a button. Pressing the latter caused a shiny silver disk to eject.

Lang took the disk into his office, a cramped space under the stairs that was a former closet, large enough only for a small table that served as a desk with a telephone, lamp and computer screen and keyboard on it, a single chair and two-drawer file cabinet. He shut the door. That made the specially insulated space both claustrophobic and immune to listening devices. Sitting at the table, he reached into the file cabinet, his fingers marching across file folders until he found the one he wanted. Extracting it, he flipped it open and ran his eyes down a sheet of paper until he came to a phone number prefaced by the Washington, D.C., area code, 202.

He pulled his BlackBerry from his pocket, remembered that the device was basically like a radio, subject to interception by anyone who had the right frequency. He reached for the phone on the table and keyed in the number. He knew the person he was calling could be, and likely was, anywhere in the world other than the District of Columbia. The number was connected to a series of electronic switchbacks and cutouts that made it impossible to trace without some very sophisticated computers.

The ringing stopped and a brief tone beeped.

"Miles, ole buddy, Lang here. I could use your help. Give me a call. Thanks."

Lang hung up.

By the time Lang had gone back to the den to refresh his scotch, his office phone rang.

He picked up on the third ring. "Miles?"

There was a half-second pause, confirmation the call was being relayed, but the softness of a Southern voice was unimpaired. "It's me, Lang. I'm here with my endless wisdom and bountiful wit to be of service."

Lang grinned. Miles Berkly, scion of one of Alabama's wealthiest families, prepped at Groton—or was it St. Paul's?—and then on to Princeton. Educated, cultured and totally without false modesty. He wore suits that would have cost a month's pay had he purchased them on his salary. He had been Lang's best friend at the Agency. Fortunately for Lang, a combination of political connections and a brilliant record had saved Miles from the post–Cold War cuts. From time to time Lang had needed favors that would have been unavailable to someone without access to the Agency's resources.

"I need a favor."

A theatrical sigh. "And I had hoped you were calling to tell me Gurt had regained her senses and left you, that she was available again. She hot as ever?"

"Eat your heart out, Miles. I've got a bit of a problem I hope you can help me with."

"That's me. Good deed a day."

Lang picked up the disk. "I've got a disk with a running sequence of a man who broke into our house. I'd like to e-mail it to you and have you run it through the Agency's face-recognition program."

A dry chuckle. "You need to talk to the Fibbies. They're the ones who keep files on your average American burglars, robbers, congressmen and other members of the criminal element."

"I think this guy is more than that."

"Divine inspiration or you have something to base that on?"

Lang turned the disk over in his hand. "If you have the time, I'll tell you the whole story."

"No need. I'll take your word for it. You know that specific technology isn't exactly open to the public. I could get in deep shit for using it for a non-Agency purpose."

"That mean you can't do it?"

"No, it means you owe me big time. Here's the e-mail address . . ."

Pétionville, Port-au-Prince, Haiti
The next evening

The restaurant was deserted. White-linen-topped tables surrounded a pool like mounds of snow around a mountain lake. Plates were in place, silverware arranged as though for some ghostly banquet. The evening's gentle breeze ruffled the surface of the blue water to the cadence of the songs of tree frogs. It was hard to believe that only a few miles away, all downhill, the city was a muggy cesspool with nighttime temperatures in the high eighties and no movement of the torpid air.

Undersecretary Chin Diem knew: he had exited the private jet and broken into a sweat before he reached the bottom of the staircase and the air-conditioned Mercedes. He had been surprised when the car delivered him not to the presidential palace but to this place—Bistro La Lantern, according to the sign in front. His questions had brought uncomprehending stares from the driver and the other man in the front seat. At least he thought they were staring. It was hard to tell, when both wore reflective sunglasses that concealed the upper part of their faces.

Diem distrusted people who wore sunglasses at night like American movie stars.

Distrust or not, though, here he was beside a pool, looking at the city below without any idea why. All he knew was that he had received an urgent note from Haiti's ambassador to the People's Republic demanding in most undiplomatic language his immediate return to Haiti. Perhaps the president for life had yet another demand. He sighed.

Something streaked the surface of the water like a fish striking prey. But there were no fish. He could see the bottom of the pool and there was nothing in there but water. He was still puzzling over the occurrence when it happened again.

The wind?

No.

Quite impossible. He had felt no sudden gust that would slash the surface as though something had been ripped through it. For reasons he could not have explained, he looked over his shoulder, seeing no one but the two men who had brought him here.

He shivered but not from the warm breeze. He hated this place. Not only the sewer that was Port-au-Prince, but this largely barren area, stripped of the lush vegetation indigenous to these latitudes. The constant sound of drums at night, the voodoo of natives who worshipped gods, *loa*, that were an equal mixture of Christian saints and African spirits, gave him the creeps even though he had been reared to believe in no power higher than the state.

The water's surface parted again, this time with an audible ripple.

Diem stood just in time to see a tiny shape, all but indistinguishable against the night, as it flitted away. A bat! The little creature was drinking from the pool in midflight. Diem gritted his teeth. He hated rodents, winged or otherwise.

His revulsion was quickly forgotten at the sound of footsteps. Another man behind mirrored sunglasses, this one perhaps the supposedly deaf bodyguard he had seen on his last trip, followed by two men in uniform with holsters on their belts.

Behind them, President for Life Tashmal duPaar, in what Diem guessed was dress uniform. More like Gilbert and Sullivan, complete with a galaxy of medals. He strode to the table as though marching to his own coronation.

As Diem stood, duPaar waved a hand, indicating the restaurant. "A good choice, is it not? Beautiful view, pleasant surroundings. And the food!" He touched his lips.

"I'm sure, Mr. President. But there are no other customers . . ."

"Aha!" DuPaar waved a dismissive hand. "Of course there are no other customers! I had the place cleared. Few are worthy of dining with the president of Haiti, and besides, other customers present security issues."

"Ah, of course."

As the two men were about to sit down, a figure dashed out of darkness to take the back of duPaar's chair. A man, a Haitian of indeterminate age, seated duPaar and said something in what Diem guessed was Creole.

"The owner. He says it is a privilege to have me dine here tonight," the president for life translated before replying in the same tongue. "I have ordered us a cocktail, as the Americans say, a taste of Barbancourt, our world-famous rum."

Diem drank little, even less when on business, but like so many diplomats, he had learned how to take the tiniest of sips, enough to be able to comment on, say, a fine wine, but far too little to reach any stage of inebriation.

When duPaar had thrown down his second glass of the amber liquid, two beer bottles appeared. Though bearing the same label, one was green, the other brown. One long necked, the other not. One was certainly, or had been, a Budweiser. Haitian brewers, it seemed, recycled the bottles of their peers in other countries.

"Good Haitian beer," duPaar announced. "Unlike some here in Pétionville who drink the finest of French wines, I am a man of the common people, drink what they drink. One of the reasons they love me so. Besides, beer will go better with the dinner I have ordered prepared."

The undersecretary saw no reason to mention the fact that few of those "common people" in the city below could afford to spend more than the national average annual income in an establishment like this, nor would he inquire why such security was necessary for a man so beloved.

The proprietor and another man placed platters before each man.

"*Lambi* with rice," duPaar announced. "Small, er, conchs dried in the sun and cooked with a spicy sauce. It goes well with beer, does it not?"

It would have gone better with CO_2 out of a fire extinguisher. The small, experimental bite Diem had taken singed his tongue and was now consuming his entire mouth. He was afraid to swallow for fear he would incinerate his intestines and stomach. Szechuan Chinese food was hot but a mere summer zephyr compared to the inferno he was experiencing.

He grabbed the beer bottle and emptied half of it at a gulp.

"As I said, the beer goes with the food, do you not agree?"

Diem was using his linen napkin to stanch the tears running down his cheeks. In his diplomatic career, he had been subjected to cuisine including hummingbird tongues, raw monkey brains and fried insects, but he had never suffered anything so painful.

DuPaar ignored his guest's obvious discomfort, continuing. "The dish, *lambi*, is a meal of the common person. The conch, of course, come from the sea and are available to all. Many of the spices grow wild."

Diem was now mopping the back of his neck.

"And the pepper . . . it is a small one." DuPaar held his thumb and forefinger about an inch apart. "Small but quite potent. I believe it to be peculiar to Haiti."

Diem passionately hoped so.

The president for life was already smoking a cigar when Diem finished moving enough food around his plate to give the maximum illusion of having eaten it. It was a trick most diplomats learned early.

He was reaching for his Marlboros when duPaar slammed a fist down on the table hard enough to overturn the beer bottles.

"It is a fraud!" he screamed. He leaned over so that his face was inches from Diem's, close enough to smell the alcohol on his breath. "Did you not think I would not run tests? Do you take me for a fool?"

The transformation from affable host to outraged victim was so sudden, the undersecretary was reduced to a stammer. "F-fraud?"

"The package, the one you retrieved from Venice."

Diem swallowed his discomfort, both from food and company, and regained his composure. "Mr. President, I can assure you . . ."

Another fist hit the table, this time making the plates jump. "Assure? Assure what, that you have given me a worthless collection of partial bones?"

"But . . ."

Leaning even closer, duPaar lowered his voice to a near whisper that Diem found more disquieting than the outburst. "As soon as I received the package, I sent small parts of it to the States for testing of DNA. The bones were of a man, a Semite, who lived in the first century AD."

Diem thought for a moment, remembering what he had learned of Western history and religion. "The Christians' Saint Mark?"

Again, the thumping on the table and raised voice. "Saint Mark? Of *course* it may be Saint Mark. It did, after all, come from his tomb. It was *your idea* that the occupant of that tomb was someone else!"

Diem made a mental note to find the person in the Foreign Office who had made that determination. If he (or she) were lucky, they would end their career in what had been Tibet. If not lucky, in prison.

"Mr. President, I understand a mistake has been made. I can assure you my government will do everything in its power . . ."

Again, the menacing lowering of the voice. "And I can *assure* you that not one additional Chinese worker, not one more Chinese soldier, will set foot in Haiti until your promise is fulfilled. It was by my show of good faith there are any here now. I should have waited until your part of the bargain was complete. Do you understand me?"

"Perfectly, Mr. President. But the, er, material already . . . ?"

"They can and will be removed!"

Without another word, duPaar stood, immediately flanked by the two uniformed bodyguards. He turned and stalked from the restaurant. It had definitely been one of the most bizarre evenings of Diem's diplomatic life. But then, Diem had been spared dealings with North Korea's Kim Jong Il, who certainly had a number of things in common with Haiti's leader. Both lived sumptuously while their people starved. Both imagined they were well loved. They shared another trait: lunacy.

Port-au-Prince International Airport
(Formerly François Duvalier International Airport)
Thirty minutes later

Jerome Place had the specially modified cell phone hidden under the mangoes. Even at this hour at night, no one questioned the man in the ragged clothes who was wandering the airport's perimeter road in an effort to sell his produce. Many such vendors had no homes, lived wherever they fell asleep.

Not Jerome. Six years ago, he had joined twenty-some other people in a voyage to America on a craft consisting of little more than boards tied across worn-out truck inner tubes and propelled by oars and a ragged sail. Few, if any, could swim.

The first day, before they even reached the Turks and Caicos Islands, two women and one of their infants had gone overboard. There had been nothing anyone could do as they sunk below the foaming waves. By the time the makeshift craft had reached the southern Bahamas, the slot between Great Exuma and Long Island, the fresh water had run out. The survivors argued: was it better to put ashore and be sent home by the Bahamian government or continue and risk death by thirst? A vote was taken.

Dehydration won over repatriation.

The third night three people died and two more simply were not present at dawn.

They were in the tongue of the ocean, that deep Atlantic trench off the eastern shore of Andros, when the high winds of a squall broke the makeshift craft apart. Fortunately for those few who had managed to somehow stay afloat, a cutter from the United States Navy Experimental Base on southern

Andros happened to be in the area and fished the seven survivors from the water more dead than alive.

Refugees picked up at sea were routinely returned to their port of origin, particularly those obviously headed for illegal entry into the United States.

Not Jerome.

To his surprise, he was separated from his comrades and packed onto a helicopter that landed on a military base he guessed was somewhere in Florida. He also guessed, correctly, that this was because he was the only survivor who could both speak and read English, a language he had studied hard during the few years he had been allowed to attend the small Catholic school in his native village before his father determined work in the little family plot was more important.

Jerome's new friends, the Americans, fitted him with new clothes, fed him and tutored him in basic computer skills, something Jerome doubted he could use in a country too poor to buy such equipment should he return home. He need not have worried. Two weeks later, he was in Port-au-Prince, equipped with a digital camera with night-vision lens, a small computer with a solar recharging unit and a thousand dollars American, more cash than a Haitian peasant would see in several lifetimes.

And promise of more. All he had to do was find a reason to hang around the airport, take and transmit pictures of arriving foreign passengers.

That was what he was doing tonight, taking and sending a series of digital photos of the man who had arrived after dark and was now returning to the aircraft. A few phone calls from people with whom Jerome had shared his wealth had alerted him to the dinner in Pétionville and the fact that this man had failed to deliver something to the president for life, information he had just passed along to the Americans. Jerome had no idea who he was or why the Americans were willing to pay for pictures of him or information as to his activities in Haiti. He could not have cared less. The money was good, but better yet, his American friends had promised him he could eventually come to the United States, bringing little Jerome, his two-year-old son, and Louisa, the child's mother.

Life would be good. People who worked hard in the United States became rich, and Jerome was certainly willing . . .

His euphoria over his good fortune had deafened him. He paid no attention to the sound of the automobile pulling up behind him. He suddenly heard the sound of a car door opening and closing.

Turning, his heart dropped into his stomach. In the lights from the airport, he could see two men approaching him. Limned by the glare of the airfield, he could not see their faces but he could tell both wore the aviator-style sunglasses that were the badge of President duPaar's Secret State Security Police. The Duvaliers' Tonton Macoute had been abolished when young Baby Doc abdicated to France in the early 1980s, but their replacement was just as feared. People who spoke unfavorably of their president for life, or who were suspected of doing so, still disappeared without a trace.

Jerome looked over his shoulder, considering making a run for it. No chance. The road circling the airport was fenced on both sides. He was not going to outrun the car whose engine was idling.

The two men approached without speaking, their silence alone menacing.

"Good evening," Jerome said in Creole. "Perhaps you gentlemen would like to take some fresh mangoes home?"

Still, neither man spoke. Instead, one grabbed Jerome by the shirt collar, throwing him to the ground, while the other dumped the fruit from the cart. Jerome's bowels constricted in terror as the man in sunglasses held up both camera and computer.

Still wordless, the man who had tossed Jerome to the

ground produced a pistol of some sort and placed it next to Jerome's head, motioning him to stand. The gun pressing against his temple, Jerome was marched to the car and shoved inside.

As the car drove away, Jerome's fear was tinted with sadness that neither he, Louisa or little Jerome would ever have a chance to become wealthy in America.

Richard Russell Federal Building
75 Spring Street, Atlanta
The next afternoon

The Reverend Bishop Groom had been delighted at the half-million-dollar bail, an amount he could raise without the assistance of a bondsman. Lang guessed the equity in the preacher's palatial home in the foothills of the northern Georgia mountains would more than cover the sum set by the federal magistrate.

Arriving at the elevators outside the courtroom, the usual cadre of television and press personalities surrounded Lang, the reverend and the long-suffering woman who was his wife. Lang had never actually heard her speak, but she held her husband's hand, smiling dutifully at the TV cameras. In an age of trial by media, appearances counted.

"When will the case go to trial?"

"Is there any chance of a plea bargain?"

"Reverend, has attendance fallen off at your church?"

Lang sensed the reverend was about to reply and stepped in front of him, preempting the camera's lens. Letting the accused make an unrehearsed statement to a voracious press was often a prelude to additional questions and disaster. "As those of you who were in the courtroom know, trial is set for early June. We intend to be ready to rebut all charges."

The standard, vanilla bravado.

A woman with blinding white teeth and a shag pageboy

too blonde to be believable shoved a microphone into the reverend's face. "There are a number of women in your church who claim you had sex with them. What is your response?"

Lang swatted the microphone away like an annoying insect. "As far as we know, the government has made no such allegations." He none too gently pushed his client toward an open elevator. "That's all the comments we have."

As the door hissed shut, the reverend dropped his wife's hand, stuffing his own in his pocket. "I don't understand why you insist I not talk to the press. I speak to thousands of people both on the air and in person every week."

"True, but you control the sound bites. The media is in the entertainment, not the news, business. If editing a statement makes a story more interesting than what the person actually said, provides a better story line, how far are you willing to trust Eye Witness News at Six?"

The reverend had no response.

At basement level, Lang exited the building two stories below a viaduct spanning what had once been neighboring rail stations. Where dozens of railroads had converged to make Atlanta the transportation hub of the South, parking lots now flourished. Long before Lang had come to the city, the Southern Railway's fanciful Moorish marvel, the Terminal Station, had been replaced by the unimaginative federal building he had just left. Lang had seen the pictures of the old building with its pair of unmatched minarets poking into a skyline that no longer existed.

Atlanta had a passion for the new over the old, a choice that had destroyed more landmarks than the railroad station. Lang supposed the trend had begun with Sherman, known locally as a Yankee a little too careless with fire or the first proponent of urban renewal.

In fact, Lang knew of a single building that had survived the 1864 burning: the Shrine of the Immaculate Conception, Francis's church. The story, perhaps apocryphal, was that Sherman had ordered the city put to the torch, including its churches. A company of New Yorkers, recent Irish immigrants, had arrived to do the job when the current priest by the name of O'Day had appeared on the steps to deliver a graphic depiction of the fate of the souls of anyone who dared desecrate his church. Fearing hellfire more than the ire of their officers, the men in blue slunk away to falsely report the completion of their mission.

Lang always smiled at the tale, but this time it reminded him of the priest's remarks about Saint Mark's tomb. He checked his watch. A few minutes after 3:00.

A limousine appeared and its driver dashed from his seat to open a rear door.

"Can we drop you somewhere?" the reverend asked as his driver helped Mrs. Groom into the car.

Lang shook his head. "Thanks, but no. Remember, no press conferences, no words to anyone regarding this case."

"I understand" were the last words the Reverend Bishop Groom spoke before he also disappeared into the interior of the limo.

It was one of those Atlanta winter days that promised, often falsely, an early spring. Knowing that the next week could as easily produce one of the region's ice storms, Lang had decided to walk the approximate mile from his office to the federal building. He could return with a detour of only a few blocks if he went easterly along Martin Luther King Jr. Drive past the county courthouse to the church. He reached for his cell phone before deciding the walk would do him good whether or not Francis was in or out tending his flock.

As had become habit in the last few days, he stopped, this time to put his briefcase down and rest a shoe on a parked car's bumper while he pretended to tie it. The gesture gave him an opportunity to check his surroundings. As far as he could tell, everyone he could see was either coming from or going to the building behind him. None of them looked Asian. Of course, there were any number of places on the viaduct where an unseen observer would have a view of the "railroad gulch," as the area was locally if less than poetically known.

The buildings in this part of town were predominantly occupied by fast-food franchises, discount electronics shops and down-at-the-heels clothing stores. There was a welcome dearth of the beggars, bums and self-appointed "guides" that populated the greener pastures of the hotel and office districts. By and large, Lang had the sidewalks to himself.

He passed the Fulton County Administrative Building, a modern tower that had been designed to hold an oasis of flowing water and stately palm trees in its lobby. The twenty-foot trees had been installed at great expense, only to die both because no one had bothered to consult the county arborist as to the proper care and planting of the root system, and leakage of the pond around which they had been planted. Additionally, the clock in the modernistic tower displayed a perpetual 3:45 and inclement weather outside the building meant an archipelago of buckets inside to catch the offerings of a leaky roof. After the finger-pointing and accusations died down, the county's elected leaders admitted the cost of construction of the building had so far exceeded budget that there remained no funds to fix the problems other than removing the dead tress and filling in the pool.

Lang crossed Pryor Street, walked along the northern side of the county-court complex and waited for the light to change so he might cross Central Avenue. The church was on the far corner. By now, Lang was surrounded by briefcase-toting lawyers, jurors discharged for the day, uniformed deputies and such other personnel as had business at the courthouse. He saw one or two Asian-looking men and women, none of whom paid him any attention.

Across the street, Lang passed the main entrance, opting for a side door into the complex that he knew led to the church's offices. He walked down a short hallway plastered with children's crayon drawings and a bulletin board heavy with notes and messages Lang suspected no one read.

At the end of the corridor a young black woman, her hair in cornrows, smiled up at him from the screen of her computer's monitor. "Yes?"

"Father Francis, is he in?"

She nodded, reaching for the phone. "Who shall I say is here?"

"His favorite heretic."

Her eyes narrowed, thinking she was being ridiculed. The door behind her opened and Father Francis stared out in obvious surprise.

"Praise be to heaven! The apostate has come to salvation!"

"More likely for a cup of coffee," Lang said.

The priest nodded to the young woman. "Tawanna, would you be so kind . . . ? One black, one sweetener only."

Lang settled into one of two wooden chairs facing the priest's desk. "Any particular reason you have such uncomfortable furniture?"

Francis sat behind a desk cluttered with books and papers, the sort of thing Lang would have expected to see had he been calling on a professor of English at one of the local colleges. "You'd have to ask whoever at the diocese provided them. My guess is that the furniture was perceived as a bargain." He picked up a printed bulletin, scanned it and returned it to the pile already in front of him. "What can I do for you today? I'm betting it has nothing to do with your spiritual side . . . if you have one."

There was a gentle tap on the door just as it opened. Tawanna pushed it wide with a hip, a steaming mug in each hand. She set them down on what little empty space the desktop had and left without speaking.

"Thanks!" Francis called afer her, handing one mug to Lang. "Now, you were saying . . . ?"

Lang tested the brew before taking a full swallow. "The

other day at lunch you made a remark about Saint Mark's bones not being what was taken from his tomb in Venice. If not his, whose?"

Francis leaned forward, resting his elbows on his desk and making a steeple of his fingers. "You want the short answer or the long one?"

"I get a choice?"

Francis untwined his fingers to pick up his coffee. "In the mid-first century, Saint Mark served as bishop of Alexandria, then the second-largest city in the Roman Empire. He was so efficient at converting the Egyptians to Christianity, the priests of the old gods stirred up a mob that dragged him out and killed him. They intended to burn his body, thereby depriving him of the afterlife in which they believed. Legend has it a miraculous storm intervened, dousing the flames that had only partially consumed the saint's remains. Somehow the Christians retrieved the body and buried it in their church by the sea. Subsequently the Church of Saint Mark the Evangelist was erected on the site.

"By 828 Egypt was under the rule of the Turks, Muslims. In the city of Alexandria, Christian churches were being looted, torn down for building material or converted to mosques. Fearing for the relics of their city's patron saint, two Venetian traders stole the bones, hid them under a layer of pork to discourage Turkish customs officials from examining the basket in which they were hidden and brought them to Venice."

Lang put his mug down on the corner of the desk. "I know. The event is memorialized in mosaics in the basilica in Venice. But so far, you haven't explained why the bones there aren't Saint Mark's."

"Gutta cavat lapidem, consumitur anulus usu."

Lang shifted his weight in an unsuccessful attempt to make the chair more comfortable. "I'm aware a drop hollows out stone and a ring wears away by use. The Roman proverb counsels patience, not endurance. If a church in Alexandria was built over the partially incinerated remains of Saint Mark and those bones were subsequently stolen and moved to Venice, why would they not still be there?"

Francis held up a finger. "Perhaps because they were never there in the first place. By the time the Venetians took whatever it was they stole, the church had long been destroyed. They claimed to have found the relics amid ruins of what they supposed had been the church, since the rubble was located by what had been known variously as Saint Mark's Gate or the Pepper Gate, the entrance into the ancient part of the city from what is now Cairo. A number of ancient travelers had described the church as being located just inside this gate as late as the mid-seventh century."

"Are you saying the relics could be anybody's?"

A shake of the head as Francis leaned forward over the desk again, coffee forgotten. "Not at all. There was someone else of note buried in Alexandria over two centuries before Saint Mark ever set foot in Egypt."

Lang stared at his friend. "Alexander the Great?"

"Indeed. His mummified body was hijacked on its way to Macedonia, taken to Memphis, then to Alexandria. Possession of the remains legitimized the Ptolemy dynasty's rule of Egypt until the Romans came along."

"But how . . . ?"

"Alexander was viewed as a god by the Egyptians, the son of Ammon. For that matter, the Greeks also deified him as a son of Zeus, and much later, he even appeared in chapter eighteen of the Koran as Zulqarnain, the two-horned lord."

"Two horned?"

"He was depicted on coins and some statues sprouting a pair of ram's horns."

Lang put down his mug half-empty. "That still doesn't explain how he got into Saint Mark's tomb."

"He didn't. The Venetian grave robbers looted the wrong tomb."

Lang started to protest when Francis waved a hand, signaling for quiet. "Both Alexander and Saint Mark were buried in the same section of the city, the palace district, which was destroyed by an earthquake and tsunami in 365 AD. There's no firsthand eyewitness account of Alexander's mausoleum after that; plus, in 391 the emperor Theodosius banned paganism. The edict would have provided a perfect excuse to loot whatever was left of the building."

"Like the golden sarcophagus?"

"One of the subsequent Ptolemys had already sold it to pay his army."

Lang held up both hands. "OK, OK. Let's cut to the chase. What makes you think these Venetians pinched Alexander instead of Saint Mark?"

Francis spun his swivel chair around to face the bookcase behind the desk. Studying the shelves for a moment, he pulled out an oversize paperback and held it up. "Andrew Chugg's *The Quest for the Tomb of Alexander the Great*." He thumbed through the pages. "Here. In describing an account of the theft of the saint's remains from Alexandria, the smell of embalming spices from the basket they used was overpowering. That was why they topped it off with pork. No way the Muslim Turk customs officials were going to touch pork.

"*Embalming spices!* The early Christians didn't embalm, but the Egyptians did in the mummification process. And Alexander was mummified, remember?"

"So were hundreds if not thousands of Egyptians."

"No doubt. But the area around the Pepper Gate wasn't a series of tombs, it was where a number of royal buildings were."

Lang smiled. "An interesting theory, but DNA testing could easily tell a Jew from a Greek, and carbon dating might establish when the body died."

"The church has already denied permission for such tests to be run."

"Why am I not surprised?"

Francis put the book on his desk. "Why the interest?"

"I figure the more I know about what was really stolen from Saint Mark's in Venice, the better chance I have of knowing who tried to kill Gurt and me. And who sent the man who broke into our house."

"Someone broke into your home? Anything stolen?"

"The, er, security system worked beautifully."

Francis leaned back, his chair protesting. "And you think this break-in had something to do with what happened in Venice?"

Lang saw no reason to mention the use of the listening device by the unknowns the night the priest had last visited. "It had occurred to me, yes."

Francis tsk-tsked, slowly shaking his head. "And I thought when Manfred came along, you and Gurt were going to settle down, live like normal people."

Lang took a final sip of coffee, noting it had gone both cold and bitter. "Trying to kill us in Venice and burglarizing my house was not my idea. Thanks for the coffee and the lecture. Interesting that you think it was Alexander's remains that were taken from the church."

Francis shook his head. "I didn't say that." He held out the book. "I said this guy Chugg postulates that Alexander's remains were taken from Alexandria. It's entirely possible the tomb robbers you encountered in Venice read the same book and accepted his theory. Stealing Alexander's remains makes a lot more sense that Saint Mark's."

"And that would be why?"

"Ancient legend has it that whoever possesses the body of Alexander will never be defeated in battle, again according to our friend Chugg."

"So now we not only have grave robbers, we have *superstitious* grave robbers."

Francis placed the book back on its slot on the shelf. "That should narrow the field as to suspects somewhat."

Ansley Park
Later that afternoon

A winter twilight was waiting on the eastern horizon by the time Lang accelerated the Porsche onto Ansley Park's meandering streets. Streetlights were stuttering on, their bluish fluorescence painting trees, shrubbery and buildings alike a ghostly hue. There were few people to be seen on the sidewalks and the winding byways. Early evening provided the temptation to unleash a few of the horses under the car's rear deck lid and enjoy handling capabilities daytime traffic curtailed.

With that possibility in mind, he had taken the long way around, entering not at Fifteenth Street at the park's southern edge but Beverly Road on the north. Only in second gear, he was enjoying the throaty burble as the tachometer whisked past 5000 RPM so much he almost missed the parked car.

Lang's house on Lafayette Drive faced one of Ansley Park's several small parks and green spaces, a strip of sculpted trees and small waterways known as Iris Garden, a venue managed by residents rather than the city in much the same way New York residents at one time maintained private parks, of which Gramercy is the last. Unlike New York, though, Iris Garden is not fenced in. The view of its ancient oaks, babbling water and seasonal shrubbery were a primary reason he and Gurt had selected their home.

Lang had planned to round the park, passing his house on the far side across the green space, and take a left-hand sweeper at the park's western edge, which would bring him to his driveway. Because of the narrowness of the street along the park's northern edge, parking at the curb was forbidden, a prohibition observed by anyone not wanting to risk finding their car a victim of an anonymous collision.

But there was a car parked there, perhaps fifty yards right across the park from his house.

Lang continued past, turning right rather than left at the street's dead end into Peachtree Circle, a wide boulevard where street parking was allowed. Pulling the Porsche over, Lang cut the engine, locked it and began to backtrack. He was careful to keep in the shadows, where the fingers of light from the street lamps did not reach.

Rounding the corner, he could see the automobile in question clearly. The lighted tip of a cigarette told him this wasn't some careless soul who had left his vehicle in a precarious position while he ran a short errand to one of the abutting houses. Whoever was in that car was there for a more sinister purpose.

Keeping in darkness as much as possible, Lang approached until he was no more than six feet from the car's rear bumper. Against the streetlights' glow, he could clearly see a single person aiming some sort of device across the park. Lang didn't have to guess. The listener was back, this time in a position not so easily observed from the house.

A dilemma: Lang could sneak away unobserved, warn Gurt the house was under audio surveillance and wait for an opportunity to find out who this snooper was. Or he could take direct action, alerting the person or persons they had been detected, and perhaps identify them.

Stooping, Lang duckwalked to the rear of the car to keep below the line of sight of the rearview mirrors. By now, he was beside the driver's door.

His knees were already protesting his cramped posture and he was about to lose feeling in his lower legs. Nevertheless, he made himself be still. How long did it take to smoke a single cigarette, anyway?

He was rewarded when the window scrolled down. A hand with the cigarette in it appeared above his head and flipped the burning tobacco away in an arc of sparks. Like a spring suddenly uncoiling, Lang stood, grabbing the arm and twisting so the man inside was forced against the dashboard. With his free hand, Lang reached inside the car, unlocked the door and dragged the man outside, forcing him facedown on the sidewalk. He struggled and Lang wrenched the arm upward.

"Be still or it comes right out of the socket," he snarled.

Still pushing the arm upward, Lang put a knee between the shoulders as he used his free hand to pat the man down. It took only seconds to relieve the prone man of an automatic in a shoulder holster and a wallet in a hip pocket. Lang stuffed the weapon into his belt under his suit jacket and the wallet into a pocket before dragging the man to his feet and shoving him against the car.

He ratcheted the arm up a little farther. "OK, who the hell are you and who sent you?"

The only answer was a groan of pain.

"You'll answer me or I'll tear it loose and beat you over the head with it."

Lang and his opponent were suddenly bathed in light. "Hold it right there!"

Lang looked up into the headlights of a police cruiser.

Swell.

Possibly, some neighbor had witnessed what was going on, and the 911 system had experienced another of its occasional successes. More likely, it was one of the rent-a-cops Ansley Park paid to beef up the virtually nonexistent regular patrols of the neighborhood.

"Back, stand back," the voice from the car commanded. "And keep your hands where I can see them."

By this time, porch lights were flickering on up and down the street.

Lang slowly let go of the man's arm and stepped back, his hands held above his head. The man beneath him struggled up, took one look at the police car and bolted.

"Stop!" the cop yelled with no effect whatsoever.

It took only a nanosecond for the officer to realize he would have to abandon one potential arrestee for another in full flight. The old bird-in-the-hand theory. A bird that required no exertion to reduce to possession.

Lang pointed at the running man. "He tried to mug me. Stop him!"

The portly officer took only a glance as the fleeing man rounded a corner, before turning his attention to Lang. "You got ID?"

Lang produced his wallet, removed his driver's license and handed it over for inspection under the beam of a flashlight.

The officer looked up. "You live around here, huh?"

"I can vouch for him, officer."

Both Lang and the cop turned to see an elderly man in an old-fashioned smoking jacket and carpet slippers. Lang recognized him from one of the few neighborhood-association functions he had attended. He couldn't put a name to the face, but for once he was going to benefit from the mind-your-neighbor's-business culture of Ansley Park.

"And who're you?" the officer demanded.

"Frank Hopkins," the man puffed, clearly chagrined the policeman didn't recognize him. "President of the Ansley Park Civic Association."

The cop nodded. "Oh, yeah, Mr. Hopkins, I recall you now. I spoke about crime prevention at the meeting at your house a year or so ago." He turned to Lang, returning the driver's license. "You say the guy was trying to mug you?"

"That's right," Lang improvised, hoping Hopkins hadn't seen all of what had happened. "He jumped out of that car right there and grabbed me. He was going for my wallet."

"Looked to me like he wasn't very successful," the cop observed, "but I'll still need to make a written report."

Lang gave a brief if fictional account of what had happened, stopping several times as the policeman filled in a number of blanks and added a written narrative. His manner suggested filling out reports of robberies, both attempted and otherwise, was nothing new. The report, Lang suspected, would be duly filed away and intentionally forgotten lest it be counted in the city's carefully edited crime statistics, numbers that uniformly demonstrated Atlanta was a safe city with an ever-decreasing crime rate, which was cold comfort to crime's victims.

"Your association dues at work," Hopkins observed proudly. "If this officer hadn't come along . . ."

It was as though he was personally taking credit for Lang's perceived rescue.

The policeman put his clipboard with the report on it back in his car and walked around the one deserted at the curb, painting it with his flashlight. "Rented."

For the first time, Lang noted the Hertz sticker just above the tag. "The name of the renter should be on the papers. Try the glove box."

The cop opened the passenger door, reached inside and produced what Lang recognized as a parabolic listening device and a set of earphones. "What's this?"

Specifically, Lang thought, *it is a DetectEar, available for just under five hundred bucks plus shipping and handling from any spyware order-by-mail warehouse. With a collapsible twenty-inch dish and only three triple-A batteries, it can pick up voices three hundred yards away.* A glance told Lang it had obviously been modified in some manner to pick up the vibrations of conversations inside, the modification that had caused the humming sound on the phone.

That there was a market for such things was not a favorable comment on contemporary American society.

He said nothing.

"Looks like some kind of spy-movie stuff" came from a group of curious residents who had gathered.

"Someone was snooping!" Hopkins's tone indicated national security might rest in the privacy of Ansley residences.

Shrugging, the policeman put it in the cruiser and pulled a sheet of paper from the glove box, holding it up to the light. "Car was rented a week ago by a James Wang of Doraville."

Doraville was an Atlanta suburb popular with Vietnam immigrants, Koreans and Chinese, so popular that the local city council had required all business signs to be in English in addition to their proprietors' native alphabets so fire and police could find them in an emergency.

"That should make it easy to check out," Hopkins volunteered. "How stupid can you get?"

If Lang was going to bet, he'd put his money on the fact Mr. James Wang of Doraville was in for a very unpleasant surprise. Either his identification or rental car or both had been stolen. Again, he said nothing.

Twenty minutes later, Lang garaged the Porsche and walked into the kitchen, where Gurt was bent over, opening an oven that emitted a delicious aroma of freshly baked bread. Manfred was seated at the kitchen table, moving a pair of toy trucks around with appropriate sound effects. Grumps, ever the optimist, was attentively watching Gurt in hopes of a stray scrap or dropped morsel. He gave Lang the briefest of glances before returning his attention to the stove.

"Whatever happened to the tail-wagging welcome?" Lang asked rhetorically before giving Gurt's rear an affectionate pat, much to Manfred's amusement.

"*Vati schlug* Mommy's ass," he chortled.

"It appears our son is learning more in school than we might wish," Lang observed, lifting the little boy by the arms and swinging him in a circle.

Gurt straightened up, a pan in her hands, and gave Lang an appraising look. "You have been to the boxing ring instead of the office?"

Following her gaze, Lang noticed for the first time that one of the seams of his jacket was ripped and his knee gaped from a hole in his trousers.

"I met someone on the way home," he said pointedly, setting Manfred down. "We can talk about it later."

Gurt set the pan on the table. No doubt about it, it was home-baked bread. She gently slapped Lang's hand as he reached to break off a piece. "And you can let it cool. Your friend Miles called. He said he'd call back at ten o'clock our time."

Lang reached to his belt and removed the weapon he had taken from the listener, laying it on the kitchen counter. He was not surprised to see that it was another knock-off Tokarev.

Gurt's eyebrows arched. "Perhaps the person you met was Chinese?"

"Too dark to tell, but that'd be my guess. Oh yeah, I got this, too."

He dropped the wallet beside the pistol. By this time Manfred's attention had returned to the trucks.

Gurt picked it up, flipping it open. "James Wang? He was the person you met?"

Lang took it from her hand and started pulling out credit cards. "I doubt it, but I intend to find out. What's for dinner, er, *Abendessen*," he said, remembering to speak German in front of Manfred. Except when the subject matter was one he preferred his son not understand.

"*Schweinefleisch mit Apfel.*"

Pork with apples.

With Manfred now in prekindergarten, Gurt spent her new leisure time preparing native German dishes contributing to both Lang's delight and his potentially expanding waistline. He put in extra time at the driving club's gym to remove the extra five pounds. Observing her domesticity in the kitchen amused him: the world's only gourmet cook who had repeatedly won the Agency's marksmanship trophy.

She rapped his knuckles with a spoon as he attempted to lift the lid of one of several pots on the stovetop. "It will be ready by the time you have a drink and watch the news," she said in German, "unless you continue to get in the way."

Evicted from the kitchen, Lang wandered into the library/den and opened the doors of a walnut *buffet de corps* to reveal a sound system and TV screen. Punching the remote, he moved to the bar and poured a liberal dose of scotch into a glass as the newscaster interviewed an official with the water department. In the third year of a drought, the city had imposed strict limits on watering lawns, washing cars or filling swimming pools. The decline in water usage had, predictably, resulted in lower water bills. The water department's solution to declining revenue was to raise rates.

Government's principal function: extorting money from the governed.

Lang was tempted to add more scotch.

Or turn off the news.

22:01

Manfred long asleep, Lang and Gurt were propped up in bed themselves, engrossed in separate books.

When the phone rang, Lang looked at the clock on the bedside table before picking it up. "Hi Miles. I was beginning to worry."

There was the usual split-second delay of multiple relays. "Sorry. You have any idea what time it is where I am?"

Lang flicked his eyes to the bedroom windows, making certain the sound shields were in place. "Of course not. I have no idea where you are. What did you find out?"

"You sure this line is secure?"

"Reasonably certain. Why?"

"You've been keeping some pretty questionable company. The guy you wanted ID'ed goes by a number of names, Wang Jianfei being most likely his real one."

"I'm not planning on Googling him."

"Wouldn't do you a lot of good. I doubt he's on Facebook, either."

"OK, Miles, what did you find out other than a possible name?"

"Nasty character. Works for the Guoanbu."

"The Chinese state-security people? Last time I looked, their spooks were busy ferreting out dissenters and other troublemakers in their own country to send to the Chinese equivalent of the gulags. Why would they go extra-territorial?"

"We'd like to know that, too. In fact, it's part of a puzzle we're working on right now."

"Care to tell me about it?"

"Not on a line I'm not one hundred percent sure is secure. Tell you what, though: I'll be in Atlanta day after tomorrow and I'll buy lunch."

"Great! Let me give you my office address."

A dry chuckle. "We're an intelligence agency, remember? I already have it."

The line went dead.

Gurt lowered her book. "Chinese state security?"

"Miles thinks the guy who broke in here works for them."

Gurt turned toward him, an elbow propping up her head. "But why . . . ?"

"Same question I asked Miles."

"He is coming here, Miles?"

"So he says."

Gurt was staring into space. "Strange. He never came back to the States the whole time I knew him. We used to tease him that he wouldn't come back to this country because he's knocked some woman down, made her pregnant."

"Knock up, not down."

"But you knock someone down, not up."

"Too bad Miles didn't know the difference."

"To come here maybe he wants something."

"Perhaps. But what?"

The question might have been answered had Lang and Gurt been privy to the phone call Miles made after hanging up.

"Ted? It's me, Miles."

"Hello Miles. In case I forgot to thank you, that was great paella in San Juan last week. What's up? But remember this isn't a secure line."

"Glad you liked the paella. Nice thing about San Juan is there's plenty of it, and Puerto Rico is geographically desirable for keeping an eye on the Caribbean. Speaking of which, you recall I spoke of a fishing trip?"

Ted had to think a moment to recall the remark. "'Fishing around' for a new asset, I believe is how you put it."

"Well, I think I have a nibble."

Law offices of Langford Reilly
11:52 two days later

Miles had changed little in the years since Lang last saw him, his wardrobe not at all. He could have stepped out of GQ. Silk foulard peeping out the breast pocket of a tailored double-breasted blazer with brass buttons bearing the seal of Princeton University, glen plaid gray wool slacks that just caressed loafers that, if you happened to be some sort of lizard, were literally to die for. A red silk tie nestled on a pinpoint oxford shirt. His hair, cut fashionably long, was parted along a streak of premature silver.

Hands clasped behind his back, he was studying the view from the floor-to-ceiling window behind Lang's desk. Seasonal winter weather had returned. Ragged patches of dirty gray clouds smeared the window with moisture. The mist parted occasionally to allow sights of the street twenty stories below. Pedestrians concealed by umbrellas scurried back and forth to get out of the bone-chilling drizzle that lasted days at a time, uninterrupted by sunlight. Lang had to make an effort not to let the monotonous damp and chill become depressing.

"Weather's the same, but not quite the view of the Frankfurt *Bahnhof*," Miles ventured.

"Thankfully."

Miles turned to appraise the office's appointments: eighteenth-century mahogany partners desk with fruitwood inlay. An elaborately carved hunt table behind it served as a credenza. A pair of leather wingback chairs with the distinctive carved-claw feet of Irish Chippendale were on either side of a small Boulle commode. To the right of the desk, a Georgian breakfront showed leather-bound books through wavy, handblown glass at least two and a half centuries old. The muted reds and blues of a Kerman rug floated on the polished wood parquet floor.

Hands still behind his back, Miles moved to study a landscape on the wall facing the desk. "Reynolds?"

Lang smiled. "Good guess. School of."

Miles waved a hand, including the entire office. "No more government issue for you! I've seen lesser antiques in museums. Any chance your clients have a clue what they're looking at?"

"Probably not, but they know they're not in the public defender's office."

"Ah, well, wasn't it Shelley or Keats who observed, 'beauty is truth, truth beauty'?"

"Keats, in 'Ode on a Grecian Urn.' Your Ivy League education is showing."

"Never could keep those guys straight." Miles helped himself to a seat in one of the wing chairs. "Well, the point is, you have these things here because you enjoy them."

"I have these things here because I charge outrageous fees."

Miles thought about that for a moment. "Nice to make money without risking your neck."

Lang grinned. "Miles, you're still with the Agency because that's what you want to do. Which includes why you're here today."

"Touché."

"Which raises the question . . ."

Miles cleared his throat. "I thought we might discuss it after lunch."

"I thought we might discuss it now, in case it makes me ill."

"Ah, Lang, where is the charm, the gracious manner of our native Southern homeland?"

Lang couldn't suppress a chuckle. "You have it all, Miles. You want something and you know I know it."

"Never could slip one by you, Lang." Miles leaned forward in his chair, elbows on his knees. "In one word, Haiti."

"Haiti?"

"You know, the western half of the island of Hispaniola. Voodoo, zombies, Papa Doc."

"Poverty, disease, corruption. Not exactly a place Club Med would locate. I can't imagine anything happening there that would interest anybody but hand wringers, missionaries and the other do-gooders."

Miles was twisting the tip of his tie between his index and middle fingers, a nervous gesture Lang recalled from years ago. "Until about a month ago, we weren't."

"And then?"

"You recall the old SAMOS-F satellite?"

"Navy intelligence, low earth orbit. One of the first to send encrypted surveillance photos. Mostly phased out years ago."

"That's the one. We have a couple still functioning."

"You're not telling me this to demonstrate how the taxpayers' money is being saved."

Miles dropped the tip of his tie. "Hardly. The one I have in mind has an orbit that covered the Caribbean. Someone noticed a series of ships transiting the Panama Canal from east to west and heading from the canal to the north coast of Haiti."

"So?"

"Since the company owned by the Chinese army has the operating contract for the canal, we monitor Panama fairly regularly. These same ships, the ones headed for Haiti, were Chinese freighters."

"Maybe the Chinese have found a way to build a car cheap enough for the Haitians to afford it."

"Cars aren't crated for shipment. Whatever was unloaded was in containers."

Lang leaned back in his chair, his hands intertwined across his stomach. "Miles, even back in the dark ages when I was still with the Agency, the resolution of the intel from satellites could distinguish a Ford from a Chevy from three hundred miles up. Whatever was in those containers should have been visible when they were unloaded."

Miles shook his head. "Should have been. But the Haitians, or whoever was on the ground, dragged them up into the mountains. Those hills are high enough to be in the clouds. The SAMOS-F didn't have the technology to photograph through cloud cover."

"I'm sure it's classified, but I'll bet we do now."

Miles was playing with his tie again. "Without saying we do or don't, I can say that wherever the contents of those containers are now, they aren't where we can see them."

Lang pondered this a minute. "What about HUMINT, human intelligence? Surely you have someone on the ground."

"Until now, Haiti didn't rate more than a single full-time asset. He disappeared. We have a stringer or two but no idea how reliable they might be. So far, whatever was in those containers might as well have vanished."

Lang stood, seeing where this was headed. "Miles, I am glad to see you, and Gurt is thrilled to join us for lunch. We'd be pleased if you could stay awhile, have you as our guest. That being said, I am not, repeat, *not*, going to Haiti."

"But what makes you think—?"

Lang held up an index finger. "You make your first visit to the U.S. anyone can remember." A second finger. "You aren't telling me this story to pass away the time until Gurt joins us." Third finger. "And you just got through telling me you are shit out of luck when it comes to assets already on the ground. I may have been out of the game for awhile but the rules never change: when you need assets, you get them wherever you can. Now, did I miss anything?"

Miles held up both hands, feigning surprise. "Did I say anything about you going to Haiti?"

Lang sat back down, smirking. "No, of course you didn't. I suppose I got some exercise jumping to conclusions. I should never have thought it would have crossed your mind to try to employ a retired agent, someone with no publicly known ties to any U.S. intelligence agency, and therefore plausible deniability, to go snoop around to see what's going on between the largest remaining communist state and one of the world's craziest dictators, right on our Caribbean doorstep. I know that's something you would never do."

"Do what?"

Neither man had noticed Gurt step into the office.

"Gurt!" Miles embraced her—a little too enthusiastically, Lang thought. "You're more beautiful than I remembered!"

"Beware of Miles bearing compliments," Lang said dryly as Gurt disentangled herself. "Our friend here wants to send me on an all-expense-paid trip to sunny skies, summer temperatures, white beaches, the whole lot."

Gurt looked from Lang to Miles and back again, aware she had missed something. "Only you? Why not us both?"

"That could be arranged," Miles said.

Lang sat back down. "Go on, Miles, explain."

Miles did, ending with, "However you two got tangled up with the Guoanbu and their man Jianfei, it may well be related to my problem."

"Just how do you figure that?" Lang asked, leaning back in his chair, hands now clasped on top of his head. "Seems like a bit of a stretch."

"Maybe so," Miles replied. "But the Chinese have historically shown little or no interest in operating in the Western Hemisphere until they took over management of the canal some years ago. We have cracked Cuban, Soviet, even Israeli spy rings operating in the country, but never Chinese. Now, all of a sudden, one of their operatives is caught in your house only a few weeks after we find they have some sort of an interest in Haiti. I know how much you, Lang, believe in coincidence."

"Not at all, but what you're suggesting is still pretty lame."

Miles held up both hands again, this time in submission. "You're right, lame as a one-term politician. I'm probably grasping at straws."

Lang narrowed his eyes. Miles wasn't one to give up so easily. "But?"

Miles watched Gurt slide into the other chair, nylons whispering as she crossed her legs. "If there's no connection between the Guoanbu's sudden interest in you and what's going on in Haiti, then you, Lang, or better yet, both of you, get a few days in the sun at Agency expense."

"And on the off chance you're right?"

"Then you'll know."

"Know what?" Gurt asked. "It is a . . . a . . . what do you say? A 'stretch' to think we will find out why Chinese state security broke into our house by going to Haiti."

"And why us?" Lang wanted to know. "The Agency must have a dozen or so employees who'd love to spend a few winter days in the Caribbean."

"Because you, both of you, can easily pass for Europeans on a holiday." Lang started to protest but Miles dashed forward. "Look, you owe me a favor, remember? I'm the one who stuck out his neck to identify those people as Chinese intel. We, the Agency, can't currently spare any Ops personnel who could pass for a German couple taking advantage of Haiti's low hotel rates."

"The rates are low," Lang observed, "because few people want to go there. And you can't spare any operatives because this is ninety-nine percent certain to come up empty."

"I have never been to the Caribbean," Gurt announced.

Lang was surprised. Not that Gurt had never been to the Caribbean but that she was showing interest in Miles's suggestion. "If you want the Caribbean, believe me, Haiti is *not* the place to begin."

Gurt gave him a quizzical look. "Is it not warm and sunny there this time of year? Do they not have beaches like I see in the magazines?"

Lang could see Miles was anticipating victory. "Yeah, but . . ."

"And is it not possible that the people in Venice who tried to kill us were Chinese?"

"Certainly possible," Lang had to agree.

Miles clapped his hands. "Good! It's settled then. I'll make the arrangements. Now, where am I taking you to lunch?"

"Not so fast," Lang cautioned. Turning to Gurt, he said, "We've just come back from several days in Venice. I don't want to impose on our neighbors to keep Manfred again so soon . . ."

Gurt turned to Miles, saying conversationally, "Lang believes his son cannot live a few days without him. When he is away, he has to call the child at least twice a day. It as though Manfred is some sort of vegetable that will perish without his attention." To Lang, she said, "Manfred will get along fine with Wynn Three, his best friend. Besides, we are keeping the neighbor's little boy for two weeks this summer."

News to Lang.

What wasn't news was the fact they were going to Haiti.
Gurt had made up her mind.

From the diary of Louis Etienne Saint Denis

December 20, 1802

The First Consul's[1] favorite sister is again troublesome!
For some years the sexual conduct of Pauline, the second
of the three sisters, has been the talk of all France. Though
charming and beautiful, the woman is without discretion.
In June of five years past, the First Consul was at Mom-
bello Palace near Milan when he walked in on his sister in
the process of having congress with one of his generals,
Leclerc.[2]

Feigning fury, the First Consul demanded her honor
be salvaged, and on June 14 of that year, they were mar-
ried at the home of the then general, all as previously de-
scribed in this diary. The couple do not match each other.
Leclerc is serious, his face in a perpetual frown, while his
bride is frivolous and quick to laugh. She continues her
flirtatious ways, while he blushes at attention from other
women.

In October of this year, realizing how tenuous is this
union and aware of the scandal already growing concern-
ing Pauline's ill-concealed infidelities, the First Consul
appointed Leclerc to put down the slave insurrection in
Saint-Domingue.[3]

---

1 In November of 1799, Napoleon, aided by troops of General Leclerc,
staged a coup, overthrowing the revolutionary government and bestowing
this title upon himself.

2 Charles Victor Emmanuel Leclerc was only twenty-nine at the time of
the nuptials. Pauline, or Paulette as she was known to her family, was
twenty-one. He was not her first choice of husbands.

3 Haiti. At this time, the name included what is today the Dominican

She refused to go despite the pleas of her new husband, who in desperation appealed to her brother. Pauline also refused him. Under no illusions as to the scope of the scandals Pauline would create if left alone, Napoleon ordered a sedan chair to be brought to his sister's home by ten of his largest grenadiers. The soldiers strapped her into the chair and marched her to a carriage in which she was sent to the port and bodily carried aboard ship, screaming and cursing.

The First Consul is well shed of her.

A strange thing happened as the ship slipped its moorings and let the tide take it from the quay. I was sitting in the carriage with the First Consul when General Leclerc appeared at the rail with what looked very much like the selfsame box the First Consul had held so dear when we departed Egypt. Leclerc held it aloft for the First Consul to see. The First Consul replied with a salute, and Leclerc turned and disappeared from view.

Republic. There is some evidence Leclerc's mission was somewhat more ambitious and included a stepping-stone conquest of what are today Puerto Rico, Cuba and then the newly independent United States by way of French Louisiana. This theory might be indirectly supported by the fact Napoleon sold Louisiana within months of France's withdrawal from Haiti, thereby ceding her last interest in the Western Hemisphere, other than an enclave in South America and a few insignificant islands.

CHAPTER THREE

Lang turned off I-20 onto Martin Luther King Jr. Drive, made a left and drove through the arch that marked the entrance to Atlanta's largest cemetery. Passing the newer grave sites marked only by bronze plaques, he entered the older section, rolling hills dotted with an eclectic selection of gravestones, statues and funerary monuments. He parked the Porsche behind a vintage Cadillac. It and the Porsche were the only cars in sight. He climbed a slight rise, walking toward a giant oak tree whose winter-bare limbs seemed to be supplicating the heavens.

A few yards to his left, an elderly woman in black leaned on the arm of young Latino in chauffeur's uniform as she hobbled up the hill, using her free hand to clutch a flat of pansies. He had seen her here on more than one occasion.

Just short of the tree, Lang stopped in front of three head-stones. Dawn, his first wife, Janet, his sister, and Jeff, her adopted son. Lang came here to visit just before every trip he took out of the country. It was as if he were saying a possible farewell to the only kin he had before Gurt had re-entered his life with Manfred. For reasons he could not have explained, he never mentioned these trips to the cemetery. Although he was sure Gurt would understand, he felt some vague sense of disloyalty to his present family that had kept him silent on the subject of visiting his previous one.

Facing the three graves, he sat on the base of a statue of

an angel, its arms reaching out as though imploring observers to follow through a closed door behind it, an early and exuberant display of early-twentieth-century family wealth by people he had never heard of.

Not far away, the old woman was directing the planting of the pansies around the marble figure of another angel, this one weeping.

If Lang could have spoken to his wife, his sister and much-loved adopted nephew, what would he tell them? Dawn, he knew, would be proud of his success in the legal world, thrilled he had the son she could not give him. Conversely, she would be less than happy about the violence that had stalked his life. Like the affair in Venice.

"Dammit," he said aloud. "I don't go looking for trouble."

Not quite true, he reproved himself. He and Gurt weren't leaving for Haiti entirely for a vacation.

"I can't just sit by," he explained to the breeze that was gently ruffling his hair. "I can't just hope those people will go away."

The woman in black interrupted the instructions to her chauffeur to glance sternly in his direction. Lang had not realized his voice had carried. He gave her an embarrassed smile.

Turning slightly, he faced Janet's headstone. A pediatric orthopedist, she had spent four or five months of the year donating her services to the children of undeveloped countries. In Central America she had encountered the small boy on the dirt streets of a nameless village, homeless and parentless. She had fought a two-year paper war to adopt him.

Lang took a deep breath. She would be proud of the foundation he had created to provide children's medical care across the globe. But perhaps not so proud about how he had funded it with an accord with the very organization responsible for her and Jeff's deaths.

Lang stood, weary of the accusations of the dead, perhaps a little angry. It always ended this way.

"I did the best I could," he said, not caring whether the old woman heard him or not.

Lang walked back down the hill, stopping for a final look at the three headstones before driving away. For reasons as inexplicable as his failure to tell Gurt of these visits, he felt he had completed a duty.

Cap Haitien
Two days later

Miles and Lang had decided that arrival in Haiti would be less likely observed if made at the north-coast port of entry. With the country's communications system still somewhere in the mid-twentieth century, there was an excellent chance they would be gone by the time the paperwork associated with their landing found its way into any central system.

Scheduled service to Cap Haitien by commercial carriers having been long abandoned, Gurt and Lang had taken Delta to Providenciales in the Turks and Caicos Islands and chartered a flight from there. Lang was in the right front seat of the lumbering antique Beech B18, nervously watching the number-two engine spew oil onto a wing whose white paint had been bleached into chalk by the Caribbean sun. There were more empty holes in the instrument panel than instruments.

Lang had mentioned this when he and Gurt first boarded the venerable old machine nearly an hour ago.

"No worry, mon," the native pilot had assured them. "Ain' no radio, no instrument landin' equipment at Cap Haitien nohow."

Lang looked apprehensively at the panel. "I don't see any GPS. How do you find it, the airport?"

The pilot shrugged. "You goes to the first ocean and turns right. Afta 'bout an hour, you looks for de tallest clouds. Haiti be unner 'em. Ain' but one airstrip on de no'th coast."

Unmollified but out of objections, Lang had uneasily strapped himself in. Before GPS, before navigational instrumentation, this was how flying was done, right? Lindbergh had made it all the way from New York to Paris with only a compass, right? Jimmy Doolittle had found Tokyo with not much more, right?

None of the above eased his concern in the least.

A flash of green caught his eye and in the next moment the aircraft banked left to parallel golden sands. On the right side of the plane jagged mountains seemed to grow from the beach's edge and claw at the clouds like the talons of a raptor.

There was a grinding sound and the Beechcraft shuttered. Lang desperately hoped he was experiencing only the lowering of the landing gear into the airstream. As if to reassure him, the plane banked again. When it rolled out, an airstrip filled the windscreen, increasing in size as the plane descended. The paving seemed out of place among what looked like postage-stamp-sized fields of sugarcane. At the runway threshold, and what Lang guessed was no more than a hundred feet, the pilot leveled off, flying the length of the strip without farther descent. At the end, on the edge of the ocean, he added power and began a 180-degree turn back toward the other end.

"What . . . ?"

"Livestock, mon," the pilot replied nonchalantly. "Natives' pigs sometimes gets loose and onto de runway. De airplane go over low, scare 'em off. You got any idea what a mess o' dis plane hittin' a pig make?"

It was something Lang had rather not consider.

The next approach was uneventful.

The instant the Beechcraft slowed to taxi speed, Lang felt as though he had been covered with a warm, wet blanket. The old aircraft had no air-conditioning and the hot, humid air filled the cabin not only with a cloying, prickly grasp but with a faint odor of sewage and wood smoke.

As the plane taxied back up the runway, two figures emerged from a small concrete-block building on the edge of the tarmac. One wore a guayabera, the short-sleeve, four-pocket shirt worn over the top of trousers, common in the Caribbean. The other was tall for a Haitian, perhaps six feet, and wore a long-sleeve olive drab uniform. Both were black. Not the browns and tans of most islands' natives but the soot black of undiluted African lineage.

"Customs and immigration," explained the pilot, hastily shutting down the left engine, then the right.

The temperature and humidity seemed to leap upward as Lang and Gurt exited the plane, followed by the pilot.

On closer inspection, Lang noted the tall Haitian's uniform was wool, yet he seemed unperturbed by the searing heat and drenching humidity. In his belt was stuck a Webley revolver, the standard British military sidearm for the better part of the twentieth century. This one looked as though it might have seen service in Flanders Fields or in the 1916 Somme offensive. Lang would have guessed, if fired, the weapon would present as much peril to the shooter as the target.

The man in the guayabera accepted a sheaf of papers from the pilot. First-, second- or third-world country, one thing never changed: the paper required by bureaucracy.

"Passports?"

Lang and Gurt each handed over the German passports they had used to exit the United States. The man compared them with the papers the pilot had given him, studying so long Lang was getting edgy even though he assured himself these had been prepared by the Agency's very talented forgers.

The customs official's brow wrinkled.

"Is there something wrong?" Gurt asked.

The man brightened, showing white teeth that seemed to glitter against the black velvet of his face. "You speak English!" He held up one of the passports. "I have never seen a Dutch one before."

Lang and Gurt exchanged glances.

"German," she corrected.

"But it says, 'Dutch.'"

Gurt stood beside him, her finger pointing to the word, "*Deutsch*. It is the German word for 'German.'"

His smile widened as he produced a stamp from his pocket and imprinted both passports. "Dutch, German. Welcome to Haiti. Do you have a hotel reservation?"

Gurt reached into her purse, producing a slip of paper. "No, but we were told the Mont Joli is quite nice."

"No matter. I do not think either hotel in Cap Haitien is full at the moment. I—"

He was interrupted by the sound of an unmuffled engine. What had at one time been a sixties-vintage Ford sedan, now painted a vibrant blue, rumbled up to the building. Its bodywork looked as though it had been modified with a baseball bat, and the tires showed more cord than rubber.

"Ah!" the customs man exclaimed. "Someone saw the plane come in. This is André, my cousin, who has a taxi service."

He turned to speak to the new arrival in a language Lang could not even begin to understand. Leaving the engine running, André dashed for the plane as though afraid it might suddenly take off on its own. He stood by while the pilot opened the nose baggage compartment and handed him two bags.

"Is that all your luggage?" the customs man wanted to know.

Lang and Gurt assured him it was.

Another burst of what Lang gathered was Creole and the cab driver lugged the two suitcases to the rear of his car, set them down and began to unwind the wire holding the trunk shut.

"Do those luggages have any tobacco, liquor or firearms in them?"

Lang and Gurt shook their heads. "No."

The customs man nodded approval. "Good. That will be fifty dollars American, landing, arrival and customs fees."

Lang and Gurt exchanged glances.

"That's over a month's pay here," Lang said softly, reaching into a pocket. "You have any dollars on you?"

"I changed some euros in Providenciales," she answered, digging in her purse, "when I bought a pair of sunglasses."

"But you didn't need another pair."

"No, but we needed someone to remember we had euros in case someone should ask," she whispered. "We are Germans, remember?"

No doubt Gurt was more current in tradecraft, Lang thought. He had completely forgotten creating a legend, the practice of leaving a series of believable clues supporting whatever identity one was using. More often than not, no one would be checking. But if they did, they would only confirm what they had been led to believe.

"Here." Gurt was proffering five ten-dollar bills.

"Fifty, all right. How big a bill did you change?"

"A hundred. I wanted to make sure we were remembered as having euros, not dollars."

"Lucky for us the Turks and Caicos's currency is the dollar."

As the cab drove away, Lang turned to look through a very dirty rear window. The man in the guayabera and the man in the uniform were dividing the money.

The road was a series of interconnected potholes, any one of which could have snapped the Ford's axle had the car been moving faster than a quick walk. A power line followed the road, periodically hosting clumps of purple orchids contrasting with the mean-looking scrub at the base of the poles. On the right, an emerald surf licked at a litter-strewn beach. Offshore, the sails of small fishing boats darted back and forth across the mouth of the bay. To the left a series of mud and daub huts faced yards of bare dirt surrounded by ragged, waist-high fences of prickly cactus. Lang was puzzled at both the choice of material and the lack of height of the cactus. Then he saw a pig with a stick tied horizontally around its neck, a stick too long to squeeze through the perimeter.

The Haitians might be poor but they didn't lack ingenuity.

A flatbed truck rumbled past, its muffler not even a memory. The sides were wooden slats painted with religious motifs and idealized scenes from Haiti's tropical forests, or what was left of them. People sat on benches running lengthwise, clutching squawking, flapping chickens or small pigs. The top was a pyramid of less-valued cargo: cardboard suitcases, furniture and bunches of both green and ripe bananas.

Tap-taps, Haiti's only public transportation.

The cab crossed a filthy creek that fanned out to make a small, gooey delta of mud and sand on the other side of the road. Mud huts with tin roofs shouldered each other to the waterline, many covered with a spiderweb of drying fishing nets. Scattered in the few available spaces, a few boats lay on their sides while owners and their families caulked or painted. The odor of open sewer filled the car, and Lang was appalled to see malnourished naked children playing in the very muck that was causing the smell.

Then the car was passing one- and two-story buildings painted every color imaginable. The predominant scent now was of charcoal coming from small braziers, around which squatting people cooked things Lang thought he would prefer not to recognize. All the women wore skirts, not a pair of pants among them. The street was crowded not by automobiles but by people, chickens and hand-drawn carts on truck tires. The impression was one of constant motion.

Then the taxi was headed up a steep hill, leaving the town's noise, sights and smells below. Halfway up, the car stopped, its engine revving furiously.

"What's the problem?" Lang asked.

The driver got out, motioning Lang to do the same. Warily, he noted the car was in park, the only thing preventing Gurt and the taxi from a quick and uncontrolled return to town. Unwilling to trust the antique's transmission, Lang motioned her to get out, too.

The driver came around the car, waving his hands "no." He then indicated that he and Lang would push. And that is how Lang and Gurt arrived at the Mont Joli Hotel, with Gurt riding like an elegant medieval lady in a sedan chair and Lang and the driver behind, pushing for all they were worth.

In the lobby, an open, airy room finished in what Lang guessed was native mahogany, a young woman imprinted his credit card.

"I'm so sorry, Mr. Lowen," she said, using the name on the passports in lilting English, "but I do not speak German."

"Just as well. Give me a chance to practice my English."

After establishing the room rates at seventy-five dollars a night if paid in dollars rather than euros, she handed him a key. "Enjoy your stay."

"What happens if I want to pay my bill in gourdes?"

From her expression, he might as well as well have suggested a particularly deviant sex act. "Gourdes?"

"Your national currency."

She ran a hand across the bottom of her chin, still agitated. "Er, it is our national currency, yes, but I know of no hotel that will accept it. If you wish . . ."

Lang waved a dismissive hand. "No problem. I was just asking."

She watched Gurt and Lang follow a porter toward their room. When they turned a corner, she pulled a cell phone from the pocket of her skirt and hit speed dial.

"*Oui?*" a male voice answered.

"We have some guests at the hotel," she said in Creole, bending over the desk to make sure those guests were out of earshot. "Guests with German passports."

There was silence on the other end.

"I do not believe they are German. His English is American. You wanted to know . . ."

"*Merci.*"

The other end of the conversation went dead.

Mont Joli
Cap Haitien
An hour later

Lang stood on the balcony outside his room, waiting for Gurt to get dressed after the shower they had shared. Immediately below him was a sparkling blue pool surrounded by grapefruit, oranges and limes dripping from trees. A huge ficus was draped in white orchids whose roots were exposed to the moist air that sustained them. The bloodred petals of a poinsettia the size of an oak reflected in the still water. Below the pool, the ground dropped off in a steep cliff to meet the sea. Turning to his right, he could see part of the town and the sweeping coastline of the bay against which it had been built. The height muted the sounds and, thankfully, the smells.

Now what?

Miles had wanted them to come to Haiti, land here on the north coast and look around a day or so before driving to Port-au-Prince if they found nothing here. Looking for what?

Miles had been less than specific: take note of anything amiss, anything unusual. Not very helpful in a place where natural beauty contrasted so sharply with the ugliness of a poverty-stricken population. It was all unusual. Everything grew in profusion, yet the people were starving, if what Lang had read was true. The flowers, the beaches, the majestic mountains rivaled anything Lang had seen in the Caribbean, yet tourists stayed away because of what was perceived as political unrest.

Gurt came up beside him, her hair still wet and gathered in a bun. "Is beautiful, no?"

Lang noticed she had changed into a skirt out of respect for the natives. Extending an arm around her waist, he pulled her up beside him. "Is beautiful, yes."

For a moment neither spoke. Then Lang pointed toward the range of jagged mountains behind the town. "What is that?"

Gurt squinted. "I see only mountains."

Lang took her by the shoulders, positioning her so she could look down his arm as if it were a gun sight. "Right there, on top of one of the peaks."

"You mean the little square knob?"

Lang nodded, gratified she could see it, too. "Yeah. What do you suppose that is?"

"A mountain?"

"When's the last time you saw a perfectly square mountain peak?"

"It might just appear square from this angle."

He took her hand. "Let's go down to the town and look around."

She wrinkled her nose. "I think I saw all of it I wanted on the way up here."

Lang chuckled. "Hey, you're the one that wanted to come to Haiti."

She sighed. "OK, but just for a short while. It is hot here." She pointed. "Down there, hotter."

On the way to the road up which Lang had pushed the taxi, Lang stopped at the desk.

The same young woman looked up. "May I help you, Mr. Lowen?"

"A question. Actually, several. First, what's worth seeing down in the town?"

She pursed her lips in thought. "I recommend the marketplace. You will see all sorts of native foods and goods. You might also want to look at the church. The carved wooden doors are considered to be works of art. And speaking of art, you will find a number of art shops."

"We were on our balcony and I noted the mountains south of town. There seems to be a square structure of some sort on top of one of them. What is it?"

Her face screwed up in thought. "A structure? On top of one of the mountains? You must be mistaken. There is nothing in those mountains other than a few mud huts."

"As I said, it just looks square," Gurt added.

Hand in hand, Gurt and Lang stepped from the area of the desk into the searing sunlight on the road. Immediately, a group of four or five men who had been sitting in the shade of a mahogany tree jumped to their feet and came trotting over.

"Need guide?"

"Very best guide, sir, madam."

"Show you Cap Haitien? Five dollar, American."

Lang had heard about these "guides." A tour of the local area was their secondary function. The primary duty was to keep at bay the child beggars and overly aggressive vendors that swarmed the few tourists like flies to rancid meat. He selected the youngest of the group. A man—boy, really—whose legs were visibly twisted by pellagra, polio or some other symptom of dietary deficiency and the country's lack of health care. Only two canes allowed him to walk, an exaggerated swagger that was painful to watch.

"How much?" Lang wanted to know as the other candidates sullenly retreated back to the shade.

"Five dolla, American."

That seemed to be the standard price.

"What's your name?"

"Paul."

"OK, Paul, what are you going to take us to see?"

"We go market, church." He nodded toward Gurt. "Then lady shop."

Despite the horribly malformed legs of his guide, Lang

was having to walk quickly to keep up with Paul, whose adeptness with his walking sticks would have been admired by a Special Olympics athlete.

Lang touched his arm, stopping him about halfway down the hill and pointing. "Paul, can you see that square thing on top of the mountain?"

The afternoon haze made the mountains little more than shadows but Paul immediately saw what Lang was talking about. "Citadelle."

"Citadelle?"

Paul nodded vigorously. "After French leave Haiti, Henri Christophe no want them to come back. Build Citadelle."

"Ah," Lang exclaimed. "So, it's a fortress of sorts." He looked closer. "But what is it, twenty miles away? It could hardly protect the town from that distance."

Paul treated Lang to a grin. "Christophe not defend town. Plan was to burn it and all crops, then go where big French guns could not reach: top of the mountain, where he could exist with five thousand people for a year, block mountain pass to interior of country. You want to see? I can arrange."

Sound military strategy, Lang thought. Leave the invading French with nothing but ruins, nothing to sustain their army that they hadn't brought themselves. "Yes, I'd like that. But, Paul, is this Citadelle something everyone around here knows about?"

Paul studied Lang's face for a second as though he thought Lang might be joking. "Everyone know about Citadelle, yes."

"OK. How do we get there?"

"Take taxi most of way. Last mile or two be by horse."

"Can we go now?" Gurt asked. "I'll need to change into pants."

Paul nodded. "Twenty minutes. Cab be at hotel. We go."

Gurt and Lang watched him move down the hill with both a speed and agility that belied his deformity before they turned to climb back toward their room.

"Why do you suppose the woman at the front desk said there was nothing up in those mountains but mud huts?" Lang pondered.

"Perhaps she was ignorant," Gurt suggested.

"You don't believe that any more than I do."

"Maybe she did not want us to be spending money outside the hotel."

A logical answer but not one Lang believed any more than the first.

Minutes later, he was watching Gurt wriggle into a pair of jeans. "Do you always buy them so tight?"

She inhaled to button the front. "They shrink after the first washing."

"So why not buy a size larger?"

Gurt sniffed, the answer obvious to any woman. "Because I wear a size eight or ten. If I bought a size larger, everyone would think I was getting fat."

Lang knew better than to pursue that. Instead, he said, "I'm not happy about having to ride horses."

Gurt inhaled again, this time for the zipper's benefit. "The exercise will do you good."

"Maybe, but I don't like anything both bigger and dumber than I am."

Milo, Haiti
An hour and a half later

Lang need not have worried about something bigger than he was. The horses gathered around a central corral were smaller than most burros. Astride one, his feet cleared the ground only by inches. The worn saddle did little to protect him from the razor back of his mount.

The town, Milo, was a small agricultural community of wooden huts amid small fields of coffee plants and banana trees. Several sheets spread on the ground displayed reddish beans that would turn chocolate brown as they dried. A second source of income was tourism or, as Paul explained, had been, before the fall of the last Duvalier over twenty years ago had precipitated a series of leaders, elected or otherwise, who were soon ousted by the next aspirant to power.

The three, Paul, Lang and Gurt, set off uphill on their diminutive mounts.

Gurt held her reins loosely. "It is as if they know where we go."

Paul gave her a smile. "The only trip they know, here to the Citadelle and back. If you let go, they go there and return."

Within minutes, the trail passed massive ruins of stone. At one time a structure far larger than anything Lang had seen in Haiti had been there.

Paul noted his interest. "Palace of Sans Souci, built by Christophe between 1810 and 1813. When he committed suicide, people pull down most of the buildings and earthquake in 1842 pull down whatever left."

Past the sloping field on which the former palace was located, the path narrowed and began to rise sharply. Lang was beginning to wish he had brought a sweater. The air was no longer pregnant with moisture, but cool to the skin. They were sheltered from the sun by increasing vegetation on each side of the trail. Vines bigger around than Lang's arm swooped low from massive branches of trees he could not identify. Unseen birds chattered in impenetrable shadows. Clearly this part of Haiti had not been deforested. At irregular intervals, the trio passed tiny mud huts squatting amid a row or two of stunted corn. Their arrival prompted naked children playing homemade flutes and drums to dance for coins tossed from horseback. Mangoes and stubby green bananas seemed to flourish without cultivation. Smiling women with huge jugs of water on their heads danced down the ragged path with steps as light as they were sure.

Twice Lang pulled his little horse to a stop and listened.

He was certain he had heard something behind them, the ring of a steel shoe striking a rock, the whinny of a horse. He did not recall seeing any other tourist in Milo, and he was fairly certain no Haitian would ride up to the Citadelle for the fun of it. There was something wrong, though he could not have enunciated exactly what.

Squeezing between Gurt's horse and the encroaching growth to ride side by side, he watched Paul in the lead. His bent, crooked legs seemed to present no impediment to his riding. In fact, he looked more comfortable than Lang felt.

Leaning over to place his mouth next to her ear, he said, "Someone is following us."

"Following?" she repeated. "It is the only path through the forest. Anyone coming this way would use it."

"But why would they come this way at all?" Lang argued. "I imagine everyone around here has been up to the old fort as many times as they might wish."

"And you intend to do what?"

Lang slid from his horse, handing the reins to Gurt. "I intend to see who's shadowing us. Go about another hundred yards and wait for me."

"Lang . . ."

Before she could voice an objection, he had used a hanging vine to climb into the dense leaves of an ironwood tree. She shook her head slowly and led his horse away.

Lang did not have long to wait. Gurt had just vanished into the twilight of the natural canopy of vegetation when two horsemen appeared. They both were dressed in khaki uniforms, and both had sidearms in covered holsters. Despite the meager light, both wore reflective sunglasses. They passed within five feet of Lang. He watched them go, then dropped to the trail and followed. With the steep grade, the horses' pace was easily one he could match.

He had been trailing them only a couple of minutes when the junglelike growth stopped as abruptly as the opening of a stage curtain. The two horsemen were silhouetted against a gray background that ebbed and flowed like running water. It took Lang a second to realize that he was at an altitude that touched the clouds.

A whiff of a breeze and the gray parted, revealing a sight he would not soon forget. Where the dense vegetation ended, it opened onto the open vista of a rocky meadow ending in a peak. Perched like a ship on an ocean wave, a massive stone structure stuck its bow into a sea of swirling mist. Lang had seen many forts, but never one with a shiplike prow. The object of fortification was not only to protect but provide a platform for heavy artillery, weaponry that could be concentrated on the enemy's positions. Here, the pointed bow achieved the opposite effect, diffusing rather than concentrating fire. But it made little difference, Lang could see. The fortress sat on a bluff with a straight drop-off on three sides. The only approach was the narrow path no more than two feet wide that crowned the slope up to the Citadelle's gate. A misstep would result in a fall of a thousand feet or more.

He could see Gurt and Paul waiting along this path, their horses nibbling at what little vegetation poked through the rocky surface. Then they disappeared in swirling gray cloud. By the time Lang could see Gurt and Paul again, the two horsemen he was following had reached them. Paul was engaged in an animated conversation. A few yards farther along toward the massive structure, two more men in uniform were approaching on horseback from the fort.

The two new arrivals reached the group at the same time as Lang. The discussion stopped and everyone turned to look at him, the only person not mounted.

"Tell them I had to answer the call of nature," Lang said to Paul, swinging back onto the little horse.

Although he was unable to understand the words, Lang could tell Paul was unhappy at what the men were telling him. The tone was getting angry and the gestures increasingly aggressive.

"What are they saying?" Gurt asked.

Paul took a deep breath. "Say we cannot enter Citadelle. Is dangerous, floors and walls not safe. We must go back. These men have orders not to allow anyone inside."

"The place has been there for nearly two hundred years," Lang argued, "and it's just now unsafe?"

"Go!" One of the men was pointing in the direction of Milo, perhaps exhausting his entire English vocabulary.

Lang took a long last look at the amazing structure perched on its lofty height. He could see guns of different sizes bristling through ports. The walls of stone rose well over a hundred feet and were smooth even though they had withstood the elements for nearly two centuries.

"Go now!"

The man knew more English than Lang had anticipated.

It was obvious no amount of argument was going to change the minds of these uniforms. Gurt reached into her purse and produced a twenty-dollar bill. In these latitudes, dead American presidents frequently spoke with more authority than mere orders.

The response was silent stares from four pairs of sunglasses.

Lang pulled the reins to his left. The little horse took dainty, careful steps to turn around on the narrow path. The animal was not only as small as a burro but just as surefooted.

"No point in arguing," he said sourly. "Let's go."

In single file, they reentered the coolness of the tropical forest. It was not until they were almost back to Milo that the trail permitted two riders side by side.

Gurt reined her horse in to let Lang catch up to her. "You do not plan to see this marvelous place, this Citadelle?"

Lang's response was a grunt. "First the woman at the hotel has never heard of the biggest attraction in Haiti, perhaps the whole Caribbean, and then we find at least four armed cops, militia, whatever, guarding the place to keep away the tourists for which the country is starving. I'd say there's something there more important than tourist dollars, something someone doesn't want seen."

Gurt smiled knowingly. "I suppose we have shopping to do, as Paul suggested."

"Indeed we do."

Cap Haitien
20:29 that evening

For dinner, Lang and Gurt had shared a pot of *tenaka* soup, vegetables done in an oxtail broth. She had the *poulet kreyòl*, he the *griot*, a highly spiced pork, all washed down with icy bottles of Prestige, Haiti's beer, served in different-sized and different-shaped bottles clearly recognizable from their former lives as containing Budweiser, St. Pauli Girl, Coors and a number of other brands stamped on the bottom of the glass, a model of recycling but more a tribute to the Haitian mentality of wasting nothing. The meal was served at the hotel's open-air restaurant beside the pool. Lang had warned Gurt to forgo the salad on the theory that in third world countries, that which isn't bottled, cooked or canned can lead to irresistible impulses to inspect plumbing facilities.

Even if there are none immediately available.

Retreating to the lobby, another open room furnished in native carved mahogany, Lang treated himself to a Cuban cigar, a Montecristo #2. It had been his favorite smoke before Manfred's arrival in his life had resulted in the second-hand-smoke treaty with Gurt, who had given up her beloved Marlboros.

"Do you not wish Cognac with that?" Gurt queried.

"Wish it?" Lang puffed contentedly. "You bet! But drink one? Not with what we have planned for the evening."

Gurt lowered her voice even though the room was otherwise empty. "We have everything we need?"

Lang contemplated the glowing ash of his cigar tip. "We checked before dinner, remember?"

Gurt stood, giving Lang a seductive look. "I think I will take a nap. Perhaps you will join me?"

Lang eyed his cigar, barely half-smoked. "Perhaps you will wait a little?"

She twisted her hips suggestively. "Poor Lang. He must choose between two of his delights."

"Haven't you heard? The president of the United States has forbidden torture."

Gurt parted her lips to run her tongue along them. "We are not in the United States."

Lang brightened. "Which means there is no such thing as a 'no smoking' hotel room." He stood. "Lead on, my lady! My cigar and I follow!"

She preceded him across a small but attentively landscaped courtyard, down stairs lit by gaslights, and stood in front of the door. Even in the poor light he could see her stiffen.

She turned and took the few steps required to stand beside him. "Someone is in our room."

Lang's joy of anticipation evaporated faster than early-morning dew in July. "You're sure?"

"The tall tale . . ."

"Telltale, the little strip of tape under the doorknob."

"It is gone."

"Perhaps the maid, turning down the bed."

"She did that while you were waiting for me at the restaurant."

Lang slid by her, squatting beside the door. He listened for several minutes before rejoining her. "Whoever it is is still there. I can hear someone moving around."

"We will have the hotel call the police."

Lang thought of the woman behind the desk who might be the only person in Cap Haitien unaware of the Citadelle, remembered his remark at dinner with the waiter hovering nearby that he intended to enjoy a cigar in the lobby afterward. "Not so fast. It might *be* the hotel."

"Lang, we cannot just burst into the room. He might be armed."

Just then, a shaft of light shone from the door. Whoever was in the room was coming out.

As though by prior agreement, both Lang and Gurt flattened themselves against the building. An indistinct shape exited their room, pulling the door closed behind it and furtively scurrying toward Lang and Gurt.

Lang waited until the person was almost abeam of him before sticking out a foot. Something tripped over it and went down amid what were understandable as curses in any language.

Lang was on top of the form, his knee pressing against shoulders as he held on to the wrists, jerking them upward. Once he had a firm grip, he stood, snatching the person to their feet. He was surprised at how light, how small, the would-be burglar was.

"Mr Lowen!"

"It is the woman from the front desk!" Gurt exclaimed just as Lang reached the same conclusion.

He spun her around to face him, pushing her toward the nearest gaslight. "Care to explain what you were doing in our room?"

Her eyes sparkled with either fear or fury. "To check your air-conditioning. Several of our guests have complained the units were not working. I knocked on your door, and when I got no answer . . ."

Lang had seen no other guests, had the distinct impression he and Gurt were the only ones. Nonetheless, he let her go.

She took a step back, rubbing her wrists. "You should be more careful who you attack," she said angrily.

"You should leave the door open when you are in someone's room," Lang countered. "It might help avoid unpleasant surprises for both you and your guests."

She gave him a glare, turned on her heel and was gone.

Inside the room, the window unit was doing a workman-like job.

Lang glanced around. "I don't see anything missing."

Gurt held up a paper bag that held the afternoon's purchases. "Perhaps not missing, but someone has moved the contents around."

At the same time, on the deserted road beside the hotel, a woman stood, talking into a cell phone.

"Yes, I looked carefully. The woman's clothes mostly have German labels. The man's . . . His jeans are American, but that means nothing. The wealthy all have American jeans. Two of his shirts are French; they still have the price tag."

She paused, listening.

"No, I found no weapons but I did find something interesting: several lengths of rope, a boat anchor—a small one—and flashlights. Whatever they plan, they plan it for tonight. They are scheduled to leave tomorrow. They saw me leaving their room, but I gave them an excuse."

Another pause.

"Yes, tonight. I would expect them tonight."

Milo
02:40 the next morning

The cab ride from Cap Haitien had been uneventful if expensive. André, operator of the vibrant blue Ford taxi, had asked no questions as to why anyone would choose to visit the little hamlet in the morning's earliest hours. If he had curiosity, the hundred dollars pressed into his palm quenched it.

As bidden, he let them out at the bottom of the hill that rose to Milo and became a mountain as it reached ever upward to the Citadelle. Wordlessly, he wheeled the old car around and headed back the way he had come. Gurt and

Lang shouldered the small backpacks they had purchased the previous afternoon.

Gurt was carefully picking her way in the ghostly light of a three-quarter moon. "You could have let him drive us into town," she observed.

"And wake everybody? The car had no muffler, y'know."

"Still, riding would not risk breaking our necks walking in the dark."

"Easy enough for you to say. Last time you rode uphill, I pushed, remember?"

They finished the gentle slope in silence. At the top, the scattering of huts was dark. Somewhere, a dog barked, someone shouted and the animal went silent. To their left, a gentle whinny led them to a low wooden fence around the central corral. Lang slipped a saddle and bridle from the top slat and was approaching a horse made skittish either by the dark or the fact he was facing a stranger.

"It will give trouble if we are caught taking horses," Gurt predicted.

"If we don't have them back by sunup, being horse thieves will be the least of our problems."

"Do they not hang horse stealers?"

Lang managed to slip a bridle over the horse's head. "That was *Lonesome Dove*. Don't know about Haiti. Whatever they do, we don't want to be here when it gets light. Now, get one saddled up."

Each leading a horse toward the increasing slope, Lang and Gurt waited until they were well past the last silent hut before mounting. The trail narrowed to the point of invisibility as it snaked upward. Lang had not been willing to follow a path he could not see with an abyss on either side, as would be the case approaching the Citadelle. Instead, he had remembered the little sure-footed horses and how they had needed no guidance from riders to find the Citadelle or home. He could only hope they knew their directions well enough to navigate without actually seeing their way.

The moon was playing peekaboo behind puffy, silver-lined clouds, drenching the mountainside in inky darkness for minutes at a time. The surrounding coolness was Lang's first clue they had entered that part of the route that passed through tropical forest. One of the horses' hooves struck a rock, and there was a sound from the side of the trail that could have been a sleeping human mumbling in one of the mud habitations beside the trail.

There was no doubt when they emerged from the canopy of trees. A panoply of diamond chips sparkled in the eastern sky, undimmed by the fickle moon. Like a stage setting, the Citadelle was an undefined mass of foreboding, black against the array of stars. For once the area was not cloaked in clouds. Lang would soon find out if the tiny horses could navigate by memory alone. Between here and the bastion the narrow path was a bridge across oblivion.

The both saw it at the same time: a pinprick of light flashed and died near the base of the fortress. Someone had lit a cigarette.

"If there's one, there's more," Lang whispered, although the distance to the Citadelle did not yet mandate silence.

The shadow that was Gurt nodded. "But how many more?"

Lang slipped from the saddle. "With a little luck, we'll never know." He edged past her horse to stand behind it, placing a hand on its rump. "I'll walk awhile, following your horse. When we get a little closer, you stop, hold my horse."

"But you cannot see."

"If I get close enough, I won't have to. I'll move on hands and knees, feel my way along."

"But—"

"No buts. If we get any closer and one of the horses whinnies or strikes a rock . . ."

Although clearly unhappy to be relegated to the role of holding the horses, Gurt knew this was neither the time nor the place for an argument. Reluctantly, she rode ahead in silence until Lang touched her arm.

"Here, wait here." He handed her the reins of his mount. "If I'm not back in an hour and a half, take the horses back to Milo and get to the hotel. I'll need help."

She started to offer a final protest, but Lang had slipped away into the darkness.

On hands and knees, Lang felt his way along the rocky path. Within minutes, his back began to throb at the unusual angle at which it was bent. Progress was slow, one hand in front of the other, making sure where he could place each knee. Once or twice, he had to stop as unseen rocks were dislodged and tumbled noisily into the void on either side. He would pause, listening for any human reaction.

So far, there was none.

After what seemed like painful hours, but his watch's luminous dial described as twenty minutes, Lang could no longer see the Citadelle's form against the sky. He was so close it filled his vision. Starting to stand, he froze in mid-crouch as an orange dot caught the periphery of his vision. Either the cigarette smoker they had seen from the trail or another nicotine lover.

Lang moved a few inches to his right and squatted, trying to pick up a silhouette, a shape, anything that might give him an idea as to the smoker's exact position. The mass of the old fortress and its shadow from the moon blacked out everything in front of him. His fingers searched the uneven ground at his feet and closed around a stone slightly larger than a softball.

He waited.

The cigarette glowed with what turned out to be the last puff before it was discarded in an arc of burning ashes against which Lang could see a single figure not three feet away.

Lang purposely cleared his throat.

The man in front of him grunted in surprise and Lang was close enough to hear the small sounds of movement.

Pebbles underfoot crunched; metal struck metal as a weapon struck a belt buckle.

Lang timed his swing with an accuracy learned on the Agency's long-ago training fields. Rock met skull with a grinding crunch and a grunt. He fell against Lang.

Quickly moving from under the still body, Lang searched his victim until his hand touched a weapon still grasped in unconscious hands. Running a hand down a stubby barrel, Lang quickly identified the gun as an AK-47, type 63/68. There was no chance he could see the markings stamped into the metal that would reveal its origins. He set it down beside him and fumbled off his backpack.

Minutes later, he was finishing binding the man's arms and legs with duct tape. Task completed, he taped the man's mouth shut and stood, slinging the rifle over his shoulder. No doubt the guy would regain consciousness shortly—he was already moaning—but Lang intended to be long gone before his companions found him in the early-morning light.

For a full five minutes, Lang stood still, listening for any evidence his presence had been detected. He heard none. Still, he didn't dare approach the fortress by the front, the site of the only entrance. Surely it would be guarded. He had prepared for a less-orthodox entry. He moved gingerly to the side of the path. Keeping a precarious balance, he reached a point where he could see a slice of the night sky, its stars outlining the wall of the Citadelle.

Climbing that wall was out of the question without some sort of help, help that just might be provided by . . .

Lang took a length of rope from his backpack and uncoiled it. Blindly, he tied a slipknot into one end. Twirling the rope above his head like a cowboy chasing an errant steer, he let it slide through his fingers. Rope met rock wall with a faint slapping sound and Lang reeled it in to try again. On the third effort, the rope settled around a cannon's muzzle protruding a foot or so from its gun port. Lang threw his weight backward, drawing the knot tight. He gave several exploratory tugs to make sure it was fast before he slung the pack back onto his shoulders and began to climb.

Unlike many fortifications that had been built with a slight slope to deflect artillery fire, the Citadelle's walls were vertical. Above the gun port toward which he was climbing, Lang could see two more, their silent barrels protruding into the night like the gargoyles of a Gothic cathedral.

His foot found a niche in the mortar between two stones. Pulling on the rope as he braced against the wall, he was able to "walk" up the face of the fort perpendicular to it. Above his head, he could see the cannon getting ever closer. Another step, perhaps two, and he would be there.

The gun was finally within his reach. Taking one hand from the rope, he stretched toward it. At the same time his foot hit a trickle of water, a patch of moss, something slick that broke the traction between his rubber-soled shoe and the rock surface, sending him swinging pendulum-like across the face of the stone.

He clung to the rope, an umbilical cord of life that held him above a drop of thousands of feet. The swing ended abruptly as his momentum slammed him into a protruding stone, perhaps the top of another gun port. The impact knocked the breath out of his lungs and blurred his vision with colorful spots that spun in front of his eyes. Gasping to refill his lungs, he felt his grip on the line slip before his concentration could return from the pain of colliding with unforgiving rock.

He drifted back and forth in space, the cannon's muzzle taunting him with unreachable proximity. His shoulder muscles were in rebellion, sending jolts of pain radiating from neck to wrist. Hands beginning to spasm from the physical tension, he forced one after the other to inch his way up the remaining few feet of rope toward the gun.

He was almost there when he felt an almost imperceptible

slack in the line. The swinging motion had somehow loosened the knot in the rope. It was coming loose.

If it did, the next stop would be nearly a half mile below.

Gurt was trying to get comfortable sitting on a craggy rock, the reins of the two horses in her hands. Her watch told her Lang had been gone only a few minutes, but the wait was becoming burdensome. They could just as easily have found some outcropping of stone to which to tether both horses. Unspoken had been the thought that the two of them, Gurt and Lang, should not be at risk at the same time. Manfred should not be in danger of becoming an orphan at a single stroke. She accepted the reasoning, but being left out of any action still rankled her.

Waiting was something she had been trained to do. The hours or days she had spent in anticipation of completing some Agency operation had taught her the virtue of patience. At a time when gratification was expected instantly, satisfaction even quicker, where information could be exchanged in nanoseconds, waiting was an acquired talent that exceeded simple inactivity. In the world Gurt had inhabited, long periods of apparent idleness could be terminated violently and unexpectedly.

Waiting, professional and useful waiting, required mental alertness behind a facade of indolence.

For all of those reasons, Gurt was sufficiently attuned to her environment to detect the sound. It wasn't the light breeze whispering among the boulders that littered the mountainside, it wasn't the exfoliation of a rock contracting as it cooled from the previous day's heat and it wasn't the sound of some stray animal. She was unsure what she had heard but it was none of those.

She released the horses, who made no effort to escape or even stray but stood dumbly, heads down as though confused as to what to do next. She lay flat, making certain she would not be outlined against the starry sky.

This time she identified the sound: horses slowly walking down from the Citadelle above. The muffled creak of leather against leather told her these were not grazing animals but saddled mounts, presumably with riders. And they were definitely coming her way, because there was no other way to go.

She could hear voices now, words she could not understand, but their inflection indicated surprise, perhaps at finding two saddled, riderless horses in the middle of the precarious trail between fortress and forest. A beam of a flashlight ran across the ground, missing her by inches. The next time she might not be so lucky.

And there would be a next time, probably in the following few seconds if the tone of curiosity she heard in the voices increased. If these men were guards of some sort, the two riderless horses would not be ignored.

She reached out, preparatory to moving as far down the slope as she could before the sheer drop-off. Her hand touched something solid, rough. A large outcropping of rock. She belly-wriggled toward it. Looking up, she saw two figures, half horse, half man, dark cutouts against stars beginning to dim as they were devoured by the moon's brighter light. She could not be certain but she thought she saw what might be a weapon slung across each man's shoulder.

She made out each careful step of the two newly arrived horses. She even imagined she could detect the impact of each hoof on the stony surface. They had to be within feet of her. The light breeze brought her the smell of horse sweat and damp leather. Could she also feel the animals' body heat on her skin?

Another beam of light swept the area, barely giving Gurt time enough to roll behind what she hoped was the protection of the rock. She seemed to have succeeded. The prying light swept by.

The jingle of tack and a grunt told her at least one of the riders was dismounting. On foot, sweeping the area with light, he would find her in minutes. She thought wistfully of the Glock 19 safely if uselessly stored in the drawer of her bedside table at home. She might not have to use it were it here, but it would certainly put her in a better bargaining position when she was discovered. So much spilt milk, as the Americans would say, though she never really understood why one would cry over spilt milk. Sour or spoiled milk, yes. But spilled?

Spilled, sour or rancid, the difficulty of getting a firearm through U.S. security at departure had seemed at the time to outweigh the possible benefits, not to mention the off chance Haitian customs might actually have an interest in luggage other than visitors' wallets.

Like most decisions with a bad result, the effect of leaving weapons behind now seemed foolish.

Foolish or not, the man was approaching Gurt's hiding place. She could see his form against the sky. Perhaps her height, maybe a little shorter. He held the light in one hand, a rifle in the other. His head seemed misshaped. No, he was wearing a short cap of some sort. Part of a uniform? Whatever, within seconds, a minute at most, she was going to be discovered. It was time to act.

But how?

She slowly got to her knees, ready to spring.

Waiting, waiting.

In a second or two, the knot would slip through, leaving Lang with a useless length of rope and a fall he would not survive. It was time to do something, even if it was wrong.

He swayed his body back and forth on the rope, gaining momentum like a child on a playground swing set. He could only hope he reached a wide enough arc before the line slipped free. On the third swing, he sensed rather than felt the slackness.

The knot was undone, the rope loose.

Ignoring the fire that burned along the muscles and

tendons of his back, shoulders and arms, he hurled himself into space.

His left hand slapped something, then his right. His fingers were scraping the cannon's muzzle, trying to find purchase on a circumference far larger than they could encircle.

He was not going to be able to hold on.

Sucking in his breath, he used what little traction he had to jackknife, sending his feet above his head like a circus trapeze artist. By wriggling, he got one leg over the cannon as far as the knee, then the other. Now he was head down, knees hooked over the cannon barrel, hanging like a giant bat in some third-rate horror film.

He tried to bend outward so that he could get his hands on the iron of the gun again. No luck. He hadn't been that supple since grammar school.

He slid the leg closest to the wall a few inches. Then the other. Already he could hear the buzzing in his ears, feel the dizziness of being head down too long. The muzzle of the AK-47 slung over his shoulder rapped the back of his head. He shoved the symptoms of inversion away, concentrating on inching forever closer to the opening of the gun port.

At last a hand touched the rough rock surface of the sill of the opening. Contorting his body, Lang twisted so his other hand could also grab hold. For a second, he hung by his arms, legs dangling in space as his feet sought purchase against the stone face.

He took a deep breath and chinned himself upward. For an instant, he hung half in, half out of the portal before he flopped inside like a hooked fish being pulled over the transom of a boat. For a full moment, he lay still, waiting for his breathing and heartbeat to return to a semblance of normal. He smelled a mixture of mustiness and the sweet air of a tropical night.

A fragile shaft of moonlight filtered through the aperture through which he had entered, a beam dividing the night into equal parts of darkness. Using touch more than sight,

Lang got to his feet. It took only a minute or two to determine he was in a small room, perhaps ten by ten. At his feet was a semicircular iron rail, the open part toward the port. Although long rotted away, the wheels of the gun's carriage would have moved along this track to cover an arc of perhaps ten degrees or so. The gun, a massive twenty-four-pounder, judging by its girth, lay amid the rusting remains of carriage-wheel rims, aiming screw and things Lang could not identify by touch. Beside the cannon, balls were neatly stacked in a pyramid near hoops of powder barrels. Lang had the eerie feeling the gun's crew had taken temporary leave and would return any minute.

The ghostly impression was reenforced as a cloud slowly enveloped the old fortress, turning what little light there was into gray fog. The sudden drop in temperature caused goose bumps along Lang's exposed skin. Or was it the spookiness of the place?

The damp shreds of the cloud reluctantly dispersed. Lang could see the rear of the room was open, allowing a gauzy film of moonlight to paint a parade ground from which mouths of similar gun rooms yawned. Above him, he could make out at least two more levels, each with openings to rooms he was certain were similar to the one in which he stood. At another time, he would have been curious as to how newly freed slaves had obtained the expensive ordnance that he had seen bristling from the Citadelle's walls the previous afternoon. There must have been at least a hundred guns here in one of the world's more remote places, almost twice as many as Henry Knox had been able to supply to the Continental Army for its siege of Boston in 1775.

Lang stood just inside the room, listening and trying to command his eyes to somehow penetrate the darkness. If whatever was here merited a guard—the one he had left bound in duct tape—logic dictated there would be others.

Keeping his back to the wall, he edged toward the courtyard, a hand feeling his way. His foot struck something along the stone just as his hand felt a wooden surface. Wood? Any wood, like the gun carriages, would have long fallen victim to the humid tropical climate and the insects that flourished in it.

Turning to face the wall, he spread his arms. Crates, long wooden crates, were stacked to the low ceiling of the gun room. This was hardly something left by Christophe's militia nearly two centuries ago.

He slipped the AK-47's strap from his shoulder, removed his backpack and fumbled in it until he touched the tiny penlight he had purchased in Cap Haitien. A larger flashlight would have been more help, but the smaller version had a concentrated beam, one less likely to be seen by other eyes. His back to the room's opening, he turned the light on, playing it across the boxes. They were marked with Asian characters, either Japanese or Chinese. Since kanji, the Japanese writing system, had been adapted from the Chinese centuries ago, the subtle differences between the Chinese *onyomi* and the Japanese *kunyomi* were indistinguishable to anyone not literate in one or both.

In light of what Miles had said, though, it was an easy guess which one he was looking at.

He switched off the light and looked over his shoulder. He neither saw nor heard any indication his presence had been detected. He went down on hands and knees, fingers searching the dusty floor. He found what he was looking for, a rusty piece of iron that could have been part of the gun carriage, a piece of the track or any number of military items.

He touched the end. Sharp enough, but had the rust of time made it too brittle? One way to find out. Using only touch, he found the edge where the lid of a crate had been hammered onto the sides. He worked the edge of his newfound tool between the two, working it up and down like a crowbar.

With an almost human groan, the nails pulled loose and

Lang inhaled a familiar odor, the sweet smell of gun oil. His fingers blindly fumbled aside an oily cloth and touched what was unmistakably a dozen or so gun barrels. The other parts would be in other crates.

He sat back on his haunches and thought for a moment. There was no way to tell how many small arms might be stored here at the Citadelle without a count he doubted he would have time to make. For that matter, the old fortress was more than ample to also contain more serious weaponry— missile components, for instance.

Now there was a happy thought: Chinese rockets with potential nuclear capability right on America's doorstep.

Almost equally disturbing was the way the rifle barrels had ben packed: with oily cloths instead of Cosmoline, that Vaseline-like substance that prevents moisture from reaching the inner working of machinery, widely used for the storage of firearms. But Cosomoline required detailed removal from intricate nooks and crannies such as firing pins and ejection mechanisms. It was not a method of storage for weapons which would see use soon.

For whatever purpose, rifles were going to be issued to someone in the near future.

What other surprises did the old fort hold?

Easing the crate's top back in place, Lang slid along the wall and into the parade ground. The night air brought him the heavy fragrance of citrus blooms, of the sea and a tiny trace of burning tobacco.

Lang turned his head slowly in hope of a visual clue as to the source of the last. The moon, now overhead, painted the interior of the old fort a monochomatic gray-silver, corners delineated by smudges of black shadow. The spasmodic breeze whispered through the open gun ports as it pushed a small piece of paper across the parade ground.

Lang could have been the only human on earth had it not been for the persistent smell of tobacco.

He unslung the AK-47 not because he feared he might

have immediate use for it as much as the comfort it gave him to have a weapon in his hands in this seemingly deserted and ghostly place. Facing the parade ground, he walked backward up a ramp that led to the next level, careful to use the shadows as cover as long as possible.

As far as he could tell, the upper gun level resembled the one he had just left. He looked around carefully before moving toward the nearest gun room. His foot touched something on the stone. Kneeling, he felt a wire, what seemed to be an electrical wire that ran from the edge of the ramp he had just traveled.

He squatted, the wire in his hand. Why would it be necessary to install electricity here unless there was some activity besides storage? There was certainly no need at the moment, as indicated by the absence of the chugging of a generator. Like the rifles stored below, wiring the Citadelle was an indication of action planned rather than undertaken.

But what?

Following the wire, he entered another room, this one without a gun port and, he estimated by touch, larger than the one he had seen below. Its lack of opening to the outside indicated its use had perhaps been that of magazine, a place where powder and shell could have been temporarily stored until distributed to the guns on this level.

The hand not holding the rifle extended in front, he touched another surface, this one metal. Exploring with his hand, Lang estimated whatever he was touching to be at least twenty feet long and four or five wide. He guessed this container held something more than small arms. A brief probe with the flashlight revealed more Chinese characters.

An idea. Returning the light to his pocket, he pulled out his BlackBerry. Now, if he could manipulate the settings . . . Ah, the screen lit up. Taking a picture was going to involve a flash, but he saw no other way of getting an image of whatever military hardware this might be to Miles. Before leaving the States, Miles had given him an e-mail address, which Lang had dutifully stored.

So, all he had to do was take the picture, e-mail it and get the hell out of this creepy place before anyone was the wiser.

Now to get the hell . . .

The thought vanished as the room was flooded with light. For an instant, he thought he had been blinded by the tiny flash of the BlackBerry's camera. Had he turned it upon himself instead of the containers?

"Drop the weapon," came a voice from behind him. "Drop it, put your hands on your head and turn very slowly."

Lang did as he was told, his eyes slow to adjust to the brilliance of two very bright flashlights in his eyes. He could make out the forms of maybe a half-dozen men, but their faces remained obscured in darkness. Likewise, he could not see who was speaking.

"Mr. Lowen," the disembodied vice said, using the name on Lang's passport, "or should I say Reilly? We have been expecting you."

"And who might you be?" Lang asked.

Rough hands grabbed him, shoving him toward the ramp he had just climbed. He tripped over the cord, his hands getting cut as they braced against the stone to break the fall.

"Careful, Mr. Reilly," the unseen voice mocked him. "We would not want you to get hurt. At least not until we have had the chance to . . . what do you say? Visit, not until we have had a chance to visit awhile."

Someone behind him found this funny, snickered, someone who was prodding Lang's back with what felt very much like a gun barrel. Hands patted his body and dug into his pockets, removing his BlackBerry, flashlight and money clip. The watch was taken from his wrist. His wallet was slipped from its pocket.

Not a good sign. Wallets were the first place investigators looked when trying to identify a corpse.

* * *

The moon was to the rear of the rock behind which Gurt was hiding. She could clearly see the man walking slowly toward her, searching the ground with the beam of his flashlight. Carefully, she edged around the stone, keeping it between him and her. She could not go much farther without being clearly visible in the moonlight to his companion, who, she assumed, was still sitting on his horse.

She got as close to the ground as she could with her feet still underneath her.

The flashlight's beam hit her face and she uncoiled like a broken spring. Her hands, open to cover as much area as possible, hit the man square in the middle of the chest. He grunted, stumbling backward in surprise.

Before he could regain his balance, Gurt shoved from the side, pushing him toward the precipice. He was waving his arms to regain some form of equilibrium when she stuck a foot between his ankles and snatched it back, knocking his feet out from under him.

He windmilled backward. Even in the dim light, Gurt could see eyes enlarged and bright with terror as he lost his footing and toppled backward over the edge.

She was surprised he did not scream. The only sound was of rocks knocked loose by his fruitless efforts to find a handhold.

She didn't have the time to find out if she could hear his body's impact below. Instead, she rushed the man on horseback. Spooked by her charge, the animal whinnied and stepped back nervously, throwing off the aim of the rider trying to bring a weapon to bear.

Before he could level his rifle again, she was upon him, tugging at his belt. He steadied himself in the saddle with one hand as he raised the barrel of the gun with the other to bring it down on her head.

It was a move Gurt had anticipated. She sidestepped, the muzzle sizzling in the air as it missed her cheek by fractions of an inch. She grabbed his wrist, and using his momentum in delivering the blow, she yanked downward as hard as she could.

His cap flew off and he seemed to leap from the saddle, performing a flip from the horse's back that would have done credit to an acrobat. Except that he landed headfirst with a lung-emptying thud.

She was on him as he shook his head and tried to stand. Before he reached his knees, she delivered a kick with all her strength that caught him squarely on the chin. He spun backward and fell on his back. This time he made no effort to get up.

Straddling the prone body, Gurt patted him down. Her search revealed a flashlight hanging by a clip to his belt and a long knife—a bayonet, she assumed—in a scabbard also on his belt.

He was starting to moan as Gurt unbuttoned his shirt and took it off. The pants were a little more difficult, requiring her to tug at the cuffs to dump him out of them. He had recovered consciousness sufficiently to mumble words she could not understand. She dragged him over to the rock behind which she had been hiding and found where she had shrugged off her backpack.

It took mere seconds to locate the roll of tape, one of two Lang had purchased. Only a little more time was required before the man was trussed like a Thanksgiving turkey. He was trying to say something as she slapped the final strip across his mouth, reducing him to grunts and squeals.

Gurt slid the shirt on over her own, trying not to notice the odor of stale sweat. The top and bottom buttoned easily, but no way was the fabric going to stretch across her breasts. She stepped into the pants, a little short at the bottom, and the belt lacked enough notches to tighten it enough to keep the trousers around her waist. No matter. She was going to be sitting anyway. She made certain both flashlight and bayonet were still in place.

It took several minutes to locate the man's rifle and his

cap. She put the latter on her head, tucking her long blonde hair under it. A soft whinny led her to one of the horses, which she mounted as she slung the rifle over her shoulder.

If whoever was in the Citadelle had sent a patrol along the treacherous path in the dead of night, it was a near certainty she and Lang were expected. They could well have been waiting for him. Besides, she had no intention of simply waiting for his return.

Just like a man to assume she would obey him simply because of his gender.

Lang was ushered into a small room he guessed had served as an officer's quarters. He was again nearly blinded by the light. As his eyes adjusted, he noted the small Yamaha generator softly chugging in a corner. The stone walls must have insulated its sound from the outside. He got a glimpse of a pair of iron cots with thin cotton mattresses. He was less than surprised to see a poster bearing the likenesses of Sun Yat-sen, Mao and Chou En-lai hanging over two packing crates that served as a dresser. Across the room a blanket hung over what Lang surmised was an entrance to one of the corridors outside the gun rooms.

Hands snatched his arms behind his back and pressed him into a reed-bottomed chair to which his wrists were tightly bound before he was spun around to face the door.

An Asian of undeterminable age peered back at him. The man wore a woodland-pattern camouflage uniform whose epaulets bore two stitched stars. His fatigue cap had a single red star pinned above the red band above the bill. If Lang remembered correctly, he was facing a *Zhong Xiao*, lieutenant colonel, of the People's Liberation Army.

The man reached somewhere beyond the angle that Lang's bindings permitted him to see and produced the mate to the chair in which Lang sat.

Dragging it to within a few feet of Lang, he reached into a pocket, produced a cigarette without removing the pack and lit it as he sat. "I am Lieutenant Colonel Shien Dow," he announced in American-accented English, "and I have a few questions for you."

Lang said nothing.

Dow took a long drag, expelling the smoke somewhere above Lang's head. "First, who sent you?"

"I came on my own."

"With a false passport? Why would you enter Haiti on a false passport? That could get you in serious trouble, you know."

"With whom? The People's Republic of China?"

The lieutenant colonel stared at him a moment, and then Lang's head seemed to explode. He never saw the blow coming. The next thing his brain registered was the chair, with him still in it, sideways on the floor. Unseen hands righted both.

"Let us try again, Mr. Reilly . . ."

"My name is Lowen and I am a German citizen."

This time he saw what was coming but was unable to prevent it. His interrogator's fist smashed into Lang's mouth and he tasted blood as the chair toppled over again.

By the time Lang was propped up, Dow was rubbing the knuckles of his right hand with the left, cigarette dangling from his lips.

He gave a deep sigh. "We know who you are. Your name is Langford Reilly; you are a lawyer in Atlanta, Georgia. We even have your address, where you and your wife live with your young son. Speaking of your wife, she came here to the Citadelle with you. If you cherish her safety, you will cooperate."

Implicit and direct bluffs? Lang suspected so. Harming Manfred or Gurt would not produce the immediate result this man wanted. Besides, Gurt should be on her way back to the Mont Joli by now, fully alerted for trouble when Lang didn't return. The question was, how did they know who he was? Some sort of face-recognition equipment used in conjunction with a surreptitious photo taken, perhaps in Venice?

Perhaps the credit-card receipt for the costume? No matter. What was important was that they *did* know who, and what did he do now? The sole weapon Lang had was to stall, to drag things out as long as possible to give Gurt time to get help. The problem was that this guy was going to use Lang as a punching bag or worse in the meantime.

He was not disappointed over the next hour.

Time ceased to exist. Only pain was real, throbbing pain from the places Lang had been hit, stabbing pain as another blow was delivered. If Lang gave them the information they sought, they had little incentive to let him live. He had to hold out, delay until Gurt came up with a plan.

He tried to withdraw his mind from this place, a technique Agency training had included. He saw the azure waters caressing the verdant cliffs of Italy's Amalfi Coast, the majesty of the Austrian Alps draped in winter white. He almost smiled as he recalled something Manfred had said, a particular wild romp in bed with Gurt.

But always the pain intruded, shattering his thoughts like a china plate hitting the floor. The pain was sapping his energy as well as his will. At some point, his resistence to it would be gone. Why suffer the agony? Tell them what they wanted now. Death would take the pain away.

And I'll never see Manfred or Gurt again.

His head snapped up from his chest and he realized with a start Dow's face was inches from his own, close enough that the spittle from his screaming mouth sprayed Lang's cheeks.

Lang was familiar with the interrogation tactic: soft voice rises unexpectedly to yelling, a sudden about-face designed to keep the person being questioned off balance. He also had a pretty good idea of what came next. If physical beating did not produce the desired result, there were two options. The first was to put the prisoner someplace where sleep and a sense of time would be impossible, nothing to occupy his mind but the dread of future beatings. Lang thought that scenario unlikely. Dow would not wait for days to find out why Lang and Gurt were here. The second option was to simply increase the pain factor: electric shock of the genitals, pull a few teeth, some form of mutilation.

The options were both limited and unpleasant.

As though to confirm Lang's fears, Dow nodded to someone behind Lang. Fingers grabbed his shirt and tore it from his body. An instant later, the Chinese colonel stubbed out a burning cigarette against Lang's left nipple.

Lang was almost deafened by the sound of a scream, a sound he hardly realized came from him.

Gurt was close enough to see the men just inside the massive entrance to the Citadelle. Darkness prevented her from making out their features, but there was enough light from the declining moon to see there were two of them, one on each side of a portal that must have been twenty feet high. She leaned forward along the narrow spine of the small horse, hoping to diminish her stature. Unless one of them chose to use a flashlight, she would appear as indistinct to them as they to her, just one more man returning from a patrol.

She entered without challenge. Her little mount picked up its measured pace, perhaps in the realization the stable and feed were near.

She was abeam the two guards when one of them spoke, a low, guttural sound with a definitely inquisitive inflection.

A question, of course. He wanted to know where the other member of the patrol was. How was she going to answer a question in a language she did not know?

Lowering her voice into what might, possibly, be the range of a male tone, she growled a muttered response imitating the sound of the words she had just heard.

The man who had asked the question spoke again, this time louder. She could see him approaching as his partner reached for the strap of the rifle slung over a shoulder.

Gurt pulled her horse to a stop, slowly slipped her right foot from the stirrup and began to swing a leg over her mount's spiny backbone in a slow dismount, the casual movement of a man weary from both the hour and his duties just now complete. From the corner of an eye she measured the closing distance between her and the question asker. It would not do to appear too deliberate or in a hurry.

She timed it so he came in range just as her right foot cleared the saddle. With her weight shifting to her left leg, she pivoted in the stirrup, her right foot swinging in a blur of an arc that connected neatly with the man's jaw.

He staggered backward, just far enough to give Gurt room to unsling the rifle from her back. Dropping both feet to the ground, she grabbed the gun's barrel and brought the stock down on the man's head with a crunch that left him sitting on the ground, too dazed to present any immediate threat.

Spinning on her toes, she faced the second guard, now moving to get around the horse between them. Gurt could easily have shot him, but the sound would have alerted anyone within a mile, including whatever garrison now occupied the old fort.

He had no such qualms, as evidenced by his efforts to bring his weapon to bear around a nervous, diminutive horse.

Gurt dropped to a squat, merging her silhouette with that of the animal and effectively disappearing in the darkness. She used part of the one or two seconds before her adversary could find her to draw the bayonet from its scabbard and test its balance in her hand.

With her left hand, she slapped the horse's rump, causing it to shy away. The man with the gun swung the rifle in her direction. She cocked her right arm. And threw.

The bayonet had not been designed for this sort of use and Gurt had not had time to explore its characteristics. Nonetheless, she had little choice but to throw it. Because of its weight, she had done so not like a knife but more like a spear, straight rather than end over end, more shoulder than the wrist action required to accurately toss a blade.

A thump and a strangled half gargle, half grunt, told her she had hit the mark.

The rifle clattered against the stone of the parade ground. She visualized the man clutching with both hands at the steel that protruded from his stomach or chest.

The rifle now in both hands, she stepped over to where he had been. A figure, faceless in the dark, sat or knelt on the ground, issuing a low moan. With a foot, Gurt pushed him onto his side, bent over and tugged at the hilt of the blade. It was caught on something. She tried to wiggle it free, eliciting a scream of pain. It stubbornly refused to come loose and Gurt doubted she had a lot of time before someone came to investigate the yell.

There was little choice, one she made intuitively on the side of safety rather than humanity. She could tape him up, taking precious seconds, or . . .

She leaned on the hilt of the bayonet until the blade went in all the way and the struggles at the other end ceased.

In a couple of steps, she was beside the first man, whose darkened form was shakily trying to get to its feet. Grasping the rifle by its muzzle again, she swung the stock as hard as she could to connect with the base of his skull. He collapsed in a boneless heap without a sound.

She paused only to scoop up his rifle and add it to the one she already had.

Instinctively, Gurt was moving toward the deepest shadows, the place she would be safest. She was almost there when she heard a scream. It was neither of the men she had encountered, no cry of alarm, but a long, wailing expression of agony more animal than human. But she knew of no animal capable of such a sound.

Whatever its source, she thought it had come from straight ahead, although the rock walls were capable of distorting

and displacing sound. She looked closely. Was that a glimmer of light leaking around the edge of a doorway?

Her back to whatever wall was available, she flitted from
one pool of darkness to another, one rifle slung over a shoulder, the other at the ready. In less than a minute, she had
traveled around half the parade ground and was at the end
most distant from the fort's entrance. She could hear a voice
on the other side of the wall, though the stone made it impossible to discern what was being said.

She ran a hand along the stone, inching her way forward
until her fingers touched wood. A quick exploration by touch
revealed a smooth surface, not the roughness and rot exposure to the elements for two centuries would have produced.
A door, a newly installed door, behind which the voice continued.

Gurt was considering what to do next. She peeled back a
sleeve and checked her watch. The grayness of predawn
would arrive in less than an hour. If she was going to find
Lang, she did not have long to do it.

She started to slide past the door when she froze, ear to
the wood.

". . . name is Rolf Lowen. I am a German citizen . . ."

Lang!

Gurt's fingers raced across the door's surface until she
found the latch, hesitated and returned to the weapon in
her hand. When she had taken it on the trail in front of the
Citadelle, she had given it the briefest of examinations. Her
touch had told her it was an AK-47. She had not had the
time to make a more thorough examination.

She opened the slide to slip a finger into the chamber, since
she could not see. Empty. She cocked it and began searching
for the safety button and automatic-fire switch. Then she
put the weapon down and went through the same procedure
with the gun strapped across her back.

Satisfied she was as ready as she could be, she depressed
the latch and kicked the door open.

The first thing she saw was Lang, strapped to a chair. His face was bloody, eyes nearly swollen shut. There were ugly marks in the skin of his bare chest.

In the instant it took for her eyes to adjust to the light, she saw movement behind his chair—two men, two uniforms . . .

No time for analysis.

Making sure she cleared Lang's head, she squeezed the trigger, a short burst. The sound of the gunfire was magnified by the stone walls but not loudly enough to cover a scream as one of the men behind Lang threw his hands to a bloody pulp that had been his face. The second danced a macabre jig as five or six bullets pinned him momentarily to the wall before he slid slowly to his knees, leaving an abstract painting of red streaks on the light-colored stone.

For an instant, Gurt feared Lang had been hit. He lunged forward, chair and all, colliding with the third man in uniform, knocking him to the floor.

Gun still in hand, Gurt closed and latched the door before drawing the bayonet from the belt of one of her victims and cutting Lang's bindings and handing him the second AK-47.

Both her and Lang's eyes were beginning to swim with tears from the acrid cordite smoke, which was confined by the low ceiling.

He took the weapon, pointing it at the man on the floor while he affixed the bayonet. "What took you so long?"

Gurt shrugged. "Trying to decide if your order to return to the hotel was suicidal or just stupid."

Lang was yanking the man to his feet, muttering, "Comedian, everybody thinks they're a comedian." He shook his head in resignation. "Gurt, this is Lieutenant Colonel Shien Dow, late of the People's Liberation Army."

"Late?"

"I have experienced his hospitality and wish to reciprocate. He's coming with us."

"But there is no time . . ."

There was a banging on the door.

Dow stood, tugging at his uniform blouse as though to straighten it. "You two are going nowhere."

Lang ran a hand through Dow's pockets and came up with his own watch, money clip and BlackBerry. He began to furiously punch the keyboard.

"Lang," Gurt said as the assault on the door increased, "there is not now the time to send all the 'wish you were here' messages you want to Sara and our friends at home. We have need to get out of here first."

"Just sharing some of the scenery with Miles." He jammed the BlackBerry into a pocket and pointed to where the blanket hung. "I think the exit is that way."

The muzzle of his rifle pressed against Dow's head, they crossed the room single file. Gurt pulled the blanket aside, revealing Lang had been correct: it was the entry into the fort proper. As the last one to leave, Lang fired a single shot into the generator, instantly turning the room into blackness. A couple more shots at the door were intended to discourage those eager to get in. It wouldn't stop anyone, but it sure might slow them down.

Behind Gurt, Lang was pushing Dow, holding the rifle against the Chinese's head with the other. "Turn left. I think there's a ramp there leading up to the next row of guns."

"But we need to get out, not up," Gurt protested.

"Right through how many armed Chinese soldiers? We sure as hell can't shoot our way out."

"But—"

"But turn here and start up the ramp."

At the top, they stood behind a circular row of entrances to gun rooms that opened off the common ramp. The outside of the ramp, the one facing the parade ground, was bordered by a low wall perhaps four feet high. Over the wall, they were afforded a view of an anthill of activity as flashlights darted back and forth in a pattern that suggested confusion more than purpose.

"Now what?" Gurt wanted to know. "We fly out like birds?"

"Not quite yet."

For the first time since leaving the lower level, Dow spoke. "Mr. Reilly, your situation is hopeless. You are surrounded by over a hundred trained officers and men of the People's Liberation Army, enough to completely search this place as soon as it is light. When they see what you have done to two of their comrades down below, I doubt they will be in a charitable mood. I certainly am in no position to guarantee the woman's safety . . ."

Lang cut him short. "You've just seen what 'the woman' can do and you're concerned about *her* safety? I'd worry about your men, were I you."

Dow bobbed his head. "You may joke now but as soon as it is light, you will find little to amuse you."

Lang shoved Dow against the wall with one hand, handing the rifle to Gurt with the other. Then he removed the bayonet, pressing its point against the colonel's crotch.

"If we're here by the time it's light, you'll be eligible for the Vienna Boys' Choir."

"Surely you don't think you can threaten—"

Lang pushed a little harder, gratified by Dow's gasp. "Get your men's attention. You are to instruct them exactly as I say."

Dow snorted. "Absurd! You'll kill me."

"Actually, I have other plans for you, but they don't have to include the first part of your sex-change surgery."

Lang lowered the bayonet and grabbed a handful of the colonel's crotch through his pants. He raised the cutting edge of the bayonet about a foot above the clump of cloth. "On three you join Eunuchs Anonymous. One, two . . ."

Dow had apparently experienced a speedy attitude adjustment. Or perhaps a realization Lang wasn't kidding. "Wait! What is it you require of me?"

Lang told him.

"Absurd! You will never succeed!"

Lang shrugged, a gesture he realized was now visible in the smoky light of predawn. "For your sake, you'd better make sure it does."

Dow stood against the low wall, cleared his throat and began to speak in a loud voice. Crouched behind him, Gurt and Lang could see the men below cease their frenetic activity and look upward to their commander.

"How do we know he is not telling his men where we are? You do not know Chinese." Gurt whispered.

"I don't, but you must admit he has a major incentive to do as I ask. Forget the hearts and minds. When you literally have someone by the balls, they are very likely to agree with you."

The light had grown sufficiently for Lang to see the skeptical look on her face. "You better be right or . . ."

The alternative was never spelled out. Below, the men fell into lines forming ranks. At a command from Dow, echoed by a half-dozen subordinate officers, the men crisply did a right face and marched toward the Citadelle's entrance.

Although they moved too quickly for Lang to count, he noted they moved five to the rank, five files to the group. He guessed he was watching between a hundred and a hundred and ten men march parade-style out of the fortress.

Dow, his face now visible in the light growing in the east, wore the expression of a man whose team is well ahead of the point spread. "I did as you asked, Mr. Reilly. My men will cross the pathway to where the forest begins. No matter what they do, they will be between you and escape."

"Can he order them to let us through?" Gurt asked.

"A little too risky," Lang answered. "If he changes his mind . . . I hope I've solved that problem."

Keeping the rifle pointed at the Chinese officer, Lang gestured with his free hand. "OK, nice and slow, let's go down and out of here."

At the entrance, Lang could see the last of the soldiers

carefully picking their way single file along the narrow crest that formed the only approach to the fortress. He guessed it would take at least thirty minutes for the last of them to disappear into the forest.

The steep sides of the path were still obscured in shadows, darkness that was retreating with reluctance before the dawn's probing fingers.

In the latitudes between the Tropics of Cancer and Capricorn, neither sunrise nor sunset is a prolonged event. Dawn comes with a grayness that seeps rapidly across the sky as though spilled from some giant container. It reaches the western horizon just as the tip of a burnished-copper sun seems to squeeze between water and sky in the opposite direction, setting aflame fleecy clouds that have ventured too close. The entire process from night to sunlight unravels in less than fifteen minutes.

"And now?" Gurt wanted to know.

Lang checked his watch. "And now we wait."

"For what?" she insisted.

"For Miles."

The surprise was clear on her face. "Miles? Here?"

"As soon as it gets light enough."

Dow chuckled. "I do not know for whom you wait, Mr. Reilly, but unless they drop from the sky, how will they get here? You have no choice: you cannot get past my men. Surrender and save us all time."

Lang looked around until he found a reasonably flat rock. He motioned Dow to sit before seating himself so the officer was between him and any potential sniper among the Chinese troops. "I believe your people view patience as a virtue, do they not, Colonel?"

Dow did not reply. Instead, he asked, "May I smoke?"

Lang nodded amiably. "Your lungs. But make sure your hand moves slowly. If I recall, your cigarettes and lighter are in your right breast pocket. I wouldn't recommend reaching anywhere else."

The three sat in silence as the light breeze of the morning succumbed to the day's increasing heat. Mist was rising from the gorge below, soon to give birth to the day's clouds, which would embrace the old fort in misty arms. Hopefully, after Miles's arrival. Lang watched his prisoner closely but the man did little other than chain-smoke, lighting one cigarette with another.

At first Lang was conscious only of a sound, a noise he could neither place nor identify as it beat like a bird's wing against the mountainsides. It was alien to the call of the birds from the forest or the whinny of horses back in the Citadelle, impatient for their morning feed. Slowly the rhythmic whop-whop of rotor blades became distinguishable. As though from a magician's hat, a black object seemed to pop out of the very ground beneath their feet as a helicopter rose from the gorge below. Someone had been skimming the uneven Haitian terrain to evade radar.

Though it had no markings, Lang recognized the machine as an old Russian Mi-8 "Hip," an aircraft that had served both as a civilian airborne office and military command post. Over ten thousand had been manufactured, enough sold abroad to make the aircraft's nationality neutral.

"As you suggested, Colonel, from the sky." Lang raised his voice to be heard over the racket as he spoke to Gurt. "Keep our friend here covered while I make sure they see us."

Lang walked away from the sheltering walls of the Citadelle, waving his arms until the helicopter hovered directly above him. The moment it stopped, the crack of a rifle, then another, echoed from mountaintop to gorge and back again. Dow's troops were not going to stand idly by.

Lang ducked behind a boulder as some sort of heavy weapon from the chopper chattered a reply. His guess was a .50-caliber mounted along the open port in the ship's fuselage. Toward the forest, he could see puffs of dust as the gun traced the tree line with lead and rock chips, deadly as bullets, flying through the air. The rifle fire went quiet.

Above him, a rope ladder unfurled to within a foot or so of the ground. The saddle between forest and Citadelle was too narrow for a landing. He turned to motion Gurt. She had already seen what was happening and was prodding Dow toward the hovering aircraft. Rifle at the ready, Lang kept behind a trio of rock protrusions until she and her prisoner disappeared into the helicopter.

As the aircraft dipped its nose preparatory to moving off, Lang dashed for the ladder. He had reached the second rung when he felt it being reeled in.

Once he was inside, a man in a uniform without insignia handed him a headset, which he put on. A nudge at his shoulder caused him to turn. He was standing less than a foot from a smiling Miles.

The grin vanished as he saw Lang's face. "Shit, Reilly," the words crackled through the earphones. "What did you shave with this morning, a meat grinder?"

Dominican airspace
Fourteen minutes later

Coffee had never tasted better, even though it was out of a thermos. Thermals, already building in the day's increasing heat, made a bumpy road of the air at an altitude of only three hundred feet just off a ribbon of golden sand, shaking the helicopter like a terrier with a rat. Gurt, indifferent to the turbulence, was dozing, leaning against the leather restraints that kept her from being thrown from the canvas seat. Dow, securely handcuffed, glared at Lang and Miles, who were seated across from each other.

"Those pictures you sent me along with your GPS position indicators, you have any idea what they were?" Miles asked through Lang's headset.

"Packing containers of some sort. I figured someone might be able to read the Chinese characters."

Miles bobbed his head. "The containers themselves told us all we needed to know."

"Which was?"

"Warheads, most likely for DF-15, Dong Feng, or East Wind missiles."

"Like, guided missiles?"

"Like. Chemical, nuclear or conventional, solid propellant, and MARV."

Lang's eyebrows rose in an unasked question.

"Maneuverable reentry vehicle. The warheads themselves can be guided as to speed and alter course to evade defensive weapons."

Lang had almost forgotten the Agency's love of technical jargon. "All of which means what?"

"Which means, once installed on a launch base, usually an eight-wheeled truck, anything within three hundred and seventy miles is a potential target."

Lang mentally called up a map of the Caribbean. "We, the U.S., is out of range, then."

"The Chinese are in the process of modifying a lot of their hardware. Wouldn't surprise me if south Florida was within range in the not-too-distant future."

"And Puerto Rico, where we still have a few military installations."

Lang thought for a moment. "You think the Chinese are preparing to attack, what, a naval refueling base and former gunnery range?"

"Not my call. The higher-ups will make that decision." He nodded toward Dow. "Along with the help of your friend there."

Lang snorted. "Over tea and crumpets with his lawyer at his side? I doubt the Agency'll get more than an ass reaming by some congressional oversight committee after a presidential apology for inconveniencing the peace-loving People's Republic of China by interrupting a perfectly innocent trade mission. Hell, if you yell at him and make him cry, you'll be regarded as a criminal."

Miles smirked, the self-satisfied grin of a man who has been dealt the fourth ace in the hole. "Were he going to be turned over to the Agency, the newer, kinder, warm and fuzzy Agency, which is obligated to share its secrets with notoriously loose-lipped politicians, what you say would be true. As it is, I am merely a private citizen doing my civic duty for one of my country's firmest allies."

Lang leaned forward in his seat. "This I got to hear."

"Very simple: I am vacationing in the Dominican Republic like hundreds of thousands of sun-loving Americans do every year. An official who happens to be a golf-playing and fishing buddy of mine mentions that Haiti, a country less than friendly to the DR, is harboring a fugitive . . ."

"But this guy, this Chinese, is no *fugitive* from the Dominicans," Lang protested. "He's probably never even been there."

Miles held up a hand, dismissing an irrelevant point. "So, the DR has made a terrible mistake. You know how these Caribbean bureaucracies can be. Now, this friend also knows I have another friend, one who was kind enough to place a helicopter at my disposal, saving me the time of driving from one golf resort to the next fishing charter. This Dominican official friend of mine asks if I would have any objection to his government using said helicopter during the three or four hours I will be on the golf course.

"What am I to do, spoil the relationship between his country and mine? Of course not. I lend him the chopper."

"But he"—Lang pointed at Dow—"is *not* a fugitive. He is an officer in the fucking Chinese army."

"I'm sure a full apology will be forthcoming."

"So . . ." Lang took up where he knew Miles had left off. "The Dominican security forces or army or whoever treat the man to the old-fashioned third degree until they get what they want, by which time the proverbial horse has departed the barn. In the meantime, you continue your golfing-fishing vacation unaware of what has happened."

"Wasn't it Thomas Gray who observed, 'Where ignorance is bliss, 'tis folly to be wise'?"

"How do you guys keep your noses from growing so long you can't get through a door?"

Beijing Olympic Tower
Two days later

Wan Ng watched the chubby general of the People's Liberation Army use a thick thumb to turn the pages of the file. In a silence loud enough to have an echo, he wondered which was worse: the disapproval of Undersecretary Diem or somehow falling under the jurisdiction of this porcine military man. Either way, his sudden recall from the States and the state of affairs with this man Reilly had less than optimistic overtones.

One thing he did know: the disaster in Haiti was somehow going to become his fault. That was the Party way, having shit run downhill. The higher ups, such as the undersecretary, blamed the fiasco on the military. Since the officer in charge of the garrison in Haiti, a Colonel Dow, was conveniently unavailable to accept blame—no one was certain where he was at the moment—the army brass had turned to the Guoanbu, state security. That made the problem Ng's. His position was not high enough to pass the blame farther down the line.

The nameless general looked up, his eyes hooded by heavy lids. "This American, Reilly, why has he not been disposed of?"

"My orders, Comrade General, were from the undersecretary himself. I was to observe him and the woman."

The general sniffed unappreciatively. "It says here you were to eliminate them should you determine they worked for the American intelligence services."

"I have not so determined, Comrade General."

The corpulent officer sighed, the intake and expulsion of breath shaking multiple chins. "After what took place in Venice and in Haiti, you still believe they are ordinary American citizens instead of threats to the policy of the People's Republic?"

Ng could have explained that his orders did not authorize terminal action upon supposition or guess.

He could have, but he didn't.

The orders would say whatever the general chose to remake them to say.

Few government workers in the People's Republic were punished for failure to properly carry out directives from above. Clerks misfiled things on computers, tasks went undone or were done poorly. That was expected in a massive bureaucracy. Problems occurred when someone of rank in the government, say, this general, felt their position threatened, whether by incompetence or just plain rotten luck.

The culprit, almost always with no one below him onto whom to pass the failure, would be accused of some heinous crime, harboring unpatriotic sentiments, stealing from the state or bribery (both of which went unnoticed without some additional offense), or the ever-popular but rarely clearly defined "counterrevolutionary activities." The accused could receive, at the whim of a revolutionary tribunal (usually influenced by the official instigating the action), anything from a term in a labor camp up to a large-bore bullet into the back of the head and an unmarked grave where his family would be unable to honor his spirit, the spirit officially disavowed by the state but very real to the people of Ng's province nonetheless.

Ng was more than painfully aware of how the justice system in the People's Republic functioned.

"How may I atone for my failure, Comrade General?"

The beefy officer took his time replying, no doubt aware of Ng's thoughts. "You will return to the United States just as you departed, by way of the Mexico-California border, so there will be no record of your entry. You will keep watch on this man, Reilly, and his family until you have the opportunity to eliminate them both, the man and the woman."

Ng nodded. "And if they leave the country again as they did when they went to Haiti?"

The general leaned back in his chair, the casters groaning under his weight. "Like most Americans, the man has a cell phone, a BlackBerry. We have ascertained that as well as the number. It is amazing what puny security measures American companies take with their information. When you return, there will be a handheld tracking device that will tell you the latitude and longitude of the location of that particular BlackBerry anywhere on the face of the earth, give or take thirty meters. See that you use it well."

The meeting was over. Ng felt a weight lift from his shoulders, a reprieve he was lucky to receive. "I will not fail, Comrade General."

The general was already looking at another file. He dismissed Ng with the wave of a hand. "See that you don't."

From the diary of Louis Etienne Saint Denis

No. 6 rue Victoire,[1] Paris
January 2, 1803

Leclerc is dead of the Siamese fever![2]
There was no means by which we could have known of the tragedy until the news arrived via a fast packet from the Indies to Cherbourg and then by horse courier to Paris.

---

1 When Napoleon first lived in the house in 1797, the street was rue Chanterine. After his victory in Italy, the département de la Seine, Paris's municipal governing body, changed the name.
2 Yellow fever. It killed more French military than did the rebels. The slaves had an immunity derived from their origins in Africa.

It was not until December 28 the frigate Swiftsure *arrived at the Hyères Islands carrying Pauline, her and Leclerc's four-year-old son, Dermide, and the lead coffin encased in cedar bearing the general's body.[3] Pauline, distraught and clad in the dreariest of widow's garb, appeared here three days later.*

With sobs, she fell into the arms of her brother, the First Consul. He greeted her affectionately but within seconds escorted her into the house's library, closing the door behind them. The last words I heard before the doors were pulled to were not those of consolation, but query as to the location of a certain box with which Leclerc had been entrusted. I could not but wonder if this was the selfsame box that my employer had taken from Egypt.

---

3 As was the contemporary custom, a separate lead box contained an urn with his heart and brain.

CHAPTER FOUR

Law offices of Langford Reilly
Two days later

Sara made a less than subtle effort not to stare at Lang's face. If possible, it looked worse than it had when he and Gurt boarded the private charter from Santo Domingo to Atlanta. His nose, broken, was a peak of white bandage between the two black valleys under his all-but-swollen-shut eyes. The bruising had turned a grotesque green and yellow. Lang was grateful she could not see the angry red sores on his chest that just today had ceased suppurating and begun to scab over.

He hoped waterboarding was the most gentle of the enhanced interrogation techniques Dow experienced at the hands of the Dominican security people.

He sat behind his desk gingerly. His legs and groin ached from muscles still protesting his time on horseback. Sinking gratefully into the embracing confines of his Relax the Back desk chair, he looked sourly at the stack of pink call-back slips. There had to be some way to respond using the computer. His nose, packed with gauze, gave his voice a tone too close to a cartoon character's to be taken seriously by anyone above the age of ten.

The phone on his desk buzzed.

"Yeah?"

"The Reverend Bishop Groom on two. You in?"

Lang sighed. Even that had a nasal sound. "I'll take it."

He picked up the receiver. "Good morning, Reverend. What might I do for you today?"

"Mr. Reilly? Is this Mr. Reilly?"

It sure as hell isn't Donald Duck, no matter how it sounds.

"I, er, had an accident, broke my nose. It affects my voice."

"You should be more careful," the reverend reproached. "I'll pray for your speedy recovery."

"Any intervention of friends in high places greatly appreciated."

There was a pause. Among his client's multitude of failings was a lack of a sense of humor.

"I called two days ago, hadn't heard back . . ." There was a note of rebuke.

Lang thumbed the call-back slips. "Yeah, I see you did. I've been out of the office. What's up?"

"I was hoping you could tell me. I mean, have we heard anything?"

Lang drew a momentary blank before he realized to what Groom referred. "The feds? No, not a peep."

"I was hoping perhaps you were negotiating with them, maybe a suspended sentence or something."

Fat chance. Lang couldn't remember the last time he had even heard of a suspended sentence in a federal case. Unlike the states, the U.S. government had endless resources to build prisons as needed. Overcrowding was not a problem. There was no need to make bargains in which the perpetrator did no time. Reduced sentences in exchange for guilty pleas saving the time and expense of a trial, yes. No time at all, unlikely. But there was no reason to screw up the reverend's day with this factoid just yet.

"Initiating negotiations is frequently viewed as having a weak defense."

"Perhaps, but I need to know what to expect, have time to get my affairs in order."

Read: before the government seized all assets it could find

for restitution to the man's victims, get as much cash as possible offshore in banks whose depositors received secrecy rather than interest.

Groom continued. "Why don't you give the U.S. attorney a call just to see what's on his mind?"

"It's a *her*." Lang knew what was probably on her mind: ten to twenty. But he said, "If that's what you want."

Minutes later, Lang was dialing a number he was surprised he remembered. It had been two or three years since he had called it. Tactical considerations had not been the only reason he had been hesitant to contact the assistant U.S. attorney assigned to the case.

"Ms. Warner's office," announced a disembodied voice.

"Er, is she in? Langford Reilly calling."

The line went temporarily dead, leaving Lang with his thoughts. In one of Gurt's several premarital absences from his life, he had briefly dated Alicia Warner. The relationship had never gotten serious and had peacefully wilted rather than died in the acrimony that frequently marks such endings.

"Well, Lang, long time no see," Alicia's voice chirped. "How's married life treating you? I understand you've got a little boy."

She could at least pretend not be so damn happy he was no longer eligible.

"Swell. And you?"

"Just fine, thanks. I must admit, though, nothing like the excitement you showed me. Haven't been shot at or kidnapped lately."

She referred to an abduction by a fanatical group of kibbutzniks who had taken her to Israel during what Lang thought of as the Sinai Affair.

"Well, yeah, I can see how that might make things a little dull."

She tinkled a laugh. "Dull I'll take."

There was a brief, uncomfortable pause.

Lang wriggled in his desk chair, one of the few times in his life he wasn't sure what to say. "Er, Alicia, I was calling about a case you have, the Reverend Bishop Groom . . ."

"Well, damn! And here I was hoping you were going to boost my ego by soliciting a sordid extramarital affair."

The wit and sarcasm he recalled was melting his uneasiness like ice on a summer day. "Maybe after the case is over."

"Maybe by the time the case is over I'll be married to the king of Siam. Oh, wait a minute. Siam doesn't have a king anymore. In fact, it isn't even Siam."

Lang felt compelled to play along. "The British have two unmarried princes."

"I couldn't take the scandals. Besides, I don't care for Eurotrash." There was a pause. "Now, what was it you were calling about?"

Lang laughed out loud. "The Reverend Bishop Groom."

"Oh, yeah. A different species of trash. Hold on."

There was the click of a keyboard, then, "Here he is: sixteen counts of tax evasion, same number of conspiracy to evade taxes, a dozen counts of mail fraud . . . Shall I go on?"

"No need. I have a copy of the indictment. You guys really like to pile it on."

"Oh, c'mon! We didn't charge him with adultery and fornication, something he's guilty as hell of."

"Only because they're not federal crimes, and I can't recall the last time a state chose to prosecute. The tender mercy of the United States attorney is well-known. I was calling to see if there might be a plea deal available."

"Sure, he pleads and the judge deals him about twenty years."

Lang inhaled deeply. "I'm serious, Alicia. The man is, after all, a preacher anxious to return to his flock."

"More anxious to fleece his flock, I'd say. He's done a pretty fair job of that, but I'll see what we can do and get back to you."

His previous discomfort forgotten, Lang was smiling as he hung up.

He began sorting the slips into three piles: return ASAP, return when convenient and the last stack on the edge of the desk, which a single sweep of the hand would send into the trash basket.

He had almost finished the task when his phone interrupted. "Lang, it's someone called Miles. He said you'd know who he was."

Lang got up, crossed the office and shut the door before he picked up. "Yes, thank you, Miles. I'm healing nicely."

There was a two count before Mile's relay replied, "Glad to hear it. How long will it take to get to a pay phone? I noticed there were several in the lobby of your building."

Lang was not even sure Miles was correct. He hadn't noticed. With cell phones more common than neckties these days, who used pay phones? Answer: people who suspected their calls, or those of people calling them, might be intercepted. The sheer randomness of selecting a pay phone made eavesdropping unlikely if not impossible.

"Same number?" Lang asked.

"Same number."

"Gimme about five minutes."

Three pay phones were, in fact, in the lobby, lined along a wall like books in a shelf. The first was clearly out of order. The second was splattered with some gooey substance, the origins of which Lang chose not to speculate upon, although he suspected it might have something to do with the homeless. Those beggars, addicts and mental cases populated the city's downtown area, using the facilities of any building whose security was lax. The chamber of commerce's pleas to the municipal government to solve the problem of aggressive panhandling went unheeded.

After all, the homeless voted, as did the bleeding hearts whose sympathies for their less-fortunate brethren did not include working downtown.

The third phone appeared to be intact and reasonably

sanitary. Lang poured in the change required for a long-distance call to the Washington, D.C., area code.

"Lang?"

"Here, Miles. I'm guessing you called to make certain my good looks will not be permanently disfigured."

"That and a minor matter of national security."

A few feet away, the body language of a couple in front of an elevator bank said they were arguing. Rather than stare at a blank marble wall, Lang watched.

"I'm not in the national-security business anymore, remember? I did you a favor going to Haiti and got my face rearranged for my troubles."

"No good deed goes unpunished. But wait till you hear what your pal Colonel Dow had to say."

The man's hands were on his hips, his head inclined forward. From his expression, Lang was glad he couldn't hear what was being said.

"I don't want to know, Miles. The only reason you'd tell me is to hook me in further. I'm retired and want to stay that way."

During the pause before Miles's answer, the woman reacted to whatever the man had said by stepping into the first elevator that opened, although it was in a different bank, going to a floor other than the ones served by the cars for which she had been waiting.

"Well, that's your business, Lang, but as an old pal, I'll give you some free advice."

"No doubt worth every penny I pay for it."

The man started to follow. He got one foot in past the door before he received a slap to the face that reverberated across the marble lobby. He jerked back as though attempting to avoid the strike of a venomous snake.

"OK, don't take it. But were I you, I'd beef up whatever security you have around the house."

A mechanical voice interrupted the conversation, demanding more money.

Lang shoved it in. "Whoa! What about security?"

"Dow pretty well spilled everything he knew after a little, ah, persuasion."

"I'm disappointed he didn't get the works, but what about security around the house?"

The man who had been slapped was frantically pushing the up button of the bank of elevators the woman had taken.

"OK, so he was probably in a little more hurt than you were when the Dominicans finished with him. Fact is, he's under guard in a prison hospital. One of the things he mentioned was, his superiors think you know something you shouldn't. You know how the Chinese handle that problem. The Guoanbu ain't good people. They're going to be on you like white on rice until somebody in the government pulls them off or—"

"I get the picture. And you have a plan to make someone call off the dogs."

"Of course!" Miles was cheerful, the way he always was when he was getting his way.

Lang sighed. Dealing with the Agency was like waltzing with the tar baby: there was no way not to get stuck.

An elevator door opened. The man got on. Seconds later, another opened and the woman got off. Lang turned to stare at the wall. It was more restful.

"OK, Miles, tell me what you have in mind."

"First, a little background. About a year ago, ECHELON picked up an exchange of messages between the People's Republic and Haiti."

Miles was referring to the system operated by the British, Americans, Australians, New Zealanders and Canadians that intercepted any message in the world sent via satellite. Landlines were becoming as obsolete as buggy whips. Consequently, ECHELON's volume was so great that computers had to search communications for key words before the number of messages of possible interest could be reduced to numbers a finite staff of humans could listen to or read.

"Since any communication by the Chinese to a country of this hemisphere is of interest," Miles continued, "we followed the conversation. China has no embassy or even trade attaché in Haiti and the two countries have no common code, so the messages were in the clear, something about establishing a trading partnership. As you remarked before going there, there's damn little Haiti exports that China wants and even less the Chinese manufacture that Haiti could afford.

"Obviously this exchange had some other meaning, so we alerted our asset in Haiti to watch the airport and see who arrived."

"Whoa," Lang interrupted. "You told me you had no assets in Haiti."

"True, we don't. We *had* a guy, but we haven't heard from him nor been able to contact him for some time. I'm afraid he's been silenced. Anyway, he e-mailed us a photo taken with a special camera we supplied of the Chinese visitor getting off a private plane. It wasn't some bureaucrat from the trade department. It was Chin Diem."

"Someone I should know?" Lang asked.

"Undersecretary for foreign relations. Pretty high up the food chain to be making a trip to negotiate the price of coffee.

"Anyway, Diem made one or two more trips. Our asset couldn't find anyone around the current prez for life who knew what was up. Our guy did lay some serious bling on a waiter in a local restaurant who served Diem and the Haitian president. Seems the Haitian, guy name of duPaar, wanted something in exchange for whatever the Chinese wanted, something the Chinese seemed to be having a hard time delivering. From what he overheard, he, the waiter, was pretty sure it was a specific object. Before we could find out what, our man disappeared."

"You're not telling me this just for my enlightenment. What do you want?"

"To find out what duPaar wants. If we can supply it, there'd be no need for him to deal with the Chinese."

Lang whistled. "Whew, pretty tall order, ole buddy. You telling me this is something the Agency can't handle? You keep forgetting I'm retired."

"Retired but incentivized. You solve the riddle, we provide the Haitian pooh-bah with whatever bauble it is he wants and the Chinese no longer have a reason to wish you ill."

Lang shook his head as if Miles could see the gesture. "I'd say they have a hell of a reason if I'm the one responsible for screwing up their plans."

"You and I both know that revenge, pure and simple, is not what drives the policy of any rational nation. It's too expensive a luxury. Once a project is dead, former threats to it become irrelevant."

True.

Lang changed the subject. "What is their interest in the Western Hemisphere's poorest nation, anyway?"

Again, the machine asking for money. Lang scraped the last change from his pocket, depositing it to the accompaniment of what sounded like an old-fashioned cash register.

Miles cleared his throat. "We believe they aren't interested in Haiti per se. It's just that the country is the most likely Caribbean nation to accept Chinese on their soil. Can you imagine the boost to the local economy a few thousand Chinese with cash in their pockets could give?"

"OK. I get it. But what does China get?"

"A presence in the Caribbean, more than likely a military one, based on what you saw there. Think of it as an unsinkable aircraft carrier or missile cruiser. But until the Chinese come up with this whatchamacallit, duPaar isn't unlocking the door, no matter how much good the deal would do his country. The Chinese will have to satisfy him before he agrees to more than the handful of troops you saw up at the old fort."

Lang checked his watch. He was due for a motions hearing in forty minutes and this was taking far longer than he had anticipated. "Thanks for the poli-sci lesson, but I still don't see what all this has to do with me."

"Lang," Miles said in a tone a teacher might use with one of his duller students, "we, the Agency, have no idea what the gizmo is duPaar wants and no way to find out, much less how or where to acquire it."

"And I do?"

"Let's say you've already established contact with our Chinese pals. They will keep in touch. Sooner or later, you'll have a chance to find out what it is."

"Or get killed in the meantime. Let me get this straight: Because the Chinese will keep trying to kill either (a) me or (b) my family or (c) both of the above, I am the person in the best position to find out what object it is the president of Haiti wants in exchange for allowing the Chinese to establish some sort of military presence there."

"Makes sense to me."

Lang hated to admit it, but the idea did present a certain twisted logic. The old baited trap. The opposition wanted to eliminate someone. The proposed victim was made to seem accessible, while covertly guarded. When the potential assassin made a move, the target's minders moved, capturing the would-be killer, hopefully someone with knowledge of facts that led closer and closer to the information sought. That was the idea. Unfortunately, failures were usually lethal.

"And just why would I want a target painted on my back?"

There was what could have been another clearing of Miles's throat or a chuckle. Lang suspected the latter. "You already have one. I'm offering you a way to remove it. Look, you know we can cover you 24-7. You can't get better security for you, Gurt and Manfred."

Lang thought of the private company he had already hired. Ex–Delta Force, ex–Marine Recon, ex-SEAL types already in discreet positions around his house. Bulletproof SUVs with armed drivers taking Manfred to pre-K, Gurt to the grocery store. He felt pretty damn secure. But for how long? The security people's incentive was to do what they were hired to do: keep the Reilly family safe. The Agency's motivation was to foil the Chinese plan to gain a foothold in the Caribbean and, possibly, end the threat to Lang as well.

Lang decided to do what any rational man would do. "I'll talk it over with Gurt and get back to you."

472 Lafayette Drive, Atlanta
21:26 the same day

A smile played across Gurt's face as she watched a water-logged Lang pour a healthy two fingers of scotch whisky. "You have had a hard time with Manfred?"

Lang contemplated and discarded a carafe of water before taking a gulp from the crystal tumbler. "What was your first clue, that I'm soaking wet?"

"That helped in the thought process, yes."

Another swallow. "Bathing Manfred can be a problem when he gets excited. But having Grumps jump in the tub, too?"

"Perhaps you should not let the dog in the bathroom."

Lang emptied the glass and was working on a refill. "If I shut him out, the damn dog howls and scratches the paint off the door, and Manfred is almost as bad. How do you separate them when Manfred goes to school in the morning?"

Gurt took a sip from her wineglass. "By force of will."

Lang snorted. "More by bribe. I note you feed the dog just as you take Manfred out the door."

Gurt picked up the book in her lap and started to read. "What is it you say, by hook and cook?"

"By hook or *crook*."

Gurt's face wrinkled in puzzlement. "I can understand hooking and cooking to get something, but crook?"

Unable to explain the idiom, Lang added a few drops of water to his glass this time. "I spoke to Miles at length this afternoon."

Gurt put her book back down, suddenly alert. "And?"

He gave her a summary of the conversation.

When he had finished, she got up, crossed the room to an ice maker under the bar, removed a chilling wine bottle and refilled her glass. "This would mean traveling to where?"

"I don't know."

"To find what?"

"I haven't a clue."

"How will you find out?"

"I'm not certain."

Gurt returned to her seat, wineglass in hand and nodding. "You and Miles have a well-planned mission."

She might not get American idioms but she has sarcasm down cold. Lang slumped into his favorite chair. "Wouldn't you say our problems with the Chinese began in Venice?"

Not sure where this was going, Girt nodded uncertainly. "Yes."

"So, it might be a fair statement that whatever it was that this guy, duPaar, wants was in that church, Saint Mark's, right? Or at least, the Chinese believed so?"

She thought a moment. "If you assume the robbers in Venice were seeking the object duPaar wants and if you also assume that object was really in the church. Did you not tell me you and Francis had this conversation before we went to Haiti?"

"Sort of. He had a theory, or had read a book, positing that Alexander's, not Saint Mark's, remains were interred in the basement of the church."

"You are telling me this man in Haiti wants someone's bones?"

"They're called relics, like Saint So-and-so's toe bone being preserved in the altar of a church. In medieval times, they not only had religious significance but were a boon to local commerce. Pilgrims would travel miles to pray before the elbow of good Saint Such-and-such. The town would prosper from what we would call tourist trade."

Gurt smiled. "I have seen everything from bones to a vial with a drop of Christ's blood to a nail from the cross. In Rome, there is a church that displays the chains in which Peter was confined, the ones which miraculously fell away."

Lang considered another refill but put his glass down on the table beside the chair instead. "San Pietro in Vincoli. Same one that has Michelangelo's *Moses*. But yeah, like that. Thing is, what would duPaar want with relics, Alexander's or Saint Mark's?"

Gurt was looking at him over the top of her wineglass. "I suppose that is what Miles wants you to find out."

Lang got up and surveyed the bookshelves as though looking for a volume. "We made a deal when you and Manfred came to live here: we were finished with the Agency. Neither of us would go romping off on adventures without the other's agreement."

"Some of the 'adventures' came looking for us. We certainly did not ask to be shot at in Venice or have our house broken into." She pointed to a shuttered window. "Neither of us wish the need to have our home guarded by a security service or use our special devices forever. Soon or late, we will want to live like normal people."

He turned away from the books, nodding agreement. "That's why I didn't turn down Miles's request flat."

"Flat?"

"On the spot. Immediately."

He could visualize Gurt filing this Americanism away wherever she kept such things. "Speak with Francis, then with Miles again. Let us talk after you have some idea what you may be searching for and where it might be."

Good idea.

Manuel's Tavern
602 North Highlands Avenue, Atlanta
19:02 the next evening

For over fifty years, Manuel's Tavern has been the gathering place for Emory University students and faculty, the local Democratic Party elite and those who would like to be either. Jimmy Carter, his hand firmly in that of the business's founder, Manuel Maloof, smiles down from the wall behind the bar that runs along one wall. Bill Clinton's autograph is scrawled across a photograph from the waist up. As a local wag speculated, perhaps a full-body shot had been discarded when closer scrutiny revealed the former president's fly was unzipped.

Across from the bar, wooden booths bear the carved initials of students and fraternities as well as graffiti in Latin and Greek as well as English and other modern languages. The house specializes in political debate, funky atmosphere, generous pitchers of beer, and cuisine that is arguably the worst in any licensed food establishment in the city if not the Southeast.

When Lang and Francis had begun their friendship, it was also one of the few places where a black man in a clerical collar could share a meal with a white man in solemn lawyer garb without drawing stares of curiosity. Among the motley clientele of Manuel's, the pair hardly drew a glance.

They entered through the back door from the parking lot.

Spurning the tables that occupied the "new" expansion to the bar that had been added nearly thirty years ago, Lang and Francis seated themselves at one of the booths that had been part of the original operation.

Francis turned to look back the way they had come. "I've got to say, riding in that SUV beats cramping into your Porsche."

Lang picked up the menu, something he could have recited in his sleep. "I'll bet you loved Max, the armed driver, too."

Francis watched the beefy bodyguard survey the room before taking a seat at the bar. "It seems impolite not to let him join us."

Lang lifted his eyes from the menu to look at his security escort. Just under six feet, with close-cropped hair beginning to streak with silver, the man moved with a catlike precision that would have revealed his special military background had his résumé not already done so. He constantly scanned his surroundings without being obvious about it. "His job isn't an exercise in manners. He can't keep an eye on the whole room sitting with us."

"You really are concerned about you and your family's safety. You've had problems like this before and you didn't hire a security service."

Lang put the menu down. "I didn't have a family, either. I'm not worried about taking care of myself, but when Gurt's busy tending to Manfred, she can't be looking over her shoulder."

"So, how long does this go on?"

Larry, their usual waiter, appeared, a foaming pitcher of beer in each hand. He set one on the table. "I'll be back with your glasses. The usual, folks?"

"Unless you have something truly fit to eat for a change," Lang muttered.

Unperturbed, Larry smiled. "Manuel's: an Atlanta tradition you can rely on."

"Like warm beer, lousy food and indifferent service."

Larry turned away with a cheery "But our prices are quite reasonable."

Both men watched him go, as did Max at the bar.

Francis repeated his question. "How long are you keeping these security guys around?"

"As long as it takes. That's part of the reason we're here tonight."

"And I thought you were yearning for ecclesiastical enlightenment."

"Maybe some other time. Right now, I need information."

Francis reached behind himself, producing a book. "You wanted to borrow Chugg's book, the one about Alexander's tomb."

Lang took it. "Yeah, that's the one. Thanks."

Francis looked around as though making sure no one was listening. What they would be discussing was esoteric, perhaps even too far-out even for the patrons of Manuel's. "It's only a theory, you know, that the Venetian merchants who thought they were stealing Saint Mark's relics actually wound up with those of Alexander, and a pretty wild one at that."

Lang was thumbing the pages. "So far, a theory is all I have. I can't imagine why the Chinese would want the relics of a Christian saint."

"Or of a pagan general, albeit perhaps the greatest ever."

"You told me, according to our friend Chugg here, the ancients believed Alexander's body was some sort of talisman, one that guaranteed victory in battle. That was one of the justifications Ptolemy gave for hijacking it. That could be why a nutcase like duPaar wants it."

Francis freshened his and Lang's glasses before holding up the near-empty pitcher. "The ancients also believed in oracles, augury and a panoply of rather ill-behaved gods and goddesses. Do you suppose duPaar also does?"

"Decided, gentlemen?" Larry had pen and pad in hand.

"The salmon," Francis said with all the enthusiasm of a man approaching the gallows. "And try not to overcook it this time."

Lang handed his menu to the waiter. "The cheeseburger. Tell the chef I'd like it somewhere between cremated and steak tartare."

Larry shrugged. "Chef? At these prices you think we can afford a chef? I just throw stuff on the stove and leave it there until I have to make room for something else."

Both men watched his departure.

"I wish I thought he was kidding," Francis said ruefully.

Lang became serious. "You were right about Alexander's remains, relics, whatever, being just a theory, but I have to start somewhere. This book is as good a place as any."

"You think that book is going to help you find Alexander's tomb? Its location is one of history's great mysteries. People have been looking for it since the fourth century AD and no one has even come close. Unless, of course, those Venetian merchants who thought they were stealing Saint Mark actually had Alexander."

"Maybe, but no one's life depended on finding Alexander before, either."

"But you don't even know if Alexander's tomb, or his remains, if they still exist, have anything to do with the incident in Venice."

Or the Chinese involvement in Haiti, Lang thought. "You're right, but I have to start somewhere. If Venice is the reason my house was burglarized, then whatever was in Saint Mark's tomb had something to do with it. Since those guys made off with Saint Mark's relics, or whatever, I'm not going to find out what it was by going back to Italy. If you have another idea, now is the time to share it."

Francis held up his hands as though to demonstrate they were empty. "No ideas here. If you plan to work Chugg's theory, where will you start?"

"Well, I think we can assume Chugg was wrong about Alexander in Venice. The Chinese are still trying to find Alexander's relics. Or at least trying to prevent me from interfering. If they'd succeeded or quit, I wouldn't need the security detail."

Francis smiled. "You're making assumptions based on negatives."

"Sometimes that's all there is to base them on."

"And you accuse religion of being illogical."

Lang had no intent of renewing that debate at the moment. "The foundation is flying a pair of immunologists to Sudan next week. I figure the Gulfstream can make a stop in Alexandria. That seems a logical place to begin, since the only thing we know for sure is that Alexander was, in fact, entombed there."

"So you figure if you find the relics first, you can put them beyond the Chinese's reach and that will be the end of the matter, they will simply go away? *Spes sibi quisque*."

Lang took a long sip from his glass. "Virgil would agree I *am* relying on myself. It's for sure no one else's family is at risk."

"And Gurt?"

"Under the circumstances, we can hardly leave Manfred with the neighbors."

"Then why not send Gurt, and you take care of your son?"

Lang stared across the table in disbelief. "I hope you are kidding! Gurt would no more leave that child while we are all in danger than . . ."

The simile failed him.

472 Lafayette Drive, Atlanta
04:12 the next morning

For an instant Lang thought he was dreaming. Then he realized the sound of shattering glass followed by the squeal of tires and a pair of gunshots were not part of a vanishing dream, but what had awakened him. His hand closed around the 9 mm Browning HP automatic in the bedside table as his feet hit the floor. Gurt was already pulling a sweatshirt over her head as Manfred's frightened voice came down the hall.

Lang almost collided with the little boy, followed by Grumps, as he threw the bedroom door open and lunged into the hall.

"Window downstairs broke," Manfred announced.

Lang squatted, his face at the same level as his son's. "You go into Mommy and Daddy's room, shut the door and stay there until we come back."

Manfred's lips began to tremble. "But . . ."

Lang lifted the child up and placed him across the threshold. In the tone that meant the order was not subject to negotiation, he repeated, "I said, stay there."

Gurt was beside him. "Lang, the child is terrified."

Lang was halfway down the stairs, taking them two at a time. "Then you stay with him."

Any answer was lost as he hit the floor of the foyer. Immediately, he smelled smoke. A quick glance around told him the fire was not inside the house. Not yet, anyway. He reached for the double dead-bolt locks on the front door, his hand stopping in midair. What better way to lure him out into the open, making a clear target, than the possibility of fire?

During the second of indecision, a heavy knock came from outside. "Mr. Reilly? It's Jake with Executive Security. Open up."

All the bodyguards looked pretty much alike, varying only in race and height. They all had that military bearing, so he wasn't sure which one of them was Jake. The voice, though, was familiar. He unlocked and opened the door.

The first thing he saw was a man silhouetted against dying flames. The front yard's winter-dry grass was smouldering, cinder black.

Jake opened the door wide enough to squeeze in and shut

it. Lang noted the M16 automatic rifle grasped in one hand. "Somebody threw the equivalent of a Molotov cocktail from a passing car. Pretty primitive. But if it had exploded inside, I'd guess the whole house would have been a furnace in a second or two. But it hit a window, broke the glass and bounced onto the lawn." He stopped, puzzled. "You got steel shutters inside the windows?"

"Seemed like a reasonable precaution when we redid the house. Did you get a tag number?"

"Nope, had his lights out. Cooked off a couple of rounds through the rear windshield, though, before I had to hold off for fear of sending ordnance through your neighbors' windows. Might've been two of them. A pickup truck parked across the street took off right behind the one that tossed the firebomb."

More likely the truck was one of Miles's men. Although Lang had seen no obvious watchers from the Agency, it would make sense that as Miles had promised, they would keep an eye on things.

Lang pointed to the back of the house. "Come on in and I'll brew a pot of coffee."

Jake shook his head. "No thanks. If I'm inside, I'm not doing much good keeping watch."

"There's supposed to be a team of two. Where's your partner?"

"I'd guess he's somewhere in the backyard, watching the rear of the premises."

Gurt, holding the hand of a pale and shaken Manfred, came down the stairs. Even Grumps seemed wary. "What . . . ?"

Lang repeated what he had been told.

Jake touched a finger to his forehead, an informal salute. "Guess I better get back to my post. You aren't paying me to be a houseguest."

As Lang pulled the door open, he caught a glimpse of a dozen or so people in the street in varying stages of undress despite the chill of the winter night. Bathrobes, housecoats, pajamas under jackets. Although it was too dark to see their faces, he was sure they were gaping. He heard a siren rapidly approaching.

The timely appearance of the Atlanta police could be depended upon when they were no longer needed.

Lang turned toward the kitchen. "Guess I'll brew that coffee anyway. I expect we'll need it."

"Lang?" Gurt asked.

He raised an eyebrow. "Yeah?"

"You don't need a weapon to make coffee."

For the first time, he became aware he was still carrying the Browning. He stuck it in the drawer of an end table. "I guess not."

An hour later, the police had run out of questions and the pot out of coffee. Wearily, Lang was shutting the front door as the eighteenth-century Birely & Sons grandfather clock chimed six times. With Manfred asleep in her arms, Gurt had a foot on the front stairs when the phone rang.

"Who the hell . . . ?"

"Answering it could well provide an answer."

At first Lang thought the caller had a wrong number. There was that instant's pause before the anticipated hang-up.

But there was no hang-up. Instead, Miles's voice, disgustingly cheery, boomed through the line. "Lang! Understand there was a little excitement around the Reilly household this morning!"

Lang was wondering how anyone could be so damn chipper at this hour before he realized it probably wasn't *this hour* wherever Miles was. "You could say that."

"My, but aren't you the sourpuss, for someone who has just cheated death! Thought you'd like to know: one of our guys followed the car that tossed the Molotov cocktail. Got the license plate."

"Let me guess—the plate, the car or both were stolen."

"How perceptive for one so grouchy at being awoken from his slumbers!"

Lang picked up his coffee cup from the a table, confirming it was empty. "You didn't call just to tell me that assassins frequently don't use their own automobiles."

"Quite so. But your security guy isn't a bad shot."

"Meaning?"

"A patrolman just called in to the APD a report of a man dead in a stolen Ford Taurus. I must say, these people have no taste in automobilia. I wouldn't be caught dead in a clunker like that."

Lang was wondering if there might be a teeny-weeny little bit of coffee left in the pot after all. He held up the cup, motioning to Gurt, who was at his elbow, listening as best she could to the conversation. "I suppose you're going to tell me the deceased is the would-be arsonist."

"According to what my guy heard on the police scanner, the back window of the car appeared to have been shot out, the dead guy bled out from a bullet wound in the back of his neck and there was a can half-full of gasoline in the backseat. I doubt he was on his way from the filling station to top off his lawnmower. Oh yeah, one more detail. He appears to be Asian, no ID on the body."

Gurt stood in the kitchen door, Manfred still draped over one arm, the other hand holding a demonstrably empty coffee pot.

"That's interesting to know, Miles."

"I thought a few facts like that might speed your decision on my little proposition."

"It does Miles, it does."

"Well?"

"I'm definitely leaning in that direction."

"Lang, do something! Think of your family. They may not miss next time."

"The thought had occurred to me. You'll have your answer before the day is out."

With parting salutations, the conversation ended.

Gurt was facing Lang. "Wherever you have to go, whatever

you have to do, make them stop it before one of us gets hurt."

That was a decision Lang had already made, Gurt's agreement or not. He just wanted her blessing before he called Miles back.

El Nozha Airport
Alexandria, Egypt
Three days later

The Gulfstream 550's tires met the runway with a satinlike kiss, a tribute to the piloting skills of its flight crew. Lang was pushed forward in his seat as the engines howled into reverse thrust and the plane came to a near stop before turning sedately onto a taxiway like an elderly dowager leaving the dance floor.

He took his BlackBerry from his pocket and called home. It would be far too early in the morning, eight hours earlier, for Gurt to have hers turned on, but the "missed call" message and his number would let her know he had arrived safely.

Lang had been watching the city as it spread out beneath him on final approach. Mostly sand-colored buildings surrounding green spaces, hardly the sophisticated international metropolis of ancient history. He rubbed eyes, gritty from the lack of sleep that always accompanied air travel. The main terminal, a low squat building, suckled aircraft of Air Arabia, Olympic, Austrian Airlines and Lufthansa. Thankful he would not have to transit what he remembered as the tiny, crowded, ill-smelling and generally filthy arrival lounge, he settled back into his seat to await the arrival of the inevitable officialdom.

The customs and immigration crew had apparently been waiting on the private aviation tarmac. The Gulfstream's door had hardly wheezed open when two khaki-clad officials climbed the short staircase and began reviewing the general declarations proffered by the plane's copilot. The deference with which the aircraft's crew and passengers were treated was far different from the arrogance that Lang recalled being shown across the field in the passenger terminal. But then, the occupants of a sixty-million-dollar private jet were more likely to be powerful people than, say, a merchant arriving from Cairo to visit relatives. Powerful or not, the language of international bureaucracy—paper—was inspected, exchanged and slipped into folders from which it likely would never emerge. Lang purchased the requisite visa stamp for the passport Miles had furnished along with matching Visa card, Mastercard and driver's permit while explaining the two immunologists with him would not be leaving the aircraft but would depart for Sudan as soon as he left the plane. The disappointment shown at the lost revenues mostly dissipated when Lang thanked the two uniformed men for their prompt and courteous service, slipping an American twenty-dollar bill into both open hands.

With a minimum of luck, these two would be satisfied that the passports did not contain a stamp from Israel, a real problem requiring Higher Egyptian Authority, and be gone shortly.

"We're in a bit of a hurry." Lang smiled. "I am expected at an archaeological excavation that is waiting for me before further exploration can take place. I hope you can speed the customs inspection process."

For another pair of twenties, indeed they could. The "inspection" consisted of brief glances about the aircraft's cabin without moving a step farther.

Lang had learned long ago that in this part of the world, government officials expected to supplement their salaries. In fact, the value of political appointments in the Arab world had little to do with the pay attached; it had to do with the opportunities to extract baksheesh. Customs inspectors, particularly those along the Sinai's border with Israel, became wealthy men.

Walking back to the small bedroom at the rear of the plane, Lang picked up a single suitcase. He reached under the mattress on which he had mostly tossed and turned the night before and pulled out the Browning HP in a leather holster. Clipping the holster to the belt in the small of his back, he probed the bedclothes again, this time producing a box of 9 mm ammunition, which he dumped loose into a jacket pocket before tossing the box into a waste basket.

Suitcase in hand, he walked to the aircraft's open door, surprised at the blast of heat that met him even at this time of year. He was thankful he would not be here in July or August. At the bottom of the steps a sleek Mercedes glistened in the midmorning sun. He gave the briefest of waves to the pilot and copilot standing at the cockpit door and then to the pretty flight attendant who had served him and his two companions three meals since departing Atlanta.

Twenty minutes later, the Mercedes was purring along the Eastern Harbor. To his left, Lang could see turreted Fort Qaitbey, built at the tip of the western edge of a peninsula in the fourteenth century on the site of the famed Pharos Lighthouse with recycled stones from the ruins of the wonder of the ancient world. Between the road and the water, a golden crescent of beach framed colorful fishing boats gently swaying at their moorings. Lang noted there were a great deal more empty anchor buoys than ships. The bulk of the fleet must already have been at sea.

To Lang's right, three- and four-story limestone buildings lined the waterfront, none of particular interest until the car eased into a parking spot in front of Le Metropole Hotel. The facade looked like the sort of North African fortress Gary Cooper, assisted to a small degree by the French Foreign Legion, might have defended in the 1939 version of *Beau Geste*.

As a uniformed bellhop opened the back door and Lang slid out, the driver, a swarthy man with a neatly manicured beard, spoke the first words of the trip. "Tell the concierge when you need the car and it will be here in five minutes. Here is my card with my cell-phone number. The service is available 24-7."

"Thanks." Lang proffered several bills as a tip.

Without looking at the money, the man shook his head. "Not necessary."

Stunned, Lang watched the car merge into the brown haze generated by a mix of cars, trucks and scooters. In his travels, he rarely could recall a professional chauffeur declining a tip. In this part of the world, unheard of.

Unless . . .

Miles.

Miles had insisted on making the hotel reservations at Agency expense and arranging for a driver. A grin crept across Lang's face as the realization dawned. Miles had arranged for much more. Lang was not alone here.

"Your only bag, sir?" the bellhop wanted to know.

Lang's attention returned to the hotel. "Yeah, I'll take it, thanks."

Pressing a few dollars into the bellhop's hand to atone for what would be viewed as unwarranted stinginess, Lang walked through revolving doors into a lobby that was a mixture of desert oasis, sheik's palace and exuberant if less-than-tasteful decor. Plastic date palms drooped under the weight of plastic dates against walls painted with life-size scenes of heroic-looking Bedouins riding camels far too clean and mannerly to be realistic. In the background, painted, burka-shrouded women obediently tended to domestic tasks, drawing water from a well and preparing meals over open fires.

To the Western eye, even more unrealistic than the camels.

Lang pretended to study the artwork as he took in the occupants of the lobby. Two men in low chairs were in intense conversation, a little table between them on which were two small coffee cups and an overflowing ashtray. The only other person other than hotel staff was hidden behind an Arabic newspaper. Pretending confusion between the registration desk and the concierge's, Lang managed a view of the reader, a swarthy Arab.

"This way, sir," a uniformed employee called from the registration desk as though shepherding a lost child.

Lang proffered the passport with the recently purchased visa. "Dr. Henry Roth," he announced. "I believe I have reservations."

The man behind the desk ran one hand over hair that could have been slicked back with axle grease. The other hand edged a finger down a list.

He spoke in British-accented English. "Oh, yes, here it is: Henry Roth. You will be staying with us tonight and tomorrow night?"

"Possibly longer, if I can. I'm not sure yet."

The expression of distress would have credited an actor. "Oh, dear. I fear we are quite full after tomorrow."

He studied a computer screen as though it might hold the solution to the problem, a solution Lang knew was elsewhere.

Reaching into a pocket, Lang palmed a fifty, placing his hand on the marble countertop so only the man behind it could see. "I trust you will do your best."

As the desk clerk reached for the bill, Lang slowly withdrew the money, returning it to his pocket. "Your best is all I can ask."

There was a meaningful moment of eye contact before the man behind the desk inhaled deeply. "I assure you, my best is what you will get."

Turning, the desk clerk faced an old-fashioned letter box behind him, the square holes in which letters and room keys were kept.

He selected a key. "I see you have a message."

He handed over both the key, attached to a heavy bronze tag, and a folded piece of paper. "If you will let me have a credit card and sign the register here . . ."

He pushed a registration form across the marble. Lang

scribbled a signature that matched the one on his passport. As the clerk entered the information into the computer, Lang unfolded and read the read the handwritten note.

Dr. Roth:
You may find me at the Catholic cemetery of Terra Santa.
                                                        Rossi

Lang smiled. Antonio Rossi, curator of the Archaeological Museum in Rome, a man he had known briefly during the affair that had ended so badly in the ancient Roman necropolis under the Vatican. Except the archaeologist had known Lang as a Mr. Joel Couch, an American from Indianapolis. But it had taken only a single e-mail to remind him that no matter the name, the American had saved him from an assassin's bullet at Herculaneum.

At Lang's request, Rossi had taken over one of the endless digs going on in Alexandria, his credentials satisfying the rigorous requirements of Zahi Hawass, the photogenic if dictatorial general secretary of Egypt's Supreme Council of Antiquities.

For centuries, if not millennia, Egypt's artifacts had been plundered. From the poaching of towering obelisks by the Romans to the relatively minor pilfering of mummies and small statues by Sir John Soane for his private, three-house museum in London in the eighteenth century, all had been available for whatever conquering power had the desire and the means to cart them off.

No more. Dr. Hawass zealously guarded his country's ancient treasures, even demanding vociferously if futilely for the return of some of the major items: the Rosetta Stone and a colossus of Ramses II from the British Museum, the swan-necked bust of Nefertiti from Berlin, a collection of sarcophagi from the Istanbul Archaeological Museum, statuary from the Louvre.

Other than native laborers, a person in Egypt needed an archaeology pedigree, accreditation and a vita Dr. Hawass approved to even be on the site of a dig. Wealthy backers were helpful.

Lang had none of the above. Dr. Rossi did.

In his room, an overdone version of some caliph's harem, Lang supposed, he took the usual check on precautions, enjoying a cold Stella larger from the minibar as he worked. The damn thing probably cost the Egyptian equivalent of five bucks, but what the hell, he was thirsty. Disassembling the phone, he made certain there was no listening device there. Nor were any to be found behind the electrical switch plates or any of the places where they could have been installed without tearing out Sheetrock. Lang had expected none but no one he knew had ever died from overcaution. He pulled the heavy drapes closed, pleased to note they were heavy satin, an excellent insulator against remote-listening devices.

Lang pulled on a pair of jeans and T-shirt and, after only a second's thought, slipped the Browning in its holster onto his belt, sliding it to the small of his back. A short-sleeve shirt, unbuttoned, and shirttails hanging outside his pants concealed the weapon.

In front of the hotel, he chose one of the city's yellow and black cabs rather than the more conspicuous Mercedes. The first thing he noticed was that all motor traffic, cars, trucks, scooters, had a common trait: they all belched out a brownish exhaust that joined the thickening layer just above the rooftops.

Within minutes, Lang witnessed the chaos of Egyptian driving. Cars charged the wrong way down one-way streets and backed up against traffic to make a missed turn. Red lights, stop signs and lane markings were deemed advisory only. Drivers' intentions were communicated, if at all, by hand. Passengers exited moving buses and pedestrians paid as little heed to the rules of the road as did drivers.

After a trip that would have compared favorably with any Dodge 'Em carnival ride, the cabby turned down the radio long enough to say "Terra Santa."

In jeans that had been prefaded just short of white, T-shirt, worn desert boots, and holding a broad-brimmed hat, Lang felt like an extra in an Indiana Jones movie. The costume was, however, a close replica of the clothing he had carefully noted in the most recent *National Geographic* article concerning desert exploration. He had originally opted for shorts rather than long pants until reading that their function was not only to protect skin from the merciless African sun but to serve as a potential shield against the scorpions who frequently inhabited Egyptian ruins.

Lang took a long glance around the cemetery as the taxi disappeared into the morning's traffic. After falling into disuse as a burial ground, the discovery of the so-called Alabaster Tomb in 1906 had given archaeologists hope Alexander's final resting place had been discovered. A cylindrical shaft lined with white marble had led down into a single room hacked into the limestone, its shape possibly Macedonian. This was all they initially found. No other chambers had been discovered. The area eventually became a plant nursery and was forgotten until 1988 and '89 when modern electromagnetic measuring revealed unexplained anomalies, cuts into the limestone large enough to have served as passages that could well have been sealed off intentionally or by an ancient earthquake.

Lang walked along a fence topped with razor wire until he came to a gate guarded by a large man seated on an uncomfortable-looking camp stool and wearing a holster on his belt. The guard lifted his eyes from the newspaper in his hands and looked Lang over suspiciously.

"Dr. Rossi . . . I'm here to see Dr. Rossi, Antonio Rossi."

Without response, the guard produced what looked like a small radio and said something into it Lang could not understand. Lang stood in the increasing heat of the sun for a minute or two, shifting his weight, before Dr. Rossi appeared.

Lang checked his watch. Back in Atlanta, it would be close to Manfred's time for school. He entered the number and was rewarded with his son's voice.

"Where are you, Vati?" the child asked.

Ever-cautious about nonsecure communications, Lang replied simply, "A long way away."

"Are you going to bring me something when you come back?"

"Only if your mother and Grumps say you've been a good boy."

Manfred was only momentarily disquieted by the prospect of being ratted out by the dog. "I will, Vati, I will!"

Rossi was tall, wearing a broad-brimmed hat, military-style khakis and worn rubber knee boots. His face was the color and texture of old leather, wrinkled from years in the sun. A queue of white hair protruded from under the rear of the hat like the tail of some small, furry animal.

"Gotta go, now. Love you!" Lang entered "end."

Rossi said something to the guard before turning to Lang, brilliant white teeth flashing in a smile. "Dr. Roth! I'm so glad you could come!"

His English was accented more by Oxford than his Italian nationality. Placing a hand under Lang's elbow, he gently led him past a group of Egyptians gingerly sifting through a mound of loose earth.

"You are Joel Couch, American newspaperman, last time I see you," Rossi gently chided. "Now you are Henry Roth, doctor of archaeology at a prestigious American university." He studied Lang's still-bruised face. "And you have met with an accident."

"You should see the other fellow."

"Had your e-mail not included the reference to Herculaneum and the fact you saved my life there, I would have discarded it as . . ."

"Spam."

"As spam. Still, it is a mystery to me how Mr. Couch becomes Dr. Roth."

Lang laid an arm on Rossi's shoulder. "Believe me, Antonio, you are better off to let it remain a mystery."

The archaeologist stopped in midstride, facing Lang. "You are also a mystery. But as you Americans say, I owe you one. What may I do to be of help?"

Lang looked around, selecting the shade of one of the few trees left. Lang could only guess how hot this place would be in the summer months. It was uncomfortably warm now.

"It's a long story," Lang began, experience warning against telling anyone more than they needed to know. "To make it a lot shorter, some people may be trying to locate Alexander the Great's tomb, more specifically, his remains. Relics, as it were."

Rossi gave a short laugh, more bark than merriment. "They and the rest of the archaeological world! The tomb itself has been lost since the fourth century AD." This time he chuckled. "Even your Shakespeare has Hamlet refer to tracing the 'noble dust of Alexander.'"

"Some say it has been confused with that of Saint Mark."

Rossi pointed to several empty crates and motioned for Lang to sit on one while he took another. "That is a long story, more of what you would call . . . supposition? Yes, more supposition than fact." He took off his hat and fanned himself with it. "We are not even certain where Saint Mark was originally buried. Reliable accounts put his tomb near what became known as Saint Mark's Gate."

Lang imitated the archaeologist, thankful for the small cooling effect. "Would that be the same as the Pepper Gate? I understand Alexander was entombed near there."

Rossi nodded. "Yes, hence the confusion. To add to it, the Roman historian Libanius gives a contemporaneous account of Alexander's body being on display just before paganism was outlawed in AD 391. There are no later firsthand accounts. Saint Mark's body surfaces at the end of the fourth century, or about the same time."

Lang forgot the heat for the moment. "Are you saying . . . ?"

Rossi shook his head. "I'm an archaeologist, a scientist. I report what I find."

"Archaeologists also theorize, fill in the gaps."

"True," the Italian conceded.

"OK, what do you think happened to Alexander's remains and those of Saint Mark?"

Rossi studied the distance before replying as though inspiration might be there. "In the early centuries of Christianity, it would have been tempting," he began, "for some official of the Alexandria church to seize the opportunity to both preserve the remains of the city's founder, Alexander, from the more fanatical Christians and at the same time give Christians a relic to encourage the faithful. Adapting things pagan for Christian use was not unknown in the early days after paganism was made illegal. For example, a bronze idol of the Roman god Saturn was melted down to make a cross. Take a look at the ancient monuments in Rome that are adorned with crosses. Pagan temples, like the Pantheon, became Christian churches. We have the words of the Venetian merchants who supposedly stole the body of Saint Mark that it was mummified like Alexander's, yet early Christian tradition insists Saint Mark's body was partially cremated in the first century AD. This is only speculation on my part."

Lang stood, facing the area where excavation by hand was progressing in ten-foot squares demarcated by strings on short pegs. "If your 'speculation'"—he made quotation marks with his fingers—"is correct, then it is Alexander who was in Saint Mark's tomb in Venice."

Rossi also stood, glancing over to where the digging was going on. "Not necessarily. One of the things we learn in studying ancient clues to a question is that we must not overlook that there are often a number of possible answers to the same question."

"Meaning?"

"Meaning Saint Mark's body was buried at a place where many were interred. It was the . . . what would you say? The fashionable place for burials, Christians on top of those believing in the Greek gods, the Egyptian gods, the Roman gods. Though mummification was rare by then, it was still practiced. Even if the remains the Venetians took were not Saint Mark's, there is no evidence they were Alexander's, either."

Lang used his sleeve to wipe his forehead. "Why do I feel I'm going in circles?"

Rossi smiled, again exhibiting perfect teeth. "Now you experience the feelings of a true archaeologist: either too many possible answers to a question or not enough."

"But I understood the area—the palace area, it was called—was not a burial ground."

"That was true when Alexander's mausoleum was built here, if this is in fact the neighborhood. In the intervening years, though . . ." He stretched out a hand to infinity. "Who knows?"

Cemetery of Terra Santa
Alexandria, Egypt
Fifteen minutes later

Lang was watching the monotonous procedure. Diggers removed soil with small trowels, filling buckets that were carried to where he had seen sifting going on. Whenever metal struck something more solid than earth, Rossi watched while what appeared to be dental tools and toothbrushes were used to painstakingly remove clay and loose dirt. In the few minutes Lang had been an observer, two or three pieces of what looked like rock had been removed, cleaned and inspected.

Rossi stood next to Lang, using a red bandanna to wipe a combination of sweat and grime from his face. "It is not as exciting as the History Channel, I fear."

"At least there aren't any commercials."

"No, my friend, the commercials come before the show begins, when I go to various foundations to beg money to support the project."

Lang was about to reply when a young woman, her denims caked with dirt, her hair covered by a scarf, approached excitedly. She spoke in quick bursts of Italian punctuated with the erratic hand movements that are as much part of the language as the words themselves.

Whatever she was saying, it must have been important, as Rossi didn't take the time to translate. He gave Lang a "follow me" gesture and took quick steps in the direction she was pointing.

Trotting to keep up, Lang came to a stop, almost colliding with Rossi's back. Before them was a circular hole, one lined in white marble. A pair of ladders was fixed to the top and disappeared into darkness.

"The Alabaster Tomb," Rossi explained. "We are searching for the possible passages discovered by electromagnetic imaging."

"I read about it on the flight over," Lang said. "Understand you think there may be more than the single chamber known so far."

Rossi gave him a look that said the archaeologist was thankful not to have to take time to explain. "As you can see, we are working inside as well as digging down to whatever the imaging shows. Come."

Before Lang could say anything else, the Italian was climbing down one of the ladders. Lang's choice was to stay here or follow.

Lang had sudden empathy for those whose jobs required descent into manholes. Sunlight lasted for about the first fifteen feet before a string of electric lights became visible, casting about as much shadow as illumination. At the bottom, Lang noted he was standing in an inch or so of water. The proximity to the harbor meant a high water table, although from the smell, Lang guessed fresh or brackish rather than salt water. He looked upward to see a vaulted ceiling over a room perhaps ten by thirty feet, the walls smooth with fluted columns carved into them.

A few feet away, Rossi was conferring with two people whose sex was indeterminable in the pale light. He already had on a miner's helmet, complete with attached light. Without turning, he handed one to Lang.

The conversation complete, Rossi motioned for Lang to follow as he led the way, flashlight in hand. "Originally it was thought this was the only chamber, hardly a tomb fit for royalty. Today we believe differently. Mind your step."

The warning was timely. Otherwise, Lang might have tripped over what he thought was only rubble next to a wall. A closer look showed the pile had probably been part of the wall that had been removed to reveal a corridor behind it.

Rossi played his flashlight into the hallway. "This was sealed off, a wall erected and made to look like the rest of the main chamber, where we entered, and disguised to look like nothing more was here."

"Why would someone go to that much trouble?" Lang asked.

From behind, he could see Rossi shrug, the answer obvious. "To conceal something from grave robbers, perhaps."

Lang's miner's helmet thumped against a particularly low place in the ceiling, making him thankful he had put it on. "Like what?"

"I hope we will find out. Someone certainly has been here before us. The entrance was opened and then resealed."

Rossi stopped abruptly, his light shining on two more workers. There was going to be a tight squeeze to get past.

"Perhaps there was more, er, loot to be had later or some other reason they did not want anyone to know they had been here."

Rossi was squatting, his light reflecting from something small on the floor. He looked up, asking a question in Italian.

One of the workers, definitely a man, nodded, holding up a palm-sized digital camera.

"We photograph every artifact in the location it was found," Rossi explained for Lang's benefit. "Otherwise, it is like taking a fact out of historical context."

Lang was looking over the archaeologist's shoulder. "What have you got there?"

Rossi shook his head. "Not sure. Has a small loop on the back. It looks like . . . a button?"

"They had buttons in the ancient world?"

Rossi was using the flashlight to illuminate the object in his palm. "Sure. Except they were usually larger than this and in fanciful shapes—seashells, animals, deities and so forth. This one is more like a modern button." He ran a thumb across it. "Until we can get it cleaned off, we won't really know."

He produced a small plastic bag from a pocket and dropped the object into it. "But this isn't what the excitement was all about. Come on."

He stepped forward. "You will note there are still scraps of plaster on the walls, or rather the cement common to many Greco-Roman structures." He paused to place the light next to the wall. "You can even see a bit of pigment still sticking to plaster. At one time, there may have been frescoes here, or at least some sort of wall paintings. One does not decorate a hallway to nowhere. A pity centuries of being under water have all but obliterated them."

"Underwater?"

"The 365 AD earthquake and tsunami moved the harbor inland, raising the water table."

"But we're dry now. Or almost."

"Pumps, my friend. We have pumps running twenty-four hours a day. Otherwise we, too, would be nearly underwater. Only the ceiling was dry when we first entered here."

The lights strung overhead along the passage terminated at what looked like the end of the corridor. Four or five of the workers whispered excitedly as they pressed against the wall to make way for Rossi.

"A blank wall?" Lang asked, perplexed.

"Perhaps," Rossi said, running a hand along it. "But note the plaster is slightly different in color than the rest of this hallway, if that is what this is. Before the advent of electric flashlights, that would not be as visible as it is now. The texture of the plaster appears to be just that, plaster. If this is the end of the corridor, why cover it over instead of just leaving the rock? In fact, I'd guess someone resealed this." He turned his light upward, revealing a series of black smudges. "Whoever was here before used candles or oil lamps."

"You mean someone before electric lights were available?" Lang asked.

Rossi nodded. "And someone or ones who worked here long enough for the soot from the lighting device to accumulate. Perhaps while they were erecting a false end of the corridor."

"But I thought this passageway was underwater since the tsunami."

"Pumps to remove water have been available since ancient times. Someone could have pumped it nearly dry just as we have. Also, they could have braced this wall against the water pressure outside while they erected this wall."

"Meaning there's something behind it?" Lang asked.

Rossi took an ordinary rock hammer from one of the observers and tapped the wall. "Meaning I intend to find out."

Half an hour later, work was halted while wire was strung both for lights and for fans to remove the dust that had reduced vision to a few feet. An extra generator and pump chugged in the darkness, forcing tepid air from the surface into the excavation and the constant trickle of water out. Lang's eyes stung and he could feel his face caked with grime mixed with sweat. Rossi and the others were dim ghosts in the gritty haze. Even though the corridor was wide enough for only one person to wield the larger sledgehammer at a time, no one was leaving. This was hardly his idea of the romance of searching for ancient worlds, but Lang could feel the tension among the workers like a close score in the last minutes of an intense football rivalry.

There was a muffled cheer as a section of the wall crumbled, leaving a hole through which a spout of water emptied into the corridor before being sucked away by the pumps. The fans could not prevent an incoming tide of grit swirling throughout. It took two or three minutes before a murky visibility was restored. Figures moved in a penumbra of dust, resembling shadows without forms.

A gentle tug at Lang's elbow turned him toward a haze of swirling particles of dust, plaster and rock as he followed Rossi into the opening. A ray of light from a flashlight, distorted by reflection, stabbed upward. Lang's eyes followed. The roof had at one time been step-pyramidal, shaped by carefully fitted stones, most of which had fallen, leaving a tangle of roots from the plants above. It had been supported by a colonnade of Ionic columns carved into rock. As visibility increased, Lang could make out what looked like a single slab of stone about four feet high in the middle of the room. Perhaps a permanent catafalque on which a sarcophagus rested?

Even in the gritty near twilight, Lang could see his friend's grin.

"This is it? This is Alexander's tomb?"

Rossi's smile faded. "Possibly. The construction is consistent with what we know of other Ptolemaic tombs." He played his light around the chamber. "And the Roman historian Lucan tells us when Caesar visited Alexander's tomb, he 'eagerly descended,' indicating something below ground. He also uses the phrase 'unseemly pyramid.'"

"*Dedecor?*"

Rossi looked at Lang quizzically. "Yes, I believe that is the word."

"It also can have the connotation, 'unnecessary' or 'useless.' That would describe an underground tomb with a pyramid-shaped roof."

Rossi chuckled. "Mr. Couch, Dr. Roth or whoever you might be, I knew you were quick thinking. You proved that at Herculaneum. Now I discover you are also a Latin scholar. I cannot but wonder what is next."

Lang ignored the remark. "What will it take to identify this as the real tomb of Alexander?"

Rossi gave the patented Italian shrug. "Months if not years. We must find things, carvings, inscriptions that can either be related directly to Alexander or at least have dates compatible with the time he might have been laid to rest here. Every archaeologist who has searched in other places, or most of them, will present papers demonstrating why this cannot be it."

Academics, Lang thought, were even more jealous of their contemporaries' success than lawyers.

Something caught his eye and he swept a nearby wall with his light. "Let the games begin. That looks like a carving of some sort."

Rossi stepped over to it, raising a hand to brush away the dirt caked around it. "It will need cleaning, but it appears to be a battle scene. I would guess Greeks versus Persians."

"That sounds like Alexander to me."

Rossi shook his head almost sorrowfully. "Not necessarily. Many wished to, er, clothe themselves in the glory of Alexander. For example, there is the misnamed Alexander Sarcophagus found in Sidon. It was carved with the exploits of Alexander shortly before his death. For years after its discovery in 1887, it was thought it had been carved for Alexander if not actually used."

"And?"

"Most likely carved for a minor puppet king, Abdalonymus, whom Alexander appointed to rule. It is the gem of the Istanbul Archaeological Museum, though."

"You're saying this tomb, if that is what this is, could be carved with scenes from Alexander's life even if the tomb was somebody else's?"

Rossi was still studying the carvings. "The Ptolemy dynasty legitimized itself by stressing it was Alexander's rightful successor. They even formed Alexander cults. They were the ones who promoted him into being seen as a god. Their tombs contain more about him than themselves."

Lang looked perplexed.

"You've seen such things in modern times. Didn't Stalin claim to be Lenin's rightful political heir even after disposing of such inconveniences as Trotsky?"

"I guess I never thought of it that way. I—"

Before he could finish, there was a dull thud from above. The whole ground, including the chamber, shook, unleashing a new avalanche of dust and dirt. Lang had an immediate vision of an explosion.

Then, the lights went out.

Worse, the generator powering fans sucking air in from above and water out was silent. It seemed to be getting more difficult to breathe.

Someone's voice shouted excitedly from the corridor behind them, echoes distorting the tone.

Lang swung his light toward the voice. "What'd he say?"

"He said the entrance to the surface is closed," Rossi said calmly. "Digging may have undercut the foundations of the old stones, caused them to fall into the excavation. Or one of the supports we erected against the outside water pressure collapsed."

"Sounded more like an explosion to me."

"No, no, my friend. We brought no explosives to the dig. To use such things would risk destroying what we hope to find."

"Now what?" Lang wanted to know.

"Now we wait for the crew above to dig us out."

Why did Lang think it wasn't going to be that simple? Was it because he was beginning to smell a whiff of that heavy, pungent, sweet odor of nitroglycerin-based explosives such as dynamite, something someone other than Rossi's crew might have brought to the site? And if that someone had blasted the opening closed, they certainly had not done so with the consent of Rossi's people above, the people who supposedly would dig them out.

Lang inhaled a mouthful of dust. No doubt about it: it was getting harder to breathe.

And water was collecting around his feet.

472 Lafayette Drive, Atlanta
9:22 the same day

From under the kitchen table, Grumps watched with palpable relief as Gurt bundled Manfred against one of those late winter storms that paralyze the city every few years. Ice, not snow, covered every outdoor surface, transforming the most humble bush into an iridescent handful of diamonds. At irregular but persistent intervals a rifle shot–like crack attested to the inability of another tree limb to bear the extra weight. As usual, schools, including Manfred's private pre-K, had announced shutting their doors as the first frozen precipitation had fallen the night before. Predictably, state, local and federal governments seized the opportunity to suspend operations along with a number of large businesses. Smaller operations, those whose bottom lines might be adversely affected by an unplanned holiday, bravely remained opened in the face of a clientele largely fearful of risking life, limb and automotive coach work on streets slick as oil.

Gurt had had enough of being confined in a house with a five-year-old's rambunctiousness despite her normally strict discipline. Manfred had lost interest in his toys, tired of his mother's reading to him from books already nearly memorized and tormented Grumps to the extent the dog had taken rare refuge from his young master and closest pal. One alternative was to turn on the television and let the magic screen absorb the child, something Gurt was loath to do. She severely limited Manfred's TV watching, certain that the mindless junk that passed for entertainment would decrease her son's IQ if not rot the brain entirely.

Gurt zipped up the child's jacket, smiling at the resemblance the bulky clothes gave Manfred to the Michelin Man. "There," she said in German, "now we will go to the park."

All Gurt had to do was dream up some activity that would both engage and exhaust her son. She shrugged into a knee-length fur coat, checked to make sure her gloves were in the pocket and started to push Manfred toward the front door. In midfoyer she stopped. Grumps had abandoned the safety of the kitchen table. His tail broke into a furious rhythm as Gurt pocketed a tennis ball.

"Wait here," she commanded both the little boy and the dog.

Grumps, now joyful at the possibility of a romp outside, skidded to a stop just short of a collision with the front door. He waited, tail wagging in impatient anticipation as she trotted up the stairs.

In the bedroom, she removed the Glock 19 from the bedside table, checking the action and magazine before stuffing it in a coat pocket. She normally did not carry a firearm when escorting or driving Manfred, out of the fear that should she need to use it, she would draw return fire, endangering the little boy. Besides, how often did a mother driving her child to kindergarten need a weapon?

But these were not normal times. After Venice and the

crude but frightening attempt on her home, she felt leaving her pistol behind was foolish.

She watched her and Manfred's step carefully as they made their way carefully down the three short but icy stairs from the front door to the brick path that led to the driveway. With canine impetuosity, Grumps made the transition in a single leap, landing hard and sliding a couple of yards on his rear on the ice-encrusted bricks. Both Gurt and Manfred nearly lost their balance as they doubled over with laughter.

By the time they reached the driveway, the stillness of the scene became apparent. Although Ansley Park was normally a quiet neighborhood, today it was totally and eerily silent. The sounds of the surrounding city, the white noise of traffic on busy Peachtree Street three blocks away, the whine of jets arriving or departing distant Hartsfield-Jackson Atlanta International, the hum of civilization, were absent as if the blanket of ice were some huge sponge that soaked up all sound.

The rattle of tire chains on pavement across the park was like a shout in an otherwise-silent church and reminded her few of her neighbors were natives of Atlanta. This transplant had brought his winter paraphernalia with him when he left Michigan, Illinois or one of those places where snow and ice were common.

The next interruption of the crushing stillness was the cough of an engine cranking. Gurt looked at a black SUV with an exhaust trail, idling at the curb. Although tinted windows prevented her from seeing the occupant, she recognized the vehicle as belonging to the security service Lang had hired.

A door opened and a man got out. She thought she remembered he had been introduced to her as Randy. The way his eyes had never left her bustline made her wonder whether this was a name or a description. He was a beefy man with streaks of gray in his fading red hair. The fouled anchor and globe of the Marine Corps was tattooed on his right forearm above the *"semper fidelis"* motto.

Randy came around the car and opened the rear passenger door. "Going somewhere Mrs. Reilly?"

Even in her bulky coat, his stare made Gurt a little uncomfortable. "No, thank you. Just over to the park. The child is restless."

She started to add that her name was Fuchs, not Reilly, decided the rebuke was not worth the effort and guided Manfred onto the driveway.

Randy turned to take a long look at the Iris Garden. "I don't feel comfortable with that, ma'am. Even with the foliage off the trees and bushes, too many places somebody could hide."

Not without leaving tracks in the sheet of ice a blind man could spot, Gurt thought. But she said, "Thank you for your thoughtfulness, but we will be quite all right."

Taking Manfred by the hand, although there was no sign of traffic, she stepped into the street. Grumps, lesson unlearned, dashed ahead, again unable to put on the brakes. This time he hit the far curb.

Randy shut the SUV's door with a little more force than Gurt thought necessary. "Then I'll have to go with you ma'am."

The thought of the man's stares made Gurt inexplicably uncomfortable. She'd been . . . what would Lang say? Ogled, that was it, ogled. She'd been ogled by men all her adult life and most of her adolescence.

Her tone had a little more snap in it than she might have wished. "I said, we will be quite all right, thank you. I would prefer to be alone with my child."

Randy shrugged. "Orders are orders, ma'am. I'm to stay with you while you're outside."

She saw no one else was in sight on this rare day when fireplaces would be more than decorative and at least half her neighbors would be home. On the unlikely chance anyone showed up to walk the Iris Garden, he would be as obvious as a wart on the nose. But she understood the necessity of obedience to orders as only those of Teutonic origin can. She herself had complied with enough of them in her time with the Agency.

She sighed, admitting defeat. "Very well, but try to keep a distance."

Randy gave her a wary smile. "I don't mean to give offense, ma'am."

"It is not you who is offensive," Gurt lied smoothly, all too conscious of the gun in her own pocket. "It is I dislike to have my child exposed to men, er, carrying firearms. There is too much violence on television and in the papers already."

"I understand. The kid won't see my gun, ma'am."

"Gun?" Manfred piped up. "The man has a *gun?*" he turned to Randy. "Can I see?"

Gurt sighed deeply, taking Manfred by the arm. "Come, Manfred. Grumps wants to play."

"Aw, Mom . . ."

"I said, *come!*"

Today Grumps was more interested in the various smells of the Iris Garden than he was in fetching the tennis ball. Perhaps the small park's resident squirrels had left a different scent or the neighborhood dogs had deposited more "pee mail" than normal, each requiring a prompt reply.

Whatever the reason, the first toss of the Day-Glo chartreuse ball only got a glance from the sniffing dog. At the second attempt, Grumps stopped his exploration long enough to watch the ball roll down one of the two slopes that formed the valley that was the park. The dog favored Manfred with a look that clearly asked, "Just what, pray tell, do you expect *me* to do with *that?*"

The little boy's enthusiasm undiminished, he followed the dog, followed by Gurt, followed by Randy.

Gurt was breathing hard, the air cold enough to slice her

lungs like a surgeon's scalpel. Cresting a small rise, she saw other human figures, those of her next-door neighbors Paige Charles and her son Wynn Three, Manfred's friend.

"I am surprised you are out in this cold," Gurt said when she was within earshot, motioning Randy to keep his distance.

Paige shook her head, a movement hardly perceptible under the fur-lined hood of her heavy parka. "It was either brave the weather or a restless child. You can't imagine what it's like to be cooped up with a kid as active as Wynn Three."

Gurt watched Manfred and Wynn Three, now playing with a compliant Grumps. "Believe me, I do not have to imagine. I—"

A sharp crack shattered the morning's cathedral-like silence. Gurt's hand went to her coat pocket as she frantically motioned Manfred to come to her.

Paige must have seen the consternation on her face. "What? That was just another limb breaking off from the tree because of the weight of the ice."

Gurt barely heard her. She had a protective arm around Manfred, her eyes searching what she thought was the direction of the sound, but she was certain only of two things: Randy was no longer in sight and she surely knew the difference between a shattering oak limb and a gunshot.

The White House
Washington, D.C.
The previous afternoon

The secretary of defense stood, hands clasped behind his back as he stared out of the Oval Office's French doors into a rose garden desolated by winter. He checked his watch. The president was twenty minutes late for the meeting. That wasn't even close to the record. The young chief executive had no qualms about keeping staff waiting an hour or so if the opportunity arose for an impromptu press conference, something he invariably mishandled. The man was a golden-tongued orator as long as he could stick to prepared notes and the teleprompter. Off the cuff, he tended to sound self-contradictory or confused. Fortunately, a sympathetic press usually edited out his most nonsensical responses, leaving only Fox News and conservative bloggers to broadcast the miscues.

Still, the man liked press exposure. Many said someone should tell him he no longer had to campaign and should get down to the business at hand.

The business at hand. The SecDef glanced around the room. An odd crew: a fiftyish female lieutenant colonel who had something to do with intelligence; the U.S. delegate to the Organization of American States; and the new head of the CIA, a former college radical, community organizer and a man who, as far as the SecDef knew, had had no experience in running anything the size of a taco stand, let alone one of the world's largest intel agencies.

But then, neither had the president.

The last chief spook had resigned in protest of the criminal prosecution of a number of CIA agents who, following the previous administration's guidelines, had inflicted what the new bunch considered torture on some very brutal individuals, extracting information that had prevented at least one and possibly more terrorist attacks on the U.S. both here and abroad.

Such was politics. The new CIA chief, along with his boss, believed sincerely, the SecDef feared, that total candor and self-abasement were the tools of successful relationships with other nations, a policy uniformly embraced in word if not in deed by America's enemies. The country's traditional allies had all but ceased to share information for fear the same would appear on the front pages of the *New York Times* or *Washington Post*.

It was enough to make the SecDef wish he had not been chosen as the sole holdover from the previous administration.

The absence today of any of the Joint Chiefs of Staff was significant as was the fact that this meeting was taking place here rather than the much larger adjacent conference room, equipped with the latest real-time technology. The president's dislike of large meetings was well-known and offered as an excuse to exclude most of the intelligence community and military, both of which he equally and openly distrusted.

His thoughts scattered as the president entered wearing his customary golf shirt and slacks, the first person the SecDef had ever seen enter this historic room in less-than-respectful business or military attire. He was followed by Jack Roberts, chief of staff, a man the SecDef thought of as the "presidential dog robber." Whatever the White House needed, be it leaking a rumor devastating to a member of the opposition, strong-arming a recalcitrant member of his own party or making it convenient for a congressional fence-sitter to come down on the White House's side of a vote, Roberts was the go-to guy.

The president motioned for everyone to take a seat as he slid behind the desk and nodded to the director of the CIA. "You wanted to see me, Jerry?"

The director nodded, turning to the woman in the army uniform of a lieutenant colonel. "Let me introduce you to Colonel Faith Romer and Jack Hanson. Colonel Romer is the military liaison with the CIA regarding the Caribbean Basin. Jack is the U.S. representative to the Organization of American States."

The president viewed Faith with obvious distaste. "Colonel, as I understand it, the Chinese military are in the process of setting up shop in Haiti. And so far this information is known only to us, the Chinese and that man . . . the president of Haiti."

"DuPaar," the chief spook supplied.

"DuPaar, yes. To no one else?"

The CIA chief nodded. "As far as we know."

The president gave him a quizzical look. "Meaning?"

The head of the CIA shifted in his chair uncomfortably. "We had to employ some nonstandard assets to ascertain exactly what the Chinese were doing."

The president's thick eyebrows furrowed. "Tell me in non-jargon."

"The people who sniffed the whole thing out . . . They were no longer with the Agency."

The president drummed long fingers on the desktop, a sign he was making a choice. He was known to demand quick decisions. He had insisted Congress pass a budget larger than all previous budgets combined in a period of time shorter than it had taken him to choose a puppy for his children.

He pushed back from the desk, turning to his chief of staff. "OK, Jack, what do you think?"

The SecDef had almost gotten used to the president's habit of seeking advice from those least qualified to give it. As far as he knew, Robert's sole qualification to comment on foreign policy was a semester spent in Spain in college.

Roberts rubbed his chin a moment as though in thought, a process the SecDef had not considered possible. "As I see it, a Chinese presence in Haiti presents a possible crisis, one we need to keep secret until we have it solved. A confrontation with the Chinese isn't something we need, with the off-year elections coming up."

The president turned to the SecDef. "Your thoughts?"

"Mr. President, the military stands ready to have unmanned aircraft destroy any and all Chinese installations should diplomacy fail."

"Bomb a small, poor Caribbean country back into the Stone Age?" the chief of staff sneered. "First, Haiti is *still* in the Stone Age, and second, how do you think that makes us look to the rest of the world?"

Fear of foreign opinion had been a major weakness in American foreign policy since World War II, the SecDef thought. But he said, "Diplomacy isn't my job."

Roberts shrugged. "Simple enough. The president meets with the Chinese, either has them withdraw or issues a joint statement of their peaceful intentions and our belief in that."

The SecDef spoke up. "Maybe you missed the part about the Chinese military."

Roberts was also the administration's spinmaster, much loved by the media. It had been he who had convinced the public—at least its more gullible segments—that increases in corporate taxes would not be passed along to the consumer. "Besides, meeting with the Chinese makes you look presidential. You can count on the uptick in the polls. But not if word leaks out beforehand. If the public knew the Chinese have slipped troops into Haiti . . ."

The president nodded. "So be it. I want a joint meeting with the presidents of Haiti and China for their assurances the Chinese mission is peaceful and to declare that America will not interfere. For the moment, we'll keep a lid on the fact the Chinese presence is military in nature. No sense in getting all those conspiracy-loving neocons stirred up. And . . ."

Why did the SecDef think of Neville Chamberlain, Munich and "Peace in our time"?

"After the meeting, I'll want to address the nation concerning the peaceful intentions of the Chinese . . ."

Roberts was studying his BlackBerry. "That isn't going to be easy, Mr. President."

The president paused in midphrase. "Oh? Why not?"

"Next week is your 'Friendship Initiative,' the visit to Venezuela and President Chavez. When you return, you have a major address to the AFL/CIO convention in Detroit before you leave to talk with the president of Iran. A week later, the Russian president comes here to commend your decision to cancel the Eastern European missile-shield program . . ."

"OK. OK. I get the picture. Work it in somehow. ASAP. In the meantime, we must be certain to do nothing that could be considered hostile to either Haiti or China. I . . ." He looked at the pained expression on the CIA director's face. "What's bothering you, Jerry?"

"Mr. President," the CIA director said slowly. "There's a couple of things you need to know."

The president's confidence seeped away like water into dry soil. He despised surprises. "Like what?"

"Like this Chinese-Haitian thing. We had an asset keeping an eye on things, until he disappeared. Then one of our best handlers recruited a former agent, the one I told you about a few minutes ago, to find out what was going on, and he did. Unfortunately, the Chinese know about it and are trying to kill him and his wife, who went to Haiti with him."

"I would think we can convince the Chinese to lay off by not opposing whatever they are doing in Haiti."

"Possibly so, yes, sir, if we can convince them before they succeed. Unfortunately we, the CIA, are protecting him and his family right now."

The presidential eyebrows arched. "You are conducting a mission in the United States?"

The director was studying the presidential seal in the blue carpet. "Well, sort of. Just providing protection for the man's family. We did sort of promise him that."

The presidential scowl was obvious. At his level of politics, promises were obstacles easily overcome or circumvented. "You know your agency is prohibited from conducting operations, any operations, on U.S. soil. Providing domestic protection is the FBI's job."

"Yes, sir. But you see, we're also providing protection for this, er, asset out of the country. He's trying to find out exactly what the Haitians want in exchange for letting the Chinese pretty much do as they wish."

The president thought that over a second. "Since we are now welcoming them, it no longer matters, does it?"

The CIA director, thankful the conversation had taken a turn in a direction other than his, nodded. "I wouldn't think so. As a matter of fact, this asset, this former agent, could become an embarrassment if what he knows became public too soon." He looked over at the chief of staff. "Even you would have a hard time hushing up an on-site report of exactly what the Chinese are up to."

"He's right," the president agreed. "Jerry, since you are providing protection to this man and his family, there should be no problem picking them up. We can detain them under the Patriot Act until I have a chance to calm the nation's possible uneasiness about all this."

The SecDef started to point out the present administration had a bill before Congress to repeal that law, the series of statutes enacted in the wave of panic following 9/11 that gave the federal government more police powers than it had enjoyed since the laws Lincoln had had enacted at the outbreak of the Civil War. Some of the similarities—suspension of the writ of habeas corpus and the prohibitions against search and seizure—were frightening.

He thought better of it and instead said, "Mr. President, do I understand you are planning to arrest and detain American citizens because they gained knowledge this country asked them to obtain but which now becomes politically inexpedient?"

"Of course not!" the chief of staff snapped. "We're simply continuing to perform promises made to these people. The only difference is we can protect them far better in a facility of our choosing."

"And if they decline your offer?"

"Then we'll have to act in the best interests of the country."

Somehow, the SecDef doubted if these unnamed "assets" would see it that way.

Cemetery of Terra Santa

Faful wondered if the four men were really Bedouins. He, like several other laborers of the excavation crew, had grown up a nomad in the Western Desert, immigrating to the city and a more settled existence when he was fourteen. These men who had appeared at the dig had removed guns from under their flowing dishdashas, robes with sleeves tied back with cord, over which they wore the vestlike aba. The head cover was the traditional kaffiyeh, bound with bright camel-hair rope. The flowing tails of the headdress were drawn across faces, leaving only the eyes showing, as though the men were in a sandstorm.

But under the dishdashas they wore saronglike skirts, something typical of nomads of the southern Arabia Peninsula, not Egyptian Bedouins, who went bare legged.

Either way, though, Bedouins would have attracted no attention on the streets of Alexandria.

More importantly, they had ordered everyone into the administration tent, the largest of several such canvas structures.

This one was where records were kept and artifacts stored until the end of each day, when they were removed for safekeeping to the basement of the National Museum of Alexandria. This tent was the only one large enough to hold the entire crew remaining aboveground, which was why they were there under the watchful eyes of two of the Bedouins. If that was what they really were.

At first, Fafal had thought these men meant to steal whatever antiquities were on hand. Bedouins were notorious for plundering unguarded archaeological sites for artifacts to sell to unscrupulous dealers in such things. But stealth, not force, was the common method. Perhaps these men were not after artifacts.

Also, the strange Bedouins communicated mostly with gestures but occasionally in a language Faful had never heard before. Perhaps they were not Bedouin at all.

Shielded from the fitful sea breeze, the interior of the tent was going from uncomfortably hot to stifling, but the men with the guns seemed not to notice. Two of them had carried a wooden box outside. Though the flap of the tent was closed, Fafal could hear their sandals crunching in the sandy soil, toward the Alabaster Tomb.

What were they after?

His question was answered moments later when the ground shook with a muffled explosion.

Faful's first reaction was even more puzzlement. Why would they blow up the Alabaster Tomb? If it was antiquities they were after, destroying the work already done at the dig was going to also destroy what they wanted. Besides, the sound would draw the police.

Unless these men had arranged otherwise.

A few Egyptian pound notes of baksheesh could guarantee the indifference of all three street-level law-enforcement agencies—municipal police, Tourist Police or Central Security Forces—to any event smaller than a nuclear blast.

That still left the question, why?

Less than a hundred yards away and nearly a hundred feet down, Lang played his flashlight on the water gathering around his feet. Only an inch or so a few minutes ago, it was trickling over the top of his ankle-high boots now.

He sensed Rossi was making the same observation. "How long do you think it will take to run out of air or drown if we stay here?"

"Do not think of such things. Our crew will dig us out before there is even such a possibility."

Lang started to say that if, as he believed, an explosion

had sealed them in, the crew above were probably not free to rescue anyone. They were either dead, wounded or being restrained from taking action.

Instead, he said, "On the off chance they can't do it quickly enough, is there another exit here somewhere?"

The fact oxygen was getting thinner and thinner in the air provided one answer he didn't want to hear.

"Wealthy Greeks and pre-Christian Romans were entombed in *sepulcra*, what we would today call mausoleums, rather than simple tombs. They were like small houses, complete with wall paintings, sculpture and housewares. We are in a rather elaborate example. It was customary to leave a small hole at the top so visitors, family and friends of the deceased might share food and wine with the spirit of the dead."

"So, there would be one here?"

The doubt in Rossi's tone was not encouraging. "Possibly, but this hole would have never been large enough for an adult to get through."

"But it would at least let in air."

"My friend, this tomb has been here for more than two millennia, below ground level for almost as long. Whatever aperture might have existed in the ceiling would have long been sealed by dirt and vegetation."

"True," Lang agreed, "but two thousand years of debris and vegetation has got to be easier digging than solid rock." He shifted his light to the ceiling. "And trying to find it beats waiting to either suffocate or drown."

"But my crew . . . ," Rossi protested.

"If they are able to dig us out, swell. I, for one, don't intend to bet my life on it."

Muttering among some of the crew who had come down here with them suggested they shared Lang's feelings.

Lang swept the beam of his flashlight upward. Where the ceiling had fallen, roots of vegetation grasped downward like bony fingers.

"I doubt you will find anything," Rossi commented.

"Better hope I do. In case you haven't noticed, the water is already halfway to my waist and rising."

Although he couldn't see it in the darkness, Lang would have bet Rossi was in the midst of a very Italian shrug. "Even if you find such a thing, how will you reach it?"

Good question.

Iris Garden, Atlanta

Gurt took Manfred by the hand, keeping her voice level. "We will go home now."

"Aw, Mom," the little boy protested, "Wynn Three and Grumps and me were just beginning to have fun." His eyes flicked to her face, noting she was unpersuaded. "And Wynn Three doesn't have to . . ."

Another look at his mother's face told him the argument, if there had been one, was over.

Paige, startled by the abruptness of Gurt's decision to leave, asked, "What . . . ?"

But she was speaking to Gurt's back.

Her hand clasping Manfred's, the other on the butt of the Glock in her pocket, Grumps grudgingly following, Gurt climbed the gentle hill, feet planted firmly through the crust of ice with each step. When she reached street level, she had a better view of her surroundings. Randy's SUV was still parked in front of her house, although the tinted glass prevented her from seeing if he was in it. After his insistence on accompanying her, she doubted he would have returned to the vehicle while she was still in the park.

She almost missed it: about a hundred yards away, a streak, a trough in the coating of ice on the hillside on the opposite side of the park, where it looked like something had been dragged. Her eyes followed the trail to a pair of frozen shallow ponds connected by a short stream, that part of the park directly across from the house. The ice on the lower pool had been broken and something was extending out of it, something that could be a fallen branch, explaining the shattered ice or . . .

Or a human arm.

The distance was too great to be sure, but she wasn't going to delay reaching the security of the house to find out. She increased her pace, almost dragging Manfred in her haste.

Then she stopped. Ambling toward her was one of Atlanta's homeless, a man pushing a grocery-store cart filled to overflowing with an assortment of rags, a clear plastic trash bag of tin cans and junk she could not identify.

Agency training had made her permanently aware of her surroundings, alert to anomalies. With ice on the ground and the temperature below freezing, anyone with a modicum of sanity would have sought refuge in any of a number of the city's shelters or, at least, found a steam vent over which to camp. His clothes, an orange ski jacket and heavy sweat pants, though dirty, were not torn, not the ragged hand-me-downs that were the uniform of most of society's jetsam. Add to these observations the fact that no stringy hair hung out from beneath the watch cap and he appeared to have shaved recently.

The shoes were the clincher, sneakers that looked like one of the more expensive Nike models. The footwear was always the giveaway. Although a torn and laceless pair would have been more in keeping with the persona someone was trying to create, no professional was going to risk wearing anything not securely bound to the foot. A fight in which a shoe might come off with a kick, a chase in which pursuer or pursued lost the race because of the loss of a shoe . . . No, shoes were the one part of a disguise no one who knew what he or she was doing would compromise.

Stifling her impulse to just pick Manfred up and flee, Gurt bent over, pretending to adjust his jacket and giving her an opportunity to look behind without obviously doing so. She was not surprised to see a second man, his lower face covered by a muffler shoved into the turned-up collar of his overcoat.

Miles?

He had promised to have a man or two keep watch, like the one who had come out of nowhere the night of the attempted firebombing. But this was no surveillance, not two men in this weather, converging at once on a sidewalk glazed with ice. She recognized the classic maneuver intended to surround an enemy before he was aware of what was happening.

For an instant, she considered brandishing the Glock. Perhaps seeing that she was armed would make whoever these men were back off. Unlikely. More probable they were armed, too. A sudden display of a weapon could precipitate gunplay with the chance of a stray shot hitting Manfred.

No, surprise was her only logical weapon, to continue as though she suspected nothing, turning on the false tramp at the last moment. Nonchalantly, she shifted Manfred to her other side, the one away from the approaching stranger.

Usually, in dangerous situations, her mind seemed to slow down as it worked out points of attack, favorable angles and the like. As she closed with the homeless look-alike, she thought about a quick shot through her coat, another at the man behind before he could react. No, foolish. What if, as improbable as it sounded, they were exactly what they appeared to be: a hobo and a guy just coincidentally walking down a quiet residential street?

Mostly, though, she was considering Manfred's safety.

And where the hell were Miles's people?

Cemetery of Terra Santa

If there had been any doubt as to their peril, it was dispelled by the sound of rushing water. The flooding of the corridor outside had apparently defeated the braces against the water pressure on its walls. Water was up to Lang's waist and he was taking two or three deep breaths at a time just to keep a minimum of air in his lungs. He was experiencing a mild dizziness, the first signs of oxygen starvation. He could hear the crew panting in the dark like a pack of exhausted dogs as the lights on their miner's helmets moved, fruitlessly seeking an escape route.

"I don't think we can wait for your people," he gulped to Rossi.

"You have a plan?" Rossi croaked back.

"Maybe."

Lang played his light around the chamber until it centered on the place the stone slab had become invisible underwater. Moving slowly to conserve breath, he sloshed through the water until his foot touched something solid. With the next step, he climbed on top.

"That will help little," Rossi gasped. "The water will continue to rise. You will drown on that piece of rock."

Lang shook his head. "Not if I'm not on it."

"But, how . . . ?"

Rossi's gaze followed Lang's flashlight to the roots hanging from the ceiling. "You cannot reach them. Even if you could—"

"I appreciate your eternal optimism," Lang snapped a little harsher than he had intended. "How about a little help instead?"

"What do you mean?"

"I'm guessing if there was a hole in the ceiling of this *sepulcrum*, it would be right over where the sarcophagus was."

"So? It is nearly ten meters high. You cannot reach it."

Rather than expend breath uselessly, Lang swung his light among the now-silent crew. Picking the smallest man he could see, he beckoned. "You, come here."

"Dante," Rossi said. "His name is Dante, like the poet."

Rossi translated and the man cautiously joined Lang on

the stone slab. Lang handed him a hand pick one of the crew had dropped and said haltingly, waiting for Rossi to translate each phrase while pointing to the roots overhead, "Dante, here is what we're going to do: you climb onto my shoulders and see if you can snare one of those roots with the pick. Do you think you can climb it?"

Dante, short, squat and muscular, listened to Rossi and nodded enthusiastically, beginning to see hope where there had been none before.

Lang continued, using his hands to illustrate. "When you get close enough, I want you to use that pick to dig just above us, *capisce?*"

He waited for Rossi's translation, just to make sure.

Dante nodded understanding again, this time smiling.

On the first attempt, the poet's namesake leaped from Lang's shoulders, pick extended, missed a large cluster of roots and splashed into the rapidly accumulating water. Though the effort would have produced howls of laughter under normal circumstances, no one even chuckled.

Dante climbed onto Lang's shoulders again, this time directing the light on his miner's helmet from one clump of roots to another before making a decision. Lang let go of the man's ankles as Dante leaped again. This time he succeeded in grasping a tangle of roots, climbing upward with the agility of a monkey. Had the task not been far from complete, Lang would have congratulated himself on his choice of men.

There was still a long way to go, and the humid air was getting thinner as the water rose.

Almost without thought, Lang transferred his BlackBerry and wallet from his pants pocket to the one in his shirt.

His one arm and his legs wrapped around the root cluster to hold him in place, Dante took a one-handed swing at the roof of dirt, roots and remnants of stone ceiling. He was rewarded by being pelted with a curtain of loose dirt. Undeterred, he took another swing with the same result. Below, the crew, the lamps on their helmets trained upward, watched in silence. The only sounds were the bite of Dante's pick accompanied by the splash of detritus freed from the earthy roof, and the collective gasps for breath.

Even if Dante succeeded in opening a hole to the ground above, only one of their problems would be solved, the almost-depleted supply of oxygen. The water would rise to wherever the normal table was and no farther, leaving them still below the surface. Anyone who couldn't swim, or at least tread water, until help arrived would be in serious danger of drowning.

Help.

Once again, Lang thought of the members of the crew Rossi had left aboveground. He had heard no shots since the explosion that had blocked the exit from this chamber, but the fact no one had come to their assistance was ominous.

Lang temporarily forgot the question of those aboveground as a crack of light appeared above his head. With Dante's next swing of the pick, chunks of dirt and stone crashed into the water below, scattering several crew members who, like Lang, had been watching the little Italian's progress.

Almost immediately, there was a grumble of crumbling earth and a shriek. Lang would have rejoiced at the speck of daylight that appeared had it not been for a falling object plummeting from the surface above. Like a bird shot in flight, a white-clad form tumbled through the hole, smashing into the water below. It took Lang a full second to recognize the object as human, someone who seemed to be wrapped in sheets. He joined the group gathered around. A man, either dead or stunned, lay in the still-rising water. He wore what Lang guessed was Bedouin robes but there was nothing Semitic about his facial features: they were decidedly Asian. The gun that had fallen with him was unmistakable. The bullpup configuration, action and trigger in front of the magazine identified it as a QBZ type 95/97, a relatively new Chinese assault weapon that was replacing the Kalashnikov knock-off that had been the primary small arm of the People's Liberation Army.

Lang snatched it from the water just as a burst of gunfire from above churned the water not five feet away, sending the gathered crew frantically splashing toward the far edges of the chamber.

Lang lunged to his left, grasping the unfamiliar QBZ in one hand. The gun had made its first public appearance when the PLA marched in to reoccupy Hong Kong, long after Lang had left the Agency and its recurring training in contemporary firearms. Happily, he still browsed the gun publications frequently enough to know what he held, if not exactly how it worked. Muzzle velocity, clip capacity and caliber were a number of details Lang would have liked to know, but now was hardly time for a familiarization lecture. The one thing he did know was that this automatic rifle would provide firepower vastly superior to the Browning in its holster at his back.

If only he could figure out what was the safety and what was the fire selector.

Another fusillade ripped the water, this time close enough to shower him.

Shit! He still wore his miner's helmet, with its light providing a perfect target. One sweep of a hand sent it spinning into dusky shadows and drawing yet more fire.

He ducked, spinning farther into the nightlike shade provided by what was left of the mausoleum's roof. Now he was standing in darkness, looking up at a patch of sunlit sky. Reaching to his belt, he removed the flashlight he had jammed into it, turned it on and tossed it toward the circle of light playing off the room's flooded floor.

It had barely splashed before a man's head and shoulders appeared at the rim of the hole above. A ragged flame of muzzle flash jetted in the direction of the flashlight.

The Chinese rifle was too short to steady comfortably against his shoulder and squeeze the trigger at the same time. One hand on the forward grip, the other on the trigger, Lang pointed and held on tightly as the gun bucked in his hands, its blast deafening in the confines of the burial chamber.

For a second, he could only hear the ringing of his ears. There was no sign of the man at whom he had fired.

How could he have missed with such a clear target?

His question was answered a split second later as a figure leaned over the edge of the opening as though to shout something to those below. It slowly tumbled through the hole. The bright light from above showed another white robe, this one punctuated with a series of red splotches.

As his hearing slowly returned, Lang became aware of two sounds. Someone, one of Rossi's crew from above, was shouting something as he tossed a rope ladder into the opening. The other was the vibrating wail of approaching sirens.

Even the Alexandria police had a limit as to how much they could ignore.

Ansley Park

Gurt was slightly more than an arm length away from the street person when he stopped. "Ms. Fuchs? I need to speak with you."

The use of her name, one she had never changed, was uncommon among her contemporary friends and associates. She had found it easier to respond to Mrs. or Ms. Reilly than explain, the reason she had not corrected Randy as they left the house . . . what, less than an hour ago?

"Who are you?" she demanded.

He gave a smile that wasn't a lot warmer than the ice on the ground. "A friend, a friend who's here to help you."

Gurt took a step back, conscious of the man behind her. "Why do you think I need help?"

The man's smile didn't move. "Because there are some very bad people who want to hurt you and your family. If you'll just come quietly along with me . . ." He pointed to a black Chevrolet Suburban that hadn't been there a second before but was now slowly cruising down the street. "We can take you to a safe place."

Gurt indicated the house with a jut of her chin. "My house is safe."

The tramp peered over her shoulder, obviously gauging if his partner, the man in the overcoat, was going to be any help. "Ms. Fuchs, I have orders to move you to safety. Your preference is not, repeat, not, a factor. You have quite a reputation for being able to defend yourself and my superiors feared you could be difficult. That's why this street-bum getup, so I could at least get close enough to speak with you, try to reason without getting an arm broken."

Gurt sidestepped onto a neighbor's lawn. "Tell your 'superiors' they were right."

The man was becoming exasperated. "Look, lady, I don't want any trouble . . ."

"Then go away and take the man behind me with you."

"No one is going to hurt you."

The voice came from behind.

Gurt turned to look at the man in the overcoat. "Tell that to the man in the pond in the park down there."

Overcoat's face became blank. "What man?"

Gurt took a heavy breath. "The man your housekeeping department is going to have to remove before someone finds the body."

Overcoat gave a chuckle that had about as much warmth as his partner's smile. "Oh, *that* man! There's no body, although there might be if he doesn't recover from the tranquilizer dart in time to get out of the water before he freezes. Now, are you coming with us?"

He made a grab for Manfred, who yelped in fright.

Whether it was the sound, the motion or both, the child's reaction caused another.

With a snarl, Grumps dove into Overcoat, sinking his teeth into the man's ankle. With a shriek of pain, he hobbled backward, dog still attached, as he tried to pry Grumps loose.

Gurt no longer had to think, just act.

With a shove, she sent the tramp's grocery cart slamming into his midsection, doubling him over with a whoosh of expelled air. Clinching her hands together above her head, she used the combined strength of both arms to bring them down on the back of his head. A few inches lower would have snapped his spine like a rotted stick of wood, but that was not her intent. Instead, she was content to smash his face into the rails of the grocery cart. She thought she heard the cartilage that was his nose snap, but she had no time to be certain.

Turning to where Overcoat was trying to both shake his leg free of the growling Grumps and land a kick with the other, she gave the grossly unbalanced man a shove that sent him sprawling on the icy ground. She took a step back and landed a kick of her own that, if it missed his crotch, was close enough for him to roll into a protective fetal ball.

Reaching down, she removed the Glock from his shoulder holster before stepping over to where the other man was still on the sidewalk groaning, hands to a face that was a bloody mask. She took his weapon, too.

"Grumps! Enough!"

An observer of the Marquess of Queensberry rules, Grumps let go with a parting bark.

"Grumps bit the bad man," Manfred chortled gleefully.

For the moment, Gurt ignored him. "Gentlemen," she called sweetly. "Gentlemen! I'll have your attention before anyone gets seriously hurt."

With eyes brimming equally with pain and hatred, they

stared at her as she slowly unlocked the clip of each gun and thumbed the bullets onto the ground. Stooping, she retrieved each and dumped them into the pocket of her coat. "Please tell whoever sent you I am quite capable of taking care of myself. Any questions about that?"

She was not surprised there were none.

"Is good, then." She tossed each man his empty pistol. "Our business is finished, yes?"

Again, no answer.

And the Chevy Suburban was gone.

Cemetery of Terra Santa

The last of those who had been trapped in the burial chamber were climbing the rope ladder out of it as Rossi put a friendly arm around Lang's shoulders. "Once again, Mr. Couch, Dr. Roth, you have saved my life."

Lang saw no reason to point out that in both instances it had been he, not the archaeologist, who had been the target of an assassination attempt. "Glad to be of service."

"Do you suppose I shall ever learn who you really are?"

This time it was Lang who shrugged. "Does it matter?"

A parade of police cars squalled to a stop in the adjacent street, their sirens muttering to silence, lights flashing.

Rossi took a glance at the new arrivals. "I would guess you do not want to be involved with the authorities?"

"You would be right."

"Then merge with the rest of the crew." He seemed to hesitate a moment before reaching into a pocket and handing Lang the small plastic bag in which he had earlier placed the object tentatively identified as a button. "I guess the police will detain us with questions for the remainder of the day. I do not want to risk losing this before we can relate it to the dig. Could you deliver this to the museum for safekeeping?"

"Sure."

Without examining it, Lang shoved the baggie into his pocket as he headed for the tent that served as headquarters and to the still-jabbering, milling crew.

No less than six cars emptied officers wearing the winter khaki of the municipal police and black of the assault-rifle-carrying Central Security Forces. They surrounded the area of the dig. Lang wasn't going to just fade into the background as he had hoped.

Two men were in plain clothes. Rossi's crew, both Italians and Egyptians, chattered in a polyglot tumult of languages and dialects. Piecing words and phrases together, Lang understood four men in Bedouin robes had appeared at the dig. Two had held the crew at gunpoint while the other two had detonated some sort of explosive. There were nearly as many versions of what had happened thereafter as there were those telling them.

Lang had left the QBZ in the mausoleum. There had been too many witnesses to his brief gun battle with the Asian in the robes. Even in the confusion that was likely to reign for hours, the police were going to seek him out at some point. His main concern was slipping away from the scene unnoticed before then. Although he had little doubt his forged passport back at the hotel would survive scrutiny, being detained had unhealthy implications. He was fairly certain the attempt to kill all those belowground had been aimed specifically at him, and at least two of the four who had made the effort were still at large. In the custody of the police, he would be an easy target.

Within minutes, Rossi was engaged in an animated conversation in English with one of the men in plain clothes while the other wore a dubious expression as he peered into the chamber below. Lang reached the tent, glancing around. He spied a camera, one used to photograph objects in situ. Slinging the camera's strap around his neck, it took him only a few minutes to find a pen and pad. So equipped, he approached Rossi and his interrogator.

He shouldered his way between them, holding up his wallet so only the archaeologist could see he was showing nothing more than a driver's license. "Dr. Rossi? I'm Ben Towles, Egyptian correspondent for the *New York Times*."

As verification of his bona fides, Lang thrust the camera into Rossi's face, snapping a picture before doing the same to the policeman. He had no idea if the paper even had such a position on its staff but he was fairly sure the Egyptian cop didn't either. Rossi's eyes opened wide in surprise, his expression showing he thought there was a chance Lang had gone nuts.

Lang didn't give him an opportunity to express that or any other opinion. "I understand you were involved in a shooting just a few minutes ago. Do you think Muslim fundamentalists were involved?"

Rossi cleared his throat, giving himself an extra second to think. "Er, I do not know. I . . ."

The policeman was taking a few seconds of his own to recover from the surprise of having a reporter interrupt a police investigation. A member of Egypt's own media would have expected to have his skull cracked for such impertinence, but the influence and power of American news was as world famous as its insolence. The last thing the officer wanted was a diplomatic incident on his hands.

He finally asserted himself, showing a badge. "And I," he said in British-accented English, "am Major Hafel Saleem of the Alexandria security police. I have many questions for this man. You may ask yours when I am finished."

"But I have a deadline," Lang protested, shoving the major aside. "What kind of fascist regime does Egypt have? Have you never heard of freedom of the press?"

It was exactly the wrong thing to say, which of course was the right thing, under the circumstances.

Major Hafel Saleem's eyes burned into Lang's as the policeman grabbed him by the shirtfront. "You are not in America; you are in Egypt. Your precious 'freedom of the press' does not run police investigations here. I do." He shoved Lang, sending him stumbling backward. "Now get out of my sight before I decide to have you arrested for interfering with a police investigation!"

Lang considered threatening a complaint to the American embassy or any of the things the American media is likely to do when confronted with a system where the Fourth Estate is treated as less than privileged. He decided he had achieved his goal and didn't need an arrest or a beating to go with it. Doing his best imitation of sullen, he slunk away to the street to hail one of the city's ubiquitous cabs.

Minutes later, the car was stalled in traffic, surrounded by exhaust fumes, noise and smells Lang did not want to even try to identify.

He hardly noticed. How in hell had those guys known where he was? He had taken a random cab to be less obvious than the Mercedes. During the ride, he had taken a look behind the taxi, making reasonably sure they were not followed. Admittedly, in Alexandria's traffic, a tail would be as difficult to spot as to maintain. He had told no one where he was going. Even if Rossi's message had been read before delivery to him . . . No, there had been no time or date.

Then what . . . ? He was recalling every move he had made since arrival here.

The call to Manfred on the BlackBerry!

How careless can you get?

The thought brought him straight up in the cab's seat. All cell phones, including this one, communicated with one or more relay facilities when taking or making a call. For that matter, the phone, even not in use, was constantly searching for the nearest relay station. Where there were a number of relays, as in a city, the search signals could be triangulated to place the particular cell phone in an area of a few square feet.

He took the BlackBerry from his shirt pocket, scowling at it accusingly. His first impulse was to throw the perfidious device out of the cab's window. Second thought gave him a better idea. He leaned forward and changed the directions he had given the cabby.

The taxi pulled up in front of a DHL office whose red and yellow logo announced its ability to deliver anywhere worldwide. The criterion Lang had requested had been somewhat more simple: the closest shipping office, FedEx, UPS or DHL. The cab stopped at the curb, provoking a cacophony of angry horns, which the driver ignored along with the shouted insults and rude gestures of Alexandria's ever-impatient drivers.

Minutes later, Lang was back in the cab, his BlackBerry on a voyage of its own. He could only hope the battery lasted long enough to complete its way to a weather station in Chilean Patagonia, that isolated end of the world where South America yields to Antarctica. He remembered the area from a map he had once perused. Spanish names that translated into things like Desolation Land, Gulf of Sorrows, Cape of Torments.

Just the places you'd want your enemies to visit.

Cemetery of Terra Santa
An hour later

Major Hafel Saleem of the Alexandria security police was frustrated. He had gotten 90 percent of the pertinent facts in the first twenty minutes of his arrival at the cemetery. The other 10 percent, perhaps the most important 10 percent, eluded him.

Four men in Bedouin attire had appeared at the site of a duly permitted archaeological dig. Nothing unusual about that. There were always these types of explorations going on around the city. The four men had suddenly produced weapons. Not as rare an event as the major would like to think. These desert nomads were frequently armed, if not with firearms, then with knives. Violence was not uncommon.

Insults, real or imagined, to family, feuds, vengeance, it really didn't matter. They killed or maimed each other on a regular basis. The only truly unusual facet of the incident was the unique automatic weapon in the burial chamber. Saleem had never seen one quite like it.

At one time it had been the major's hope that Egypt's Bedouins would eventually be so successful in killing each other, there would be none left. But alas, they moved to the city and took up city ways, peacefully stealing and cheating each other instead of killing.

But the men with the weapons at this site had not come to kill other Bedouins. In fact, the dead man and the one who had fallen into the hole weren't Bedouins at all. Though the dead man, the one shot by the American, was beyond the major's interrogation techniques, the living one was not. The fact he had broken a bone or two in the fall would ensure he would answer questions with less effort on the major's part.

Saleem was confident that before calls to evening prayer blared from the mosques' minarets, he would know who these men were, why they had attempted to either drown or suffocate a dozen or so people, and other matters of interest, particularly who the American was.

Antonio Rossi, the Italian in charge of this dig, had been cooperative but less than helpful. The American's name was Henry Roth, supposedly an archaeologist from one of those big American universities, the one in California. Saleem had phoned this information into his staff for verification by Internet or otherwise, only to learn within minutes (1) there were several big universities in California, (2) none of them were currently involved in a dig in Alexandria, Egypt, (3) all but one had never heard of, much less employed, a Dr. Roth in their archaeological departments, and (4) the university that did employ a Dr. Roth (whose name was Harold, not Henry) insisted he had been on campus that very day.

The major's Dr. Roth was a guise, then.

So, who was the American who had done the shooting and, if not one of the scientists, why was he here?

The suggestion that Dr. Rossi's complicity in allowing the American, posing as a reporter, to vanish would prevent him from ever obtaining another permit to dig in Egypt had elicited only scraps of information, the most useful of which was that he, the American, had arrived today.

Assuming this elusive American had used the same name, all the police had to do was check the registrations reported by the city's hotels.

This American might or might not have committed a crime, but he certainly had information Saleem wanted, information he would get once the American was found.

Le Metropole Hotel
At the same time

Lang entered the hotel and headed straight for the elevators. He had almost crossed the lobby when he noted the desk clerk frantically signaling to him. Lang detoured.

The clerk gave Lang an obsequiously oily smile. "Wonderful news, Dr. Roth! I have personally had some things . . . how do you Americans say? Moved around? Yes, moved around. I had things moved around and your room will be available the rest of the week."

Lang had forgotten his earlier request. "I've had a change of plans. How quickly can you get my bill ready? It shouldn't take long, as the room was prepaid."

The smile vanished as if by magic, to be replaced by a petulant frown. "Dr. Roth, I and my staff . . ."

Lang held up a silencing hand, digging in a pocket with the other. "I can imagine the effort involved." He produced a money clip and peeled off fifty American dollars. "Have my bill ready to pay by the time I get back here from my room and it's still yours."

How hard could that be? He'd only had a single beer from the minibar.

The return of the smile was like the sun peeking out from fading storm clouds. "Of course, Dr. Roth. Shall I send someone to fetch your luggage?"

"Not necessary!" Lang called over his shoulder as he dashed to beat the closing doors of an elevator.

In his room, he stuck a hand in his pocket, groping until he remembered the BlackBerry was no longer there. He cursed silently as he snatched his open bag from the closet and began to hurriedly repack the few items he had taken from it. That cop from the cemetery would be looking for Dr. Henry Roth in the near future, and Dr. Roth had sudden urgent business elsewhere.

His bag nearly packed, he glanced into the spacious bath. He would have loved a soothing shower, letting steaming hot water remove the grit of the dig as well as the patina of mud from the rising water. No time. He'd have to settle for washing his face and a quick change of clothes. No telling when the local fuzz might show up.

He splashed cold water on his face and, eyes closed, groped for a towel. He grabbed his discarded shirt and pants to cram them into his suitcase before zipping it shut. He felt something small and hard in a pocket. The thing Rossi had found in the corridor before the trouble had started.

He took it from the pocket, opened the baggie and dumped the object into his palm. Sure looked like a button, but he couldn't be sure because of all the dirt caked on it. His curiosity battled against his desire for a speedy exit. He needed to leave now, but when would he have the chance to find out what he was really holding?

He stepped back into the bath, turned on the sink's spigot and held the object under it. Using a thumbnail to help scrape away the grime, he soon saw metal tarnished the color of mint. No doubt it was a button, a brass button. On the front was the number twelve, surrounded by branches of . . . what? Olive? Laurel?

He was not sure he could have told the difference between the two if he had held real leaves in his hand, but the design was one he had seen before.

He turned it over, holding it up to the light to make out the letters. "Fonson & Co." arched across the top. Under the loop by which the button would be attached, "Brux."

But where?

No time now.

Returning the button to its bag and both to his pocket, he zipped the single suitcase shut. Then he picked up the room's phone, entering the number for the front desk.

"Yes, Dr. Roth?"

"I'd like for you to make a call for me."

"Certainly, sir."

Lang took the limo driver's card from his wallet, reading the number. "And would you tell him I need him in about five minutes?"

"Certainly, sir."

Downstairs, Lang retrieved his passport—or rather, that of Dr. Roth—and handed the clerk the credit card that had come with the passport. The clerk turned to put the plastic in one of those machines that stamps a receipt while he punched numbers into a telephone, presumably to verify the card. The procedure was one Lang had not seen in the U.S. for years.

The desk clerk turned to face Lang, puzzled. "Visa says the card has been cancelled."

Cards issued by the Agency were never cancelled, at least not until the mission for which they were issued was complete. "I'd guess either you or the company made an error."

The clerk gave him a suspicious look. "Do you wish me to try again?"

"Yeah, sure." Lang looked at his watch. It had been over an hour since he had escaped from the cemetery. The cops would be looking for him by now. How much could the damn beer cost? "No, never mind." He pulled a wad of bills from his wallet, counting out the Egyptian pounds.

The clerk gave him a look that said his suspicions had been confirmed, took the money and stamped Lang's copy of the bill. "Will there be anything else?" he asked in a tone that contrasted with his previous ingratiating manner.

A man who had just had his credit card cancelled was a man unlikely to be a generous tipper.

"Yeah," Lang nodded. "I asked you to call the limo for me."

The desk clerk gave a sigh, at his patience's end in dealing with this pretender. "The number has been disconnected."

Lang felt a hollowness in his stomach as though all nourishment had been sucked from his body. Some sort of electronic glitch could have fouled up the card, but the limo driver's phone? Lang was not a believer in coincidences, and the cancellation of the card and disconnection of the phone had the earmarks of an operation being rolled up.

But this one was in midstride.

It wouldn't be the first time the Agency had cancelled an affair early. Many operations could be kept secret just so long before an overzealous member of some oversight committee leaked them to the Agency-hating press or the purpose of the business became averse to a sea change in policy. As the light of publicity hit the media, operatives scattered like cockroaches, seeking the safety of anonymity. Some didn't make it. Jobs were lost, careers destroyed, all in the name of political expediency.

This was not a problem for Lang. He no longer depended on foreign policy that shifted with each election. He did, however, need to know if Miles was covertly covering his backside as originally indicated. More important, were his people still keeping watch over Gurt and Manfred?

Damn! If he had his BlackBerry, he could call Miles. He glanced at the row of house phones across the lobby.

He was pondering the possibility when two cars pulled out of traffic and stopped in front of the hotel. All but one of the men getting out wore uniforms.

Time to exit stage left.

As the police entered the lobby, Lang had already reached the adjacent dining room, where a few guests were having an early dinner. Ignoring the maître d's question as to his preference of tables and offer to keep watch on his single suitcase, he headed for the kitchen, nearly colliding with a waiter. The surprised cook staff watched him walk briskly to the rear and exit a door. He found himself in a short hall leading to a loading dock. In seconds, he was in an alley. Scabrous dogs competed with rats the size of cats among trash cans overflowing with rotting food that smelled bad enough to bring bile to the back of Lang's tongue.

A couple of the dogs growled defensively at the potential rival as he hurried to the daylight at the end. He reached a street just as one of the city's aging yellow three-car trams made a stop at a corner fifty feet or so away. Yellow meant the tram was part of the east line, toward the terminal. Blue would have denoted west line, or so Lang remembered from the brief information he had read on the flight. Since the numbers and routes posted on the front were in Arabic script, he could not be sure of the destination. The important thing was to get away from here, not where he might be going.

He was careful to approach the first car, not the middle, the one reserved for women. Reaching in his pocket for a handful of piastres, he climbed aboard and held out his palm for the motorman to select the fare. No doubt the man would include a generous tip for himself, but Lang was not in a position to haggle.

The car was full, its worn seats crowded. Lang stood as the car clanked along its rails at a walk. Periodically, he twisted around for a glimpse out of the dirty windows. No one seemed to be following, and if he was having trouble seeing out, any pursuer would have equal difficulty looking in. At last, the tram reached Ramla, the main downtown terminal. If Lang remembered the city map, the bus depot was not far away.

The bus depot reminded him of a stockyard he had seen in Texas: teeming, noisy and odoriferous. In fact, the stockyard smelled better. The good news was that the destinations were posted in multiple languages. It took fifteen minutes for him to reach the front of the line and purchase a ticket to Cairo. Other than a few municipal police vainly trying to keep order, he saw little in the way of an official presence. He had arrived at the depot before the security police had had time to post men at all departure points.

A few minutes later, he boarded a bus that could have begun life as a 1950s Greyhound, definitely not one of the "Superjet" buses of the Arab Union transport company, with the impala on its side, which boasted all the comforts of air travel including videos and hostesses walking the aisle to sell high-priced snacks. He could not afford the luxury of waiting for more suitable transportation. Sooner or later the security police would be covering the bus terminal.

The moment he shoved his bag into the overhead rack, he was assaulted by a cloying heat that only the movement of air through the open windows would diminish. The price of a ticket apparently did not include air-conditioned comfort. A quick glance toward the back, the women's section, confirmed it did include toilet facilities, though how functional remained to be seen. Lang was glad he had not succumbed to the temptation to down another cold Stella before departing the hotel.

His seat was on the aisle next to a bearded man wearing a white skullcap. His fingers constantly moved a string of beads through them as his lips moved in silent prayer. As Lang slid into his seat, the man paused long enough to give him the disdainful glare a true believer reserves for the infidel.

Ah well, Lang hadn't been looking for a chatty seatmate, anyway.

As the bus rumbled through Alexandria's outer slums,

Lang remembered Rossi's button. Hadn't taken it to the museum, hadn't exactly had time to. He took it out of his pocket, emptied it into his palm and frowned at the encircled *12* on the front and the inscription on the back.

Where had he seen that before?

The possibility dawned like an Old Testament prophet's revelation. A long-ago visit to Les Invalides in Paris, site of Napoleon's elaborate tomb. The upstairs of the former military hospital was a museum of French military glory with battle flags, uniforms and arms. Each room represented a different period. The largest by far was of the Napoleonic era, the rooms dwindling in size in proportion to France's military prowess. World Wars I and II were little more than the average bedroom, Indochina and the siege of Dien Bien Phu by the Vietcong a closet.

The largest display, that of the Napoleonic Wars, included some of the uniforms worn by Bonaparte's troops. Lang had marveled at the diversity that had been implemented in 1811. Red pom-poms, for instance, on line troops, red plumes on the shakos of fusiliers, yellow lining on the lapels of others. He supposed the different battle dress had served as a form of communication, allowing the commander to actually see what parts of his army were where. The differences, though, even applied to the smaller details of the uniforms, like this button. Numbers had been fairly common, denoting the wearer's organization, in this case the Twelfth Brigade.

He turned the button over again. "Fenson & Co. Brux." The *Brux.* was an abbreviation for the French word for Brussels, home, most likely, to Fenson & Co. He leaned back, trying to find what little softness remained in the shabby bus seat. Most of the seat's foam stuffing had spilled out through a series of cracks and tears long ago, and the Browning in its holster was jabbing at his back. At the same time, he turned the significance of the button over in his mind. A Napoleonic uniform in what was possibly a Macedonian tomb that predated Bonaparte by over two millennia?

The idea wasn't as absurd as it first seemed. Someone had intentionally sealed off the main burial chamber, someone who had had to use a smoking candle or oil lamp. Hadn't Napoleon spent time in Egypt? Of course he had. It was his troops, or one of the scientists, the savants, who accompanied them, who had found the Rosetta Stone. It was highly probable they had found and explored the tomb in Alexandria as well. But why close it off?

He stared across his seatmate, now gently snoring, and watched the desert glide by, occasionally replaced by palm-fringed green fields along the sluggish brown Nile. Where the river was hidden by levees, its course was marked by the triangular sails of feluccas, small craft virtually unchanged since the time of the Pharaohs.

Lang forgot the scenery. It was time to devise a plan.

From the diary of Louis Etienne Saint Denis, secretary to Napoleon Bonaparte, emperor of France

Tuileries, Paris
June 1, 1815

The mob cheered the emperor today as they have each day since his return from Elba.[1] He has all but completed the restoration of his officer corps who have, in turn, reor-

---

1 At his forced abdication and May 1814 exile to an island off the Tuscan coast, Napoleon was given the duty of ruling it and its twelve thousand inhabitants. He arrived with his mother, his sister Pauline and one thousand men who agreed to go with him, including Napoleon's mistress and their illegitimate son and Saint Denis. Napoleon's second wife and their legitimate child refused to come or, for that matter, answer his letters. By means still not certain, he eluded over a hundred guards and a British frigate, escaped the next February and returned to Paris March 20, 1815. The recently installed Bourbon king, Louis XVIII, fled. The police sent to arrest Napoleon knelt before him and joined his army which, like the phoenix, quickly arose from the ashes of its own destruction.

ganized the Imperial Army, men who served with the emperor before and will gladly do so again.

It is good to be away from Elba. We had barely arrived when we received news of the death of Joséphine.[2] Though the emperor took his duties as the island's ruler seriously, making many improvements,[3] he soon tired of such banal chores and longed to return to the task he viewed as given him by fate, uniting all of Europe.

Once, brooding upon this unfinished task, he asked his mother what he should do, to which she replied he should fulfill his destiny. I know not if these words inspired him to complete his escape plans, of which few of us were aware.

The Congress of Vienna[4] has declared the emperor an outlaw and is raising armies to meet him. It will not be long before he must take to the field again. It was with this in mind, I believe, that he spoke to me last evening.

After the usual polite inquiries into the health of myself, my wife and children, he remarked upon the uncertainties of war, a fact I suppose is much in his mind of late. I bespoke my certainty of his success in the coming campaigns.

Then, he spoke most strangely, saying, "Saint Denis, you have been a loyal servant. It is in your name I leave that which is my most dear possession."

---

2 May 29, 1814. Though she and Napoleon had divorced so he might sire a son, they continued to exchange letters. He spent the last days before his exile at her home at Malmaison.

3 The water-delivery system, for instance.

4 The first such gathering of representatives of European states since the days of the Holy Roman Empire (see the author's monograph, "The Holy Roman Empire: Neither Holy, nor Roman nor an Empire," University of Paris Press, 2006). The Congress of Vienna had been convened to decide how to undo what most crowned heads of Europe viewed as the damage Napoleon had done to the old status quo, most particularly, the institution of royalty. They were in session when Bonaparte escaped from Elba, and placed the English Duke of Wellington in charge of an international force to try to put the genie back in the bottle. Hence the "Hundred Days" campaign leading up to Waterloo.

I took this to mean he intended to bequeath to me some treasure for my long service upon his death and endeavored to convince him I expected his demise no time soon. I much desired, though, to know the nature of this legacy to be bestowed upon me.

He must have sensed my eagerness to know more, for he added, "It is upon the heel of a return from anonymity."

At first, I thought I had not heard correctly, the phrase was so odd and seemingly out of context. Before I could further query, one of the emperor's generals, I believe Marshal Ney, insisted upon an immediate audience.[5]

---

5 Michel Ney (1769–1815). As noted earlier, Napoleon conferred the title "Marshal of France" on a number of his generals. It had mostly an honorary significance. Ney, however, was marshal in both the military and honorary sense. He and Napoleon might have had much to discuss. Ney had been among those demanding his former commander's exile and had served the Bourbons before rejoining Napoleon upon his return from Elba. He was hotheaded and heroic, and many blame Ney's rash actions for the loss at Waterloo.

CHAPTER FIVE

472 Lafayette Drive, Atlanta
11:35 the same day

Almost dragging Manfred by the arm, Gurt reached her front door and fumbled in her pocket for the keys. What the hell was happening? Although those two men had not expressly said they were from the Agency, how else would they have known her real name and her Agency reputation? The tactics, poorly executed as they had been, were typical Agency, too. Miles had said he would have someone keep an eye out, not try to abduct . . .

Movement at the corner of her vision caused her to drop Manfred's hand long enough to grasp the butt of the Glock as she turned, mindful of the ice on her doorstep.

A wet and shivering Randy slowly made his way up the drive. Water sloshed from his shoes and she could see him shivering from where she stood. Steam from his body heat enveloped him as though he were some spirit materializing on the front lawn.

He shook his head, chagrined. "Sorry, Mrs. Reilly, I don't know what happened. One minute you and the little boy were in full view, the next I was floating in a fishpond. Some sort of tranquilizer delivered by . . ."

"By a dart gun," Gurt finished for him, ignoring his surprise as she finished opening the door.

"Yeah, I guess that could have done it," he admitted sheepishly. "But I don't understand—"

She interrupted him with a motion. "Come. Inside before

you die of hypothermia. You can take a hot shower, take some of Lang's clothes."

He crossed the threshold, visibly savoring the warmth. "Thanks. But first I need to call the office for reinforcement. Whoever knocked me out was obviously going after you. Are you all right?"

"Quite," she assured him. "I saw the men responsible. You can call whoever you wish after you have shed those wet, cold clothes."

His professional curiosity overcame his discomfort. "You *saw* whoever . . . ?" He glanced round. "Where . . . ?"

"They give no longer a problem and will not be back soon. Now, the hot shower."

To the sound of water running upstairs, Gurt checked and rechecked the house's alarm and security features before she called Lang's BlackBerry. Perhaps he could explain what had happened. She got a cheery recording assuring her that if she left a name and number, he would call her back. Next, she called Lang's office. Sara had not heard from him in two days. Unusual but not unheard of.

If only she knew how to contact Miles. Lang had his number around here somewhere. But where? Relenting and letting Manfred turn on the television as he ate a hastily prepared peanut butter and jelly sandwich, she left him to enter the closet under the stairs Lang referred to as his office. A five-minute search of the file cabinet produced a list with Miles's name and a Washington, D.C., phone number.

She called it, leaving her name and BlackBerry number. Before she got back to where Manfred was teasing Grumps with the remainder of his sandwich, he called back.

"Gurt?" Miles's voice lacked the normal breezy self-assurance. "I've been trying to contact Lang. I've gotten no answer."

"I also," Gurt said. "But that is not the only difficulty. Not an hour ago, two men tried to snatch Manfred and me."

She paused, waiting for an explanation.

When none was forthcoming, she said, "The two were from the Agency, I am certain. What is happening, Miles?" she added pointedly.

"Er, I'm not sure. The reason I was trying to get hold of Lang was to tell him I was ordered to drop protective surveillance of him, your house and family. No explanation."

"Miles . . . ," she began with more than a trace of accusation.

"No, no, I swear! That's all I know, really."

"But why?"

"I told you. I don't know. Would I lie to you and Lang?"

As long as you have been employed by those people, in a heartbeat.

"It is possible the reason has been concealed from you?"

A snort. "Of course. No one is told more than they need to know. Surely you remember that."

"It is also possible there has been some change in the policy that made protective surveillance desirable."

"True," Miles admitted, "but it would have to have been a change from outside. I get the internal memos."

Gurt thought for a moment. "Outside? You mean . . . ?"

"Anyone from the State Department, the White House, Defense. The possibilities are endless. It's not the *who* that bothers me, it's the *why*. As in *why* would this anonymous policy maker suddenly want to take you somewhere?"

"They said there were some very nasty people."

"So, what's different? There always are. No, my guess is they want to make sure you stay quiet about what you know, don't go to the press."

"About what?"

Another snort from Miles. "I'd guess this Chinese-in-Haiti matter. For whatever reason, some branch of government wants a lid kept on it."

Gurt was truly puzzled. "But why?"

"Above my pay grade. If I knew that, I'd be heading up some government department, meeting with the prez on a daily basis. For the moment, I'd suggest you keep your head down."

"What about Lang?"

"Lang will have to look out for himself. He has a pretty good record of doing just that. I hear from him, I'll let you know."

"But, Miles . . ."

He had ended the call.

Cairo International Airport
21:49

Lang had been unable to figure out what, if any, pattern there was to the bus's stops. It seemed that a man waiting on the road's shoulder merited stopping to let him aboard, as did a lone camel who preferred macadam to sand, or a herd of goats crossing the pavement. At last, the livestock delays diminished as darkness grew. At various points, a rider would stand, remove his luggage from the overhead bin and make his way forward to speak to the driver, who would then bring the bus to a wheezing halt to allow the passenger to disembark into the darkness. At each stop, whether or not someone was getting on or off, the door opened, admitting a hot cloud of swirling sand particles stirred up by the bus itself.

Lang had been relieved to hear the roar of a jet overhead, a noise that got louder with each takeoff or landing. When he could see signs in multiple languages bearing a pictograph of an airplane, indicating the road to the airport, he stood and retrieved his bag preparatory to getting off. By the time he reached the driver, two other men were also exiting the bus, both in blue short-sleeve shirts, dark pants and wearing identity tags around their necks. There was not enough light to read the cards, but Lang would have bet they indicated employment by one of the airlines.

Lang followed them as they dismounted and walked toward what looked like some sort of transportation shelter, a
roof but no sides, like the bus stops in some American cities.

"Does a bus to the airport stop here?" Lang asked, hopeful
one or both spoke English.

"Yes," they said almost in unison before the smaller of the
two continued. "The bus circles both terminals, the one we
call the new airport, where Western European and American airlines are, and the old airport, where Eastern European, Arab and African airline gates are. We are going to
the new airport."

Lang sat beside them on a wooden bench, waiting until
the bus chugged to a stop. All three boarded. In minutes, he
was following the two into the terminal.

Due to the late hour, the chaotic mob Lang associated
with Egyptian transportation hubs was absent. There were,
however, the police with automatic weapons common to air
terminals everywhere outside the U.S. A quick glance revealed two of these officers were showing an unusual degree
of diligence in inspecting the papers of every person passing
through the single security checkpoint while two more
watched.

Normal procedure, or had the Alexandria security police
alerted Cairo? He knew Cairo's security was among the
world's toughest if not necessarily the most competent. Instead of random checks, every passenger's background as
shown by his passport was scrutinized, his carry-on searched
as well as x-rayed.

Either way, Lang had a problem. If he used the Roth passport, he would be risking instant detention. His own would
lack the Egyptian entry visa, raising questions he certainly
didn't want to answer.

His back to the rest of the terminal, he studied the TV
screen of arrivals and departures. There was an Air France
flight to Paris that departed in the morning and a Heathrow-
bound British Airways plane half an hour later. He could

buy a ticket now in his own name, but that would not only involve the missing visa, it would also give any Egyptian official scanning airline computers five- or six-hours' notice of his intentions if the Alexandria police had discovered his identity.

There was no line at any of the ticket counters, most of which bore "closed" signs.

Handing his Roth passport to a brightly smiling young woman behind the British Airways sign and logo, he said, "I hope you have room on your flight to London in the morning."

He listened to the click of a keyboard before she looked up, smile still in place. "Tourist or first-class?"

"First-class."

At roughly twenty cents to the Egyptian pound, the number representing the cost of the ticket was astronomical. Lang reached for his wallet and feigned surprise and embarrassment. "I seem to have left my credit cards in my other pants."

She gave a shake of the head, still impressed by the fact someone would pay that sum of money to ride in comparative luxury for four and a half hours. "No problem, Mr. Roth. I have the number from your passport. Here it is back. I will note that you will pick up the ticket two hours before departure tomorrow morning. Your seat will be reserved until then."

He thanked her and exited the terminal but not before stopping by the electronic billboard of hotels. At the cabstand, he directed the driver to deliver him to the nearby Novotel with an intermediate stop at a nearby pharmacy. He was familiar with the worldwide chain of inexpensive lodging, clean rooms and little else. At the desk, he gave his own passport to the sleepy desk clerk, who, as expected, simply swiped it through the copy machine without noticing the absence of a visa and returned it. Lang was betting if his papers were checked against immigration records at all, he would be long gone before the discrepancy was discovered.

He gave the clerk a healthy tip and requested a wake-up call. Once in his room, he searched his wallet for the international calling card he always carried but had not used in over a year. Manfred answered on the first ring. "Hi Vati! Where are you?"

Resisting the temptation to visit with his son, Lang said, "I need to speak to your mother. Right now."

He sensed the little boy's disappointment from the silence before he heard him calling Gurt. Unfortunate, but the longer he was on the line, the better chance the call could be traced by anyone with the minimal equipment and know-how to tap a phone.

"Lang?" There was anxiety in Gurt's voice. "I could not get you on your BlackBerry."

"It's on a South Pacific cruise at the moment with emphasis on *south*."

"I do not understand."

"No time to explain. You and Manfred OK?"

"Yes. You?"

"I'm a moving target at the moment, but yeah, I'm OK."

She told him about the men on the street and Miles's thoughts. The whole thing fit uncomfortably snug with the cancelled credit card and the sudden unavailability of the driver Miles had provided. For whatever reason, the Agency was more interested in their silence than the help Miles had originally sought.

A sea change indeed.

"OK, here is what we're going to do," Lang said deliberately. "You and Manfred take a few days, go to the farm."

The "farm" was a shack on farmland in middle Georgia Lang had purchased in a foreign corporate name some years ago. Its remoteness plus neighbors who were highly suspicious of intruders had proved it to be an invaluable hideout before, and Lang had improved it since its last use.

"We are having an ice storm here."

"You are also having four-wheel drive on your Hummer. I'd risk the road before I'd depend on the weather to keep the Agency at bay. Next time they may send someone experienced enough to anticipate your tricks. And not to forget our Chinese friends. You can bet they still have us in mind. Oh yeah, don't mention any of this to Miles."

"You think . . . ?"

"I'm not thinking anything; I just don't want to take the risk that you and Manfred get stuffed into some Agency hideaway until whoever is calling the shots thinks different. I'll call you on the neighbor's phone when I can. Oh yeah, don't use your BlackBerry. There's a good chance somebody can triangulate."

Lang hung up to a background of Manfred indignantly demanding to speak to him.

He woke up minutes before the call, the growling of his stomach reminding him he had not eaten since . . . when? Breakfast on the plane yesterday? Putting aside the growing protest, he carefully disassembled the Browning. He put the metal barrel component in his shave kit and distributed springs and catches among his shirts. Clips went into the shoes in his bag. In Egypt, firearms were prohibited, whether in carry-on or checked baggage. Breaking up the recognizable components of the weapon should defeat the curious eyes of the x-ray machine trained on even checked baggage. Ammo he sealed in plastic bags that he hoped would frustrate any sniffing mechanisms, chemical, mechanical or canine, looking for explosive compounds. He could only hope he had no need of the gun before his departure.

His next task required somewhat more care. Using a razor blade purchased at the pharmacy last night, he cut the page from the Roth passport bearing the Egyptian visa. Noting the page was the one with a picture of a Mississippi River boat on it, he razored the same from the real U.S. passport. Now the tricky part: using just a touch of the paper glue he had also bought at the pharmacy, he substituted pages. The alteration was not going to withstand careful inspection and it surely would be detected by electronic means upon reentry to the States, but that was not his problem at the moment.

He stopped in the lobby long enough to help himself to luscious-looking figs, dried dates and nuts from the hotel's small breakfast buffet. His stomach cried out for more substantial fare but he did not have the time.

Back at the new airport, he joined the tourist-class line in front of the Air France counter. As he shuffled his bag along, he noted the British Airways desk thirty or so feet away. Two uniformed and armed security police were checking the passports of every male in the queue. Two men, conspicuous in their dark suits, watched. Lang thought he recognized Major Saleem before turning his back. Given the opportunity, he would bet the gate from which the plane to London was to depart was equally well covered.

Finally at the front of the line, Lang purchased what he was told was the last available seat on the Paris flight, paying with his American Express card. He hated leaving a record. The Chinese had proven adept at following him by credit-card receipts, but the alternative was more immediate: buying a ticket without prior reservations and paying cash almost guaranteed drawing the attention of either the security or drug-enforcement people.

Almost as unpleasant was the thought of checking his suitcase. Modern transportation had made it possible to have breakfast in New York, lunch in Paris and baggage in Tehran. Plus, standing at airport carousels waiting to determine the winners and losers in the luggage lottery tied him to one place when circumstances might dictate faster movement. Checked bags, though, did not get the thorough inspection carry-ons did. If he wanted the Browning in Paris, he had little choice.

He reluctantly watched his bag disappear on the conveyor

belt. He'd get out of Egypt and worry about his problems later. The answer to some of them might well be in Paris.

472 Lafayette Drive, Atlanta
The previous evening

Gurt was also dealing with luggage, piling it into the maw of the Hummer in the garage. She had no idea how long she, Manfred and Grumps would be gone. The hour was late and the little boy was up past his bedtime. The novelty of a reprieve was beginning to wear off, leaving him cranky.

"Vati wouldn't talk with me," he said irritably, referring to Lang's brief phone call. "I want him to come home!"

Me, too. But Gurt made soothing sounds. "He will be home soon enough. But while he is gone, we will drive to the farm."

The child brightened. "Can we go fishing?"

There was a small pond on the property from which Manfred took great delight in catching bream with his own small fishing rod. He was less eager to eat them, however, resulting in most being thrown back.

Gurt had a brief picture of standing in the winter wind waiting for some unfortunate fish to find the worm-baited hook in the muddy water. "We will see."

Manfred's face squeezed into a pout. He was old enough to recognize the expression as meaning he would likely be told no, later.

A tapping on the garage door prevented potential unpleasantness.

"Mrs. Reilly?"

"In a moment," she answered, recognizing the voice of Jake of the security service. The hapless Randy had been furloughed with the beginnings of a bad cold.

"Let me in."

Turning off the lights that would have illuminated the garage like a theater's stage, Gurt pushed the button to lift the door. "What . . . ?"

Jake ducked under the door before it had fully lifted and pushed the "down" button with one hand, waving a device that looked like one of those used by security screeners at airports. "Just want to sweep your car."

"Sweep? *Ach!* Of course. For homing devices. I cannot see how someone could have gotten in here . . ."

"You went to the grocery store yesterday. It's possible we didn't see someone hide a bug." Jake was waving the device around the SUV's perimeter, a Merlin of electronics with his magic wand, casting a contemporary spell. "Can't be too careful."

Moments later, the Hummer backed out of the garage, tires crackling on ice, and the door rolled shut. There was a certain security in being in a vehicle that was larger than some pickup trucks. Its very mass was the reason she had selected a car whose appetite for gas was insatiable and whose very size made it difficult to park. Its weight, she felt, formed the maximum protection for Manfred, securely strapped in his child seat. He would be unharmed in a collision with anything smaller than an eighteen wheeler. As the SUV reached the street, a Cadillac Escalade pulled in behind and another took its place. Gurt knew four armed men were in the following vehicle. They would stay in her wake until certain she was not being followed. She had insisted a car remain in front of the house to give the appearance of normality. Over Jake's protests, she had also demanded the escort be broken off at a prearranged place if there seemed to be no need for it.

Four husky men in suits driving a shiny black SUV with tinted windows would draw as much attention in Lamar County as a painted fancy woman in the local Baptist church.

In the car's mirrors, Gurt saw lights blink once, a periodic signal that the vehicle behind was Jake's. The security men followed her through a tortuous course that took advantage of Ansley Park's meandering streets and byways. So far, no other vehicle had joined the two, but Gurt was not satisfied. She took another tour of homes to be certain.

She made a left on Piedmont Road, one of the main streets of the northern section of the city. The traffic was moderate, making a tail difficult to spot. When she pulled through a service station to reverse course, only Jake's vehicle followed.

Once southbound on the interstate, she was relieved to note the ice had melted except for a few dark patches along the exit lanes. The rhythm of the tires soothed her and put Manfred asleep in his child seat. Grumps snored from the back. Every two minutes, the blink from Jake. He was still in place behind her. Twice she exited the expressway only to drive back up the entry ramp and reenter.

No one other than Jake followed.

Once outside I-285, the perimeter surrounding the city, traffic became decidedly lighter, but it still would have been difficult to notice a car following them.

Aware of the problem, Gurt exited the four-lane, choosing a two-lane state highway instead. As shabby storage buildings and truck stops melted into a semirural landscape, there were a series of flashes in Gurt's mirrors. Two plus two plus two.

Jake had picked up a possible tail.

As planned, she hit the accelerator, sending the big car rocketing down a short straightaway before braking for a curve. Jake's headlights were fading quickly. He was slowing to block whoever might be following.

Gurt rounded the curve, praying she was now south of the effects of the ice storm. At this speed, she would not have time to avoid the slick patches. She shifted into four-wheel drive. Thanks to modern technology developed on the Formula One circuit, she would sacrifice no speed and be less likely to wind up in a ditch. But she was no Michael

Schumacher; sooner or later she would have to slow down if road conditions did not improve.

She need not have worried—the decision was not hers.

Accelerating out of yet another curve, her headlights painted what she first thought was some sort of mirage: Two cars were pulled across the road. One had the markings of a local sheriff's department, its Christmas tree of lights flashing malignantly. The other was an unmarked sedan, its very anonymity threatening. As she streaked closer, she could see two men in uniforms. Four others wore dark windbreakers with yellow lettering: FBI.

Charles de Gaulle International Airport
Roissy (just outside Paris)
10:42

Lang was in the CDG 2, the airport's second terminal, waiting for the Metro train into the city. He had much for which to be thankful. His passport had received no more than a glance, his bag had not ventured off on an excursion of its own and he was clear of Egypt. Apparently there was no international "want" on him, not yet anyway. He guessed Major Saleem would query the English authorities first, unwilling to admit the British Airways reservation had duped him.

As soon as he cleared customs and passport control, he had retreated to the nearest men's room to reassemble the Browning now comfortably at his back. He looked around, taking in the people sharing the platform. One or two tourists, noses in guidebooks, who had accepted the city's miserable winter weather in exchange for deeply discounted airfares. Several businessmen armed with briefcases, suits sharply creased despite airline seats. Two families trying to quiet small children made restless by the inactivity of flight.

The sight made Lang think of Manfred. He missed his

son and really should not have cut Manfred off last night. Ah well, Paris was full of toy shops that would buy childish forgiveness. He smiled, visualizing the joy his son demonstrated when Lang came home from a trip.

Yeah, so does Grumps, and you don't have to bring him gifts.

Two train changes and forty minutes later, Lang exited the Opéra station into the cold drizzle that characterizes Paris's winters. His suitcase trailing behind him, he dodged traffic crossing one of the city's busiest intersections, the place de l'Opéra, and entered a nondescript building facing the ornate Opéra Garnier. Inside, Lang passed an antique birdcage elevator to climb steps covered in worn carpeting. At the top he turned right, facing an old-fashioned glass door. He knew the opaque glass was the hardest bullet and blast proof available. He lifted his head, and the dim light reflected dully from the lens of a camera almost hidden in the shadows that hung from the ceiling like dull drapes.

Had he any doubts that the person he sought was still here, they were resolved.

A knock on the door caused it to silently open, leaving him facing another, this one of steel.

"*Oui?*" a woman's voice asked from a speaker.

"Tell Patrick Louvere, Langford Reilly is here to see him."

The voice switched to English. "He is expecting you?"

"I doubt that very much. Just tell him."

Patrick Louvere was head of Special Branch, Direction Générale de la Sécurité Extérieure, DGSE, France's equivalent of the CIA. The bulk of the counterespionage organization had years ago been moved to the fort at Noisy-le-Sec. Only Patrick's division remained in the city. During Lang's employment, the Agency had a long-standing distrust of its French counterpart. Operation Ascot, a plan to stir separatist action in Canada, had been devised by de Gaulle and carried out by DGSE's predecessor. In 1968 the same organization had supplied arms to secessionists in Nigeria's Biafra region to wrest control from U.S. and British oil companies at a cost of over a hundred thousand lives. All of that was long before Lang's time. He had worked with Patrick in the days of the Cold War and they had become close friends. It had been Patrick who had performed the sad duty of informing Lang that his sister Janet and her adopted son Jeff had died in a blast in the place des Vosges in the Marais section of Paris, where she was visiting a friend. Patrick had also helped cut a great deal of the red tape associated with shipping their bodies back to Atlanta.

The steel door swung open, revealing a man in a dark suit of Italian cut, the creases of the pants razor sharp. His shirt was crisply starched and his shoes gleamed with polish. Lang and his first wife had often joked that Patrick had to change clothes two or three times a day to always look so fresh.

The two men stared at each other for perhaps a half a second before Patrick's salon-tanned face broke into a smile of perfect teeth. "Lang! It is the great surprise."

In the next second he held Lang in a bear hug of an embrace. Lang was thankful his friend remembered his aversion to being kissed by another man even if it was only on the cheek.

Patrick stepped back as if to confirm it was, in fact, Lang he held in his arms despite the still-visible cuts and bruises from Haiti, injuries about which Patrick was too polite to inquire. "You have come unexpectedly to Paris, yes?"

"I didn't plan to be here until yesterday, yes."

"But you did not let Nanette and me know." Patrick clucked his disapproval. "We would have made the big dinner, opened the finest wines."

"I hope we have time to go to dinner together."

The Frenchman dropped his arms to his side, nonplussed. "Surely you have the time to make the dinner, no? Nanette will be furious if you escape Paris without seeing her."

Lang glanced around, aware he was probably on several

different cameras. "Actually, I have a bit of a problem I'd hoped you could help me with."

"A problem?" Patrick's bushy eyebrows arched like a pair of dancing caterpillars. "A problem of the heart, a woman, perhaps? It is a subject we French know well."

Only then did Lang realize that Patrick didn't know about Gurt and his instant family. "Er, not exactly. Can we go into your office to talk?"

Twenty minutes later, Lang was finishing his story as Patrick ground out the butt of a Gitane despite the no-smoking signs outside his office. The French tended to view government attempts to regulate personal conduct as unworthy of notice.

The part of the story the Frenchman found most interesting was that Lang was now living in what was domestic bliss with Gurt, a woman Patrick had more than once compared to one of Wagner's Valkyries.

"Your recent adventure explains something I thought strange." Patrick clicked the keyboard on his polished desktop, intent on the computer's monitor. "Ah, here we are! Your Federal Bureau of Investigation has asked Interpol and police in a number of nations to be on the lookout for you. Is that right, *lookout?*"

In view of what Gurt had told him, this should not have been a surprise, but the words still hit Lang like a punch in the stomach. "Huh?"

Patrick turned the screen so Lang could also view it. He was looking at a picture of a much younger version of himself, a photograph from his Agency days.

Underneath was a caption.

Wanted for questioning by the Federal Bureau of Investigation as suspected part of criminal conspiracy to defraud and related crimes. Possibly armed and dangerous. Use extreme care. Detain.

Lang had never believed you could feel the blood drain from your face. Now he did.

Patrick used a finger to pull down a lower eyelid, the French gesture of incredulity. "So, my friend Lang is a big-time criminal, maybe like Al Capone?" He pantomimed firing a tommy gun. "No?"

Lang was far from amused. "No."

The Frenchman became serious. "It is a measure of how badly your government wants you that they would turn on you. The question is, why?"

"There are a limited number of reasons why my government would want me and Gurt in custody," Lang said. "The only one I can think of is they think we know something they either want to learn or don't want to become public. As I told you, Gurt and I are the ones who gave our friend at the CIA this information about what's going on in Haiti."

Patrick pulled the blue box from a coat pocket and shook out another Gitane. "So, you cannot simply swear to say nothing?"

"You are in the business. Would you take someone's word not to divulge that sort of information?"

Patrick lit the cigarette with a gold Ronson, sending a plume of blue smoke toward the ceiling. "It is not the same. In France, just like your friends the English, we would have put you under oath and warned of our official-secrets act. Violations of the act are punishable by prison. In your defense of free speech, you Americans have no such laws. That is why the most delicate of international affairs sometimes appears up on the evening news. That is also why your own people are trying to find you and Gurt." He chuckled. "All governments are more alike than different, professing free speech while trying to limit it by one means or another."

"I may or may not agree with your philosophy," Lang said, "but I do need your help."

Patrick, opened his arms wide, another Gallic gesture, this one of expansiveness. "But of course! You will stay with

Nanette and me. No point in risking giving your passport to some hotel clerk to report to the authorities. But our hospitality is not the reason you are in Paris?"

"No, although I appreciate you risking problems with your government by not turning me over to mine."

Patrick laughed as he stubbed out the Gitane. "Your CIA wants you. I believe it is the best interest of France to keep you for me to debrief on the serious situation developing in Haiti. Unless there is some formal extra, extra . . ."

"Extradition."

". . . extradition request, France is not obligated to meet every American demand, no?"

Lang was well aware of the glee the French took in frustrating its supposed allies, a tendency dating back to the Crusades and continuing through two world wars and the Cold War. He supposed there was a word for it. More important, for the first time, he was thankful for it.

Patrick continued. "You have told me your story but you still have not told me of your reasons for being in Paris, since you assure me they are not romantic."

Lang stretched out in his chair and groped in his pocket, producing the small plastic bag. He dumped the button on Patrick's desk.

Puzzled, the Frenchman turned it over in his hand. "A button?"

Lang nodded.

"With number twelve on it. Twelve what? Could it be from the uniform of a flick in the Twelfth Arrondissement?"

"I don't think Paris cops have the specific arrondissement on their uniform buttons."

"But it is a military-type button, no?"

Lang returned the button to the baggie and the plastic bag to his pocket. "I think so. I believe it is from the uniform of Napoleon's Twelfth Brigade. I found it in an ancient tomb in Alexandria. Bonaparte's savants must have employed the army to do the heavy lifting in their archaeological work. I think they, the savants, may have found, or at least thought they had found, Alexander's tomb."

Patrick's interest increased visibly. "And you think the tomb's relics are what this man in Haiti, duPaar, wants in exchange for letting the Chinese set up a military base there?"

"It's possible. DuPaar wouldn't be the first person to believe whatever country possessed Alexander's mummy could never be defeated. It's the kind of legend a deranged dictator would love. And I'm fairly certain the Chinese didn't rob the church in Venice for Saint Mark's remains. They thought they were getting Alexander's."

Patrick pursed his lips, doubtful. "Alexander the Great in Saint Mark's tomb? That is . . . what do you say . . . a pull?"

"A stretch. But not as much as you might think."

Lang explained the theory set forth in Chugg's book.

By the time he had finished, Patrick was shaking another Gitane out of the box. "And you believe if you can find these . . . ?"

"If I can find the mummy, or whatever remains of it, or prove it no longer exists, duPaar will no longer tolerate foreign forces in his country."

Patrick took a thoughtful puff, smoke streaming from his nose. "And that would hardly endear you to the Chinese, my friend."

"Perhaps not, but if they no longer can keep a foothold in Haiti by reason of Alexander's mummy, remains, whatever, they have very little incentive to continue efforts to get rid of me and Gurt. Like them or not, they are practical. Likewise, if the Chinese pick up their toys and go home, the U.S. government no longer has to worry about what I might say. In fact, they can take credit for avoiding a threat."

Patrick opened his center desk drawer, poking through it with a pen as though he anticipated he might encounter something venomous. "Nanette has a friend whose husband teaches history at the Sorbonne, a pudgy, officious little aca-

demic. Nanette tells me he has just finished editing for publication a diary of someone, Bonaparte's personal secretary,
I think. Supposedly, this lecturer in history discovered a
number of previously unknown facts about the emperor.
Ah! Here is his card!"

Patrick held it between thumb and forefinger, the way one
might hold a dead rat by the tail.

Lang took it, scanning the spidery print. "I'm not sure
what he can—"

Patrick shut the drawer with a slam. "The man may be an
ass but he has won several prizes for historic research. If
Bonaparte's savants found anything relating to Alexander,
he would know about it.

"I will call to let him know you will visit him." Patrick
consulted a large gold Rolex. "But first, the oysters at the
Restaurant de la Place de l'Opéra are superb this time of
year. They arrive daily from Honfleur. Come."

It was obvious Patrick was not going to focus on anything
beyond lunch, not until he was sated with Norman mol-
lusks.

A rural highway in Georgia
The previous evening

The men blocking the road had given the matter some
thought. They had chosen a place the highway narrowed
slightly just before a bridge over some nameless creek. There
was no chance Gurt could pull around them without hitting
the bridge abutment or going into the water itself.

She gave the latter possibility an instant's thought. The
big Hummer's high ground clearance and four-wheel drive
just might be enough to get it across the water. She dismissed the idea. She had no means of knowing how deep
the water was but it was a certainty winter rains and any ice
melt had not diminished its flow.

Instead, she kept her foot on the gas despite frantically waving flashlights and the echo-tinged shouting of a bullhorn.

Two questions occupied her mind as she bore down on the blockade: where was the weakest spot and did the government want her badly enough to use deadly force?

The second was answered by a burst of automatic rifle fire well over the Hummer's roof, warning shots only. The staccato blast brought Manfred wide-awake with a yelp of fear. She had only a fraction of a second to take a hand from the wheel, reach behind the front seat and make sure he was secure in his child's seat.

"Mommy!" he shouted in terror.

There was no time for him to say anything else.

Gurt was aware of figures scattering like a covey of frightened birds as she aimed the Hummer at the narrow space between sheriff's cruiser and the unmarked car. Now she would find out if the massive Hummer's superior weight would push through the lighter vehicles. With a sound of shrieking sheet metal, the Hummer split the two apart like an ax cleaving a log. The impact tried to snatch the wheel from her hand.

Then her world went white as the air bag exploded into her chest, driving her back against her seat and blinding her forward vision. Using the edge of the road she could see through the side window, she kept on the pavement as she used one hand to tug the balloonlike air bag aside. Ahead, she could see into multiprismed fractions as the windshield had become a spiderweb of refracted light.

She could feel something dragging against the right front wheel. A fender, she guessed. Manfred was howling with fear but otherwise seemed fine. A thin trail of steam was jetting from a radiator even the big grill had not been able to completely protect. A quick glance at the gauges showed engine heat creeping toward the red as oil pressure fell off. She must have ruptured a line or holed the oil pan.

She next checked the mirrors. It was too dark to see exactly what damage she had caused but it was apparently enough to prevent pursuit for the moment. She needed to put as much distance between her and the people at the bridge as possible before the engine seized.

She took the first dirt road she could see by her one remaining headlight. Cresting a small rise, she saw another, smaller unpaved path, actually no more than parallel tracks leading toward a shedlike structure.

She turned in, the scraping sound against the right front wheel louder. She stopped in front of a ramshackle wooden building, shifted into park, put on the brake and got out. She left the engine running for fear it would not restart. In the beam of the single light, she saw a tractor and an aged pickup truck. She had arrived at some farmer's machine shed.

Shifting her attention to the Hummer, Gurt could now see the grill had been pushed back into the radiator where the spume of steam was hissing. A fender had indeed been crushed against the right front tire.

None of this interested her as much as what she could not see.

Crossing in front of the car, she opened the passenger door.

Forcing herself to ignore Manfred's pleas to be freed from his car seat, she removed a flashlight from the glove box, knelt and began to examine the underside of the SUV.

It took her less than a minute to find a soap-bar-sized box just under the driver's door. She recognized it as one of a number of commercially available wireless devices with GPS capabilities, the kind used by long-haul trucking companies for both security and driver location. It could be tracked by anyone with Internet access and a password. The following car Jake had spotted was only closing the rear door of a preset trap once she had entered a section of the highway with no turnoffs. Like chasing fish into the net.

But hadn't Jake swept for just such a homing device a few hours ago? A closer look showed a wire from the contraption running forward. Although she could not see from where she was, she would bet it was connected to the Hummer's starter, activated only by turning on the ignition. With the switch off, there was nothing to be found by the kind of sweep as Jake had performed.

Her thoughts were interrupted by the thumping of rotor blades. Her pursuers might have been disabled on the ground but they had managed to get a helicopter airborne and this locator beacon was going to lead them straight to her.

From the rate at which the sound was growing, they would be here in minutes.

Place de l'Opéra, Paris

The Honfleur oysters had been as good as promised but gastronomy had hardly been on Lang's mind. He had hardly savored the *fruits de mer*, a whole lobster, crab, shrimp, mussels, clam and whelk with tart shallot-vinegar sauce, warm loaf of rye bread and dairy-fresh butter.

"Only a single glass of Muscadet?" Patrick asked. "It is a marvelous vintage."

Lang looked around the ornate, rococo dining room complete with mural on the ceiling. Most of the patrons were men in business suits. Several had much younger women with them. Lang would have bet this was not the French version of National Administrative Professionals Week.

He would have liked nothing more than to get a little tipsy on the sweet wine and retire for a nap. "Regrettably, I have a busy afternoon, what with seeing professor"—he reached into a pocket to remove the card—"Henri D'Tasse."

Patrick had shamelessly helped himself to the last of the Muscadet, shaking the bottle slightly to make certain not a drop remained. He gave a reproachful look that reminded

Lang that at table, the French do not favor discussions of anything not pertaining to the food, the wine or the cheeses. Comparisons with other dishes or meals, the last time that particular vintage had been enjoyed, which establishment did the best version. Lang had actually witnessed a couple screaming threats of divorce sit down to dinner. The conversation immediately switched to a calm debate of the relative merits of Livarot versus Pont l'Évêque cheese.

"A pity," Patrick said. "Perhaps I might interest you in a second bottle . . ."

Lang held up hands of surrender. "We Americans don't function as well as you French do after a heavy meal and several bottles of wine."

The Frenchman shook his head. "It is because you are weaned on McDonald's and hot dogs."

Lang grinned, shaking his head as he pushed back from the table and signaled for the check. He reached for his wallet. "We can argue American junk foods later. I appreciate your taking my suitcase home with you."

"No need for you to carry it about when you are staying with us anyway."

Patrick motioned the waiter to decline Lang's money, tendering a credit card in its place. "It is a government card. Let the people of France thank you for the valuable intelligence you have brought with you. Shall I call a taxi?"

Lang shook his head. "No thanks. I need to walk this meal off before I go to sleep."

Patrick lowered his voice. "And to make sure you are not followed. Do you have . . . ?"

Lang put his fist to his mouth to stifle a burp and touched his back in the place he could feel the Browning in its holster. "I have."

Forty minutes later, Lang sat in a small Left Bank bistro on the quai d'Orsay at its intersection with boulevard Saint-Germain. The sole entrée seemed to be pizza for a few American tourists. Through the moisture-streaked window, he could see a fountain with a statue of Saint Michel, and behind it, follow the pewter-colored Seine to the misty ghost of Notre Dame, its gleeful Gothic spires stabbing the belly of low gray clouds.

He was not here for the postcard scenery.

He nursed the cup of coffee that would give him license to remain here as long as he liked. He was watching, making sure he had not been followed. The use of his own passport and credit card had been an unfortunate necessity, one the Chinese would discover sooner or later. Then they would come looking for him. Happily, Paris was a very large city.

He was reluctant to give up the dry warmth of the bistro, even though a lined Burberry purchased just minutes ago promised some degree of comfort against the cold drizzle that characterizes Paris's winters. Slipping a euro beneath his cup's saucer, he tightened the belt of his Burberry, got up and went outside to begin the uphill trek to the Sorbonne. He passed the fifteenth-century mansion of the Abbot of Cluny, built over Roman ruins and now a museum housing the world-famous unicorn tapestries. The Luxembourg Gardens, its normally lush grounds in winter drab, abutted the Luxembourg Palace. Headquarters for the German *Luftwaffe* in France during World War II, it was now home to the French senate. The architecture, more Italian than French, had been dictated by Marie de' Medici, widow of Henry IV, to remind her of her native Florence.

At the top of the hill, Lang faced the Pantheon, designed originally to be a church dedicated to Saint Genevieve, the patron saint of Paris, by Louis XV in gratitude for his recovery from an illness. Unfinished by the time of the revolution and the rebellion against anything of a religious nature, the building's facade was converted to a copy of a Roman temple and dedicated to France's heroes.

Lang took out the professor's card, reminding himself of the address, and began a slight descent along the left side of the building. This area had been the seat of the University of Paris since its founding as a place for sixteen poor students to study theology in the 11th century. In 1969 the university had been divided into thirteen different departments and disbursed throughout the city. Some lectures were still held in the building at 47 rue des Écoles. From the card he held in his hand, Lang supposed history was one of them.

The street still had the slightly shabby, down-at-the-heels atmosphere common to neighborhoods where students congregate, with discount stores and bistros advertising low prices. Number 47 was a two-story brick building with little to distinguish it other than a pair of huge wooden doors. Lang entered a stone-floored foyer whose only feature was a spiral staircase. The stone steps were worn from centuries of student feet. Upstairs was a single corridor lined with doors with opaque glass above unvarnished wood.

Lang read the names in chipped black letters until he found the one marked D'TASSE. He knocked gently.

"*Entrez!*" came from within.

Had Lang asked a film company to create an office for an absentminded professor, they might have produced something very much like what he saw. A wooden desk was stacked high with a jumble of papers, single sheets, periodicals and notebooks. Behind it, a floor-to-ceiling bookcase sagged with the weight of dusty volumes, magazines and more papers. In the corner, an electric heater hummed in a futile effort to dispel the room's clammy cold. At the desk was a man in a black turtleneck sweater. A sharply pointed Vandyke beard did little to minimize the chubbiness of the face. He peered at Lang though narrow slits of glasses.

"Professor D'Tasse?"

The man stood to a height that could not have greatly exceeded five feet. He extended a hand the size of a child's. "You are Mr. Reilly, the American my good friend Patrick Louvere called me about?" he asked in accented English.

Not exactly how Patrick described the relationship.

Lang shook the hand. "Yes. He said you could help me."

The professor sat back down. "Any friend of Patrick's is, as you Americans say, a friend of mine."

Lang looked over to where a straight wooden chair served as the depository for a stack of books. D'Tasse nodded and Lang moved them to the floor to take a seat after slipping out of his new coat.

"You have recently edited a diary of, I believe, Napoleon's personal secretary?"

Behind the glasses, D'Tasse's eyes narrowed. "What is your interest? I already have a publisher, and a number of American universities are interested. In fact, it has been previewed . . . is that the correct word, *previewed*? Yes, previewed in *American University & College Review*." He held up a pack of printed pages. "I have had made an English-language translation to send them."

Lang cleared his throat, giving him an added second to come up with a plausible story. He couldn't. "Let us say I have a very practical interest in Napoleon, one I am not at liberty to divulge."

"Ah, a secretive friend of the ever-so-secretive Patrick!" He put the papers down and leaned across the desk, resting on his elbows. "See here, Mr. Reilly, I must guard my work. It should be available to all at no cost. Protecting scholarly research from capitalistic exploitation is a duty of the academic community."

More like academic penis envy.

D'Tasse continued. "I can tell you story after story of colleagues of mine who shared their work, only to see it for sale in some commercial publication."

How many copies of People Magazine would the diary of Napoleon's secretary sell?

Lang tried not to show his annoyance. Patrick knew a pompous ass when he saw one. "I can assure you, professor—"

The sentence was never finished.

The door slammed open. Lang swivelled his neck to see

two men standing on the threshold, overcoat collars tuned up, caps pulled low. Lang's first guess was that they were students, students very pissed off. Perhaps about a grade.

Then he saw the guns in their hands.

Somewhere in middle Georgia
The previous evening

The helicopter was approaching. Already Gurt could see a cone of light sweeping an adjacent field as it flew circular patterns, the standard search procedure. She guessed she had less than two minutes to do something.

She stood to reach inside the Hummer, turning off the remaining headlight. She then hurried to the rear passenger door and fumbled with the buckles on Manfred's child seat. Whoever had designed the thing did not have a speedy exit in mind.

"Mommy, the copter's coming," he chortled gleefully, his fear now forgotten. "I want to see it!"

His hand in hers, she unlatched the rear compartment, letting Grumps out. He sniffed at the frozen grass, undecided where to leave his next pee mail.

Gurt pointed. "Manfred, take Grumps to that shed over there and stay inside."

"But I want to see . . ."

"MACH SCHNELL!"

His mother rarely raised her voice to him but when she did, particularly in her native tongue, Manfred knew there would be no subsequent conversation.

Taking a second to make sure she was being obeyed, Gurt watched the little boy, followed by the dog, trot inside the rickety structure. Boards were missing and, she was certain, so was part of the roof but it should shelter both from the probing skyborne eye.

She started to bend down and disconnect the tracking

device. No, no good. The chopper was close enough to find her without it. Better to use their own weapon against them.

Climbing back into the Hummer, she snatched off the brake and shifted into drive while watching the helicopter's pool of light skim ever closer. Thankful the cold weather had delayed the engine's seizing, she stepped on the gas, easing the bulky vehicle back onto the dirt road. Once there, she shifted again into park. Using her seat belt, she lashed the steering wheel to hold the car straight in the road before slipping the gearshift again to drive. She grabbed her purse by the shoulder strap and jumped free as the Hummer lumbered forward.

With a little luck, the Hummer and its tracking device would be a mile or so down the road before loss of oil and coolant brought it to a stop.

By that time, she intended to be gone.

Where and how, she was not sure.

She made it back to the shed just before the light from the helicopter swept overhead, the aircraft's twin-turbine engines roaring malevolently. She watched as the pool of light moved away before going outside to the pickup truck. Rusty hinges complained bitterly as she opened the door and felt for the ignition switch. She was grateful the truck was an older model without the complicated antitheft mechanisms. She was fairly certain she remembered Agency training for how to direct-wire the ignition, bypassing the switch itself. What was it Lang called the procedure? Hot-wiring, that was it. Now if only the battery in this dilapidated scrap heap was working.

There was something else in the training for doing this . . .

Oh! Her instructor had mentioned the surprisingly high percentage of drivers who left the keys in their cars. Perhaps the same was true of pickup trucks.

A quick search found a key on the driver's sun visor. The

owner had taken for granted his vehicle would be safe at a remote spot on his own property.

Gurt leaned over to search the sky, saw nothing and inserted the key in the ignition. Her fears swam to her mind's surface when the engine whined as it turned over. She took her foot off the gas, fearful of flooding the fuel system.

On the next try, the engine gave a wet cough, whined again and caught.

Gurt reached for the lights and caught herself just in time. Instead, she felt out the manual transmission and eased it into first gear, inching toward the shed.

In less than a minute, Manfred was beside her, Grumps on the floor at his feet.

"You forgot the car seat, Mommy!" the little boy giggled, glad to be free of the restraint. "Vati will be mad if he finds out."

That's a bridge I'll jump off of when I come to it.

"Why aren't we in the Hummer? Whose truck is this? Did you ask if you could take it? What about our clothes and stuff?"

Gurt searched the night sky. Wherever the chopper had gone, it was out of sight.

"When will we get to the farm?"

Gurt was thinking about the cars she had smashed into. Surely there were others available. But there were a number of crossing highways shortly past where she had taken the dirt road. Did they have enough men and vehicles to cover all possibilities?

"Mommy, will Vati be at the farm?"

And the truck. It would be reported stolen. But with this weather and in the winter, she guessed later rather than sooner. She wondered if the farm's pond was deep enough to conceal it.

"Mommy, why did we leave the Hummer?"

Manfred, like most small children, tended to ask questions

not so much out of curiosity as for attention. For once, Gurt found them comforting. They kept her from thinking about what could have happened.

The Sorbonne

One of the two men in the doorway gestured with his weapon, speaking French to the professor. His harsh tone gave a sharp edge to words Lang did not understand. D'Tasse's eyes went to the manuscript he had just shown Lang.

The first man saw the glance and stepped forward to reach for it. Whoever these people were, they apparently kept up with articles in *American University & College Review.*

D'Tasse snatched the papers up, holding them out of the man's reach. The academic "duty" he had described included resisting armed robbers? Pompous or not, the little man had guts.

The first man spoke to the second in another language, one Lang thought might be Chinese.

Motioning Lang away from the door, the second man went to help his comrade, obviously thinking Lang presented no clear threat.

That told Lang two things. First, neither was the same man who had tried to firebomb the house in Atlanta. That man would know what Lang looked like from observing before he struck. Second, there had been a real failure to communicate by the People's Republic. These would-be thieves of academic treasure, if they were even aware of the problems Lang had caused, had not expected him here.

The first man grabbed D'Tasse by the turtleneck, the collar of his overcoat falling away. Lang was not surprised to see he was, in fact, an Asian. So was the other.

As the first man used the hand not holding the gun to drag the diminutive professor across the desk by his shirt, the other tugged on the papers D'Tasse had clinched in his fist. Lang felt powerless. If he attacked either one of the assailants, he or D'Tasse or both were likely to get shot. If he pulled out the Browning, gunfire would follow, with the same result.

Before he could decide on a course of action, the decision was taken out of his hands. With the sound of ripping fabric, D'Tasse's shirt tore, the inertia of his resistence sending him backward and into the bookcase behind the desk. With a crash, the bookcase slammed forward, showering D'Tasse as well as the other two men in a paper avalanche.

In an instant, the Browning was in Lang's hand. A single step brought him next to one gunman still struggling to free his feet from the pile of books. Lifting his pistol above his head, Lang brought the barrel down sharply on the gunman's wrist.

The crunch of shattered bone merged with a howl of pain as the man's weapon hit the floor and spun across the room.

Lang whirled to face the second man, whose gun was already coming to bear. Lang squeezed off a shot, the sound physically assaulting his ears in the confines of the small office. His target staggered toward the door as a red splotch grew on his light-colored overcoat. His weapon dangled from his hand as though forgotten. Then he turned, raising it. Before Lang could fire a second time, the man's knees gave way and he sunk to the floor and lay still.

D'Tasse yelled something, pointing. Lang turned just in time to see the other man sprint through the doorway, one hand holding both the smashed wrist of the other and the manuscript. Go after him? What was the point? What would he do even if he caught him? Besides, there was the possibility these two intruders had left backup outside.

"My article!" D'Tasse shrieked. "Do not let him get away with it!"

Lang holstered the Browning. "He only has the English

copy. What's the problem? I doubt he'll have much luck selling it to *Playboy*."

"It is my intellectual property," the professor said huffily. "Allowing it to get into other hands almost guarantees it will be pirated."

A man is possibly dead, another crippled, a second ago you were staring down the muzzle of a gun and you can only think about a few pages of paper being stolen?

By now, D'Tasse had a cell phone in his hand, talking—no, shouting—into it. It was more than an even bet he had not called a friend to describe his good fortune in still being alive. Lang guessed the police would arrive shortly.

The stinking cordite fumes were bringing tears to Lang's eyes, a man was bleeding on the floor, the office was a wreck and it was definitely time to take his leave unless he wanted to spend the rest of his time in Paris answering questions in whatever the current version of the Bastille might be. D'Tasse was so intent on yelling into his phone, he did not notice when Lang slipped one of the French copies of the manuscript into a pocket as he shrugged into his coat. Lang cautiously peeked out into what proved to be an empty corridor. The professor was so intent on making sure the police knew what had happened even before their arrival, Lang doubted he even noticed his departure.

On the first floor, Lang proceeded to a door with wc stenciled on it under the standard figure of a man. Inside, he took a stall and removed the Browning from its holster, transferring it to the pocket of his Burberry. If he had to use it, he was not going to have time to remove his overcoat.

He had not gone two blocks before a white police car wailed past, blue light flashing, in the opposite direction, followed only moments later by two more. A half block farther, half a dozen police carrying automatic weapons were walking up the hill, checking out every business as they came. A quick glance told him he was the only pedestrian in sight. Had the professor given a description of him?

Abruptly turning in the opposite direction would attract attention. Lang spied one of those street flower vendors common in European cities in the summer. Where this one had obtained her inventory this time of year was a mystery, perhaps North Africa. But the flowers' source was not what interested Lang. To the flower seller's surprise and delight, Lang purchased the first dozen roses he saw, paying full price without the haggling that takes place with those who do business on the streets.

Just as a pair of cops reached him, Lang continued the way he had been going, roses in hand. He drew no more than a cursory glance. A man carrying a handful of flowers along a Paris street was hardly a man escaping from just shooting and possibly killing someone. He was a man on his way home to please his wife. Or more likely at this time of day, his mistress.

24H rue Norvins, Montmartre, Paris
That evening

Lang remembered Patrick's third-story walk-up flat. On the city's tallest hill, it was equidistant from Paris's last vineyard, also on the hillside, and Sacré-Coeur, with its odd, ovoid domes. The church, built in the late nineteenth century with private funds, was visible from nearly anywhere in the city.

Montmartre had been a center for Paris's artistic community for two hundred years. Géricault and Corot had painted here at the beginning of the nineteenth century. On any day it was not raining, almost every corner had its impromptu gallery displaying everything from copies of old masters to photographically real scenes from the city to contemporary blobs of undecipherable meaning.

Patrick's wife, Nanette, had chosen the area, Lang suspected, with her husband's less-than-enthusiastic agreement.

An artist herself, she had spent her earlier years here before her talent brought her to the attention of one of France's largest advertising firms, where she had put her ability to work in a commercially successful if less-inspiring career.

Since French law strictly mandated a thirty-five-hour-maximum workweek and four weeks minimum vacation, she still had ample time to paint, as evidenced by the artwork decorating the walls of the apartment. She embraced Lang at the door, thanked him profusely for the dozen red roses and insisted on opening a bottle of reasonably good champagne in his honor.

Lang watched her pour two flutes. She was almost as tall as Gurt, slender with a face slightly too narrow, a feature emphasized by shoulder-length dark hair that he knew she wore in a chignon with dark business suits for work.

Stem glass in hand, Lang inspected the paintings that covered every available bit of wall space, murmuring appreciation of each. As usual, he silently marveled at the ability of Europeans, particularly those dwelling in large cities, to live in spaces Americans would consider claustrophobic. Two small bedrooms and a single closet of a bath opened off of a living room/dining area of less than three hundred square feet. Standing at the stove, no part of the kitchen was out of reach. Yet Nanette, Patrick and their son, Gulliam, seemed quite comfortable.

Gulliam. The boy would be about the same age as Lang's nephew, Jeff, had he not . . .

Don't go there. You have a son, a wife and life is good.

"Patrick will be late," Nanette announced in flawless English. "Something to do with a shooting at the Sorbonne. A refill?"

Lang held out his glass, saying nothing.

He went to the sofa, his bed for the night, and shuffled through the pockets of the Burberry he had tossed there upon entering the apartment. "While we're waiting, I wonder if you could translate something for me?"

"I will try."

Lang handed her the French version of D'Tasse's work. "Thanks. If you don't mind, just read it to me in English."

She went to a desk and took out a pair of glasses. Lang did not recall her using them before. But then, he had never seen her read anything other than a menu. He supposed vanity had prevented her from wearing them in public.

Leaning over to catch the light from a lamp on a table, she studied the first page before she began. She had been reading for only about five minutes before Patrick's key rattled in the lock and he entered, overcoat draped over one arm.

"Sorry I am late." He went the armoire against the far wall and carefully hung up his coat before giving Lang a meaningful look. "There was a shooting at the Sorbonne this afternoon. D'Tasse's office. The police wanted to question you."

"Question Lang?" Nanette asked in confusion. "Surely they don't think . . ."

Patrick shut the armoire's doors. "*Wanted* is the past tense, no? It is a matter of national security, since we believe the victim is employed by the Guoanbu."

Lang guessed the French had a picture-ID system like the Agency's.

Patrick continued. "It is a matter for the DGSE, not the local police."

Lang wondered how much weight Patrick had thrown around to accomplish that.

"The Guo-what?" Nanette asked.

"Chinese state security," Patrick said, taking the champagne bottle from the ice bucket and inspecting the label. "Strange. They wanted an article written by a professor, something about Bonaparte. And were willing to take it at gunpoint."

Nanette looked from the manuscript in her hand to Lang and back again. "Could they not simply read it when it was published?"

Patrick was pouring into a flute. "We believe they did not want to wait until the article became public. We do not know why. The inscrutable Oriental, no?"

Nanette held up the papers in her hand, puzzled. "Why would Chinese want . . . ?"

Patrick forgot the champagne. "Is that it? Is that the article on Bonaparte by your friend Henri D'Tasse?"

Even more confused. "Yes, yes it is. I was translating it for Lang."

Patrick sat on the sofa, glass in one hand, the other fishing for the box of Gitanes. "Please, start at the beginning and read it to both of us."

Twenty minutes later, she finished.

Lang was staring into space. "He left his most prized possession to his secretary's namesake? Who would that be? And what was it he left?"

Patrick held up the champagne bottle, ruefully noting it was empty. "There is a computer on the table in our bedroom. The answer to your first question could be sought on Google. But first there is the matter of dinner. On the other side of Sacré-Coeur there is a bistro with the best *moules frites*, mussels and fried potatoes, in Paris. We can easily walk there."

Jesus, does this guy ever get tired of seafood?

Seated at a small and dimly lit table, Lang barely noticed the muted hubbub around him. His thoughts were on Saint Denis' diary. What could Napoleon have had that was so precious to him? The obvious answer was the contents of the box that kept reoccurring in the diary's frequently disjointed passages, the box that was brought from Egypt, was taken to Haiti by Leclerc and returned by his widow. But what was in the box? Alexander's mummy—or what was left of it? Of everything Napoleon possessed, that would be a macabre favorite. Was its present location somehow revealed by his secretary? The Chinese must have thought so; otherwise what would they want with a soon-to-be-published scholarly article?

And Saint Denis' namesake.

A son?

Lang stopped, a mussel speared on a fork halfway to his mouth.

Wait a second.

The diary did not mention a namesake; he had just assumed that was what was meant. The words were *in your name.* Was the distinction important?

"You do not like the *moules?*" Patrick asked, interrupting Lang's thoughts.

Lang ate the one on his fork. "No, er, I mean, yes. They're quite good."

Nanette studied Lang's face. "I think perhaps he has . . . what is the phrase? Something on his mind."

"I was thinking about Saint Denis' diary and what Napoleon meant when he said he was leaving his most precious possession." He paused a moment. "What does the name Saint Denis mean to you?"

"It is the location of the Paris football stadium," Patrick answered immediately. "The Pomme de Pain there has closed, to be replaced by a McDo's . . ."

A popular version of French fast food, a sandwich chain, had been replaced by McDonald's, "McDo" in Parisian slang. Lang wanted to head off a discussion of American fast food, which the French blamed for, among other things, the current world economic problems, global warming and the collapse of Western civilization. In spite of the antagonism, KFC, Subway and Pizza Hut, to name a few, attracted a large following in Paris.

"The football stadium," Lang repeated. "Is Saint Denis the street address?"

"It is the area where it is located," Nanette interjected, "a suburb north of Paris. It is also the location of a very old church, the one where all but three of the kings of France after the tenth century were buried in the crypt."

"Could Napoleon have left his prized possession to a church?" Lang asked skeptically. "I mean, the revolution was anticlerical."

"It was he who returned the building to the church. The revolutionaries had confiscated all of them," Nanette said.

Patrick used a paper napkin to wipe the mussels' juice from his lips. "Not only did they confiscate the basilica of Saint Denis, they opened all the royal tombs in the crypt and dumped the remains into a common pit. Later, when the basilica was restored to the Catholic Church, it was impossible to tell which was which. The various relics went into a common ossuary." He glowered at Lang and Nanette as though this disposed of the matter and there was no need to continue this breach of French dinner-table etiquette. "Now, who would like another glass of wine?"

Unabashed, Lang asked, "So none of the kings are in their tombs?"

Patrick looked at his wife, daring her to answer.

She did anyway. "Not quite so. Ironically, the last two Bourbons are the only ones who have their own resting places today."

"I thought Louis XVI was dumped in an unmarked grave with his wife, Marie Antoinette, following about nine months later," Lang said.

"True," Nanette responded. "Their bodies, along with about twenty-eight hundred other victims of the guillotine, were disposed of in that way."

"Then how did they wind up in Saint Denis?"

"A lawyer, a secret royalist, lived nearby. He saw both the headless royal bodies dumped there and marked the places in his mind. Later, he bought the little garden where they had been treated so rudely and planted trees over the site. When Louis XVIII came to power after Bonaparte was defeated the first time, he had the bodies removed to Saint Denis and a monument erected in January of 1815. There were only skulls and a few bones and part of a lady's garter left because the bodies had been covered with quicklime."

Patrick put down his fork, disgusted. "This talk of bodies and guillotines does not go well with dinner, no? Let us discuss it afterward."

Lang thought a moment, either not hearing or ignoring his friend. "A monument after a mass grave? That would be a return from anonymity, would it not? And Saint Denis, the church, would be 'in the name of' the guy writing the diary. And what better place for Alexander's mummified body, or whatever is left of it, than a crypt?"

He stood, forgetting his half-eaten meal. "How long will it take to get to this church?"

Patrick looked up at him as though Lang had uttered some particularly vile blasphemy by suggesting the meal not be finished. "The church would be closed by now. Sit, enjoy your dinner."

Another thought made Lang sit. "But how could Napoleon put anything there? He was on Elba until the spring of 1815."

"He had many followers eager to do his bidding, as witnessed by how quickly he raised an army after his escape," Nanette offered. "And he returned to Paris straight from Elba, presumably with full access to Saint Denis or any other church in the city. But do not consider going to Saint Denis at night. The area is not safe."

Lang was on his feet again. "You can bet the Chinese aren't worried about safety. We have to get whatever is in that church before they figure out what Napoleon meant."

He signaled frantically for the check. "I can't wait."

With a sigh of resignation, Patrick stood. "And I cannot allow you to go to the Saint Denis area alone and at night."

2 rue de Strasbourg
Basilique Saint Denis
An hour later

Stopping only for Patrick to go by his apartment and re-trieve two flashlights and his PAMAS G1 with two extra clips of ammunition, it still seemed to Lang that the Metro took forever to deliver them to Saint Denis. The station was one of the few he had seen that was dirty, littered, and streaked with graffiti, a preview of the shabby neighborhood it served. The small number of passengers disembarking the train here appeared to be of North African descent, the women with heads covered and the men bearded.

Outside, the buildings had the dispirited look of public housing. Behind chain-link screens, the few store windows displayed cheap household appliances against backgrounds stark enough to proclaim any hope of good fortune had long since departed. Scruffy cars were parked along the curb, many with flat tires indicating they had taken up permanent residence there. Lang immediately noticed the occasional pedestrians traveling in groups, who glared resentfully at him and Patrick.

He was grateful for Patrick's company.

Turning the corner around a particular grim high-rise decorated with hanging bedsheets and other laundry de-spite the sporadic drizzle, they faced the Basilica of Saint Denis. It was like discovering a prize rose growing in a weed patch. Lit by a battery of floodlights, a single tower reached heavenward, oblivious to its dowdy surroundings. The church was a pleasing combination of Gothic and Romanesque built of what Lang guessed was white limestone, burnished to gold by the surrounding lights.

"Is beautiful, no?" Patrick asked. "But what is your plan to get inside?"

"Get inside?" Lang asked. "They lock the church?"

"My friend, in this neighborhood, that which is not securely locked at night has been looted by morning." He pointed to the left portal, two massive doors secured by a heavy chain and large padlock. "I think it would take some time to get through that."

Lang fished in his pocket, producing a ring of keys. "Then we'll just unlock it."

"You have the key . . . ?"

Lang held one up. At first glance, it resembled any ordinary key. Closer inspection revealed a series of bumps along one edge.

"A bump key. Most people have no idea how simply the normal pin-tumbler lock can be defeated. Watch."

Lang approached the huge doors, noting with surprise the ornate carvings on the stone frame were signs of the zodiac, more pagan than religious. Holding the big padlock in one hand, he inserted the key and then sharply rapped the bottom of the lock against the wooden door. There was an metallic snap and the lock sprung open.

Patrick was looking over Lang's shoulder. "That is a very convenient thing to have in your pocket."

"Us former Boy Scouts come prepared. Now, lets get inside and close the doors before someone gets suspicious and calls the cops."

Patrick chuckled dryly. "It would take more than a suspicion to get the flics here at night. Even so, they will not come unless there are a number of them. The residents of Saint Denis do not like policemen."

Once inside, Lang reached through the cracked-open doors and managed to drape the chain back into position along with the open lock. It would require a detailed examination for a passerby to notice the church was no longer secured.

The outside lights shone through huge, airy windows, creating a chiaroscuro of lofty arches soaring far above and columns with the circumference of redwoods marching in soldierly ranks. Lang regretted the outside lights did little to illuminate what he was certain would be exquisite stained-glass windows.

Their footsteps echoing against the marble floor, the pair made their way past candles flickering in front of side chapels from which pained saints suffered a variety of martyrdoms.

At last, Patrick tugged on Lang's sleeve. "The entrance to the crypt."

The ambient light from outside created as much shadow as illumination. Still, no matter what Patrick had said about the indifference of the police, Lang hesitated to use his flashlight for fear someone outside might see the flicker. Extending a hand toward Patrick, he felt an iron rail about waist high. Behind it, Patrick seemed to be sinking into the floor. Only when the Frenchman was beneath the level of the church did he turn on his light, revealing a set of steps that ended somewhere in darkness.

"It is OK to use the torch here," Patrick said. "The crypt has no windows."

As Lang descended, he could feel a dampness and chill that made him pull his new overcoat more tightly about him. There was the smell that he associated with places where there was little air circulation, a mustiness reminiscent of dust and cobwebs. The sound of outside traffic vanished; the stillness was like a tangible curtain between present and past, demanding any speech be in whispers.

Straight ahead, a low wooden door emerged from the gloom. There was no knob, only a rusted metal plate with a handle about two feet from the floor, below which its ancient keyhole yawned for a key far larger than the one in Lang's pocket.

"Someone's afraid the occupants will escape?" Lang asked in surprise.

"To keep out vandals?" Patrick suggested.

"Locking the barn door two hundred years after the horse is gone," Lang muttered.

Patrick pushed on the iron plate with no result. Then he pulled the handle, surprising both himself and Lang when the door opened an inch or so toward them. Another tug and the door groaned on its hinges and opened another few inches. In seconds, the entrance stood open.

"Look." Patrick was pointing with his flashlight's beam. "The key is on the inside."

Lang contemplated the iron key. The part outside the lock was nearly a foot long. "Either the residents insist on their privacy, or someone wanted to make sure the original key didn't get swiped by some souvenir hunter."

Inside, he played his light to his left. Like icebergs in an Arctic sea of darkness, sarcophagi floated in random groupings. Most displayed recumbent likenesses of the original occupant. One, a large mausoleum, depicted a well-dressed royal couple contemplating their nude likenesses. Many had been chipped, cracked or otherwise defaced, the handiwork of revolutionary vandals two centuries past.

It was clear the crypt, like the church itself, had been built in stages. He and Patrick had descended into the older portion, as evidenced by relatively crude barrel vaults. A short distance away, slender Gothic arches opened into dark emptiness.

The previous resting places of Charles Martel and Saint Louis immediately attracted Lang's attention. He was trying to find an angle with his light that would make the words carved below the latter's effigy legible.

"We are not here for a history lesson," Patrick hissed. "We are here to look at this one."

The tomb of Louis XVI and his queen stood in the beam from Patrick's light. It was easily identifiable. All other likenesses were prone, as though sleeping. The unfortunate Bourbon monarchs knelt in prayer, the queen facing Louis' left side. The statuary was placed on a plinth about two feet in height so that even in prayer, both faces were roughly even with the viewer's.

Patrick ran the beam of his light over the carved marble. "There is nothing here but dust, no?"

Kneeling, Lang was studying the base of the plinth. "There is dust, yes." He rubbed his hand across the base's surface, leaving a deep furrow. "And we can't tell much in this light."

Patrick's impatience was showing. "We can come back in the daytime when the lights are on down here."

"The Chinese may not wait that long."

The Frenchman sniffed his disagreement. "I do not understand why Bonaparte would have played such games, hiding things in churches."

Lang was running a hand over the effigy of Louis. So far, all he had produced were dust motes that seemed to sparkle in the light of the flashes. "Remember, the whole time he was on Elba, his wife, the Archduchess Marie Louise of Austria, the woman he divorced Joséphine for in order to have an heir, refused to return his letters. He had not even seen his son, who was, by the time of his escape, what? Four or five?"

"So?"

"I'm guessing, but I'd say Napoleon knew he was soon going to be fighting the combined armies of Europe and maybe his chances weren't so good. For sure he knew that after his escape from Elba, any future exile would be much harsher, no thousand men to accompany him. In fact, he may have guessed he would be killed."

Patrick began to show a glimmer of interest. "Killed?"

"Hair taken from Napoleon's corpse was tested, oh, maybe ten years ago. There were definite traces of arsenic, probably administered in gradual doses."

"You can never trust the English."

"Perhaps. But also perhaps Napoleon wanted to make sure his prized possession was delivered to the son he never saw again. What better way than to hide it from those who wanted to destroy every trace of the French emperor, trust it to a friend to deliver at the appropriate time. A friend who for whatever reason was unable to do so."

"But a secret hiding place in a church?" Patrick was skeptical. "Why not just give this . . . this whatever to someone to deliver?"

"Perhaps that wasn't possible at the time. Besides, Napoleon was a master of the dramatic. You will recall, he took the emperor's crown into his own hands to place it on his head himself."

"And you believe this treasured item to be the mummy of Alexander? Hardly a gift for a small boy, yes?"

"A small boy in whose favor the emperor of France abdicated after Waterloo."

"But, my friend, Napoleon II never ruled."

Lang was examining the stature of Marie Antoinette. "His father could never have known that would be the case before being banished to Saint Helena. What better gift to leave his heir than the remains, and hence a legitimate claim to the legacy of the greatest warrior that ever lived?"

Patrick shivered, whether from the increasing cold or boredom, Lang couldn't tell. "All a very interesting history lesson. But this crypt is not a schoolroom. You have examined the statues and they have no secret, yes? Let us go before we die of pneumonia from the cold."

It was a tempting suggestion. Lang stepped back to survey the carving in its entirety. "What were Napoleon's exact words? Something about 'on the heel of a return from anonymity'?"

"It is but a figure of speech, it . . ."

Lang was circling the memorial. "The heel. You can't see Marie Antoinette's heels; they're under the folds of her dress. One of Louis' heels is covered by his cape."

Patrick's bored expression, or what Lang could see in the reflection of his flashlight, seemed to change. "You do not think . . ."

Reaching across the effigies, Lang grasped the heel of the marble shoe. "I can feel a crack between it and the rest . . ."

He tried to twist it clockwise. The other direction produced a sharp click.

Patrick jumped back in surprise. *"Merde!"*

At his feet, a tray had popped open from the base of the plinth.

Lamar County, Georgia
The early-morning hours of the previous evening

Gurt was having a problem keeping awake. On the interstate, the temptation would have been either to pull off for a few minutes' snooze at a rest stop or visit one of the fast-food joints that lined the exits for a dose of caffeine. Either would have been a mistake. No doubt the FBI had wasted no time getting an all-points bulletin out for reports of any sightings of her, quite likely with the usual "Believed to be armed and dangerous" the Bureau routinely added for effect.

The thought of herself, Manfred and Grumps as some latter-day Dillinger Gang made her smile in spite of her weariness. Or more appropriate, Bonnie and Clyde. Weeks earlier, Gurt had become enraptured by a series on the History Channel dealing with the Depression-era gangsters: Pretty Boy Floyd, Baby Face Nelson, Ma Barker, Al Capone, as well as Dillinger and Bonnie and Clyde. They all seemed much more interesting than their law-enforcing nemeses. Melvin Purvis and Eliot Ness were simply colorless, boring men. What kind of an American mother named her son Melvin, anyway?

Those criminals had made the FBI what it was today, had forced reforms in law enforcement. But the 1930s Bureau was nothing like the sophisticated, highly technical machine with which Gurt had cooperated a couple of times while with the Agency.

Now, millions, if not billions, of dollars worth of high-tech equipment was being used to track her down. It would have been intimidating had she not realized that as long as she kept away from public places, did not use her cell phone or credit cards, she would he untraceable, no matter how many high-resolution satellites circled overhead, how many helicopters searched the highways or how many listening devices probed the ether for any communication from her.

As long as he has a well-prepared hole, the rabbit always has the advantage over the hound. And this hole had been prepared to hide from enemies from her and Lang's past, should they reappear. A simple wood-shake cabin of no more than fifteen hundred square feet housed a cache of at least a month's food. A computer covertly routed through any number of others, a tract of land in middle-Georgia farm country owned by an untraceable offshore corporation. A series of well-hidden remote cameras set off by motion. Gurt had long tired of watching the parade of deer, beaver, fox and other creatures who regularly appeared on the real-time show, but she realized its potential value.

Better than any electronics was the man who operated a small farm on the adjacent property, Larry Henderson. As a former marijuana grower whom Lang had defended from federal prosecution a few years ago, Larry not only was highly suspicious of strangers, particularly trespassing strangers, he was intensely loyal to Lang and knew how to handle the variety of firearms he owned. Plus, he and his wife pretty much knew whenever a new face popped up on the local scene.

In Lamar County, he was better than Jake's security service.

Dillinger notwithstanding, Gurt wasn't going to be caught at Chicago's Biograph Theater or its middle-Georgia equivalent.

At last, the truck's headlights picked up the first of the series of NO TRESPASSING signs that delineated Larry's property.

The next driveway, nearly obscured by brush intentionally left uncut, would be the turn into the farm and the end of searching the sky and rearview mirror. Tomorrow, she would dispose of the truck and ask Larry to go into nearby Barnesville for any needed supplies.

For the moment, all she wanted was not to wake Manfred when she carried him inside and to get some sleep herself. Both the late hour and tension had drained her.

For the moment, she was safe.

Basilique Saint Denis

Lang shone his flashlight on the tray that had popped out of the plinth. "Spring release?"

Recovered from his initial shock, Patrick knelt for a closer look. "Hardly room for a mummy."

Lang squatted, placing the light in his mouth while he used both hands to reach into the tray, and removed a wooden box. "If these are Alexander's remains, I suspect it's less than the full body." He examined the metalwork. "The hinges are rusted shut." He touched a keyhole. "And there's no key. I don't have anything with me that would open it. We may have to just force it . . ."

He cut the sentence short as both men froze. There was no mistaking the sound of footsteps above.

"Do you think the Chinese have already figured out what Bonaparte meant?"

Lang pushed the tray closed and was searching for the best hiding place. "At this hour, I doubt we're hearing early arrivals for mass."

Nearest the stairs, he spotted the congregation of tombs he had first seen, circled almost like a wagon train under attack. From the brief glance before cutting off his light, he fixed the position of the older part of the crypt, that closest to the staircase, in his mind.

He tucked the box under his left arm. With his right, he slipped the Browning from its holster at his back.

With Patrick's hand on his shoulder, Lang groped his way toward the place he had chosen. The thin light filtering through the basilica's windows from above spilled down the stairs, outlining vague shadows that had equal chances of being merely ethereal or hard, unforgiving marble. With the hand holding the Browning extended in front of him, Lang found something, a tomb, and pulled Patrick down beside him.

They had no time to ascertain just where they were before footsteps echoed from the stone stairs. One, two, three, four shapes drifted down the stairs to merge with the darkness like specters descending into Hades. There were muted whispers, and two lights swept the gloom. Lang ducked, expecting to be caught like one of those unfortunate World War II British bomber pilots pinned to the sky by a German searchlight. One beam swept over the sepulcher, painting the adjacent dusty sarcophagus with a brilliance it had not had in over a millennium. Lang got a flash of a reclining woman, arms crossed over her breast, with an animal, a dog, at her feet, before the light passed by.

Next to him, Patrick was attempting to rise up enough to see. Lang tugged at his arms. Lips next to his friend's ear, Lang whispered, "Wait."

He had a good idea what the Frenchman was thinking: four men, undoubtedly armed, with possibly a couple more keeping watch in the basilica above. Not good odds. If the undone lock on the church's left door had not tipped the intruders off someone had been here before them, if they had entered by one of the two other portals, something else would. Lang tried to think. Had he unintentionally left some other sign of his and Patrick's presence?

Too late to worry now.

Relying more on sound than sight, Lang guessed the new-comers had divided, two men with each light, as they edged deeper into the crypt. For the moment there was nothing to do but cower in the darkness amid the group of tombs.

Slowly, the lights passed them by, traveling farther into the necropolis. Then there was a cry, something in a language Lang could not understand. Daring to raise his head above the stone figures, he saw both lights illuminating the Bourbon monument. Four men surrounded the statuary, the reflected light revealing Asian faces animated in conversation.

Lang gave Patrick a gentle shove. Now was the time to get out of here.

Patrick understood. Lang could see his dim outline on hands and knees, ruining his impeccably tailored suit, as he made for the exit. Lang followed, the box in one hand, Browning in the other.

They had almost reached the open door when Patrick blindly smacked his head on someone's tomb, eliciting a grunt of pain. Had the accident happened a split second earlier, the chances were the sound would have gone unnoticed, but it came at that precise moment when the men surrounding Louis and Marie Antoinette suddenly went quiet.

Both lights caught Patrick and Lang at the door.

Both men made a dive for the opening as one. In the confined space, two muzzle flashes were instantaneous, with the sound of gunshots close enough for the ears to feel as well as hear. Lang's cheek stung from a marble splinter.

Both he and Patrick rolled through the doorway as bullets thumped into the door itself. Reaching up, Lang reached back to snatch the key from the lock. For an instant, it would not come loose, a delay that brought another volley whining over his head. With a frantic twist, he freed the heavy key and kicked the door shut.

On his back, Lang reached up again, this time to insert the key on the outside. With surprising ease, it turned as the bolt went into place and several more bullets hit but failed to penetrate the thick wood.

Lang took a deep breath and gave thanks to medieval man. First for being so much shorter than his contemporary cousins that a keyhole was only a modern arm's length from the floor, and second, that his builders chose the stoutest of oak for doors, even if they were so low he had had to stoop to get through.

Standing, Lang turned to the steps. In front of him, Patrick was frozen. There were two men at the top with weapons extended.

Boulevard Carnot, Departement of Seine-Saint-Denis
Moments earlier

Gardien de la paix Jules Carrier had drawn the short straw careerwise. Only two years out of the police academy, he could expect to be placed on the eight-hour shift from 2300 hours until 0700, the hours least popular with those with more seniority. He would not have expected to be partnered with a *stagiaire*—intern, one-year graduate—as a partner, though. Almost always, the younger officers were paired with more experienced partners. But then, nothing went normally for those unfortunate enough to be assigned to Saint Denis, one of the three Paris suburbs that came under the jurisdiction of the Paris Prefecture of Police.

Saint Denis was the black hole of police work, both figuratively and literally. Populated largely by immigrants from France's former North African colonies, the district was heavily Muslim. Some of its residents practiced the extreme customs of their religion, such as female genital mutilation, intersectarian murder, honor killing and tribal feuds. Then there were the commercial enterprises such as meth labs, heroin dealing and fencing stolen goods. Lesser problems involved slaughtering of goats on public streets, dumping refuse on the sidewalks and setting fire to establishments that sold alcohol. There were almost-annual riots involving the

burning of automobiles, smashing the few windows not secure behind steel curtains and automatic weapon fire at
anyone unlucky enough to be in uniform when the trouble
started. Jules was certain law-abiding, peaceful Muslims existed too, sometimes they just seemed outnumbered in and
around Saint Denis.

Only a fool of a police officer would volunteer for duty
here, and only a short-lived fool would wander far from the
well-lighted main streets unless he had a substantial and
well-armed force with him. Even the army was hesitant to
venture into the narrow streets and alleys. The general, if
unspoken, opinion around the Paris prefecture was that it was
far wiser to make only a gesture of police presence around the
perimeter of the worst areas than to risk the lives of good officers in a vain attempt to establish order in a place that was
more war zone than neighborhood.

That was why Jules and his partner Lavon had chosen a
relatively peaceful spot across from the Hotel Sovereign to
sit in their diminutive Peugeot 307 and drink coffee, hoping
to pass the shift without someone throwing a brick or worse
through the car's windshield. They paid no attention to the
car's radio when the first report of gunfire crackled through
the airwaves. Why should they? Hardly a night passed without some son of Islam taking a shot at another. Narcotics
deal gone bad, perceived or actual insult, home invasion.
You name it, the provocations for murder and mayhem by
and against the locals were endless.

A second report followed the first.

Jules was getting uneasy. What if they received orders to
investigate? Walking the streets of this district in a police
uniform was tantamount to pinning a target on your back.

Even relatively inexperienced, Lavon knew that much.
"Perhaps we should find an automobile accident in a far location or take our break now?"

Good idea.

"We can get fresh coffee over there at the hotel," Jules

suggested, reaching for the door handle. "Tell the prefecture we will be on break."

It was as if the radio operator could hear. Her voice called their unit number.

". . . at the basilica, multiple gun shots coming from the basilica. Proceed at once."

Too late.

Jules slowly picked up the microphone, toying with the idea of claiming the message was breaking up. Probably no use. A dozen other units would have heard it.

"Backup?" he asked hopefully.

The radio assured him it was on the way.

But the church was only a kilometer or so south of their position, minutes away. The last thing Jules wanted was to be the first to arrive at a darkened church where some zealous Muslim fundamentalist was shooting up the place of the infidel.

"Check the weapons," he instructed Lavon.

That should afford a minute or two's delay.

The weapons consisted of each man's SIG Sauer SIG Pro 2022, which had within the past year replaced the standard Beretta, a Taser and a Browning twelve-gauge pump shotgun with a choice of rubber bullets or number-two buckshot. Lavon confirmed the firearms were loaded and the Taser charged.

By this time, radio chatter confirmed at least two other cars really were on the way. Waiting at the scene for their arrival before entering the basilica would not only be prudent, it would be standard procedure.

Backup or not, Jules still had a bad feeling as he turned on the siren and pulled away from the curb.

Basilique Saint Denis

Even in the watery light filtering through the church's windows, Lang could see the two men at the top of the stairs were Asian. He could also see there was no cover. Unless he and Patrick could sink through the stone floor, they were at the others' mercy. As one, Lang and Patrick dropped their pistols and raised their hands.

Lang fully expected to be shot where he stood.

The eyes of the taller of the two Asians flicked to the box in Lang's hand. He pointed and said something in what Lang guessed was a Chinese dialect.

His companion, gun trained on Lang's forehead, took a step closer. "The box," he said in understandable if accented English. "He wants the box."

Lang knew Patrick was thinking the same thing: if Lang could use the box to lure either man close enough . . .

Lang held it up. "Come and get it."

Even in the poor light it was obvious the English speaker's smile did not reach his eyes. "If I have to take it from your corpse, I will do so. Now, reach up the stairs as far as you can and place the box there."

Shit, a professional.

Lang hesitated.

The non–English speaker's finger was tightening on the trigger.

"OK, OK!"

Just as Lang leaned forward to comply with the demand, there was a series of loud thumps on the door behind him. The men in the crypt had heard voices and guessed what had happened.

"First, do as I have said. Then you will unlock that door."

Lang felt Patrick's elbow gently jab him in the ribs. The similarity of training between the Agency and the French organization had been a topic of discussion between the two friends in times past. Lang could only hope there was a concurrence in this situation.

Stretching forward, he placed the box on the next-to-top step before slowly straightening up.

"And now the door."

Lang turned to fumble with the key. He didn't know if Patrick could see in the poor light, but he winked anyway.

The door swung open quickly, probably because one or more of the men inside was pushing on it. In unison, Patrick and Lang stepped back as though to make room.

As the last two men, guns in hand, came through the opening, Lang and Patrick stepped behind them, grabbing each with one arm locked around the neck, the other holding his opponent's gun arm. Shielded by their captives' bodies from the weapons of the others, both Patrick and Lang slammed the hands with the guns against the steps' iron railing.

The pistols clattered to the stone floor.

The first two men through the doorway turned, trying to maneuver into a position to get a clear shot without hitting their comrades. The stairwell was too narrow. The man Lang held was struggling, and Lang knew he could not hold him indefinitely. At some point he and Patrick would have to recover either their own guns or those that had been dropped by the men they held.

And there was no way to do that without exposing themselves to the fire from the men at the top of the stairs.

Patrick cursed as his man broke partially free, giving the men at the top of the stairs a target. Before they could react, Patrick made a dive for the small space at the bottom of the stairwell just as the sound of a pair of shots smashed against Lang's eardrums.

Patrick grunted in surprise. *"Merde!"*

With Patrick exposed, Lang released his man, raising his own hands in hopes there would be no more shooting. In the cramped confines of the staircase, even a ricochet could be deadly.

Lang sensed uncertainty in the two men at the top of the steps. The English speaker bent over, reaching for the box.

Then the lights went on.

For the instant it took for eyes to adjust, Lang and the

Chinese froze in blindness. Lang shoved the man he had let loose forward, at the same time stooping to reach for the spot where he thought he had seen someone's weapon on the bottom step seconds before.

By the time he came up with it, the two at the top of the stairs were gone and the other four were scampering up the steps.

Shouts echoed from the arches overhead, magnified by the natural acoustics built into medieval churches. The four men who had been in the crypt were at various levels on the stairs. The two at the top fired toward the front of the basilica before turning as though to make a run for it.

The one in the lead jerked and fell as a burst of automatic-weapon fire reverberated throughout the cavernous church. The remaining man at the top dropped his pistol and flung his arms into the air. Behind him, the remaining two made a quick decision and raised their arms, too.

Pushing by Lang, Patrick climbed the stairs, his right arm grasping his left shoulder. It was only when he came out of the shadows of the stairwell that Lang noticed the left shoulder of his friend's suit was darkened with something wet. A splatter of crimson on the marble floor told him Patrick had been hit.

Following Patrick, Lang emerged into the floor of the cathedral. Between him and the portal through which he had entered were six police. Two held short, stubby automatic weapons, another was pointing a shotgun. The remaining three were in a two-handed shooting stance, pistols aimed in Lang's direction. At least two of them were too nervous for Lang's comfort. All were shouting commands in French.

No interpretation needed. He dropped the pistol and raised his hands.

"My inside pocket," Patrick said, gritting his teeth against obvious pain. "Get out my wallet."

"You're hit."

"Yes, yes. And we are both likely to get shot if you do not show them my identification."

Lang removed the ID wallet from his friend's inside coat pocket. It was slippery with blood. Moving slowly with the wallet held up for inspection, Lang handed it to the officer who looked as though he might be in his early twenties, the oldest of the group. The other five edged closer, dividing attention between what their elder was holding and their prisoners.

"DGSE?" the cop asked, confused as to what a member of France's counterespionage agency would be doing in the Basilica of Saint Denis in the early-morning hours.

A brief exchange in French followed. From Patrick's increasing irritation and the few words Lang understood, Lang gathered the policeman was asking questions and Patrick was invoking state security.

He hoped someone here understood English. "In case you haven't noticed, this man has been shot. Can we get him to a hospital before he bleeds to death?"

Patrick, his face blanched, was holding on to the stair's railing for support. He rattled off what sounded like commands before translating. "I told them to find the two missing Chinese." He looked around. "And where is the box? What happened to the box?"

Lang scooped it up from the floor, holding it aloft like a trophy. Patrick did not see. He had collapsed on the floor.

Hôpital Cognacq-Jay
15 rue Eugène Millon, Paris
Two and a half hours later

Lang and Nanette shared a tiny room only a few feet from the hospital's surgery. Fearing the worst despite Lang's assurances, she had left her son in the custody of a neighbor. As in any such institution, the air was heavy with the odor of antiseptic. An occasional murmur of an intercom system was the only break in the silence.

Lang furtively glanced at his watch.

"It is a long time for such what you call a small wound," Nanette observed tartly.

"Look, Nanette, I'm sorry. Patrick insisted . . ."

The conversation stopped with the entry of a woman in hospital scrubs.

Nanette stood on shaky legs, her question unspoken.

Lang could not understand the woman's French, but her smile and Nanette's obvious relief told him all he needed to know.

"She says Patrick is fine." Nanette beamed as the doctor left. "He is a little . . . what do you say? Woozy. He is a little woozy from the anesthetic from removing the bullet, but he is asking for both of us."

Following a nurse, Lang and Nanette walked down a short hall, stopping at the last room on the left. Compared to U.S. hospitals, the room was small, barely space for the two beds mandated by France's national health care. One was empty. Above the other, a monitor beeped in the muted tones of a regular heartbeat. Patrick, his left shoulder swaddled in gleaming white, was sitting up, a broad grin across his face.

Before he could speak a word, Nanette was embracing him gingerly. "Does it hurt?"

Patrick gave what would have been a typical Gallic shrug had he been able to employ both shoulders. "Not so much. They say they will release me tomorrow."

Nanette's expression said, not if she had anything to do with it, but Patrick's attention was on the box in Lang's hands. "You have opened it?"

Lang shook his head. "I thought I'd reserve that honor for you."

With his right hand, Patrick pointed to the bandages.

"You may have to wait a few days. Why do you not do it for me?"

Lang reached to the side of the bed, unfolding a tray across it, and placed the box on it so that Patrick could see the contents once it was open.

Patrick lifted a corner with his right hand. "It weighs little. How do you plan to open it—with your magic bump key?"

Lang withdrew his key ring. "Afraid not. The hole is too small." He passed several keys, stopping at a small version of a Swiss Army knife. Opening the blade, he worked it under the lid like a diminutive crow bar. There was a squeal of protesting wood as Lang pried upward. Then a popping sound as the lock mechanism broke. Patrick's eyes grew large as they met Lang's when the latter lifted the top from the box.

The smile on Patrick's face morphed into open lips of astonishment. With his good hand, he turned the box over, dumping its contents onto the collapsible tray.

Lang had to lean forward to see. At first he was unsure of what he saw. Two lumps of what might have been brass, tarnished green, what looked like a neatly folded stack of clothing and a small gold cross on a chain.

Patrick held up the metallic objects. "A French general's epaulets!"

He shoved them aside to spread the clothing out on the tray. "And a French general's uniform, size petite!"

Next, Patrick grasped up the cross. "The gift from his mother."

"Are you saying that uniform, cross and those epaulets were Napoleon's?" Nanette spoke for the first time since the box had been opened.

"Of course they were," Patrick smiled. "This would be the uniform and insignia he wore before becoming marshal of France, perhaps at the time he turned cannon on royalists who were besieging the National Convention."

"Then those are priceless, er, artifacts. They should go to the museum at Les Invalides," she suggested.

"Not quite yet," Lang said, drawing the attention of the other two. "Such a donation would surely make the press, and the last thing we—or I—want is to tip the Chinese to the fact that box does *not* contain Alexander's relics. I'd much rather let them think what duPaar wants is beyond their reach."

Patrick puffed his cheeks, expelling his breath in a gust. "But these items are valuable, too valuable for us to keep ourselves."

"No need," Lang said. "When the president for life of Haiti sees he won't be getting what he wants, I'd guess the Chinese will be leaving the country. Once they're out, you can put the whole story on the front page for all I care."

"But what stops the Chinese from making another, er, deal, from coming back if they ever find Alexander?" Patrick wanted to know.

"Hopefully, good intelligence and the United States Navy."

Presidential palace
Pétionville, Port-au-Prince, Haiti
Five days later

Tonight Undersecretary Chin Diem was in no mood to enjoy the view of the city below. Failure seemed a small enough price to pay to assure he would never see the madman duPaar or this pestilence-ridden tropical hell again. But would that be worth the price of failure at home?

He turned from the window as duPaar and his bodyguard entered.

The president for life plopped down behind the desk. "You have something for me?"

"Mr. President . . . ," Diem began. "I fear I have bad news, a temporary delay."

DuPaar leaned across the desk, scowling. "Explain."

"The container we believe holds the remains of Alexander is in the hands of the Americans."

The following pause was so long, Diem thought the man had not heard. "We tracked them to a church in Paris when—"

"You do not have them and have no certain prospect of obtaining them." DuPaar spoke so softly the secretary had to lean forward to hear. "I ask for the relics of Alexander. You bring me excuses instead."

"I'm sure—"

The president for life's voice escalated from a whisper to a near scream, spittle flying from his mouth. "Do you take me for a fool? Do you think I will accept failure as fulfilling our bargain? Just what do you think?"

"I would think, Mr. President," Diem began in his most reasonable voice, "that the word of the People's Republic—"

DuPaar was back to a near whisper again. "Idiot! Do you not understand? Alexander was the world's greatest warrior. The country who possesses his remains cannot be defeated in battle. It is a fact Ptolemy knew and Perdiccas found out to his dismay when half his army drowned in the Nile." He sneered. "The People's Republic does not keep its word!"

He paused as if catching his breath.

"I am sure we, the People's Republic, will be able—"

DuPaar leaned across the desk. "The People's Republic will do nothing! Nothing other than getting out of Haiti!"

"But, Mr. President—"

"*Out!*" DuPaar was pointing to the door. "Out of this place, out of Haiti. You will leave here immediately. All Chinese troops will be off Haitian soil in ten days or I will go before the UN, appeal to the United States to free us of this invasion . . ."

Diem had served in the diplomatic corps of his country for over fifteen years, but he had never seen a display like this. "Invasion? But you invited—"

"I invited a peaceful trade mission! Now I learn you have occupied the north coast of my country with military! I will invite the United States to send troops!"

Diem had never dealt with a man quite so crazy before. Admittedly, the North Korean dictator had been nuts, but not as bad as this. With as much dignity as he could muster, he marched toward the door the bodyguard was holding open.

If he was deaf, how had he known to do that?

The White House
Five days later

The president looked up from his desk as Chief of Staff Jack Roberts entered the Oval Office. "You said you had news for me?"

Without waiting to be asked, Roberts slouched into a chair. "Yeah, I do, boss. Two days ago the techies maneuvered one of our Misty-2 satellites into a new orbit."

The president picked up a pen and was rolling it between his hands. "That's the one that can see through clouds and is supposed to look like space junk?"

"Yep."

"OK, so it's in a new orbit. I assume it can now see the Caribbean. Don't make me pry the info out of you, Jack."

Roberts grinned. "No need. The spy in the sky has confirmed the Chinese are leaving Haiti. Their withdrawal should be complete within the week."

The president leaned back in his chair and grinned right back, showing teeth famous worldwide. "Perfect! That should be shortly after I meet with the president of the People's Republic. Set up a major news conference immediately afterward. I want all the networks' big guns there when I announce this administration discovered the secret presence of Chinese military in Haiti and, through diplomacy alone, had them peacefully withdrawn. That should boost our polls before the midterm elections."

The chief of staff stood. "Not to mention taking off the front page the fact your economic programs haven't succeeded yet. And you did it without lifting your little finger."

"No need to tell that part." The president's chair snapped upright and he put down the pen with which he had been toying. "I'd rather be lucky than good any day. Oh yeah, there's one more thing."

"And that would be?"

"Those people the FBI was protecting, the former Agency people. Did the Bureau ever find them?"

"I don't think so, no. You want me to call off the dogs?"

The president nodded. "It would seem now we don't care what they know or might say."

Roberts cocked his head. "Should we tell them we no longer want to detain them?"

The president frowned, bringing his eyebrows together. "*Detain* is an ugly word. I would not want anyone to think this administration is in the business of 'detaining' innocent citizens. Simply tell the people over at the Hoover Building we have no further interest in them."

From the *New York Times*

TOMB OF ALEXANDER FOUND?

ALEXANDRIA. *One of history's most enduring mysteries may be on the verge of solution by an Italian-led team of archaeologists. Dr. Antonio Rossi, curator of Rome's Archaeological Museum, and Dr. Zahi Hawass, general secretary of Egypt's Supreme Council of Antiquities, announced yesterday that a heretofore-unknown chamber* had recently been discovered off what had been known as the Alabaster Tomb, a location earlier archaeologists had discarded as the site of the final resting place of Alexander the Great.

Modern electronic equipment led Dr. Rossi and his crew to reevaluate the site and they discovered part of the tomb had been sealed off, probably by scholars attached to the army of Napoleon Bonaparte.

"When he was forced out of Egypt," Dr. Rossi speculated, "Napoleon intended to return. He did not want his enemies to get the credit for discovering what had been lost for two thousand years, so he tried to cover his tracks."

Rossi explained that using careful archaeological methods of excavation, his team could still be weeks away from determining if this is really the place Alexander was buried.

"We will never know for certain if this is Alexander's tomb," Rossi said, "unless we actually find the body, in this case, a mummy."

Alexander, known as "the Great," was king of Macedonia, and died near the ancient city of Babylon in 323 BC.

472 Lafayette Drive, Atlanta
Sunday evening, a month later

Lang Reilly had to step over a snoring Grumps to toss a log on the sputtering fire. "There! That ought to keep it going awhile longer."

Father Francis, seated on the couch, looked up from the one of the sections of the Sunday edition of the *New York Times* Lang had given him. "So, Alexander's mummy might still be in Alexandria after all these years?"

Lang retrieved his glass from the mantlepiece. "Who knows? The only thing certain is that it is not and probably never was in Venice or Paris. Or for that matter, Haiti."

"You're basing that on the president's announcement that Chinese troops are leaving that fortress . . ."

"La Citadelle."

"The Citadel. The Chinese are leaving, ergo duPaar didn't get what he wanted—Alexander's relics."

Lang finished off the contents of his glass and crossed the room to the bar. "Elementary, my dear Watson."

Francis held up his glass. "Watson is thirsty, too."

Lang tinkled ice into the priest's glass, followed by a generous measure of scotch.

Lang lifted his glass. "To my health, which I have seriously damaged, drinking to yours!"

Francis was about to reply when Manfred appeared in the doorway, solemn faced, to make an important announcement. "Mommy says dinner is ready."

Lang stepped back to let Francis through the library/den's entrance into the dining room. "I hope what we are about to receive is sufficient compensation for your missing the Women's Guild Potluck Supper at the church tonight."

"A lot more pot than luck. Bless them all, but I've had enough cold fried chicken, potato salad, baked beans and banana pudding to last me the next fifty years."

"The tribulations of Job."

Francis took his customary seat at the table. "Not Job but perhaps the culinary equivalent of the hermit's cave of Saint Jerome."

Gurt emerged from the kitchen, a ceramic Dutch oven held in gloved hands. "You will have 'pot' again. This time pot roast."

Manfred followed Gurt. With Francis engaged in the newspaper article rather than in the games the priest and small boy normally played, he had "helped" his mother with dinner. Without his assistance, Lang guessed, the meal would have been on the table a half hour earlier.

Lang turned to Francis. "OK, padre, you're on, but remember, no one wants cold pot roast."

After a mercifully short blessing, everyone busied themselves with filling their plates. Grumps, ever the optimist, lurked nearby in hopes of spills.

"One thing I don't understand," Francis said between bites. "The box. I mean, Napoleon carries a box with epaulets from Egypt, sends it to Haiti and winds up hiding it in a secret compartment in a funeral effigy? Doesn't make a whole lot of sense."

Lang speared a potato with his fork. "Maybe not to us. Remember, Napoleon was what today we would call a superstitious man, had an astrologer available at all times to consult as to the most propitious times to invade, go into battle, et cetera. The contents of that box, the stuff he associated with his rise to power, was his talisman, his good-luck charm. Sort of like lending out your lucky rabbit's foot."

"Which is less than lucky for the rabbit."

"Whatever. I'm guessing Napoleon thought the articles from his past, the gold cross, the epaulets from his first general's uniform, would bring luck to Leclerc."

"So why did he hide them in a church?" Francis wanted to know.

"I think he knew there would be a wave of reaction to anything having to do with the empire, at least among the victorious allies. Prince Metternich of Austria was leading the Congress of Vienna, composed of the allies, in that direction, dismantling Napoleon's empire. He hid what he thought was valuable so his son might have it. Unfortunately for him, the plan somehow misfired."

They were silent for a few more minutes before Francis looked over at Lang, a tray of hot rolls in his hand. "We were so busy discussing Alexander and Napoleon, I forgot to ask. What's in store for that charlatan, the Reverend Bishop Groom?"

Lang sighed deeply. "I thought forgiveness was part of your shtick, Francis."

"I forgive all charlatans but I'm hoping the law won't."

Lang accepted the bread tray. "He's pondering an offer to plead to two counts of tax evasion and one of mail fraud. I did a hell of a job getting the U.S. attorney to make the offer. The feds usually won't bargain. He should be a free man in five or six years."

"Enough time to repent."

Gurt changed the subject. "Do you think your friend Rossi will find Alexander's mummy?"

Lang shrugged. "For his sake, I hope so."

"For your sakes, I hope not."

Both Lang and Gurt stopped with forks halfway to mouths and stared at Francis.

"Why not?" she wanted to know.

"You're joking! Surely there's not a religious reason not to discover the greatest pagan of them all?" Lang added.

Francis put his silverware down and looked from one to the other. "Of all the people in the world who should know better, you two should. Alexander the Great's mummy—if it exists—has brought nothing but trouble to those who searched for it. Alexander's general, Perdiccas, lost an army trying to get it. Napoleon lost Egypt. You two could have lost your lives."

Lang forgot his dinner for the moment. "Are you saying there's a curse on it, like King Tut's curse? Talk about pagan!"

Francis calmly returned his attention to his plate. "Pooh-pooh all you want. Within less than a month of opening Tutankhamen's tomb in 1923, Lord Carnarvon, the expedition's financial backer, was dead."

Lang wiped his mouth and put down his napkin, fascinated Francis could believe in such hogwash. "The curse of the mummy? The twenty-six other people present, including Howard Carter, the man who found Tut's tomb, survived. Surely you don't believe in curses?"

Francis was unperturbed. "Of course not. I *do* believe some things are inherently evil, including grave robbing, even of pagan graves."

Lang started to respond but caught a slight negative head shake from Gurt—*No, don't go there.* Francis was by far the brightest person Lang had ever know. But sometimes there were issues that simply could not be discussed within the framework of their friendship. Faith could be neither explained nor rationalized. Intrinsic evil was not an arguable subject.

Gurt broke what could have become a heavy silence. "If Alexander's mummy is found, then what?"

"The Egyptian, Hawass, will claim it for his country," Lang said.

Francis smiled, reaching for another helping of pot roast. "Let us hope it stays there."

Although Lang didn't agree with his friend's idea of evil per se, he hoped so, too.

Author's Notes

Andrew Michael Chugg's book, *The Quest for the Tomb of Alexander the Great*, provided both the idea of Alexander's mummy being mistaken for Saint Mark's and a great deal of historical background. Nicholas J. Saunders's *Alexander's Tomb* was also helpful.

Louis Etienne Saint Denis was a real person. Described variously as Napoleon's "second manservant," copyist and librarian, he was the son of one of the servants at Versailles and, unusual for the time, educated. He was with Napoleon on both Elba and Saint Helena. He returned to France, residing in Sens, and lived out what has been described as a "middle-class" life. He was never, as far as I know, Napoleon's personal secretary, but somebody had to fill the role in the plotline, so why not Saint Denis?

My apologies to what may be an unfair characterization of Haiti, a country in which I have spent more than a little time. As of the writing of this book, Haiti is occupied by UN peacekeeping forces and the unfettered (and much-televised) violence is largely a thing of the past. The country, or at least the north coast, is one of the more spectacularly beautiful places in the Caribbean, and yes, the old fortress exists as described, along with the bone-jarring ride up to it. Interestingly enough, one of the major cruise lines has a regular stop at one of the islands just off Haiti's north coast, hopefully a sign tourism will eventually return, although the line doesn't tell its passengers they are in Haiti.

Special thanks to my friend and office landlord, Mike Maniaci. Without his patience, help and computer skills, I would have deleted or lost this story many times. Thanks also to Don D'Auria, my editor, who can spot a hole in my plots instantly. His thoughts are always an improvement to my books.

As always, thanks to Suzanne, my wife, for her ability to unearth little-known (to me, anyway) facts.

October, 2009

INTERACT WITH DORCHESTER ONLINE!

Want to learn more about your favorite books and authors?
Want to talk with other readers that like to read the same books as you?
Want to see up-to-the-minute Dorchester news?

VISIT DORCHESTER AT:
DorchesterPub.com
Twitter.com/DorchesterPub
Facebook.com (Search Pages)

DISCUSS DORCHESTER'S NOVELS AT:
Dorchester Forums at DorchesterPub.com
GoodReads.com
LibraryThing.com
Myspace.com/books
Shelfari.com
WeRead.com

CPSIA information can be obtained at www.ICGtesting.com
Printed in the USA
BVOW040442151111

276143BV00001B/17/P

9 781428 511125